ODD PARTNERS

MYSTERY WRITERS
of AMERICA PRESENTS

ODD PARTNERS

An Anthology

EDITED BY

ANNE PERRY

BALLANTINE BOOKS

NEW YORK

Copyright © 2019 by Mystery Writers of America, Inc.
Introduction copyright © 2019 by Anne Perry

All rights reserved.

Published in the United States by Ballantine Books, an imprint of Random House, a division of Penguin Random House LLC, New York.

BALLANTINE and the HOUSE colophon are registered trademarks of Penguin Random House LLC.

Individual story credits are located on page 351.

LIBRARY OF CONGRESS CATALOGING-IN-PUBLICATION DATA
Names: Perry, Anne, editor of compilation. | Mystery Writers of America.
Title: Mystery writers of America presents odd partners:
an anthology / edited by Anne Perry.
Other titles: Odd partners
Description: New York: Ballantine Books, [2019]
Identifiers: LCCN 2018053271 (print) | LCCN 2018059337 (ebook) | ISBN 9781524799366
(ebook) | ISBN 9781524799359 (Hardback)
Subjects: LCSH: Detective and mystery stories, American. |
American fiction—21st century
Classification: LCC PS648.D4 (ebook) | LCC PS648.D4 M97 2019 (print) |
DDC 813/.087208—dc23
LC record available at https://lccn.loc.gov/2018053271

Printed in the United States of America on acid-free paper

randomhousebooks.com

2 4 6 8 9 7 5 3 1

First Edition

Book design by Jo Anne Metsch

Contents

Introduction

I have really enjoyed putting together this anthology, and I think you will enjoy it, too. When I was invited to edit it, I was also given the chance to decide on the subject that would bind all the stories together. Several ideas were put forward, but I was passionate about the idea of "odd partners." I had in mind any two beings who had to cooperate with each other, willingly or by force of circumstances, to solve a crime.

I had already read with great pleasure Charles Todd's series of mysteries featuring an officer from World War I who was haunted by the ghost of a man he was forced to execute, whose voice he still heard in his head, advising him on current cases. That was a fascinating and uncomfortable "other." Charles Todd was the first person I invited to contribute a story. Happily, he accepted.

There are endless possibilities to work with. Partners may be "odd" because they are of different races, cultures, beliefs, or even have different purposes for solving a crime. Conflict, internal and external, is the heart of drama and perhaps the soul of its resolution. Conflict can provide insight into anything, but particularly into people, and into yourself.

The journey is eventful because all sorts of clashes can happen. There can be quarrels, misunderstandings, anger, and forgiveness. And, of course, always, the crime must be solved: who, why, and how? After all, we are the Mystery Writers of America!

I placed no limit on time or place, and there is a wide variety. More importantly, there was no restriction on the nature of the awkwardness or differences between the two people. Or that they had to be two people! Why not an animal? Especially a dog. Where would the police force, or the army, be without dogs—or horses? Cats are another subject, and make for a different kind of story, and detective—but never forget cats! Or wild animals. William Kent Krueger has contributed a marvelous story whose odd partners are a lover of the land and its life and beauty, and a wolf in the wild. And yet they are partners in this instance. It is a beautiful story. I read it smiling, with tears in my eyes. I will definitely read it again.

And there are other wonderful stories by writers you know, such as Joe R. Lansdale, Allison Brennan, Jeffery Deaver, Robert Dugoni, Jacqueline Winspear, and Ace Atkins, which you will love, and others by writers you will come to know. They each address "oddness" differently, some with wit, some with tragedy, others as triumph. Cooperation can be willing or unwilling.

Naturally there can be other kinds of odd partners as well. If you can have a ghost or a wolf, why not a diary that tells you things you didn't know, and perhaps didn't want to know—but now you do, you have to deal with it, and it leads you to the solutions of old crimes and new ones. The same could be true of a bundle of old letters or even a portrait painted by a particularly perceptive artist.

The odd relationship can lead to anything—or nothing at all.

But the heart of a story is the journey toward understanding of others, and, most of all, of yourself.

I hope you get as much pleasure from reading these stories as I did when I collected them.

—ANNE PERRY

ODD
PARTNERS

Reconciliation

ANNE PERRY

Jack had to find Private Richards before he did something stupid, and irrevocable. Damn the men who had tormented the new recruit with what they had said was his cowardice. They might have thought they were teasing him, teaching him to stand up for himself, but Richards was barely seventeen. It was too soon—only a couple of months ago he had been a school boy! Now he was a soldier in the Flanders trenches, with a rifle in his hands.

Jack rounded the bend in the trench, keeping his head low. But Richards was nowhere in sight along this stretch. He was not among the men sitting on the duckboards, smoking their Woodbines, reading letters from home, making bad jokes. They knew how to hide their fear. Richards didn't, not yet. He was frightened out of his wits, deafened by the noise of gunfire, sick with the smell of death clogging his senses, and above all trying to do the right thing, trying to belong.

Jack Barrick was a veteran; he was twenty-three and had been here since the beginning, two years ago, at the end of that blazing hot summer of 1914. Home by Christmas, they had said. Over a million casualties later, it looked as if they would be here forever. Some of them really would be, God help them. Buried in the Flanders clay. What is forever when you are seventeen and the average life expectancy is a matter of weeks?

But Jack was not going to lose Richards because some irresponsible idiot had made him think he was a coward and not fit to be one of them.

Everything was quiet now, Jerry must be taking a nap! Jack's feet rattled on the duckboards. *Think! Where would Richards go? Where would he feel safe? Double back to the supply trench.* Jack went down the connecting trench, still keeping low. A careless hand—or worse, head—could still attract a sniper's bullet.

Jack asked everyone he passed if they had seen Richards. No one had. But then he encountered a worried-looking sergeant far too concerned with his own problems to listen to anyone else's.

"Ah! Captain Barrick," said the man as he grabbed Jack's arm. "You seen anyone come this way carrying a gas canister? Probably had it wrapped up in something. Could look like anything—clothes."

"You missing one?" Jack caught his alarm. Gas was everyone's nightmare. Ever since it had first been used at Ypres last year, the thick, poisonous fumes haunted them all, worse than drowning in the mud, or being caught on the barbed wire, riddled with bullets. Equal, maybe, to the sapper's fear of being trapped in the endless tunnels beneath no-man's-land in a flood or a cave-in, slowly crushed, unable to breathe. Jack knew that fear personally. He was a sapper himself.

"Yes," the sergeant admitted. "Saw a young soldier hanging around, you can always tell the latest lot. The fear in their eyes that isn't quite the thousand-yard stare, but you know that if they live, it will be. He could have taken it; stupid little sod might not realize what it is."

Jack felt a knot tighten in his chest. "About my height, fair hair? Seventeen?"

There was no relief in the sergeant's face. "Yes. That's him."

Jack wanted to doubt, but the sick certainty inside him left no room. "Which way did he go?" he asked, although he knew already.

"Toward the front." The sergeant indicated the front line, and no-man's-land and the German lines beyond. "Do you know him? Where's he gone?"

"Just lost, I hope," Jack said fervently. "Please God—"

The sergeant still had hold of Jack's arm. His grip tightened. "Lost? You want the poor little devil lost? What's wrong with you, man?" He was almost shouting.

Jack freed his arm. "I'm hoping he's wandering around trying to think what to do. Or better still, how to get the gas back without anyone knowing."

"But?"

"But I'm afraid I know where he's going—"

"Where? God in heaven!" The sergeant's face was white now. "He's not going to gas those stupid gits who were teasing him, is he?"

"No . . . I think he's hoping to prove his courage by going into the tunnels and letting the gas out . . . on the other side." Jack remembered the taunts he'd heard and some harebrained idea that gas in the German lines would decimate them the same way they had decimated us. Only nobody had the guts to take it there. It was just stupid talk.

But Richards had heard it. He had even asked where the entrances to the tunnels were from this side. No one had answered him. It was a carefully guarded secret. Only the sappers went down there, new men, and the remnants of those who had dug them. Sappers' casualty rates were high. It was something Jack knew but refused to think of.

The sergeant was staring at him. "What do you want me to do?"

"Keep quiet for the moment."

"You going after him?"

"Yes."

"Would it . . . would it be so bad if he put a gas canister in their trenches for a change?"

Jack closed his eyes to conceal his fury. "It would be very bad indeed, Sergeant," he answered quietly. "Our trenches are a little lower than theirs. Slope of the land. And we dug a bit deeper. It gives us an advantage in some ways. The friable topsoil where they are tends to collapse more easily. Ours is more clay, thicker, less likely to give way. And wetter, of course. Water finds its own level—"

"I know all that," the sergeant interrupted.

Jack opened his eyes. "Do you also know that the gas is heavier than air? That it finds the lowest level it can? It will start off in their tunnels and then seep into ours—"

"Through the earth?" The sergeant's disbelief was thick in his voice—doubt, mockery.

"No," Jack said patiently. "Through the places where the tunnels come close to one another. Through the walls that are so thin in places, we can hear them talking to one another as if there were just a piece of plaster board between us and them. Sometimes we accidentally break into one of their tunnels, or they do into one of ours. If he lets the gas go in one of theirs, you can bet your last penny it will end up in ours, too. Would you like to be trapped underground in a dark, narrow tunnel where you have to stoop to miss hitting the roof and carry a lantern to see where you are going—there's no light underground, Sergeant. Absolutely none at all. Then smell gas? Would you?"

"Oh, sweet Jesus." The sergeant crossed himself, his face pasty white.

"So which way did he go?" Jack repeated.

"You're not . . . going down there after him? You can't!"

"No, I'm just going to let it happen," Jack snapped. He could not bear to think about it and then do it. He could do it only if he thought about something else.

The sergeant grunted without saying anything else.

Jack went straight to the camouflaged entrance of the nearest tunnel. To his mind, it seemed the most likely one for Richards to have found. Although the thought that the boy had stumbled across it so quickly was worrying. It was obviously not as well hidden as he had believed. Something to pay attention to another time.

He pulled back the sacking over the entrance and went in, letting it fall back into place after him, concealing it again. He shone his lantern ahead of him. The corridor was long and low, rising at the end until the way forward became invisible. His eyes would get used to it.

He breathed in slowly. Even now, the smell of wet earth almost suf-
focated him. It brought back too many memories, going far into his
childhood and time spent with his father down the coal mines of
Durham County, in the mining village where Jack was born. He could
remember the huge, ragged wind-torn skies, the endless views from
the moors, and place names that haunted you, like Pity Me. Mining
country.

Miners were hard men. They had to be. Hard men with soft hearts.
Funny how many of them could sing so gloriously. You didn't know
music till you had heard a Welsh male voice choir. Break your heart, it
would.

Jack was walking firmly now, as if he were on a well-trodden path.
And so he was. Other men like him had built this tunnel, going far
under no-man's-land, right under the German lines—men from other
mining villages in England and Wales. Lots from Wales, from the
richly coal-seamed valleys. It didn't really matter where a mining village was, they all had something in common—England, Wales, even
Germany. The soil was different, but the darkness was the same, the
sense of the earth tightening itself against the invader, closing in. And,
of course, the incessant dripping of water.

Water is necessary for life, and yet, underground, it is also the
enemy. Over time, it rots all the wooden supports that hold up the
cross beams. You could not always see it in the half-light. You had to
know the places where it collected. Water goes down, following the
way of least resistance. He was sure some preacher had made the most
of that in a sermon! Look for the rot where the water collects.

Jack had to think of something other than the light almost invisible
around him, and the fact that he was going deeper all the time. He had
to keep out of the way of the German tunnels. Last thing he wanted
was to break through into one of theirs! Of course, better straight into
it than over, and fall in on top of them. An injury down here was
worse than in the open. Easy enough to do. The worst of all would be
a rockfall pinning you down, trapped here forever. Who would dig
you out? Touch the walls where they had given way and you could
bring them all down.

He came to another arch built of timber. He could remember building this one. He and Colin had worked on it. Seemed like a long time ago. And Colin had been dead a year now. Still down here, somewhere. A cave-in. There was nothing they could have done.

He did not want to think about it. The sight of the arch had brought it all back. He touched it with one hand, as if in some way he were touching Colin himself, forever built into this tunnel. He even spoke to him. Stupid thing to do, as if he could hear.

Jack looked at the ground. Was there anything at all to indicate that Richards had come this way? What would tell him? Footprints? Hardly. How would you tell the marks of one army boot from another? There could be a hundred thousand men with a size ten boot, and every boot was near enough the same.

Did Richards expect to come back? Yes. To tell the men who had accused him of cowardice that he had gone through the tunnels alone and put gas right where the enemy lived. Then he might have made some mark to recognize on his return and know that he was going the right way.

It was five impatient minutes before he found it. Just a tiny *DR* scratched on the upright, above eye height. You had to be looking for it. Miners tended not to be tall men. Short, stocky, could laugh hard, and weep hard, and sing like angels.

Jack had a pretty good sense of direction. If you work underground, you have to have that. There's nothing to guide you. No stars, no shadows except your own, cast by the lamp.

There were no sounds either, except occasionally the scurrying of rats' feet. He hated rats. But at least if they were alive it meant the air was fit to breathe. Gas you couldn't see was the hidden enemy. That's why the miners carried little animals, like mice or canaries. They were small enough to fall unconscious before a man would. They were sent down only a certain number of times, and if they survived, they were pensioned off. Too bad the men didn't get to do the same.

He should have brought a stick. It was the simplest of devices to detect if anyone was digging close by. Just push it into the ground and put the other end between your teeth. You'd feel the vibration if there was anything near you. Such a simple thing, but there were few sticks of any sort near the front of these trenches. Nothing lived, no plants, no birds, except carrion creatures, of course. Plenty of them. And mud. Everywhere mud.

There was no sense of time down here. It could have been yesterday that he and Alec had been here, telling silly stories to hide the fact that they were scared. There had been a bad collapse, and three sappers were killed. One of the lower tunnels was completely flooded. They had all escaped that, then got caught when a support gave way and fifty yards of roof caved in. It had seemed to happen in slow motion, and yet was probably a matter of only a minute or two. He remembered running and falling. It was Alec who had helped him up.

Where the hell was Richards? Jack must have been under no-man's-land by now. He was breathing too fast, fighting the claustrophobia. Was it really summer outside? He was going upward again, but it was definitely wetter now, the dripping coming faster and little trickles of water carving through the mud on the floor.

He passed a tunnel off to the right and followed it a little way until he came to the last set of wooden supports. He looked up, slightly above eye level, to see if he could find the *DR* carved. What did *D* stand for? David? Donald? Douglas? Who had named him? His mother?

He put the thought out of his mind.

Sean, who had taught him so much, had taught him better than that. The ghosts of the dead are not always with you. What makes you think you are so damn important? They've got their own business to mind. Jack remembered Sean laughing. He had a very individual laugh. Always sounded surprised. "Who'd want to stay around here?" he had said, and laughed some more.

He was gone, too. Gas. Better not even to think about it. Did anybody expect to walk away from this? Too many that he cared for had fallen already, and who knew how long this would last. He did not want to remember Sean, and yet down in these dripping tunnels, with the sound of gunfire faint above him, how could he not? He could see Sean's smile, hear his voice saying, "Don't do it, boyo," with the lilt to it that so many Welshmen carried, like a kind of music in itself.

Lost down here. Not even bodies to send home. There was something ludicrous in weeping because you could not bury a friend, because he was buried forever deep in the earth.

He heard a rumble of gunfire above him, and then another. But it was not that that froze him rigid against the wall. It was a much smaller sound, and much closer. A rat? No. He knew the scrabble of a rat's feet. This was soft, the movement of a much heavier weight. The weight of a man.

Jack stood frozen on the spot. Then quickly he doused his lamp. The darkness became almost solid. Not even a deepening of shadows, but a total absence of light everywhere.

There was the sound again, just a footfall, but now he was sure it was a man. How far was he from no-man's-land? Near enough to the German trenches? What was Richards thinking? More scared of being thought a coward than of dying alone down here. What the hell had they said to him? And why? Why would you do that to anyone?

The footfalls seemed closer now. Definitely a man. There was a long, straight run ahead, slightly uphill. Definitely getting close to the enemy lines. If they passed by a German tunnel, or worse, a dugout with men in it, he would hear them talking. He could speak a little German. They sounded so ordinary. So like his own men. Quite a lot of the words were even the same: house, man, hound . . . the familiar things.

Were the soft footfalls any closer? They sounded like it. But sound was distorted underground. He might be a long way off. Forty or fifty yards. If he kept traveling without a light, they might actually bump into each other! That thought made him break out in a sweat.

Could it be Richards? Changing his mind and returning, please heaven!

Suddenly, a light appeared ahead and to the right. Somebody coming along a connecting tunnel. Richards?

The man reached the main tunnel too quickly. The farthest rays of his lamp touched Jack's feet. The man stopped and spoke suddenly, "It's no good. The water's getting deeper." Only he said it in German. Jack could understand that easily. "Good" and "water" were nearly the same in both languages.

Seconds ticked by.

Above them there was a rumble, as if a train were going overhead, except they both knew it was heavy shellfire.

A clod of earth shook loose and fell from the roof. One of the supports six feet away cracked and bent a little. A trickle of water appeared.

Jack gulped, but his mouth was dry.

He looked at the man at the same moment that the man looked at him. He was German, a short, stocky man, as miners tended to be.

"Water?" Jack asked in German. *"Wasser?"*

The man answered in German, then translated it into English. "Yes. Behind me. Which means it's coming this way. Not much yet, but it's increasing." He looked sideways and up at the support that had cracked. He did not need to say what he feared. If the support gave way under the weight of the crossbeam, the whole roof could collapse here. And would alter the weight and the balance of the rest of the tunnels.

Jack relit his lamp and held it higher. A couple of grains of dirt fell on him.

"Did you come down for this?" the German asked. "It's a long way from you. Is it worse your way?"

"No. A young man came down here. I want to get him back."

He saw the disbelief in the German's face.

"It's the truth. It's just not all of it," Jack explained. He needed to make the man believe him. "We'd better see if we can find a strut to reinforce this. If it gives, we're both lost. And anyone else who's down here."

Indecision flickered in the German's eyes.

Jack understood. He would have felt the same. Richards was a reality to Jack, but to the German he could be an invention.

Jack held his hands out, clearly empty. "If I were here to sabotage your tunnel, I'd have brought something to blow it up after I'd gotten the hell out of the way!"

The German smiled. He had a good face, nice teeth. "We say all you English are mad, but not that mad! That side tunnel doesn't go very far, we could take one of the uprights from there and add it to this."

"Dangerous," Jack said, thinking of the difficulty of removing an upright without jarring the whole thing and bringing half the roof down.

"If that tunnel goes, it doesn't matter. A cave-in here would take out the entire passage," the German pointed out.

A larger piece of dirt dropped onto Jack's face, then a trickle of water. He put out his hand. "Jack Barrick."

The German took it and gripped it hard. His hand was strong, callused. A miner's hand. "Karl Bucholz." He turned and gestured for Jack to follow him.

Ten yards into the side tunnel, they saw the first set of supports. The earth was soft around it. The Germans, on higher ground, often faced this problem of more friable earth. It was easier to dig, and made their tunnels easier to fall.

Could Richards have come this way?

"How far does it go?" Jack asked.

"Twenty meters," Karl replied. "Your runaway is not down there."

So Karl had understood him! He must have gone along this way before Jack had reached this far. Silently they began working together to loosen the upright. It was slow, digging and gouging with knives, but it was all they had.

"Where are you from?" Jack asked.

"Little village in the Saar Valley. You?"

"County Durham. Bishop Auckland." With both of them working, the wood was coming loose.

"Not Wales?"

"No. Not valleys at all. Big, high, open land. Sometimes think you could touch the sky."

"Only touch the sky if it falls on you," Karl said with a twisted smile. "And sometimes I think it's going to."

"Been here long?"

"Since the beginning."

"Me, too," Jack replied. "I suppose that makes us veterans? I don't want to be a veteran at twenty-three."

"Better than the alternative," Karl said dryly. The wood was really coming away now. A heavy shower of dirt came with it. "What's the matter with this young man of yours? Why'd he come here? Running away from something?" He said it with more pity in his voice than contempt. Perhaps he, too, had his own ghosts. What man with any imagination hadn't?

Jack did not answer, but concentrated on getting the heavy timber out of its bed without bringing down the rest of the arch. In the wet earth, the whole thing would collapse soon enough.

Karl took the weight of it on his back. Jack shifted quickly to take the other end. They moved it as gently as they could, back along the way they had come. He could feel the muscles knot in his neck. His clenched teeth eased a little, until at last they reached the next set of supports and were back in the main tunnel.

Without speaking, they set about putting it in place, upright, to shore up the weakened timber, which was already looser. They were born to the same craft, the same heritage of mining, with its courage, loyalty to their own. The same history of disaster and survival.

At last it was in, as far as they could get it. Karl nodded with satisfaction. "Good."

"As good as we can make it," Jack agreed.

"Then we'd better go and find your runaway."

"I'd rather go alone," Jack replied. It sounded abrupt.

"Can't let you do that." Karl smiled, but there was no yield in him.

"I'm not going to . . ." Jack began, and realized it was pointless. What was he going to do when he found Richards? Say that he had to come back? That people didn't really believe he was at fault for what had happened? They were just thoughtlessly cruel, or too afraid to make sense? Wanted to see someone even more frightened than themselves?

Karl was looking at him steadily.

"He's got a canister of gas," Jack said slowly, measuring each word. "I've got to get it from him before he opens it . . ."

Realization slowly came to Karl's expression, imagination of the disaster, of the terror that drives out all sense. He had been here for nearly two years, just as Jack had, and had seen it all. He must have seen friends die. He, too, would have lain awake in the freezing mud, wondering if this was his last night alive. Every day someone died. For what? Home, family, a place you loved, a chance at life? All the things you hadn't tasted yet?

Karl was the first to break the silence. "We've got to find him. He doesn't really want to do this."

"I'm thinking," Jack replied. "That side tunnel only goes fifty yards in. I didn't pass him. You didn't. We might be able to work out where he is."

Karl thought for a moment or two. "Has he any sense of direction—underground, I mean?"

"I don't think he's ever been underground before. He's not a sapper. He's only been here a couple of weeks."

"But is he a miner?"

Jack felt the desperation rise inside him. "No," he said quietly. "He's from Hertfordshire, near London." He refused to let his imagination see the wooded countryside, sunlight on the grass, the quiet farms he imagined Richards was from. This was a bloody, useless, senseless goddamn tragedy. He had to find this boy and get him back to their own lines so he could be killed next week or the week after. It was meaningless, a gesture of defiance against insanity, a few more days of being alive.

Karl said nothing, but Jack believed he understood. He wanted to think that he did.

They walked one behind the other, Karl leading them toward the German lines. They moved slowly, looking for anything that might tell them if Richards had passed this way. Mostly it would be some mark or other that he would recognize on the way back; that was on the assumption he intended to come back. Jack saw another roughly scratched *DR* and pointed it out to Karl, but it was just before the side tunnel off to the left.

Karl brought an iron coin out from his pocket and tossed it. Jack called tails. The rusty ten pfennig side came up in Karl's palm.

They went down the side tunnel—Jack's choice. That was when it happened. They were both looking so hard at the support struts they did not notice the loose soil at the side until it slid out in front of them, giving way, and Karl found himself up to his knees in water.

Jack lunged forward without even thinking. For a moment Karl was not a German, he was just another sapper, like Jack, caught in an underground river.

The water rose quickly, pouring in from the side, filling the dip in the ground. Jack grasped Karl and pulled him back again, scrambling back up the slight incline the way they had come. The earth crumbled behind them, and water gushed in.

For long seconds Karl was dead weight. Then he recovered his control and pushed himself forward up the incline. Minutes later, they were both on more or less firm ground, shaken, wet, and ice cold, but safe, for the moment.

"I guess he didn't come this way," Karl observed wryly.

"He could be ahead of us . . ."

"Not in the last hour, or he'd have been the one who dislodged that and brought it down." Karl climbed to his feet, offering Jack a hand. "Do you think he'll really open that canister?"

"God knows," Jack said honestly. "He's . . ." He dropped his voice, almost as if he didn't want to say, didn't want anyone to hear him. "He's young . . . other men's opinions of him matter too much. It's easy to say that what's inside is what counts, but when you're far from home, knowing you might never go back, friendship is about the only decent thing left, all that means anything."

His mind went back unwittingly to when he had felt the first real weight of war. He had seen a man he knew blown apart from shellfire. One moment he was a human being, funny, irritating, laughing at anything because he was afraid. A moment later, he was just blood and unnamed bits of body on the ground, no dignity, no life, but still warm.

How did you deal with that, except by staying close to the living, feeling that you belonged, you were part of something that mattered, that somebody else cared what happened to you and would remember you, even if there was nothing recognizable left?

Did Karl know all this as well as he did? Had he, too, once been so young, so terribly overwhelmed by horror and needing to belong? Comradeship was the only thread back to sanity, the only meaning in the darkness.

What had those fools said to Richards that had sent him off to find gas and go into the tunnels? Had their own fear driven out every decency in them? It could. He had seen it before. What did you fight it with? He wanted to beat the hell out of them. That was his own rage, not a cure. Should he let them think they had killed him? Did they care? They would one day, if they lived.

"You've got to believe in something," he said. "At least that you are not alone. Comradeship. A light that you've seen somewhere, even if it's gone out now. Remember where it was."

Karl listened in silence. A single touch on the arm to acknowledge that he understood. No words were necessary in either language. They made their way back along the tunnel and off into the one to the left that they had not tried. It was slow going, much of it not recently used, and every few steps needed testing to see if the ground was still firm. There were patches that were alarmingly wet.

"What are you fighting for if not some kind of truth?" Karl asked quietly.

Jack swung round. "What? You bloody . . ."

"German," Karl supplied for him. He was smiling.

Even in the lamplight in this filthy tunnel, Jack could see that. It was a real smile, at absurdity. There was both pity and kindness. His anger went as suddenly as it had come. He felt empty.

"There's another *DR*," Karl observed. "What are you going to say to him?"

"What?"

"What are you going to say to him?" Karl repeated.

Jack needed to answer, not to Karl, to himself. He turned and started to think about it.

It was getting wetter under their feet.

Jack was choked with anger that he could do nothing to change what was in the dark down here or in the light above. It was all too much. It went on senselessly week after week, month after month. Now it was year after year.

They heard a brief sound ahead, a splash louder than a piece of earth falling would have made, unless it was a very big one.

They both froze. Was it Richards? And even more urgent, did he still have the gas canister?

Karl gestured for Jack to go ahead. Filthy as they were, Richards, if it was him, could tell a British uniform from a German one. God willing he would hesitate before hurling the gas at another English soldier.

For another ten minutes they moved silently forward, slowly, testing each step before they put their weight on it. Increasingly, the soil gave under them. They were going slightly downward. Then Jack saw the figure ahead of him. It had to be Richards. He must have heard them. He swung round, the canister of gas in his hand. His face was white, his body rigid. He slowly raised his hand to show the canister.

Jack stood still. "Richards, it's Jack Barrick. You can't let that go in here—"

"Yes, I can," Richards called back. His voice was high, as if his throat were too tight, even painful. "All I have to do is open it, and throw it . . ."

Jack took a deep breath. He was shaking. "If you let the gas go here, it'll go back onto our own lines—"

"No, it won't! I'll throw it at them!" He glared at Karl with wide eyes.

"Gas is heavier than air, Richards. It doesn't matter where you put it, it must go down. Like water. You can't stop that. It's gravity. In this section, our lines are lower than the Germans'. Or is that what you're doing, aiming at us? At the men who belittled you?"

"No! No, of course not . . ." Richards looked totally confused, and desperately young.

"What are you trying to do? Prove that you're not a coward?"

"I'm not! I was going to kill some Germans. Show those men I'm not afraid . . . that I can do my bit. . . ."

"I know that," Jack said levelly. "They're fools, and I'll tell them so. Worse than that, they're disloyal."

"They won't believe you . . ." Richards's voice cracked. He was close to hysteria. His hand holding the gas canister was shaking. Jack feared he would drop it and it would roll downhill, back to the British tunnels.

Jack took a deep breath and let it out slowly. Deliberately lowered his voice. "They are lying to you, trying to push you into doing something stupid—to cover their own fear."

He watched Richards carefully, the confusion in his face, the terror—he was fast slipping out of control.

"They are only words," Karl said quietly in English. "They are trying to make you do something they wouldn't dare. Their fear has made fools of them. You are a better man than they are, and they know it."

Richards was confused. He looked from one to the other of the two men facing him, one in British uniform, one in German.

Jack took a step forward. "Put the canister down, Richards," he said quietly. "Come back with me. No one else need know about the gas."

"They'll find out . . ." Richards looked utterly wretched. He raised the gas canister even higher, as if someone were holding on to him and slowly letting go. He lost his balance. The earth under him was crumbling. One of the uprights bent, and there was a tearing sound. Like ripped cloth, only it was wood. Soaked through with slow, creeping water.

Richards lost his balance. His face filled with terror as his legs buckled underneath him.

Karl lunged forward, taking the weight of the splintering upright on his back and pushing Richards onto the firmer ground behind him.

The gas canister fell out of Richards's hand and rolled away. If the upright fell on it, it would break open. Jack leaped after it, landing hard, twisting his ankle and cutting his hands, but he got it. It was cracked already. He caught the smell of gas. There was only one thing to do with it.

He took it to the fearsome crack where the upright had come away. He threw the canister as hard as he could, and watched the crumbling earth swallow it almost immediately.

There was a cry from Richards, high in his throat, choked with anguish.

Jack turned in time to see Karl disappear and the rock fall as the whole section crumbled to pieces and collapsed into the tunnel below it.

Richards stood ashen-faced in the thread of lamplight.

Jack felt a sense of loss so profound it was as if part of himself had gone under those crashing rocks to be buried deep in the earth forever. It could so easily have been him.

Was Karl an enemy? Or only his own face in a mirror? He stood still, numb with loss, until Richards spoke to him.

"What are we going to do?"

Jack turned slowly. Richards looked like a child, bewilderment in his eyes, tears on his face.

"We're going back to our own lines," he said quietly.

"It's too late . . ." Richards began.

"No, it isn't," Jack argued, with no idea if he was right. "There's comfort in loyalty, even to stand together in the wrong. And there can be a lot of loneliness in the right. You're too young to have to make a decision like this. But time won't wait. Karl died for you. I dare say he didn't mean to, but he did it anyway. You are coming back with me, and you are going to keep silent about this, but you are going to re-member it. You are going to help those who are more afraid than you are, and you are going to be a bloody good soldier. Even if you are terrified, you're not going to give in. You've got debts."

Richards stared at him, his eyes wide with fear.

"We're all scared," Jack said gently. "But you can sleep if the things you're scared of are outside you. When they're inside, you never lose them. Come on, we're going out. We're going to put this right."

Richards looked at him for a long moment, then he turned and faced the fallen earth behind him, under which Karl was buried. He gave a small, tight smile, then came smartly to attention and saluted.

Jack swallowed hard and did the same.

The Nature of the Beast

WILLIAM KENT KRUEGER

I am Neanderthal. Part of me anyway. Or so say the geneticists who have studied Eurasian DNA. I think of this ancient ancestor of mine as brutish, but that's not how I see myself. I'm a modern man, educated, sophisticated. Still, I know that even modern men have a brute in them somewhere. If you're lucky, you never have to come face to face with this beast out of time. But luck has never been my strong suit.

Often, in the gray of first light on summer mornings, I leave my house in St. Croix Falls and head to the Balsam River, a lovely flow of water a few miles south of town. It's a good trout stream that runs through a broad meadow bordered on the north by an enormous stand of old-growth white pines. In northern Wisconsin, most of those giants were cut a century and a half ago, felled to feed our nation's insatiable appetite for cheap lumber. That great stand, which us locals call Weyerhausen Woods, was spared by the great lumber baron Lucius Weyerhausen, who maintained a cottage in the heart of the forest, a little hermitage. The woods and the hermitage, which long

ago fell to ruin, passed down to his family, along with the broad
meadow where the trout stream runs. Generation after generation,
they've left all that beautiful land untouched.

It was a warm June morning. I stood in the middle of the Balsam
River, casting my line. I was trying out a new fly that I'd tied myself.
The stream was clear and clean, as it always is. The air was fresh and
scented with the tang of pine. I felt lucky. Not just in what I might
catch that morning, but lucky to be in such a place, a rare kind of
Eden. I had just cast, dropping my fly at the upstream edge of a little
pool. That's when I looked up and saw that I was not alone.

He stood at the edge of the woods, eyeing me warily. At first, because we were so far from any house, I thought he was just a stray dog.
But his size made me think again, and I studied him more carefully.
When I understood what I was looking at, I wondered if I should be
afraid. I'd never seen a wolf in the wild.

I was concerned that any movement I made might startle him, but
my line had drifted far downstream and I began to pull it back in. The
wolf didn't move. I cast again and studied the animal more closely. His
fur was mostly gray but with a bit of white, and a snowy patch on his
forehead shaped roughly like a star. Although I knew nothing about
wolves, the animal seemed unhealthy, far too thin. I wondered if hunger was a part of the reason he had ventured so close to civilization.

Then a trout struck my fly. I began playing the fish, and my attention shifted away from the wolf. When I pulled the trout from the
stream and held it aloft, the wolf stepped nearer, his blue eyes steady
on my catch. He limped as he moved, favoring his left forepaw, which
was covered with dried blood.

I'm normally a catch-and-release angler, but after I'd removed the
fly's barbless hook, I tossed the trout toward the wolf. At that sudden
movement, which must have seemed threatening, he shied away, but
when the trout landed in the wild grass near him, he froze. He eyed
me and he eyed the flopping trout, and his hunger gave him little
choice. He lunged for the fish, snatched it up in his jaws, turned, and
made quickly for the woods, where he melted among the great pines
and disappeared.

. . .

"A wolf?" Robin said. My wife was at the stove, frying eggs for us both. I was sipping orange juice at the breakfast table as I told her of my encounter that morning.

"One of his paws was hurt," I said. "I wondered if he'd been caught in a trap."

"If he was desperate, he might have attacked you."

"I don't think so." But what did I know? Maybe she was right.

"Wolves travel in packs, don't they? Maybe there were others, and if they were all hungry, how safe would you be then?"

A question worth considering, I supposed. But it didn't stop me. I returned to the stream the next morning. I angled, but my real focus was on the stand of white pines. The wolf didn't appear. Which was probably safest, I told myself, but I was disappointed nonetheless.

I turned my attention to my casting, and after a while, a trout took the fly. It gave me a satisfying fight as I worked it in. When I lifted it from the clear water, the wolf was there, at the edge of the stream, eyeing not me but the fish. I tossed the trout into the grass on the bank, the wolf snatched it up and limped back to the pines. Before he vanished, he turned the white star on his forehead toward me and gave me an ice-blue stare. Then he was gone.

I went back to the stream that evening, this time taking a big, raw, bone-in ribeye that I'd put in my creel, and that I'd refrained from mentioning to Robin. I angled for a bit, but it wasn't long before the wolf appeared. I waded to the bank where I'd left the creel, took out the ribeye, and heaved it to the far side of the stream. The wolf didn't shy at the toss. He limped to the steak, took it between his teeth, gave me another long, penetrating look, and returned to the woods.

Over the next couple of weeks, I brought offerings, morning and evening. I wasn't sure if this was the wisest course, but the animal's thin look began to improve, and his limp grew less noticeable. I made no mention of this to Robin or to any of our friends. Partly this was because I was sure that feeding a wild animal this way, particularly a wolf, was something they might object to. And partly it was because I didn't want anyone to intrude.

One evening, well into our relationship, I brought a big ham bone with lots of meat left on it to throw to the wolf. But when he came from the forest, I saw that he held a rabbit in his jaws. He approached the bank of the stream, studied me, and let the rabbit fall. He remained a few moments, then returned to the dark among the white pines. I waded the stream and accepted what I believed was an offering.

The next morning, Armand Grogan showed up. And that's where this story takes a dark turn.

I didn't see the big man until he hailed me from the meadow. He came wading through the tall grass and the wildflowers, leaving a path of crushed vegetation in his wake. I judged him to be maybe sixty, with a broad, tanned face and an enviable head of silver-gray hair that had been razor cut. He was huge and lithe and moved with an athletic grace, such that I thought he might have been a pro football lineman in his younger days. Or an action movie star because of his good looks. He wore khakis with a knife-blade crease down each pant leg. His shirt was tailored to fit the broad expanse of his chest exactly. His shoes were of some fancy Italian design.

He paused on the bank and smiled at me as I cast my line in the middle of the stream. "Catch anything?"

"Not yet," I said, trying to sound congenial, although the truth was that I bridled at his intrusion in this place which, over the years, I'd come to think of as my own little sanctuary. I'm not the only angler who fishes the stream, but everyone knows this spot is mine. Also, I hadn't seen the wolf yet, and I figured that, because of this intruder, I wasn't likely to.

"Any idea who owns this land?"

I told him the name of the family.

"Do they live around here?"

"Chicago," I said.

He turned toward the old-growth white pines. "Haven't seen trees like this before."

"Not likely to again," I said.

"Chicago," he said. "Thanks, friend." He turned back the way he'd come, but instead of retracing his steps, he waded through the meadow following a different route, crushing more lovely flowers as he went.

We received word a week later. Armand Grogan, who I learned had been the intruder that evening, had made an offer on the land, which the Weyerhausen family was seriously considering. Grogan, we understood, intended to build a luxury Northwoods lodge among the white pines, with a view overlooking the Balsam. It would require roads and the felling of many of those beautiful old pines, devastating news to all of us in St. Croix Falls, even those who didn't angle for trout. We'd all grown up picnicking along the river and exploring Weyerhausen Woods.

We held a hastily called town meeting, and our collective decision was to make the Weyerhausen family a counteroffer. As a community, we would buy the land to ensure its preservation. We weren't certain how we'd raise the money, but putting a halt to Grogan's plan was the first order of business.

While we awaited a reply from the Weyerhausen family, I continued fishing the stream, morning and evening, and the wolf was often my companion. I didn't need to offer food anymore. He no longer limped, and I could see that he'd fattened himself to a healthier look. I honestly didn't know why he showed up, except that maybe he was the proverbial lone wolf, and even a lone wolf craves companionship once in a while. He would sit on his haunches, watching me cast, and sometimes I found myself talking to him, as if he could understand. One of the things I talked about a lot was the uncertain fate of Weyerhausen Woods, and so of him.

The family rejected our offer. They explained it was all business, and Armand Grogan had countered with an offer of his own. The family gave us two weeks to decide if we wanted to make another, better offer.

In the time we considered our options, which were dreadfully few, I found solace in angling the Balsam River. I was out there one evening when Grogan himself showed up, wading through the meadow, which had recovered from the destruction of his previous passage. He came to the riverbank and stood watching me a long, silent time, as if making some important assessment. Whether it was of me or my activity or the river, I couldn't say. My line jerked and I played in a trout, removed the hook, and returned the fish to the stream.

Grogan shook his head and finally spoke, in a congenial tone. "Never saw the use of fishing if all you do is throw the damn thing back."

"In large measure, it's a contemplative exercise," I told him.

"Fancy name for a waste of time."

"Do you ever find yourself in deep contemplation of anything, Mr. Grogan?"

He laughed, flashing teeth perfect and even, like tight rows of white marble gravestones. "I learned a long time ago never to think about a thing too long or the chance to strike is gone. A philosophy, my friend, that's taken me pretty far in the business world. Do you have a name?"

"Perry Palin," I told him.

"I'm afraid I have some bad news for you, Mr. Palin." The look on his pretty-boy face was grievous, and his tone reminded me of maple syrup dripping down a stack of cakes. "As much as it pains me to deprive anyone of such an obvious pleasure, I intend to close the river to public fishing when this land is mine. I'll have to reserve that privilege for the guests of my lodge. I'm sure you understand."

He gave me a smile that appeared warm but chilled me like ice water, then turned away abruptly and wandered along the riverbank, where he flushed a covey of quail. He lifted his arms as if sporting a shotgun and pretended to fire. I mimicked him with an imaginary rifle of my own, and put an imaginary bullet in the back of that handsome, empty head.

He kept strutting along the apron of the meadow that separated Weyerhausen Woods from the Balsam, a privileged squire surveying his estate. I watched him, then swung my gaze to the woods. In the shadowy dark under the trees, the wolf watched him, too. When the man was far away, the wolf turned his glacial-blue eyes to me and we stared at each other for a long, thoughtful while.

In the two weeks given us, the good folks of St. Croix Falls couldn't muster the financial wherewithal to better Grogan's offer, and the land was sold. Our county commissioners held an emergency meeting to discuss what might be done legally to preserve the integrity and beauty of our little Eden. Practically the whole population of our small town was there.

Grogan somehow got wind of the meeting and came up from Minneapolis to attend. He brought his wife with him, a woman of great beauty, easily thirty years younger than he, a trophy bride, but with the look and attitude of a muzzled animal on a leash. She sat quietly through the meeting, her eyes never once making contact with anyone in the room. I felt sorry for her. She made me think of a beautiful creature in a cage. He also brought a lawyer from one of the best firms in the Twin Cities. The commission considered zoning regulations, taxes, estoppels of any kind they could think of. The lawyer had a legal counter to them all. In the end, it was quite clear that Grogan had us by the throat, and there was nothing to be done.

At meeting's end, the big man stood and said to the gathering, in a voice so unctuous I wanted to throttle him, "Believe me, I do understand how you must feel. And I hope you understand that there's no personal malice in any of this. It's just what I do. I see something I want and I take it." He shrugged, as if in resignation to a force over which he had no control. "The nature of the beast." He smiled, a savage grin with no charm in it at all. "But I'll tell you what. Any of you I decide I like, you'll be welcome to visit Grogan's Northwoods Lodge. And"—his eyes settled on me—"if I like you and you fish, I might even allow you access to the trout stream once in a while."

It took the surveyors a few weeks to show up. In the meantime, I continued angling on the Balsam River. Although the beauty of the place didn't change, my sense of it did. A heaviness lay on me, as if a death sentence had been handed down. Dying doesn't require that a beating heart be stilled. The spirit of a place can be killed, and what's left in the wake of its passing is an emptiness sad enough to make the angels weep.

The wolf remained my companion for a while longer. He was another reason for my concern. What would happen to him when the big machines came to cut the trees and bulldoze the land? Sometimes he sat at the edge of the woods and watched. But occasionally he would come to the very edge of the river and lie in the tall grass and wait for me to throw him a leftover ham bone or the last part of a pot roast or the occasional trout. He didn't need my handouts. He'd healed and had become a hunter again in full, a powerful predator from the look of him. But he still accepted my offerings.

When the surveyors arrived, he vanished. It didn't surprise me. His territory was being invaded and there was nothing he could do about it. I knew that feeling. I was pretty sure he'd gone back to wherever it was he'd come from, probably the safety of the deeper forests farther north. And then I heard news that sent an arrow of sadness deep into my heart. A wolf had been killed fifty miles north, shot by a farmer who claimed it had brought down one of his sheep. For several days after that, I wandered Weyerhausen Woods, thinking that maybe it was a different wolf that had been killed, hoping I'd catch a glimpse of the wolf with the white star on his forehead. Eventually I was forced to accept the truth, and I found myself grieving, shedding tears as if I'd lost a brother.

Still, my search of that ancient forest wasn't completely in vain. Near the end, I found the carcass of a deer, a young buck with its throat torn out and its bones stripped of flesh. I could see that the animal had been dead a good long while, well before the wolf had vanished. It was frightening to think of the violence that must have been involved in that kill. But as I stood there, staring down at the empty cavity beneath the white arch of the rib cage, I felt something in me stir. Something ancient and brutal and startling in its appeal.

And I thought that the wolf and I and my far-distant Neanderthal ancestor were not so different after all.

My first idea was to shoot Grogan, lie in wait somewhere in the woods when he came to check on the progress of the surveyors, and put a bullet from a hunting rifle through his heart. It happens all the time in Wisconsin, this kind of fatal accident. But it usually happens in hunting season, and that was still far away. Besides, I wasn't a hunter and had no idea how to fire a rifle accurately. So hit and run, maybe? An ATV accident as he strolled through the meadow? But there were problems with that, too. For starters, I didn't own an ATV. Also, I knew they were noisy little machines and there was no way Grogan wouldn't hear it coming. And even if I did manage to run him down, there was no guarantee it would kill him. I'd probably have to hit him several times, and I couldn't see that scenario playing out easily. No, dead immediately was best. If I were truly a Neanderthal, I thought, I'd simply smash his head in with a club.

That's when I remembered an incident on the Balsam River many years ago. A neophyte angler had slipped on mossy rocks along the riverbank, fallen, and hit his head. He'd tumbled into the stream and had drowned in three feet of water. I rolled this over and over in my head and finally decided that if I planned it right, with one swing of a club, I could let the Balsam do the rest of my dirty work.

"You invited him to fish with you?" Robin looked at me as if I'd lost all good sense.

"Not exactly. I said that I would be willing to show him the spots for angling so that his lodge guests might have a better chance at being successful, if fishing is what they have in mind."

"Those places are sacred to you, Perry."

"Were sacred," I said.

She eyed me carefully. "There's something in it for you." She put down her dinner fork and considered what that might be. Then her eyes widened. "You're not hoping to weasel your way into his good graces so that you can continue to fish the stream?"

I looked away.

"Oh, Perry, tell me that's not true."

"That's not true," I said without conviction.

"Trout fishing is so important to you that you'd sell your soul to that devil?" She got up from the dinner table and left the dining room.

The next morning, the stream and meadow and woods were as beautiful as I'd ever seen them. The sky was liquid sapphire. The song of the larks reminded me of the sacred chants that greeted each day in ancient monasteries.

In the middle of the Balsam, I cast my line again and again, the fly lightly touching the surface of the water in exactly the same spot each time, a skill from a lifetime of angling.

Grogan arrived long after first light, his loud passage through the deep meadow grass making the larks fall silent.

"Goddamn dew," he said shaking the water from the soaked cuffs of his pant legs. "First thing I'm going to do is lay an asphalt path along here."

He stood at the edge of the stream, waiting for me to acknowledge his presence, but I continued to cast.

"I haven't got all day, Palin." Now that he had what he wanted, he dropped all pretense of civility.

"That's the thing about trout fishing, Grogan. It takes you out of time for a while. Nothing matters but you and the stream and the trout. It's harmony."

"Did you bring me out here to feed me some poetic crap, or are you going to show me where to point my guests who want to catch trout?"

"I see you wore expensive shoes. Italian?"

"What the hell difference does it make?"

"They might be nice in a business meeting, but you have to be careful here. A few years ago, a man died in this river. Slipped on rocks just like those at the edge of the riverbank where you're standing, hit his head, fell in, and drowned. A freak accident, but if you don't watch yourself in a trout stream, Grogan, anything can happen."

"And you're telling me this because?"

"Just figured you might want to warn your guests."

I reeled in my line slowly and made for the bank. When I'd arrived that morning, I'd set my creel in the grass near the spot where Armand Grogan now stood, growing visibly impatient.

I set my rod on the ground and lifted the lid on the creel.

"Let's get on with it," the big man said. "I haven't got all day."

"Have you ever seen a trout in the water, Grogan? Beautiful thing. A creature wholly suited to its environment after eons of evolution. It belongs there."

I was talking too much. I could feel my heart hammering, my breath coming in shallow intakes. My hands were shaking as I stood looking down into the creel, which was a fine willow design, and which Robin had given me on my fiftieth birthday.

"Goddamn it, Palin," Grogan said. "This is too much. I've had it with you. I've changed my mind. You're never fishing this stream again. You can say goodbye to your precious fishies."

My mouth was almost too dry to speak, but I said, "Take a long look into the water. If you're careful, you can see them, holding themselves steady in the stream, their perfect muscles working against the current. It's a lovely sight, one I promise you'll never forget."

"Screw the fish."

"Just do it, Grogan," I said in a guttural voice that startled me, a voice that was not mine but that of an ancient ancestor.

The tone seemed to take Grogan by surprise, and he did as that brute voice commanded. He turned away from me and bent over the stream.

I reached into the creel and came up with the pipe wrench and swung it against the back of Grogan's head. But he didn't tumble into the stream as I'd intended. That block head of his was thicker than I'd imagined.

He straightened up, looking stunned, and stumbled backward, the weight of his huge body carrying him away from the river. When he fell, it was into the grassy apron. He lay there, looking up at me, his eyes glassy. I raised the wrench again and prepared to bash in his skull.

In the moment of lifting that weapon, however, I hesitated. The first blow had come from a place inside me, ancient and brutal. Killing was all I'd had in mind, and I'd swung with a full heart. But now, seeing him helpless on the ground, another more evolved and humane element of my being took over, one that stayed my hand so that I couldn't bring myself to strike the fatal blow.

Which was all Grogan needed. He swept his leg, as powerful as a rhino's, and knocked me off my feet. In the next instant, he was on top of me and had gripped my wrist and forced the wrench from my hand. He bent down inches from my face, his hot breath breaking over me. Blood from the wound I'd delivered ran down the side of his head and dripped onto my cheek.

"Not your nature, Palin?" he growled. "Couldn't follow through with the kill? That's what separates the sheep from the wolves. Oh, I'm going to have so much fun ruining your life. I'm going to put an end to everything you love."

His eyes were afire with the thrill of the kill. He pinned me for an eternity, his blood falling drop by warm drop onto my face, before he finally lifted his great bulk and stood above me, his hands fisted on his hips.

I rose slowly, a man defeated, and gathered the wrench and my creel and my rod, and left the field of battle. While I slunk away, he laughed cruelly at my back. I turned once and saw that he stood with his legs spread wide, his arms raised in victory, in exactly the pose, I imagined, of a gladiator who'd just finished the slaughter of some poor schmuck in the sand of the arena.

When I got home, Robin took one look at me and her face filled with concern. "Didn't go well?"

I slumped into an easy chair. "Do you know the name of a good lawyer?"

Robin knelt and gazed up into my defeated eyes. "What do you need a lawyer for?"

"Neanderthals used clubs," I said. "But I'm a modern man, and modern men, I guess, use lawyers."

It was the surveyors who found Grogan's body, their attention drawn to the deep meadow grass by a huge cluster of noisy crows, which scattered at their approach. I never saw any photographs of the scene, but in several newspaper reports I read graphic descriptions of how Grogan's throat had been savagely torn out.

Over and over in my mind's eye, I have imagined how it must have been: *That handsome brute of a man leaves the stream and starts through the meadow. In the dark beneath the pines, the wolf waits, powerful muscles tensed, all his senses tuned to the movement of his prey. He has hidden himself in the forest long and well, hidden himself from all men's eyes, even mine, patient as a good predator must be. Now, at the perfect moment, he launches, a streak of animal fury, gray against the green of the tall meadow grass. He hits Grogan with the full force of his body. The man topples, the wolf all over him. Grogan's great hands struggle to keep the sharp canines from his throat, but the wolf is a blur of savage movement, an inexorable killing machine, the result of millions of years of perfect evolution. Grogan never stands a chance.*

The death of Armand Grogan became legendary in my neck of the woods. Man killed by wolf. The state's wildlife authorities launched an intensive hunt, but they never caught even a glimpse of the wolf with the star on his forehead. For a while, we were all cautioned against going near Weyerhausen Woods or fishing the Balsam, but I paid no attention.

Grogan's widow, his trophy bride, had no interest in pursuing her husband's plan to build the lodge. She donated the land to the county, which created a preserve. I have always suspected that she wasn't particularly sorry to be rid of a husband like Armand Grogan. Self-preservation is part of the nature of us all. If there were ever a person born to crush the human spirit, it was Grogan.

I'm a modern man. But here's the thing. Always in my imagining of

Grogan's demise, when the wolf has finished his terrible business and stands with blood dripping from his jaws, he turns his head and fixes me with his glacial-blue eyes, and before he returns to the forest, a look of perfect, ancient understanding passes between us and something deep inside me whispers, "Brother."

Sad Onions

A *Hap and Leonard Story*

JOE R. LANSDALE

M e and Leonard were cruising back from a fishing trip.
We'd been at a cabin that Leonard's boyfriend, Pookie,
owned on the lake. Pookie couldn't make it, but we had the key, and
we spent a partial day and a lot of the night sitting in lawn chairs on
the cabin's deck where it overhung the water, sitting with big glasses of
ice tea, now and again casting our fishing lines. During the day we hid
under the shadows of our wide-brimmed straw hats, and pushed them
back on our foreheads at night to feel the cool breeze blowing off the
lake, rippling the dark water.

We caught four fish and threw them all back. Those fish would
have stories to tell. Hope word didn't get back to Aquaman. Things
might turn nasty.

Of course, the trip wasn't about fishing, it was about me and Leonard hanging, without distractions, talking. We had both been through
the mill as of late, and some time off was doing us good, and it probably wasn't hurting my wife's feelings either. She and my daughter were
spending a day doing pretty much the same thing Leonard and I were
doing, minus the fish.

Now it was over and it was deep night and I was driving us home. The moon was a silver slice. Shadows hung from the trees on either side of the narrow road like crepe paper at a funeral. We were fifty or sixty miles from home. I was driving Leonard's pickup and he was dozing on the passenger side. There were a lot of curves in the road and the headlights danced around them. I wasn't driving real fast, but I wasn't messing around either. I was ready to be home and in my own bed with Brett.

The road straightened out finally, rose up a hill where the trees were thick on my left and thin on my right. As the truck's headlights topped the hill a woman showed up in my lane, waving her hands.

I swerved and crossed into the left lane, wheeled around her, found the right lane again, skidded to a teeth-rattling stop that nearly sent me off the edge of the road, where I would have bumped over a short drop of weeds and rocks, and possibly would have fetched up against a barbed wire fence. If the fence snapped, they might have found us and the pickup wearing a couple of cows.

Leonard came awake with a shout, looked at me. I didn't say anything. I got out of the truck and rushed back to where the woman stood in the road, wringing her hands, crying, and yelling, "He's down there."

She was as pale as I was, had her blond hair up in a pile. Strands of it had slipped loose and fallen across her face like leaking vanilla. By moonlight, and I assumed by any light, she had a very nice face. She was carrying a white purse. It was draped over her shoulder by a long strap. She was wearing an expensive-looking white dress and had on a silver necklace and matching double bracelets on both wrists; they clattered together like the wagging tail of a rattlesnake. She wasn't wearing any shoes.

By that time Leonard was with us. His black skin looked like sweat-wet chocolate in the bright moonlight. It was that kind of weather, even late at night.

I said, "I'm going down for a look."

"I'll get her out of the road," Leonard said. "Come on, lady."

Leonard gently touched her arm, guided her toward his pickup. I watched them go away, him walking slow, her balancing on her naked toes like a ballerina, trying to put as little of her feet on the blacktop as she could manage.

I went down the hill. I could see a white Lincoln at the bottom of it. A ridge of trees stood in front of it, and between the trees I could see the barbwire fence that ran behind them. The car was mashed up primarily against a sweetgum tree, though part of an oak had got into the act. White smoke was hissing out from under the hood. The windshield was shattered, but still in place, the front of the Lincoln was as crumpled as an accordion.

I looked through the driver's window. There was an elderly black man behind the wheel, the side of his head resting against it, a semi-deflated air bag pushed up against him; it made him look like a man hugging an oversized pillow. His face was turned toward me and the front of his bald head was warped so bad it looked like some kind of special effect. His face was coated in blood, his mouth was open, and there were teeth missing. One of them had nestled on his blood-covered chin.

I tried to get the door open, but it was locked or jammed up. I went to the other side and that door came open. I crawled across the seat and touched my fingers to the man's neck. He was as dead as my youth. When I got out of the car, I noticed the lady's high heels were there by her door, where she had left them to better climb the hill.

I climbed up the hill and got my cell out of my pocket, tried to call 9-1-1 but there wasn't any service.

I went to the truck and spoke through the open driver's side window.

"Listen," I said to Leonard. "You take her into town, or get to some place where there's service and call. I'll wait here."

"How is Frank?" she said.

"We'll let a doctor decide," I said.

She burst out crying. She sounded like a banshee. Leonard said something soothing, then wheeled them out of there, leaving me beside the road, standing in the moonlight, smelling the heat from the Lincoln's engine as steam rose up the hill in thinning white plumes.

. . .

I went back down the hill, hoping I was wrong about him being dead. Nope. He was so dead there needed to be two of him.

As I walked around the car, I noticed there was a mark on the back end of it, and as I continued around it, I saw the front left tire was blown. On the passenger seat, there was blood. I hadn't noticed any on the woman, so I presumed it was the man's, thrown there by impact and gravity. I noticed too that some of that blood had got on my pants when I crawled across the seat.

By the time I climbed up to the road again, something was itching at the back of my brain.

Leonard came back not long after, but the ambulance and the emergency crew got there first, followed by the law. It was that county's sheriff's department, and we didn't know any of them. We are usually detained or arrested by someone we know.

The entire hill was lit up by emergency lights. It looked like a nightclub up there. I answered some questions, gave the deputy, a stout black woman named Celeste Jones, all the information I had. She didn't look down the hill at the car. I guessed she wasn't the one for that. She made it easy for us and let us go.

Going home, Leonard driving, I said, "How was she?"

"Said she was Terri Parker, and she seemed to be rolling with the punches pretty good. She's twenty-seven, and the dead man is her husband, Frank Parker."

"You have that curious tone," I said. "Like the one you get when you realize you have on mismatched socks."

"I'm thinking I got another pair just like them at home. Hell, I don't know, Hap. I got a funny feeling is all."

"You and me both, brother."

When Leonard dropped me off at home, the porch light was on. I used my key, slipped in quietly. My daughter, Chance, had stayed over. She was sleeping on the couch. It actually folded out, but the thing was far more comfortable if you didn't bother with the fold-out bed, which could feel a bit like a torture instrument from the Inquisition.

Her long, dark hair was hanging off the couch, touching the floor. I couldn't see her face. I had only known about her for a short while, never realized I had a daughter until she was an adult. It was pretty wonderful.

I went quietly into the kitchen, got the milk, poured myself a glass, found some animal cookies on one of the shelves, sat down at the kitchen table to snack on them in the dark.

After a while, I crept upstairs to the bedroom, slipped into the bathroom to brush my teeth, pulled on my pajama pants, and climbed into bed.

Brett rolled over and put her arm across my chest. I could smell the sweetness of her hair, strawberry shampoo.

"Catch any fish?" she said.

I thought she was asleep and was surprised when she spoke.

"We caught them, looked them over, and sent them home. There was something else, though."

She rolled over again and stacked her pillows behind her head, sat up against them. She didn't turn on the light.

"Like what?" she said.

I told her about the woman, the car, and the dead man, ended with, "Something didn't seem right."

"You said the passenger seat was bloody?"

"That's right."

"Did she have blood on her dress?"

I thought about that for a long moment, remembered the shimmering whiteness of it. "I don't think so."

"She had her purse, but left the high heels at the bottom of the hill?"

"Yeah."

"Shock can make you do all kinds of funny things, but why didn't she carry the shoes with her is my first thought? Seems staged."

"That's pretty good for not being there," I said.

"I'm amazing. Now I'm sleepy again. Good night."

Brett readjusted her pillows, put her arm across my chest again, and went back to sleep.

I lay there thinking, which can be pretty painful on most occasions, but at that time of night when I should have been sleeping, it was akin to an injury.

I eventually slept.

I didn't go into the office of BRETT SAWYER'S INVESTIGATIONS until ten. By that time Brett had already gone to work and Chance had gone home. Chance left a note.

DADDY. YOU ATE MY ANIMAL CRACKERS.
LOVE YOU. BUY MORE.

When I got to the agency, Brett and Leonard were there. Leonard was having his morning vanilla cookies, dipping them gently into coffee. Brett had her long red hair clamped back and she was sipping from a mug of coffee about the size of a fish pond.

When I closed the door, Leonard said, "Brett asked me about the blood, and I got to say, like you, I didn't see a drop on her."

"I think she didn't want to sacrifice the dress," Brett said.

"Yeah," I said, "something about this whole thing stinks."

"Did you shower this morning?" Leonard said.

"You know what you can do?" I said, and then I told him. It was anatomically impossible, but I told him anyway.

We spent the day tapping pencils against things, looking out the window, wondering what we would have for lunch. No one came in with a job. No one came in to ask our opinions on anything. There was nothing outside the window but a parking lot, and across the street some houses, and in the oak by the lot a squirrel jumped about now and then, but it was more like it was squirrel duty, no real enthusiasm there.

Brett made another pot of coffee and we sat looking at one another some more, saying nothing. Arguing politics wasn't going to cut it. We'd been there before. Leonard was the only black, gay Republican I knew who was a Vietnam War hero and only listened to country music. There are others I didn't know, of course.

Talking religion wouldn't work either. We were all atheists. So, we talked about the night before, kicked that around a bit, and since it was really none of our business, we got right on looking into it.

Leonard drove me out to the wreck site while Brett stayed at the office and looked into the dead man, Frank Parker. Out at the hill, we parked off the road and made our way down to where the car had been.

It had been hauled off, but in the daylight we could see clearly where the tires had made deep marks in the earth as the car jetted off the road. My phone may not have had service there, but it took good photographs and I took a lot of them.

"One thing I realize now is the tree impacted on her side," I said. "But it was Frank who was all messed up. She came out pretty un-scathed. And as has been noted, she wasn't covered in blood, even though the seat where she would have been sitting was. It was a hard-enough crash to make the bag pop, but was it enough to kill him? He had quite a lick to the front of his head, where the bag would have protected him."

"It do be curious," Leonard said.

"Let me add something else," I said. "The back bumper, I could see well enough last night to see it was banged up."

"Like someone had used a car or truck to push it?"

"Could have been a bang from a previous accident, but . . . And another thing, there are tire marks as the car goes off the road, but no skid marks."

"Yeah," he said. "Add it to the other stuff, it starts to paint a dif-ferent picture. And you know what else I think?"

"She had help."

"Bingo."

.   .   .

Back at the office Brett said, "Frank Parker founded Sad Onions."

Chance worked with us part-time and she was there, too, her pretty face alight with youth, framed by that lovely hair, dark as the far side of the moon.

She said, "Sad who?"

"It's a chip company," Brett said. "They dry out onions into chips, and the chips are in a kind of . . . I don't know. Droopy shape. Anyway, Frank called them sad onions, because they're droopy. It's stupid, but hey, it caught. Company also makes chips out of other vegetables. Get this, after the onions, their biggest seller is made from a dried turnip."

"Who eats that crap?" Leonard said.

"I've had them," Brett said, "better than you think. Some of them are salted, some are peppered, and some are straight dehydrated veg-etables with no frills. Frank Parker started out an onion grower, over around Noonday. Soil there is supposed to be great for onions. Makes them sweet. Anyway, he figured out how to dehydrate them and turn them into chips before every other company was doing it, and he got rich. And he got married."

"Terri," Leonard said.

"Yep. He was seventy, and she's twenty-five," Brett said.

"And a hottie," I said.

"Watch it, Buster," Brett said.

Chance snickered. She liked it when I was in trouble.

On the way to the sheriff's department that had investigated the crime, Leonard said, "I don't think that woman was ever in the car, that's what I think. She was down there waiting for someone to come by. Standing down there today, a car went by, and I heard it a long time before it got there, because that's how sound is at the bottom of that hill. She left the shoes there to support the idea she had been in the car, and to climb the hill faster."

"I think you're right."

"That's a first," he said. "Next thing you'll learn to love guns and quit supporting liberal politics."

"I don't think so," I said.

At the sheriff's department they let us cool our heels in an interrogation room, something we were professionals at. It was a full thirty minutes before Deputy Celeste Jones came in.

"You wanted to see me?" she said, and took a chair at the table across from us.

"We don't think that wreck was just a wreck, and we don't think the lady fair is true and blue," I said.

Celeste turned her head and cracked her neck. I almost expected it to fall off.

"Yeah," she said. "Why are you thinking that?"

We gave her our thoughts on the matter, showed her the photos on my phone. She got out a pad and wrote down some notes, then it was over and all three of us were walking toward the front door.

Celeste said, "Something stinks, gentlemen, but the sheriff thinks it is exactly what it looks like. He's not the sort to disbelieve a pretty, blond white woman."

"But you are?" Leonard said.

"Sometimes," she said. "But I'll tell the sheriff what you said, how you feel. Up to him to figure out what to do about it."

It was about nine the next morning when we heard someone coming up the outside stairway to the office. I went to the window that overlooked the lot and took a gander. There was a sheriff's car from the next county in the lot, with a crunched front end. The law showing up is seldom good, even if they're out of their jurisdiction.

There was a gentle knock. I opened the door. There was a young, lean, black man standing there holding his white cowboy hat. He wore a sheriff's outfit and a deputy sheriff's badge. He had hound-dog eyes and a soulful look, a smile with enough fine teeth an alligator would have envied him.

I invited him in. He shook hands with all of us, sat in front of the office desk, and looked across at Brett, which was a view I envied. I sat in a chair at the corner of the desk, next to Leonard, who had his butt parked on the edge of the desk.

"My name is Journey Clover, and really, that's my name."

I figured that was remarked on a lot and he wanted to clear up questions right away.

"Okay, Deputy Clover," Brett said.

"I came over to tell you that the whole thing with the wreck, the thing you fellows came across, has been wrapped up."

"You came all the way over here to tell us that?" Leonard said.

"Seemed the polite thing to do, considering you came by yesterday to voice some suspicions. I'm here to tell you we have done a thorough investigation, and it was nothing more than an unfortunate accident."

"That's a quick investigation," Brett said.

"We have good people," he said.

"They must be damn good," Leonard said. "Two days later and it's done?"

"Simple case," he said. "Listen, I don't want to be impolite, and we appreciate your concern, your ideas about this, but people, it's done. It was nothing more than an accident."

"And you'd rather we not poke our noses into it?" Leonard said.

"I suppose that's right. I knew Mr. Parker well, by the way, liked him. I used to be an insurance salesman before I went to work at Sad Onions. Sold him some insurance. He seemed like a really nice guy, did lots of charity work."

"What insurance company did you work for?" Brett asked.

"Regency Mutual," he said. "I wasn't much of a salesman. Sold Parker a policy, liked him, and went to work for him in the office. I have an accounting degree. But it didn't suit me, so I ended up in the sherriff's department."

"That means you knew his wife as well?" Leonard said.

"Not much, a little. On sight, that sort of thing. She came into the office, of course, went to lunch with Parker. But, hey, that's all I got. Celeste wanted to keep you in the loop. She said she had suspicions, too, but the investigation closed them out. She feels it's all been answered. Well, got a bit of a drive, so nice to meet you. Just wanted you to know."

After Deputy Clover left, Brett said, "Tell me I'm not the only one that found that odd."

"You're not the only one," Leonard said.

I nodded. "Yeah. Drives all the way over here to tell some civilians how things turned out. Usually you can't get a thing out of the law, even if you're the victim."

"It do be peculiar," Leonard said.

"Yes, it do," Brett said. "Follow the money. Meaning I'm going to talk to some insurance folks I know, then see what I can find out about Mrs. Parker. You and Leonard check up on Clover?"

Me and Leonard drove over to Clemency, which was the town where Clover's office was located. Leonard was at the wheel and I was sitting in the passenger seat watching the scenery rush by.

"Front end of Clover's car was smashed in," I said. "Wonder what the story is on that?"

"You're thinking like me. What if Clover gave Parker a little push from behind, sent him down that hill into those trees."

"I was thinking what if Parker was dead before he went over the edge in the car. His head was really bashed in, and it seems to me the airbag would have prevented a wound that bad. I think they killed him and stuffed him in his car and he bled like a stuck hog. Also thinking since Clover knew him and his wife, maybe Clover wanted to be in the clover, decided to help the wife bump the hubby for some insurance money, and she came with it?"

"But why would he leave Sad Onions, become a deputy, if he wanted to be near her?" Leonard said.

"Husband could have got suspicious, so Clover needed to put some space between them."

"Maybe," Leonard said.

We stopped in at a greasy spoon that looked like a railroad boxcar. We had caught it at a time when no one was there but us. We bellied up to the counter, ordered coffee and burgers.

The server who brought us our food was a middle-aged white lady with a tired face, but a sweet attitude. She wore an old-fashioned waitress hat that was precariously perched on her hairdo, which was intended to be blond, but looked like an enormous wad of pink cotton candy.

If anyone knows the citizens of a town, it's a café worker, a barber, or a bartender. I gave her my most heartwarming smile.

"We're wondering about an old friend of ours, Deputy Clover. You know him?"

"I do," she said, "and if you're such good friends, why are you wondering to me?"

"Touché," I said.

"Thing is," Leonard said, "we're insurance investigators."

"Yeah?" she said. "So, not old friends."

"There was an accident outside of town, on that high hill. A man was killed," I said. "We're looking into some possibilities."

"Possibilities?"

We didn't respond to that.

"Cutting to the chase," Leonard said, "you ever see Mrs. Parker come in with Clover?"

"Nope, not once, but she didn't act like much of a wife."

"No?" I said. I tried to say it like the idea of infidelity was something I had never considered or even heard of.

"Way she hung on that woman when she was in here, in the back booth there. . . . I just don't get it. Two women?"

"What woman?"

"The black deputy at the sheriff's department."

Click.

. . .

Outside in the car I said, "So, what did we learn?"

"We learned that waitress doesn't like two women together, so I have to make sure to bring my Pookie here for lunch someday and rub up against him, see how she likes two men."

"You are such a devil," I said.

"We also learned that Deputy Jones talks a good game, but by acting concerned about the event and then clearing it as an accident, it seems she may be throwing suspicion off herself."

"But what about Clover? He's the one that came over to talk with us, and his car has a banged bumper. Might have come from pushing Parker's car off the road."

"You know, we ought to go to the department, thank Deputy Clover and Deputy Jones in person for keeping us in the loop. See how that plays."

We drove over there, didn't find Deputy Jones, but Clover was still around.

In the breakroom at the sheriff's department, Deputy Clover said, "You came all the way over here to thank me for what you already thanked me for? We talked yesterday."

"We're very polite," Leonard said.

"Sounds to me like you're piling up something I might need hip boots to walk through."

"Your cruiser, man, it took quite a lick to the front," I said.

He studied us for a moment. I kept expecting him to pin us and mount us on a board.

"That's Deputy Jones's car. Borrowed it while mine had some general inspection. Just did a favor for her, letting you guys in on things."

"Where is the good deputy," Leonard said, "so we can thank her in person?"

"Her day off. I'm starting to try and figure how I can make things difficult for you boys."

"Boys?" Leonard said. "You call an alligator a lizard?"

"You should go now," Clover said.

. . .

When we were in the car, the phone rang. It was Brett. I put the phone
on speaker.

"Insurance payout for Parker's death will be plenty," she said.
"Enough to live on for the rest of your life."

"Would it be enough for two?" I asked.

"Maybe for four or five, as long as they didn't trade their Maserati
in every year."

I told her what we'd found out.

"Hang on," she said.

I could hear keyboard keys clicking. In a bit she came back and
said, "I got Celeste Jones's address for you."

Deputy Jones lived in a simple house outside of town, somewhat se-
cluded. There was a cruiser parked in front of the house. There was no
garage or carport.

We went up to the door and Leonard knocked. While we waited, I
glanced at her cruiser. It was in good shape. Had it already been fixed?

No one answered the door.

"You know, Hap, I'm not feeling good about this."

I walked over to one of the windows, cupped my hands together,
looked inside.

"You're about to feel less good," I said.

Leonard came over for a peek, said, "That's not good."

"No, sir, it isn't."

We could see Deputy Jones sitting on the couch, her head thrown
back. She looked very comfortable, not a care in the world, and this
was due to the fact that she was as dead as Christmas past.

We hustled around back and used my lockpick to enter through the
back door. Deputy Jones hadn't become undead and gone into the

kitchen for a soda. She was still in her position on the couch. She had a small bullet hole right between her eyes.

"Up close and personal," Leonard said.

"I think Mrs. Parker may have decided she didn't want to share the money," I said.

"Bingo," said a voice sweet as Georgia honey. It was Terri Parker, of course. She was holding a shiny little revolver, and it was pointed at us. "Sit on the couch."

"By her?" Leonard said.

"Yeah," she said, "by her. She won't bite."

We sat on the couch, away from the blood as best as possible. Terri stood near us, held the gun like someone who knew what she was doing.

I heard a car drive up. From where I sat I could see directly out the window. It was another sheriff's cruiser. I felt a moment of hope, but when I saw Clover step out of the dented car, I knew we were in a deeper pit than expected.

Terri unlocked the front door and let Clover in. He looked at us and the deputy on the couch.

"Should have left things alone," he said to us.

"I'm thinking kind of the same thing," Leonard said.

"I had to shoot Celeste," Terri said to Clover. "She grew a conscience. Then these two losers came in."

"That's all right," Clover said. "Splits better two ways."

It clicked then. It had really been Terri and Clover all along, and the whole thing with Deputy Jones had been a cold-blooded attempt to make her sympathetic, help clear up the investigation. But Jones got covered in guilt, so she had to go.

And now, so did we.

When night had settled in good, we were walked out to Clover's cruiser, forced into the backseat, along with Deputy Jones's body, which we had to carry. We propped her up between us.

Clover had wrapped Jones's head in towels and then put a black trash bag over it, tightened it around her neck with a bathrobe belt. Leonard and I were both put in handcuffs. I wished for a moment that I had just taken the chance before that was done, been shot out in the open and had it over with.

As Clover drove, Jones's body rocked between us.

"You two have made things kind of messy," Clover said through the wire grating between the seats.

"That's our bad," Leonard said.

"However, there's a nice old abandoned gravel pit full of water where I think Jones and you two will be real comfortable," Clover said.

As Jones wobbled between me and Leonard, I managed the lock-pick out of my front pants pocket, and was casually using it to unlock the cuffs. They went easy. When Terri glanced away, I passed Leonard the pick across Jones's body. He sat quietly and looked out the window, but his hands were working.

The car stopped at the end of a narrow road in the depths of the woods. We were near the gravel pit. We were eased out of the car at gunpoint. We could see into the pit, and it was filled with water; it was near big as a lake. The moon was up high and it had grown a little fuller. Its image lay on the dark water like a slice of fresh cantaloupe.

We had the cuffs draped over our wrists and we held our hands close to us. I was shuffled from my side of the car to the other by Terri and her six-shot accessory.

"Drag her out, drop her in the water," Clover said to us, nodding toward Jones's body.

"That's messed up," Leonard said, "us dragging her out and then you shooting us and putting us in the water."

"No," Clover said, "we'll shoot you on the edge of the pit. We won't have to do any carrying."

"Well, you thought that through, didn't you?" Leonard said.

"Get the body," Clover said.

"Sure," Leonard said, moving toward the open back door, "but Hap, first, the elephant of surprise."

That had become a kind of code for us. It meant do something, anything, and do it now.

I wheeled, let the cuffs drop, went low, clipped Terri at the knees, sending her flying over my back. I turned in time to see Leonard fling the cuffs in Clover's face and kick him in the crotch.

Clover staggered, but didn't go down. He fired awkwardly and missed. By that time, me and Leonard were running like gazelles down a wide path and into the woods. The path turned behind a thickness of trees. Several shots were fired at us. They rattled through the leaves like rain, and one of them nipped at my hair.

A moment later, we heard the cruiser fire up, and lights were cutting through the trees. Clover was driving the cruiser back down the path, trying to find us.

The trees were too thick with briars for us to hide in, so we ran down the curving trail until we came to where it ended, the gravel pit, dark water, and the floating moon. It was about twenty feet down to the water and there was a lot of garbage visible. Couches, washing machines, a broken dresser. It had become a dump, and that crap was probably stacked all the way to the bottom. Jumping wasn't going to turn out any better than being shot.

The car came around fast. We were trapped at a dead end. Me and Leonard split up. He went left, and I went right, into the woods on either side where the briars had thinned.

Clover skidded to a stop, got out with his pistol. Terri stayed in the car, slid behind the wheel. The window was down on the passenger side, and I could see her waving her gun through the open window. She couldn't wait to shoot somebody.

"I'm going to make you suffer if you make me hunt you," Clover yelled out, like it was incentive for us to just come on out and be shot.

I looked around, found a piece of pipe that had been tossed into the woods, tried to pick it up, but it was nothing but rust and came apart in my hand. Then I saw an old baseball that had been thrown out. I picked it up. The cover was mostly off but it was firm enough, and it was all I had.

Clover was moving close to where I was hiding. I couldn't go toward him, because of the gun, and to go through the woods behind me would lead to the pit. I was between a killer and a wet spot.

I cocked the ball back, stepped between two trees, into the open. Clover saw me. I flung the ball. It was a good throw. There was some real meat behind it.

It sailed beautifully across the moonlit trail, and glided over Clover's shoulder. I felt like an idiot.

Clover looked at me, grinned, raised the pistol.

That's when someone screamed.

Clover wheeled to look, and I dropped back into the woods, out of the line of fire, near the edge of the pit. From my hiding spot I saw the source of the scream was Terri. Leonard had come out of the woods on the driver's side, surprised her, and grabbed her gun arm, which she was hanging conveniently out the window.

Clover stepped to the center of the road, aimed at Leonard, and fired. But the shot went wide, punched a neat hole through the windshield. I saw Terri's head fly back, and then, dying, she reflexively stretched out, stomping down hard on the gas.

The car jumped and Clover didn't. It hit him so hard it knocked him flying ten feet in front of it, over the edge of the quarry. The body of Deputy Jones flew forward and hit a wire grating, dropped out of sight.

I watched as Clover's body hurtled down and smashed against a washing machine with a cracking sound like a rotten limb. It bounced over some more junk and slid into where the water was deep.

The car came right after him, shot downward like a bullet, right where Clover had gone under. The car hit with a splash and the moonlight shook on the water. The impact drove Deputy Jones's body back against the rear windshield. Her bagged head hit it hard enough to cause a spiderweb of cracks, and then she fell toward the front of the car and the car went under.

I walked into the road, stood on the edge of the quarry, and looked down. Leonard joined me. The car's taillights creeped beneath the gurgling water, where they glowed momentarily, then went out. The water rippled for a time, finally went still, and it was done.

The Wagatha Labsy
Secret Dogtective Alliance

A Dog Noir Story

JACQUELINE WINSPEAR

PART ONE
The Assignment

Let's cut to the chase. Tom and Livvy—Dude's humans—are missing. Gone. It's a big deal, because people don't just up and vanish in our 'hood. And *anything* that goes amiss on our patch is a big deal. It's an action signal for the Wagatha Labsy Secret Dogtective Alliance. We don't have an agency, per se, but we're sort of allied. We do what we have to do because we're the only ones who can do it. Who'd leave the solving of mysterious goings-on around here to a pack of humans?

Before we go any further, you need to know who's who in the 'hood—which is in a small town twenty-five miles north of the city of San Francisco. Location-wise, that's all you need to know—we protect our privacy.

There's Wagatha Labsy, aka Wags, Aggie, Waggy-girl, and The Wagster. I'm sure you know that all dogs have at least four names assigned to them by people like yourselves. Humans. I'll get to my own monikers in a minute. Wagatha Labsy has a day job. Works narcotics.

Mainly SFO—that's the airport—and the docks. She used to be on the fruit, nuts, and meat beat, but jeez, she felt bad, you know, sniffing out an apple some old lady forgot was in the bottom of her bag when she flew in from Madrid or Paris, maybe London. But now Wagatha's nose is finely attuned to illicit substances, from recreational herbs to the hard stuff, though she says what they're really after now is something called fentanyl. And she don't just work the airport and docks—she's a *numero uno* trained asset and is deployed on all the big busts, which is why she has a few days R & R this week—K9 snooze time. There's only so much an efficient olfactory system can handle. Oh, and in case you didn't guess—she's a Labrador. Black. Like soot.

I'm Rebel. Aka Rebsy, Rebbo, and sometimes just Reb. Pure German Shepherd. Former SFPD K9. Took a hot one in the shoulder while in pursuit of a perp. The boys rushed me up to UC Davis. Lights and sirens. CHP outriders all the way. We take care of our own, and Davis, in case you don't know, is the big university veterinary hospital, where I had the best docs working on me. I pulled through, but the department had to retire me. Big ceremony, medals, party—the whole deal, plus press photo call with me and Ed, my human partner. He got a stomach wound on the same job, and the perp got him in the leg, too. He was in the hospital for a while—not the same one, duh! Then rehab.

We've both had a hard time adjusting. Ed's now on what they call "PR duty." He goes around to schools talking about the safety stuff that kids should know and how not to get into trouble. If he's expecting a tough crowd—and you know what they're like, these kids—he'll take me along. One sassy comment, and I get up, slink along real low, and stare down the little shits. No one, but *no one* talks back to Ed on my watch.

Okay, down the line here, and I'll make it snappy. In the house across the street there's Penny Lane, and it's anybody's guess what she is—Aussie Shepherd, bit of Corgi, maybe some sort of oodle in the mix. I tell you—those oodles get everywhere. You buy any brand of oodle, and in my humble opinion, you've been had. Got yourself one overpriced mutt. Not that I'd mention it to Penny Lane, aka Penno,

Pensy, Pen, and—get this—Pen-E-Lope. That's what her mom calls her. Pen-E-Lope. And Pen's a bit off-kilter, for a dog. Rocks out to the Beatles' *White Album* when she thinks no one's looking, but—take note—she sees more than she lets on, which is why Wagatha called her into the Alliance. She's not as stupid as she is strange-looking.

Hank's up next. Lives two houses along from Pen. Hank's a New-foundland. Big black, hairy giant, looks like a walking rug. Guards the refrigerator. Never takes his eyes off the refrigerator unless his people go to the cupboard. Then he's there, at the cupboard, waiting. Do not—I repeat—do not leave any rations anywhere near Hank. You won't even see him get into your bowl, he's that fast. Hank's in the gang because he's huge—like Hagrid, the big hairy guy who keeps an eye on Harry Potter. I'll get to the matter of dogs and reading later. Oh, and Hank—the Newfie, with webbed feet designed to save people from the sea? Terrified of water. Go figure.

Wrigley—aka Wrigs—is on my side of the street. Another big black Labrador. WTF is it with these Labradors? Former seeing-eye dog, just didn't make the grade. If he'd gone out with a blind dude, the poor guy would've ended up dead. Wrigs gets distracted. But you know, he has a nose on him, and we like a good nose, so Wagatha okayed him joining. I heard the gal who named him was a fan of the Chicago Cubs.

Next we have Ella from the 'Hood—and you should see that little gal. White terrier crossed with something else that's got a lot of 'tude. Ella's human dresses her in dog coats from freaking Armani, Gucci, and—get this—Chanel! You could say Ella (aka Ella Bella, Ella-roo, and sometimes even Sweet Ella) cleaned up real good, because her human doesn't know that, before she rescued Ella, that dog was known as Rats, and she owned—yes, owned—Bernal Heights until it went upscale, courtesy of all those Googlers moving in. Ella's one fearless little fighter, and she's on the team because Wagatha said she was fast off the mark when it came to a scrap. Ella from the 'Hood is our ammo.

Ladybird is our go-between with the coyotes on the hill. She wanders at night and there's nothing escapes her notice. She comes back with serious intel and reports to Wagatha every day, which is how we keep the 'hood clean—not mean.

Moving right along there's Dude. Aka Doody-boy, Dooley, Doody-do-do. His people—Livvy and Tom—are the young couple on the street. Thirtyish, both work for tech companies, so they ain't short of greenbacks. You see them out on their mountain bikes on the weekend—and we're talking top of the line. Josie, Ed's girl—she's with CSI—says those bikes probably cost more than her horse. Livvy and Tom have got their own business stuff going on the side, so they're working 24/7, according to Dude—he says they're into developing apps or whatever the hell.

Wagatha gets it because her department liaises with the data protection and fraud guys, and she okayed Dude for the Alliance because we needed a techie hound. He watched and he learned. And like all you humans, his people don't know his capabilities. Only problem is his . . . well, let's call it his "attire." Makes Ella from the 'Hood look underdressed. His people taught him to ride a skateboard, and they bought him some shades and a baseball cap with holes for his ears to poke through. Goes with the image, I guess. I said to him, "Dude, why'd you put up with it?" and he says to me, "Keeps my people happy—and I've got a good gig. If it ain't broken, I ain't gonna fix it. They get me high-quality kibble, treats from a fancy puppy store in the Embarcadero Center, so what do I care?" I could see his point.

Maya's probably mostly Labrador, but there's something else in there, too. Something suspect. I'd say pit bull—just a spoonful, enough to give her an "I can take care of myself" edge. She hangs out with Ella because they're both rescue dogs. Maya would never start a fight, but boy, does she know how to finish it. Do not mess with Maya. She's sharp as a whip and together with Ella, they are our sniper force. They can go in, take out whatever needs taking out, and get home without anyone being any the wiser.

Now I get to the final member of our gang. But he's still on probation on account of his age. So, here's how it goes. Ed comes home a couple weeks ago, strokes me on the head and says, "You need a pal, old fella." I didn't like the sound of "old fella." As Wagatha might say, it did not bode well.

Ed goes out to the car and comes back with a crate. First thing that goes through my mind is, *Oh shit. Now what the freaking hell is this?* Yeah, you know what it is—it's a freaking kid! And not only that—Ed has completely lost it because it's a Border Collie pup!

I give Ed the look that says, "Ed, partner, my buddy, Ed—you've got more sense than this. You do not bring home a Border freaking Collie unless you also have a freaking sheep or two in the backyard! He is going to drive us out of our minds!"

Even Josie says, "But Ed, these dogs are herding dogs." What she left out was "Where the f%*k is his herd?" But Ed just brushes it all aside, and calls him Angus. Something to do with his heritage. Whatever that is.

Now to the case. "At last," I hear you say. Yeah, but you've gotta know who you're dealing with in the Wagatha Labsy Secret Dogtective Alliance first, haven't you? Otherwise you'd've been stopping me and asking me who was who. Or whom.

Wagatha had just come off a big job—pulled in a shipment of cocaine coming up from the south. All the narcotics guys were on it. So, like I said, she's on R & R right now, though her handler don't get the vacay. I guess I left out most of the human names, but they're not what you'd call germane. But Tom and Livvy are important because they vanished.

As I was saying, Wagatha had just come off an all-nighter, and her human was opening the passenger door to let her out of the car, when they saw Wrigley and his person across the street with Dude. Dude was downcast—you know, droopy eyes, all "Oh, woe is me"—so there was a conversation about what was going on, and Wrigley's person said that the back door of Tom and Livvy's house had been left open, and she'd heard Dude howling in the kitchen—in a crate. Wow.

Wrigs told me that the minute the story started, you could see the hair on Wagatha's neck go up. Just like that—you know, full-on hackles. That's when me and Ed came along for our morning walk. I don't need no leash. I know my place and I am right there, by his side—where I've been since basic training. Which is more than can be said of freaking Angus. "What part of 'heel' are you not getting, you little shit?" I growled. Before we could say "Cute Puppy Approaching," the humans were all over little Angus. And Wagatha's handler should have known better, having just been given serious intel and letting it slide. Wagatha nodded to Wrigs and me, and we did some sniffing of one another and Dude—we didn't want the humans to know what we were communicating about. At this point I will say that I do not know what Wrigs gets into, but it has to be cat scat, because he just stinks. At both ends.

Wagatha brought us up to speed about Dude's people. Dude one-pawed his skateboard back and forth, so it looked like he was playing.

"Did you see anything suspicious?" asked Wagatha. "I mean, Dude—you must've seen something."

"Nothing much, because I'd chewed some good shoes yesterday and was confined to crate."

"A crate?" said Wrigs. "What kind of shoes were they? Livvy's new trail runners?"

"Wrigley." Wagatha raised her nose. He shut up.

"You didn't hear anything?" Wagatha pressed the Dude.

"I had my headphones on," he said sheepishly. "I caught a look at one guy, came to the door."

"Wassup?" Ella joined us. She was wearing a new Kate Spade coat. Her person was distracted by Angus and was all, "He's just the cutest!" If Ella hadn't been more interested in us, Angus would have been chow. I sighed in relief—I didn't relish having to protect the little bro from Ella's fangs.

Wagatha summed up the story, then said, "If Tom and Livvy haven't been located by lunchtime, the Alliance meets at the top of the fire road, under the redwoods. Twelve hundred hours. You know what to do." She looked at me. I'm her lieutenant—did I tell you that? "Reb, we'll need Ladybird for reconnaissance into C-territory. Bring

Penny, and someone tear Hank away from the Wilsons' fridge—
Ladybird will need backup if this goes dark. Ella, make sure Maya's
with you—I want sniper presence."

"Ten-four, Wagatha," I said. The others raised their noses.

The human talk came to an end. The professionals—Ed and Wagatha's human—agreed that Tom and Livvy would probably be back
later, but they'd check in anyway. No one wanted to sniff them out at
their day job—might cause embarrassment—but they'd call if they
had to, maybe just to tell them they forgot to lock the back door, but
Dude was okay because he was with Wrigs.

"They're employed by one of those strange places where the people
all sit around on multicolored plastic blocks, like it's preschool," said
Ed, laughing.

Wagatha looked at me. It was her grave look, the sort she has when
the smell of something amiss is under her nose. We knew—we'd all
got the vibe—that the strange place right now was our street. And it
was our duty to protect it. Semper Fi.

PART TWO
Coyote Grove

Samba, the Rhodesian Ridgeback/Great Dane, who lives closer to
town, reported that there was nothing to report. He'd ambled up the
road to find out what was going on and said he'd post lookout—he
can see right into the local police department from his living room.
There was nothing doing. Samba wants into the Alliance, so he's been
providing intel lately. I don't blame him—he's alone sometimes when
his human goes off on business trips, though on the other hand he
kinda likes it because he gets to walk with Wrigs, and he's got that
Ridgeback independent thing going on. But his human lets him have
the run of the house, so he hangs out in the living room, watching.
Wagatha says he'll probably make it in the next recruitment go-round,
after I've given my field performance report.

At 1200 hours we met under the redwoods. We were all there—the boss, me, Penny, Hank, Dude, Wrigley, Maya, Ella (coat by Stella McCartney), and, yes, right there in my shadow, Angus. Ladybird crawled out of the bushes. Angus gave a yap and began circling.

"Angus. Angus, will you just get over here now!" My lip was curled above my gums.

Ella went for him and he yelped.

"Ella! No!" said Wagatha, hackles up. Ella opened her mouth to complain, but Wagatha had already turned to me. "He should begin his lessons, Reb—he can't go on like that."

"I know. I'll start him tonight."

"On what?" said Dude. *"Lassie Come Home?"*

"I said I'd deal with it," I snarled.

"I've some information," Maya piped up. She was a dog who liked to get the job done. No messing around. "I heard my people talking this morning—about Livvy and Tom. Before we knew they were gone."

Ella snarled at Angus again. I felt him lean into me.

"Go on," said Wagatha.

"Talk was that they've been doing well—and I mean *real* well. My man works in the same biz, and met Tom for lunch. Couple days ago. Little bistro south of Market."

"What'd they eat?" Hank pushed forward.

"Hank, would you shut up?" said Penny.

Wagatha took down Penny and Hank with one look.

"There's this stuff called VC money. Means venture capital, and it's a lot of cash given to someone to invent something, or when they've invented it, for the big-money guys to buy in," said Maya. "There was a lot of interest in what Tom and Livvy had. Whatever it was."

"Dude—Tom and Livvy ever mention anything to you?" Wagatha knows people talk to their dogs—tell them a lot they wouldn't tell their best friend. Or their doctor.

Dude shook the shades off his nose, let them drop. Eyes filled up. "I knew they'd had some serious cash coming in. All those Embarcadero Center treats—they don't come cheap. They bought me a new bed. Memory foam. Thick and soft. And another for the crate, so even if I'd been a bit, well, bad, I wouldn't suffer."

"When did you ever suffer, you shit," said Ella.

Maya rolled her eyes. "Ella, don't mind me saying, but—"

Angus came closer. If I was a kangaroo, he'd've climbed into my pouch.

"Go on, Dude," said Wagatha.

"There was new furniture—and I don't mean Ikea. Top-of-the-line stuff—real comfy couch. And last week a Sub-Zero refrigerator was delivered."

"Sub-Zero!" Hank shot over to Dude. "Why didn't you tell me?" He looked at Wagatha. "New refrigerator means major grocery shopping. I'll watch the Dude at his house tonight."

We all growled. Hank backed off.

Wagatha nodded, taking in Dude's description of the change in Tom and Livvy's fortunes. She raised her head, shot a look at Ladybird. "Are you ready for the coyotes?"

Ladybird seemed to slink lower. She was ready.

"Okay," said Wagatha. "Ladybird, you go up the hill, but I want Reb and Hank as backup a few paces behind. Maya and Ella—on the banks either side of the path so you're flanking the team. Watch Ladybird like a pair of hawks—any trouble and you go in." She paused. "Ella—lose the jacket."

"Pen, pull this thing off me, would ya?" said Ella.

"Angus, you stay here," she added in a soft voice. "And do not move at any point. Unless you want to be coyote chow." She went on. "Dude, you're emotionally involved, so you stay with the boy. Penny and Wrigs—second tier behind Hank and Reb—and keep your distance. If they're down, you go in—understand?"

They nosed the ground. They were ready.

"As soon as Ladybird gives the signal, I'll approach."

Wagatha pawed the tarmac and we started up the hill, just like she said. Ladybird first, then me and Hank. I heard him breathing hard.

"You've gotta get some cardio going, Hank—you'll be dead before you see a Sub-Zero."

"It's my undercoat. Needs combing out—it's like I'm wrapped in a duvet."

Ladybird turned. Lifted her right front paw, the signal to stop. "Wait until I've made contact."

Four more paces and she began to yip, just like a coyote. I could feel everyone's hackles go up. Ladybird was not of this world. She was—well, she was weird. Out of the corners of my eyes, I saw Maya and Ella take up position. Any trouble, and we would all go in.

A big red-and-gold coyote crept out of the undergrowth, his snout like a dagger topped with coal.

"He ain't missed any rations," whispered Hank.

"And you have?" I snipped.

Ladybird and the coyote circled each other, and we heard her yip and he yipped back, and then four more coyotes came from behind. Ella and Maya moved closer, crawling down the banks toward the path—just one false move, that's all it would take.

"What're they saying?" said Hank.

"Would you shut the f—" I started to say when Ladybird turned. "They'll talk. Signal Wagatha to come forward."

Penny and Wrigley moved aside, then fell in behind Wagatha. Hank and me, we kept real close to her, so she was protected. Ladybird crouched nearer the ground, exposing her neck—she was demonstrating Wagatha's standing in the Alliance.

Our leader put her head to one side, then the other. "We come seeking wisdom from you."

"WTF?" said Hank, real low. "What wisdom does that mange bucket have?"

I ignored him. It's the only way sometimes.

"Ladybird says you were seeking sustenance in the trash cans on our street in the early hours. We want to know if you saw something unusual—humans lurking."

The coyote nodded, his eyes on Wagatha. "We might have. Depends upon what's in it for us."

"Of course," said Wagatha. She let the silence hang. Five seconds. "We'll leave rations near every trash can tonight. Good stuff. High quality."

The coyote looked around at his pack, then back at Wagatha.

"Agreed." He paused. "There was a black moving monster with four round paws."

"WTF is that shit talking about?"

"SUV. A sport utility vehicle, Hank," I snarled.

"Outside the house of the one with black eyes and wheels on his legs," added the coyote.

"That's Dude's house." I heard Wrigley behind me.

Wagatha was calm. She was a cool one—all those narcotics busts, you need to be real easy with the trigger.

The coyote started again. "The humans spoke in an unfamiliar tongue." He coughed, his red coat shimmering as the sun shafted through the redwoods. He coughed again, yipped, and described what he'd heard.

My ears went back, and I cleared my throat. "I know the rhythm of that language, ma'am."

Ladybird cast me a look—I hadn't been approved to speak.

"What is it, Reb?" said Wagatha.

"It's Russian, ma'am," I said.

I heard the collective whining behind me. There was muttering, a few growls, and I could have sworn I heard Ella cussing from her place on the hill. That Ella's got a potty mouth.

"You know what that means, don't you, Reb?" said Wagatha.

I pawed the ground. "Yes, ma'am." I could hardly speak. "The Borzois. It means we've gotta go talk to the Borzois."

"Oh heck," said Hank. Only he didn't say "heck"—it just had the same sort of sound. "Those skinny Russian sh—"

Wagatha glared, then motioned Ladybird to come closer. "We must secure safe passage through the coyote grove to see the Borzois. Can you do it? If anyone has intel on Russians, it's the Borzois—it's imperative we speak to them." She uses words like "imperative."

Ladybird walked back to the coyote. The pack yipped and Ladybird returned.

"We can move on through the coyote grove at 1800 hours. They'll be resting before nightfall hunting. It's our best chance."

"But that's freaking dinner time!" Hank whined beside me.

"Listen, you big-assed lug, if you want to get chucked off the Alliance, you're going the right way about it."

That shut him up.

Ladybird agreed on the terms—more food left by the trash cans over two nights—and we all backed up down the hill without turning around. Never, ever turn your back on a coyote.

When we were clear of the redwoods and home on our street, we reconvened.

"The Borzois! That's a whole new bowl of kibble," said Wrigley.

"I'm scared," whimpered Dude.

"You've got to watch those Borzois," said Ella. "Foreign to the core."

"Pedigree all the way through, though," said Maya, which was probably the wrong thing to say to Ella.

"It's certainly an unforeseen impediment," said Wagatha. She was thoughtful. "Ladybird, Rebel, and I will range into the coyote grove, and Hank, we need you there, too—there's always the chance of a renegade coyote. Ella and Maya—as before, you keep to our flanks on the hills either side of the path. Wrigley and Penny—go no farther than the line into the grove. Dude—keep watch on Reb's house and make sure Angus remains inside. This is no place for a child."

She looked up at Samba, who had kept back. "Samba, if you're with us, I want you to make your way up around the other side of the hill, in position above the House of the Borzois. Keep watch from there and give the alert if anything is amiss." She looked around the circle. "This case has only just started, and already we are in dangerous territory. Let us give the signal for danger, so our collective voice memory is refreshed."

We pointed our noses to the sky, to the clouds above us, and we howled. Even little Angus looked up and was doing his best to howl, one paw raised like a true member of the Alliance. Then, as one, our emergency siren-call ended. That's when Angus started running circles around the pack.

"That boy needs some sheep," growled Samba.

PART THREE
The Russians

Angus was down for his nap when I left to meet the Borzois. Ed was home, in front of the TV watching the game—sort of. He was asleep in the chair. And we'd taken in Dude for the night. You guys think you know where we are at all times, but really, you are so in the dark about what your dog is up to.

Maya and Ella fanned out as Ladybird went ahead and spoke to the coyote sentry. We were cleared for safe passage through the grove. And I can tell you, it's not for the faint-hearted. Every cracking twig sounds like a leg breaking. Every branch caught by the breeze could be a coyote ghost. We moved with speed, but stealth. From the track through the grove there's a staircase up to the Borzois' dacha—140 wooden steps to the perimeter of their territory.

They were waiting for us when we got there—Vasily and Nina. They leaped toward us. If you didn't know them you'd be terrified, but these two are like a pair of dancers from the Bolshoi Ballet. Borzois do not walk or run. They prance.

"Comrade," said Vasily. "What brings you here?" One word slid into the next, in the Russian way.

Wagatha raised her nose. "We come to ask for help. One of our pack has lost his people—taken from him. And we believe there was some . . . some interference from humans of your kind." She took her time, let the words sink in. "If you have any information at all, we would be grateful."

"How grateful?"

"Not again—tell them we'll leave out a couple of dead coyotes."

"Hank!" I nipped his flank. Got hair in my teeth—jeez, that undercoat!

"Tell the Canadian to leave," said Nina.

"What?" said Hank. "Oh yeah, I know—they're still sore about that hockey game at the Olympics. And what about Labrador? That's Canadian."

"Hank—move on back a few feet," said Wagatha. Hank sloped back three paces.

She turned again to the Borzois. "That's as far as he'll go—we only return through the grove as a pack."

Nina nosed the air. "There is something we've learned. I cannot reveal our sources. We were at a show yesterday—a meeting of Russian dog owners. There was talk."

"What kind of talk?" asked Wagatha.

Nina and Vasily looked at each other. Vasily spoke. "About people in your ranging zone. Specifically, the humans belonging to the one who has wheels."

A low growl went through the Alliance.

"Where are they?" That was me, cutting to the chase.

"We don't know—but it seems they have come to the attention of some powerful people," said Nina. "And it's all to do with something called. . . ." She turned to Vasily and they jumped around a bit.

"What's that all about?" said Wrigley.

"He's telling her to keep her mouth shut, no more telling, and she's asking why and saying it's only fair to help us," said Penny.

"Hold on a minute. How the heck do you know that?" I had my eye on Pen now.

"I've heard 'Back in the USSR' in Russian—my people have got Beatles recordings in all sorts of languages. They started learning some Russian, and I just kinda picked it up."

"Now she tells us," I growled.

Vasily and Nina stopped prancing. Vasily approached. "Okay. Here's a morsel. We overheard the Samoyeds. The words I heard were 'data collection.' I know no more."

And with that the Borzois turned and danced away, but not before we'd heard the words: the Samoyeds.

"All I can say is, I think the Russians were poor losers," said Hank.

"Shut up, Hank!" we howled in unison.

Wagatha growled us to attention. "It's time," she said. "It's time to bring in the humans. Tomorrow we see Dr. Lacey and Bill."

No one argued. Not even Maya and Ella, who had joined us for our return to the 'hood.

And just so you know, Dr. Lacey Cashman is our veterinarian. She's ex-army, so she's seen action—taking care of our kind deployed in Afghanistan. At the end of her military service, she became our vet, and all I'll say about Dr. Lacey is that she has a heart of gold—but she knows when you're faking it, and she doesn't like sass. You don't mess with the good doc. She also understands us. And then there's Bill— the only mailman who loves dogs, and the dogs love him right back. Go figure. He understands, too. Some humans are gifted that way.

Maya and me were earmarked to find Dr. Lacey in the morning. I stayed with Wagatha for a few minutes to talk strategy.

That night, after Ed had turned in, and—I should add—after a formal "missing persons" report on Tom and Livvy had been filed with the local police department, I settled down for the night. I was tired and my shoulder hurt. But my day wasn't finished yet.

I called Angus from his crate and pulled a book from the shelf. *The 101 Dalmatians* by Dodie Smith. The little fella's education had begun. I'd get him onto *Call of the Wild* as soon as it was age-appropriate.

PART FOUR
The Human Factor

I went with Maya to see Dr. Lacey. We skipped out in the morning while our people slept. Josie came over last night so, well, you know, she and Ed wouldn't be getting out of bed anytime soon. And Dr. Lacey gets into the office real early. She said it was on account of being in a war zone—incoming kept you awake at night, so you learned to catnap. I didn't like the sound of that—never met a cat I could trust. Well, with the exception of Delderfield but she's gone, and sadly missed. Honorary member of the Alliance, and even Ella howled when the big C got that little calico. She served us all her days. Oh, and if you're wondering how me and Maya got out before sunup—hey, you've gotta be kidding! A dog can always get out, if it wants.

We barked at the back door of the veterinary office until Dr. Lacey answered our call.

"What're you two doing here?" she said, kneeling down to ruffle our ruffs. Maya curled into her—she was one tough rescue dog the good doc had helped tame. And because of their bond, the doc can see Maya's pictures real clear. "Looks like you're on a mission." She closed her eyes as she touched us, and we pulled up the pictures into our heads. That's the only way to describe what we do—like running a movie behind our eyes, and Dr. Lacey can see the same thing. It's how she knows when Hank has been at a slice of banana bread with chocolate chips—he cannot get that stuff out of his head.

"Tom and Livvy gone? Is that it?"

Maya yelped, going all paws down.

"Has Ed been to the police?"

Maya and me, we yelped together.

"But what's this about Nina and Vasily—which reminds me, they both need their leptospirosis shots and anal glands attended to."

That was way too much intel.

"Oh—Russians—you think it's something to do with Russians!" She was getting there.

We yelped again.

"Okay, I'll talk to Ed. Make up a story about how I know."

Thank Dog for the doc. Maya and me, we barked our thanks, snuggled in for a hug, and ran home. We split up on the street.

"I'll report to Wagatha," I said. "Thanks, Maya—we needed your pictures to get Dr. Lacey on board."

"Part of the job, Lieutenant," said Maya. "But what was that about the Borzois and their anal glands?"

"Don't even go there, Maya—don't even go there."

Dr. Lacey called Ed and shared her intel. Maya found Bill delivering letters on a neighboring street, and brought him up to speed with her mind-pictures. She reported that Bill said he'd delivered an official-looking document postmarked "Russia" to Tom and Livvy last week. But who uses snail mail with two techies? The plot was definitely getting thicker.

I heard Wagatha's call, and snuck out the back door to meet her between the two big cypress trees.

"We need a lot more information, Reb. We must expand our investigation," she said. "I'm sure the Borzois know more than they're telling. And I don't like the fact that they mentioned the Samoyeds. They can be ruthless."

"Ed's going down to the town PD with what we got from the doc and Bill—Doc spoke to him, so he's in the picture. But the clock is ticking—Dude could lose his people."

We agreed to expand our reach, which would mean some serious roaming. Easy for Ladybird, who was always on the prowl, but long-term absence can be noted. Ed wanted to check out Tom's workplace. I leaped into the car as soon as my partner opened the door. Angus started whimpering about being left for Cruella de Ville to find him. It was time to elevate his education, so I went back inside and pulled *The Art of Racing in the Rain* off the shelf—you know, the one about Enzo, the dog who comes back as a . . . wait, better not tell you. It's a bit of a tough story for a pup, but I think he's ready for it, and it'll distract him until I'm home.

Oh, and just so you know—dogs can read, but we don't do words. No, what we see is pictures. We turn a page and we see pictures in our heads. You know that old saying about putting your nose into a good book? Came from a dog. True.

Tom's company was way cool. Guy at the reception desk—called a greeting circle—took us into what he called a "meeting pod." Didn't even bat an eyelid about me being there, because they are a dog-friendly environment. His words. And as if to prove it, a big fluffy Goldendoodle comes out to say hi. Now, I'm not one to cast aspersions, but a Goldendoodle asking me if I'd like some refreshment feels a bit strange. I wanted to say, "No, let's go outside and lay in puddles, then we'll see what that coat looks like."

But back to the pod. So, we're in this transparent sort of round tube, like being in a big fat water glass, and a "human resources parent" (I know—the names they come up with, like all these people need another mom!) joined us to ask if we had news about Tom, because he's not been in the office, and they assumed he was working from home. I mean, Hello! What sort of place is this? Wasn't it cool to call Tom to find out?

Ed asked a few more questions, but didn't get very far. I think he was thinking the guy was keeping something back. I just thought he was a bit, well, dopey. And I wanted out of that pod!

By the time we were back in the 'hood, some big stuff was going down. I heard the call—the Alliance was in the Redwood Grove. Wagatha brought me up to speed. Nina had danced down the hill earlier and met Penny, who was rocking out to Sergeant Pepper in the front yard. Nina and Vasily had been taken to another Russian dog show last night, after we'd seen them, and they'd discovered that there were people "staying" at a house in the city owned by some Russians—real Russians, from Russia, not just people into Russian dogs or whose ancestors came through Ellis Island, like, one hundred years ago. And apparently those Russians don't live in that house—they just use it.

"Where is it?"

"Russian Hill," said Wagatha. She looked down. "I should have considered the possibility earlier."

"Don't blame yourself," I said. "Who knew Russians lived on Russian Hill?"

Wagatha cast a grateful look in my direction—what good is a lieutenant if he can't support his leader? She pawed the ground.

"Dude, I want you to go home—just for as long as it takes for some pictures to come into focus. I believe you were too upset to receive any before, but now we must have a clearer vision of what happened in the house. Hank and Samba—go with him; he'll need your support." Our leader gave Samba a special look before turning to me. "Reb, Nina gave Penny a picture of the house on Russian Hill, so she'll know it when she sees it. Bill should be along to deliver our mail in half an hour. That gives Dude enough time to receive pictures while Maya and Ella go to Dr. Lacey. Is Ed at his desk in the city?"

"Planning a special conference on violence in schools," I said. "Getting kids, teachers, and police involved." I sighed one of my big-dog sighs. "Sad, that's what it is. Plain sad that it even needs to be talked about."

"Can we get him?" asked Wagatha.

"We'll ask Dr. Lacey to call him."

"Okay, Reb. Let's go over the plan."

We closed our eyes, put noses together, and to a dog we saw Wagatha's pictures in our heads. We knew what to do.

"I can get you all in my van," said Bill. "This street is last on my route today, but don't get your paws on the outgoing mail."

We were loading up when Dr. Lacey came down the street in her truck, Maya and Ella riding shotgun. She leaped out, dogs following. She knew Bill was like her—could see a dog's thoughts.

"Looks like they've done a lot of work, Bill. Can you get everyone in?"

"Almost, Doc. You following?"

"I'll take Hank and Samba so you have more room. I called Ed. Made up a story about an emergency patient coming in and the owner mentioning a house on Russian Hill. I'm sure he suspects something."

"I've some pictures to share," said Dude. You can tell his people are of that strange generation, you know, everyone's sharing and all that stuff. No one can just give someone a call anymore—they have to do this reaching out thing. Really confuses a dog, I mean, our language never changes.

We all concentrated on Dude, and the pictures started coming. The doc gasped. "They had guns! Oh dear—and they took the computers, too."

Bill was shocked. "They didn't even let them change out of their pajamas." He turned to Dude. "Any idea what was in those files they took with them?"

Dude shrugged. "I tried not to get too involved. I thought it was best I didn't know what they were doing—because I knew it was something important."

Wagatha licked his ear. He liked that.

"Okay. Time to hit the road," said Bill.

PART FIVE
The Dognouement

Our mailman drove fast toward the city. Me, Maya, Penny, Dude, Wrigs, and Ella were aboard with Wagatha. I'd managed to lock Angus in his crate, and threw in a copy of *Oogy: The Dog Only a Family Could Love*. It was time he was introduced to memoir, and there's nothing more inspiring than a dog who'd made it up from the streets to become a beloved family pet. It's a tear-jerker, but Angus needs to know that he's got it good—no one is asking him to be a bait dog for the fighters. Maya and Ella wept when they read Oogy's story—they know how it goes when you're a rescue dog.

"This is it—stop!" barked Penny.

We were first to the house on Russian Hill. The street was quiet, just a few cars parked.

Maya whistled. "Check out this pad," she said. "How many rooms do you reckon they have. Twenty?"

"This ain't the Tenderloin, that's for sure," said Ella. She growled.

Dr. Lacey pulled up, releasing Hank and Samba.

"All he talked about was freaking food!" said Samba.

Wagatha called us to attention.

"We have to follow the humans now," she said. "But as soon as we're in—spread out fast. I can see there are three floors, so Maya, Ella, take the third. Dude, Penny, and Wrigs, take the second, and

Samba comes with Reb and me to the first. Hank, you stay on guard at the front.

Dr. Lacey checked her phone. "That's a text from Ed. He's on his way in a black-and-white with another guy from the PD. Busy day—it's all he could get."

My heart sank. I knew what happened. He's a wounded desk jockey now—no one listens to him. It's like he's an old guy—at forty.

Bill rang the doorbell, a package under his arm and his signing device in his hand. We waited behind his van with the doc. I felt hackles go up along the line. We were all trembling, ready to roll. No answer. He hit the bell again. The door creaked, then opened to reveal a tall guy, bald, dressed in a suit, blue, and his jacket bulged at the chest. He was carrying. I'd say it was a Magnum.

"Your lucky day, sir. Anyone's birthday?" Bill smiled at the guy, who frowned.

"Nothing was ordered. We are not expecting a parcel."

Russian. Definitely Russian.

Dude whimpered. "It's him. It's the guy in my pictures."

"Well, I can't take it back with me, sir. You gotta sign for it right here." Bill was firm, and held out the device.

The guy opened the door a little wider and reached for the package, which Bill conveniently dropped.

"Oops," he said.

That was our sign. The pack moved with lightning speed, knocking the Russian over. Doc Lacey ran to Bill's side, a roll of Vetrap in her hand—you know, that bandage stuff they use to keep a dressing in place—and a cone. Before the guy could utter, *"Privet, tovarich,"* we were in the house, splitting up like Wagatha instructed.

Hank sat on the Russian, who started going on about Canadians, so Hank sat harder, putting a paw on his face while the doc coned and tied him. I heard the black-and-white's siren in the distance: Ed was on his way. Maya and Ella had taken down another Russian on the stairs, and he wouldn't be going anywhere anytime soon—knocked out cold. Wagatha, Samba, and I searched the first floor—couple sticks of furniture, and crates stacked everywhere. Wagatha yelped at the crates—she knew what was in there: *fentanyl.* We could hear Wrigs, Penny, and Dude above us, so we launched up the stairs. That's when we heard a commotion coming from the third floor. Doc Lacey was right behind us.

"WTF is going on?" That was Ed in the distance, as he reached the doorstep.

What followed happened fast. Maya and Ella had taken down another two guys, and Wrigs and Penny were keeping them there. Dude was scraping at the foot of a door, the last in a long hallway. Wagatha went to his aid, and I was right there with them. Doc Lacey told us to stand back, then—I swear to Dog, I would never have believed this—she took a flying kick at that door and it caved right in. And there they were, Tom and Livvy tied to chairs, their mouths bound, and they were still in their jammies. Dude rushed up, but Wagatha and me, we turned around—we'd been on enough busts between us to know it couldn't be this easy. And it wasn't. Big Russian guy was pointing his piece directly at the doc.

"One move, just one step, and she dies."

"Does this guy know he's talking to dogs, and that he sounds crazy?" I whispered to Wagatha.

I could see a shadow in the hallway. It was Ed, pacing toward the room real slow. With one swift move he held his gun against the Russian's temple.

"Drop that piece now or your foreign brains will be all over my dog, and I really, really don't want to bathe my dog tonight."

And he don't want no bathing either, I thought.

The Russian dropped his weapon. Doc Lacey went straight to Tom and Livvy, pulling tape from their mouths. But before they could speak, Ed's partner came into the room.

"Whoa there, this is really so freaking weird. We got a mailman at the front door having a smoke while what looks like Big Foot is pinning down a Russian guy with a cone on his head. And we got dogs sitting on Russians all over the place, and now you got dogs in here. Oh, and don't tell me—she's a veterinarian!"

"You got that right, Sherlock," said Ed. "Let's get everyone down to the precinct and we'll get to the bottom of it."

· · ·

And here's the bottom of it. Turns out Tom and Livvy had developed an app to make it easier to process and ship stuff throughout the U.S. of A. and overseas. Kinda like Uber for packages. Not sure of the finer points and how it all works, but anyone can sign up to take packages if they're going to another place—gives them some pocket money when they get there. Sure, there's companies doing the same thing, but this is different. Bigger. And it could seriously dent the coffers of your FedEx and your UPS, to say nothing of putting Bill out of a job. Suddenly, anyone could be a part-time delivery person, and without having to wear brown shorts.

They had documentation and security issues resolved, and serious interest from all the big online outlets. We're talking Amazon, Walmart—and they'd landed what they call "first round funding" from one of those venture capitalists. It was, as Ed said, a slam-dunk straight into the billionaires' club, brunching with Jeff Bezos and Warren Buffett. Who knew? Trouble is the Russian Mafya knew—and don't correct me. It's not Mafia, because they're not Italian.

Anyway, they figured it would be easier to ship contraband—there's an old word for you—across the seven seas. And the Russians not only wanted in, they wanted it all, and in a very big way. So they decided to nab Tom and Livvy and get their hands on everything they knew, or would know in time, holding them hostage until they were no longer useful—and we don't want to even think about what they'd do when they were done. But what the Russians got right was knowledge of the human-dog bond. "As soon as they took us away from Dude," said Tom, "I told them we'd do anything to get home. No decent person leaves their dog."

"Even if that dog chews brand new trail runners," cooed Livvy, her arms around the Dude.

It was enough to make a dog roll in something bad.

· · ·

So, it's been kinda quiet ever since Tom and Livvy came home, except for the celebrations. There was a big old street party, with dog treats from that cool place in the Embarcadero Center. Dr. Lacey and Bill received medals, and so did every dog in the Alliance—nice ceremony at the SFPD. Ed got a promotion.

That night, I settled down in our living room and looked out the window. I was reading *Suspect* by Robert Crais for the hundredth time—jeez, I love his Maggie, the German Shepherd who never left her partner when he was down. I'd given Angus *The Call of the Wild*, and told him Jack London was turned away by a lot of publishers after he'd written that book, and then it became a bestseller. Humans love a dog story.

As the moon lit up our street, I could hear the strains of "Hard Day's Night" coming from Penny's house. I saw Maya's person take her for the last-thing-at-night amble. They stopped and chatted with Ella and Wrigs and their people. Wrigs absconded into Penny's yard, so Maya and Ella brought him back. We all know Hank's sleeping by the refrigerator. Samba went home happy because he passed his review, and Ladybird was in the shadows, slinking toward the coyote grove for a midnight yipping. And Wagatha Labsy was at her window, keeping watch. She looked across and our eyes met. We raised noses.

All was well in the 'hood. For tonight, anyway.

Glock, Paper, Scissors

SHELLEY COSTA

New York City

Here is what I will remember from the moment I shot him:

A bloated half-moon in the cold dawn. The hydraulic wheeze of the garbage truck up the block. A short recoil. A whooping siren that—so soon—had nothing to do with me. The sound of the gunshot peeled a few layers off my old skin, and I was grateful I came to this moment already half deaf. No new loss. Not for me.

He, on the other hand, lurched from the 9mm round and went down inelegantly.

I got close enough that a single shot was all I needed. If I failed with one round, I wasn't doing my job, and my job was stepping up close to this killer. I wanted to be close enough for no mistakes. Close enough for him to know me. He died there on the street. As I had always hoped he would, only many lifetimes too late. Mine. His. And, most of all, hers. Before I turned away from the mess he had always been—now he was just a mess in an Armani coat—I caught a glimpse of his strange marble eyes where death had cut off his stunned recognition of me.

Never had I felt more like my twelve-year-old self, and my heart leaped. I had missed this twelve-year-old girl. I slowly tucked my gun hand back into the soft folds of my long coat. From the other pocket I pulled the carefully folded paper I had opened only twice since that terrible afternoon in July of 1942.

My fingers teased the folds open. I gasped, "Ah," in the carriage lights flanking the entranceway, and I bent over the mess. Finally, I had found a use for him. I smoothed out the priceless paper on the dead shoulder. There it was. There it was, for what would be the last time, and I was content.

The piece of special white silhouette paper she always used for her paper cutting was softer to the touch than ever, and lightly tinged with seventy years of gentle decay. So was I. My skin was paper, my bones were paper, my mind was paper. All this paper life made me light once again, weightless as the homeless twelve-year-old girl I had been when the world blew apart and I went on the run.

Paris, July 1942

There were the careful snips she had made with her scissors hand, the twirling manipulations of the paper with her other hand, the robust swell of Caruso singing *"Nessun Dorma"* on the phonograph as we sat with our china cups of Darjeeling tea, stirring in ginger drops for extra flavor. The final image of what I knew would be an exquisite papercut was obscured until the very end, tiny clippings falling like everlasting snowflakes around her, the fairy tale princess.

"Do Jews have fairy tales?" I asked shyly while she worked, just three nights before the end none of us could see.

The paper twirled, the embroidery scissors snipped. "We have fools and monsters," she said finally.

"So do we."

"We learn from ours."

What she held up, then, was very nearly done, twin silhouettes of us both, back to back like equals, our heads sharing the centerfold. In the cutaway spaces of her half-page were her large dreamy eyes and full and slightly parted lips, always at the edge of a kind word. She had expertly cut out the look of my smaller face, my narrow, suspicious eyes, what she called my Gallic lips, closed tight for fear of letting something slip.

A survival skill.

And not the only one.

At twelve, I had short brown curls. At seventeen, she had long blond waves. We admitted we preferred each other's hair. Then, with a practiced hand, she eyed me and folded my half of the papercut over hers. The cutaway places overlapped. Together, the silhouettes made a single, new person, and my breath caught in my throat.

"We can be partners!" I cried. The idea was so brilliant that the flat she shared with her father, the diamond merchant, brightened.

She sat back. "Partners?"

I spun it grandly for her: "You can snip and I can sell. Up in Montmartre!" My fingers itched. "The tourists are crying to be separated from their francs," I blurted.

She gave me a keen look—those dark eyes slipped to the tear in my pullover that I had pinned—and I sank into a chair, afraid my Gallic lips had let too much slip, after all.

Finally she laughed. "You make it sound like a crime."

"No," I said, raising my chin, "not a crime"—no more crimes— "business partners." We stared in silence at the double silhouette.

"Together," she remarked, tipping her head this way and that as she studied her handiwork, "we are less dreamy and, I think, more wise. *D'accord,*" she announced, giving her tea a vigorous stir, "partners it is."

I cried and hurled myself at her, hugging her tight. If I didn't get it right, since only wind and fear ever held the likes of me, I would never know.

New York City

And in the light snow that was falling now, nearly a lifetime later, I saw tiny flakes land on the eyes that couldn't blink them away. I studied him. Money, I decided, is no proof against the sleek purpose of the Glock pistol I had bought off a street kid in the Bronx thirty years ago. This pistol, this gray polymer lightweight wonder, was an eternal truth. Like fools and monsters.

I lifted the dead arm, slipped the papercut double silhouette from Paris underneath, and let the arm fall. It was a great chance I took, leaving the papercut like a receipt for a long overdue service, but now, in my eighties, there were so few real chances left to take.

Not like lightening my hair later that long-ago day in Paris with peroxide stolen from a chemist's shop in Rue de Rivoli. Not like stuffing my thin, stained chemise with blue powder puffs stolen from a flat where I knew the Jews had been cleared out weeks ago. Not like sticking doorstop wedges in my shoes for extra height before heading for the Gare de Lyon and a night train to Rome. Now, all these years later, I might stand an inch too close to the edge of the subway platform on my way home from this shooting. I might just toss my cane into the Department of Sanitation truck as I passed. I might even add the Glock.

At least, if I didn't get very far, I would have a story to tell.

And it would begin, "My name is Simone Halévy."

And so was hers.

Paris, July 1942

"Take whatever you like, Lisette," she tells me with a smile that fades, "whatever you can use." Then she adds with a choked laugh, "Whatever you can make off with."

Standing in the arched doorway of her bedroom, I murmur thanks. I hardly know what's happening. I only know that in the parlor, she and her gentle father stand hunched over the table and exchange strangled half-sentences. He hears a roundup, clearing the Marais. She hears the velodrome, but only temporarily. He is dressed in the neat black day coat he wears when he goes out to business in the first arrondissement—although, these days, he hardly dares. His graying hair under the skullcap is uncombed, and his fingers fidget over the diamonds.

She pushes personal papers into a neat little stack and her voice is tight when she asks him how they are getting away. Just yesterday a rock broke the front windows, and the two of them knew better than to take the time to clean it up. I am slim and faster than a breeze and used to shadows. I sleep in confessionals and pee in the parks. My ghost fingers pull my livelihood straight from the pockets and purses of others.

From time to time, my brother, Rémy, meets me in our favorite sewer a block from the cathedral. We compare, we tell stories, no longer knowing what's true and what's not, and we yearn for the big score. I whisper about my new friend in the flat with many grand rooms who lets me wash up in their clawfoot tub. I whisper about her father's kind eyes and the red velvet pouch filled with white fire.

"We are going to be partners," I tell him in a casual boast.

"Partners?" he snorts. "She's a Jew and you are"—he sneered—"street trash."

Hearing his scorn all over again, I stiffen and turn back to the chifforobe in her bedroom. My fingers move through the padded hangers of silk and brocade, lightly fingering the beautiful, fine clothes as though I were turning the pages of a priceless book. I count ten pairs of shoes and half a dozen hats. In a satin-lined drawer is a thin jewelry case with her initials, *SMH*, embossed in gold in the lower right corner. How can I choose? How can I carry? And—most important of all—where do I bring these gifts? I have no chifforobe. I have no bedroom, no flat, no family beyond the sly Rémy.

On the nightstand is what she has told me is a prayer book in lettering that looks like dancing figures. The book is encased in an engraved silver cover, with colorful gems inset. My hands shake just to hold a book so valued that it is decorated with garnets and amethysts. Next to the prayer book is a table cigarette lighter made out of porcelain with a design of pink flowers on a curling vine. I shake it. Empty. I am attempting to twist it open, not to refill it, but because I feel my mind shrinking into disappearance at the thought that they are leaving, my friend and her father. No, they are more than leaving. They are fleeing. That much is clear. And all I can do is help myself to mementoes. And steal a safety pin to repair my pullover, its hole from the yellow star on the breast of a Jew up the block, dead from age and exposure.

I am even poorer than I had thought.

Suddenly there are heavy boots on the steps in the hall. In one moment of terrible paralysis, we three look at one another a room apart. *"Trop tard,"* she cries, and again, *"trop tard"*—too late—turning, frightened, into her father's arms. My cunning tells me it's one soldier only, one pair of heavy boots, my ears know the difference—but how can that be? Usually they arrive in pairs, or gangs.

I am fog, slipping silently into the chifforobe, leaving the door open a sliver no bigger than the finest of cuts she makes with her sharp little scissors with the tortoiseshell handle. Barely breathing, I position myself so I can see the parlor. At first I hear no pounding, just the door wrenching open, softly thudding against the wall. I hear no barked commands, no terrible slurs, but she and her father stand, amazed. With a flicker of his eyes toward the table, her father moves slightly to cover the view of the red plush velvet and white fire behind him.

It's the gun I see first, jerking the father and daughter back, back. And it's not a Walther, the Nazi service pistol. Something smaller—

And when the gunman moves into sight, I clap a hand over my mouth, terrified. The sheaf of yellow hair badly cut, the scar on his neck from the knife fight over turf, the slight limp from his tough birth, when nature had second thoughts. My brother. Two gunshots—*fft, fft*—and they go down in blood and silence. As she falls, she half whirls—my teeth sink hard into my hand—and a flung arm scatters the diamonds that were meant to set them up in a new life.

Rémy steps over the bodies, one hand plucking diamonds off the table, dropping them into the red velvet pouch. This he stuffs, with the tender pats of a proprietor, into a breast pocket. With the anxious clearing of his throat, in case he has something to explain to anyone he meets on his way out—a quirk I know well—he is gone.

I weep in the sad, fragrant darkness of her beautiful things. I have wet myself. I have bitten my hand bloody. *Take whatever you like, Lisette,* she had said. *Whatever you can use.* Am I fog? Will I slip away and live for all my days in corners underground?

I step out of her chifforobe with a small leather valise in my hands. My fingers are quick, my bloody hand nearly dry. One dress, one pair of shoes, one hat. Into the valise they go. Along with the prayer book and the empty cigarette lighter. In the parlor, I gather up the personal papers—which include railway tickets, passports, identity cards— into a folder, and last of all I slide in the precious papercut of our double silhouette.

With her embroidery scissors, I crouch, trembling, and snip a lock of her hair, which I wrap in a handkerchief. I drop the scissors into the valise. Fingers as soft as fog gently close her eyelids. And then her father's. As I stretch to reach him, something glints in the useless, useless light—there, next to the foot of the table. It is a diamond. A diamond the killer has missed.

Whatever you can use. With the back of my wounded hand, first I touch her cooling cheek, and then I set it against her chest, where the bloodstain with none of the finery of cut paper has spread.

Anger begins.

So does a plan.

I open the porcelain cigarette lighter with the pink flowers . . . and drop the diamond inside.

New York City

It was just three weeks ago that he slammed into me on West 47th Street as he emerged from a diamond merchant's shop. More than seventy years after the murders. Hatless, he had a sheaf of well-cut white hair, and as he scowled at me, too fast for any recognition, Rémy adjusted a Burberry scarf, and there it was. A knife scar. With a gasp in the cold air, I ducked into the wind, my hood hanging low over my head. Pretending to gaze at the merchandise on Lucite tiers in a window decorated with cotton ball snowdrifts, I caught sight of him, at ninety, having a rear door to a tawny Rolls held open for him by an impassive uniformed driver. Brushing his lapels free of the contact with the clumsy old woman outside the diamond merchant's shop, he folded himself inside.

As the Rolls pulled away, I hailed a cab, and spent the next three weeks following the creature. I learned his habits. I made slow and thoughtful notes on his ways. Each night I returned to my apartment off Delancey Street, where I had lived for more than seventy years. There I had learned to read the beautiful dancing figures in the prayer book with the gem-studded cover. There I had lighted Shabbat candles for a lifetime with a gentle husband who, until he died, made sonorous blessings over the wine. There I had embroidered challah covers for three children as they married, using a pair of scissors with a tortoiseshell handle to snip the colorful threads. There I made a practice of what we Jews call *tikkun olam*—repair the world. I have taken up *scherenschnitte*, the art of paper cutting, which I teach at the community center.

The evening before I waited in the cold dawn outside a fine building on East 79th Street, the Glock pistol deep in my coat pocket, I cut a particularly beautiful silhouette. Dreamy eyes. Parted lips. Ripples of long waves that drifted off the paper into memory.

"A self-portrait, Simone?" my son-in-law asked.

"Or a portrait of someone else?" asked my granddaughter, her eyes teasing me.

In a world where truths struggle to breathe—and not all of them should—I realized that I held two.

"Yes" was all I said.

Blood Money

An Inspector Rutledge Story

CHARLES TODD

London, 1920

Inspector Ian Rutledge walked out of his flat into May sunshine. He'd just reached his motorcar when Hamish MacLeod, the voice he'd carried in his head since the Battle of the Somme, said, "*Ware.*"

He turned to look toward the corner of the quiet street just as an older woman, her hair in some disarray, called to him.

"Inspector Rutledge? I'm so glad I caught you. Will you come, please? There's a cat up the tree in front of my house and her crying kept me awake all night. Can you bring her down?"

Groaning inwardly, Rutledge went to join her beneath one of the plane trees that lined Melbourne Avenue. Mrs. Gregg had lived alone since her husband's death in early 1919, and every able man in the street had been called upon to help her in one way or another. Since his return from the trenches, he himself had dealt with a chimney clogged with a bird's nest and a jammed window rope.

He could hear the soft, piteous mews of the cat now. Looking up, he could just see her, white with splashes of bright orange, half hidden among the leaves. She was very small, even accounting for her long fur. She peered down at him, her amber eyes pleading with him to do something.

But the lowest limbs of the tree were beyond his reach. He turned to Mrs. Gregg. "It's best to call the fire brigade—" he began, just as Constable Harris turned the corner.

Mrs. Gregg had also spotted him, and she hurried over to beg his help as well.

The constable touched his helmet to Rutledge, looked up, and sighed. "I'm a good deal heavier than you, sir, and not as tall. But I'll give you a boost to that branch, if you like."

There was nothing for it but to accept, although Hamish reminded Rutledge that he had a meeting with Chief Superintendent Markham in an hour, and needed to be presentable. "A torn cuff or a broken leg willna' do."

He handed his hat to Mrs. Gregg, glancing ruefully at his polished boots.

The constable cupped his hands, and Rutledge was able to catch the lowest branch, and with a grunt, swing himself up into the tree. He hadn't climbed since he was twelve, in his parents' back garden. Apparently, the knack of it hadn't been lost in the intervening years.

He got himself from branch to branch until he was just under the small cat. She'd nervously watched his approach, pacing up and down her own limb, and Rutledge had the distinct feeling she was about to go higher, beyond his reach.

But when he put out a hand to grasp her scruff, she didn't struggle, and he was able to lower her against his chest. She began to purr softly as he tucked her inside his coat and began his careful descent. Below, Mrs. Gregg clapped her hands in delight.

He got himself and the cat down the tree with only a few scrapes to his hands and face. The next problem was how to make those last ten feet without breaking an ankle. He managed it somehow, lowering himself by his arms until he could safely drop to the ground.

He could feel the cat's sharp claws dig through his shirt into his chest, but she made no effort to leave the safety of his coat, and when he landed, he lifted her—still purring—out.

Constable Harris backed away. "Cats make me sneeze."

Mrs. Gregg pointed. "She lives just there. With Sergeant Johnson."

Two houses down from hers, white with a dark green door. Rutledge had seen the occupant a number of times but had never spoken to him.

Leaving Mrs. Gregg with Harris, Rutledge carried the cat up the short walk to the door, but no one answered his summons. He went round to the rear of the house, taking the narrow service alley, and opened the gate that led into the back garden. Like those of the other houses on the street, it was shallow, with a shed to one side and a flowering tree by the back wall.

There was no one about, but the cat jumped out of his grasp and ran across the grass to the kitchen door. Brushing himself off, he was about to turn away when he realized his shirt front was streaked with what appeared to be rusty splotches. He looked back at the cat, and saw that her underbelly was the same shade—nowhere near as bright as the orange patches on her head and back.

She was standing at the door, waiting to be let inside, her tail twitching from side to side. Rutledge went forward, tried the door, and it opened under his hand. The cat trotted inside, mewing, and after a moment he followed, stepping into the entry before moving to the half-open kitchen door. He pushed it wider.

A man dressed in shirt and trousers lay on the floor in the shafts of sunlight coming through the tall windows facing onto the back garden. The back of his head was bloody—drying blood, not fresh. The cat trotted over to the man and curled up at his feet. The house was quiet around him as Rutledge crossed the room and knelt, feeling for a pulse, although it was clear enough that the man was dead.

"It must be Johnson. Yon cat doesna' fear him."

Rutledge moved the man's head slightly. "Yes. Johnson." He'd answered Hamish out loud, as he often did in times of stress. The voice had been there since 1916, although he knew the Scottish corporal was buried in France. They had all come close to breaking by that August, exhausted, their dead often underfoot. And then he'd had to order Corporal MacLeod shot for openly refusing to lead his men into heavy enemy fire one last time. Military necessity, but he'd felt the guilt even so, and he'd brought Hamish back to England in the only way he could, in his head.

Looking around the room, he saw the poker from the hearth lying in the shadows of the table. "And that, no doubt, is the murder weapon. There's blood on it."

Rising, he found a dish in a cabinet, filled it with water to lure away the cat, then stepped past the body to a door that was shut. The room beyond had been tossed with little concern for contents: a broken lamp lying in a pool of water from a cracked vase, the tulips crushed under foot, and chair cushions slashed with angry force. Even the carpet had been lifted and tossed aside. What had someone been searching for?

The upstairs rooms were also ransacked, with increasing frustration. It was this, then, that had frightened the cat. But whoever it was had put her out. Why?

He went down to the front door and called to Constable Harris. Leaving him in charge, Rutledge reassured an anxious Mrs. Gregg, then left to inform the Yard of the murder.

Chief Superintendent Jameson frowned at Rutledge's report. "Can't have our inspectors climbing trees in such a respectable part of London. What will people think?"

"If I hadn't, it might have been days before the body was discovered."

"Then deal with it fast as you can," Jameson told him, resignation in his voice.

It was while Rutledge was out speaking with the doctor and the undertaker that Sergeant Gibson tracked down what he could about the late Alexander Hickson Johnson.

When Rutledge returned to the Yard around six o'clock, the file on

Johnson was on his desk. According to the doctor's preliminary report, the victim had been killed toward midnight, the cause of death had been blunt force trauma to the head, and the weapon was likely the poker. The body had been transported to the morgue, autopsy still unscheduled. According to Constable Harris, who had spoken to the neighbors, Johnson had lived quietly, apparently within his means, and seldom had visitors. But he often left the house on Wednesday evenings, ostensibly to attend evensong. The man had no hobbies nor vices, as far as the neighbors could tell, although he had enjoyed golf before the war, and had played once a month at a club in Surrey. But not, they thought, since the war. He'd come home a quieter man than he'd been when he'd enlisted, except for his Wednesday evenings. The cat appeared to be his only survivor.

When Rutledge called on Gibson in his lair, a small room filled with reports and boxes of evidence, the sergeant took out a sheet of paper and handed it across the desk. Rutledge could almost feel Hamish standing at his shoulder, reading it with him.

Gibson was giving a running commentary on his findings. "No police record that we can locate. Born in Gloucester, came to London at the age of twenty when his father died and left him a small inheritance. Wounded at Passchendaele in 1917, and again in late '18. War record clean. A neighbor confided he was one for the cards, but Johnson's bank manager informed the Yard his accounts seldom varied by more than twenty pounds over a year's time. Either he was unlucky, or he kept his winnings elsewhere."

Hamish spoke, jolting Rutledge. "The way yon house was turned over, his killer didna' find what he was after. The winnings?"

He coughed to hide his reaction. "If not money, what about secrets?"

Gibson shook his head. "If he had any, we've not uncovered them."

But Johnson had *something* that someone else had wanted badly— and believed to be in that house.

Rutledge went back there, using his torch to find a lamp, then lighting it. There were still smears of blood on the kitchen floor, and

the little cat was huddled forlornly under the table, anxious and uncertain. Rutledge found part of a roast chicken in the larder, and cut
up a portion into a bowl. She went to it at once, purring as she ate.
And what am I to do with her, he asked himself, *when the inquiry is finished?*

He went to the parlor and began to sort through the wreckage.

Hamish sighed. "No' here."

He hadn't expected it to be—not in such a public place—but he
couldn't be certain until he'd looked for himself.

Rutledge climbed the stairs to the bedroom. It offered no insight
into the murder, but showed him a solitary man's life that reminded
him of his own. Books from a bookshelf littered the floor, along with
bedding and the contents of a slashed mattress tangled with shirts and
underwear and stockings pulled from drawers. A small desk lay on its
side, contents scattered. Golf clubs were tossed around the room, the
bag empty.

A military chest was overturned, uniforms and souvenirs spilling
out. He could confirm what Gibson had learned, that Johnson had
been a sergeant in a Wiltshire regiment, and digging deeper, Rutledge
found medical discharge papers—Johnson had lost the sight of one
eye and several toes, his war ending in September 1918.

Looking at the books, Rutledge found that Johnson had an eclectic
taste, from Dickens to Conan Doyle, biography to travel. A man of
many interests . . .

What was his killer searching for?

The other two rooms on the first floor were less personal, but they
too had been tossed, bedding dragged off and trampled underfoot,
pictures taken down from the walls, even the window curtains pulled
off their rods. The second floor, used as a box room, was in no better
shape, the few oddments of furnishings stored there overturned, seats
of chairs slashed, the lining of valises shredded, a trunk upended, the
contents scattered across the floor.

Returning to the bedroom and ignoring the chaos, Rutledge asked
himself where he would hide something he didn't want to be found.
His own medical records, for one, showing shell shock . . . Dr. Flem-

ing had destroyed most of them, but there must have been a few still
locked in cabinets of clinic records. Testing the floors, he didn't find
any loose boards, nor did the wardrobes have false bottoms.

His thorough search of the house had yielded no secrets, and trim-
ming the lamp wick, he began again. It was nearly eleven o'clock when
he stood in the center of the bedroom and cast a final glance around
him, prepared to call it a night. A new man, Constable Turner, was
posted at the front door to make certain no one else was allowed in.
Tomorrow . . .

His gaze paused at a box of playing cards barely visible in the top
of one of a pair of army boots. Cards. Johnson was a gambler. . . .

He retrieved it, set an overturned chair back on its feet, and sat
down to draw the cards from their water-stained box. They were Belgian, he realized, a souvenir from the war, and not likely to be used for
general play. He was about to put them away when Hamish said, "Just
there!"

He turned the face cards over. Nothing. Fanning them in his hand,
he realized suddenly that there was writing on the lower number cards.
Crossing to the lamp, he stared at it. Names. Nine of them. In different fists. And beside each, a number.

Now what the devil did that mean?

The cat came upstairs to wind herself around his feet, then curl up
on a half-torn pillow, preparing to sleep.

Rutledge took out his notebook and wrote down each name and
each number. Looking at them on the page, he could see that they appeared to represent an accounting of some sort. But of what?

Hamish commented, "The box wasna' hidden."

Rutledge put the cards in his pocket, closed his notebook, and
went down the stairs.

At the door, he said, "Good night, Constable."

"Good night, sir."

Rutledge walked down the street to his own flat, and after a whiskey, took out the cards and the notebook again.

Who were these men? No rank was given, but he had a feeling, given the fact that the cards were Belgian, that they had to do with the war.

Hamish said, "Yon sums. What each man owed him?"

"Owed? Gambling debts that he hadn't collected?" Rutledge answered aloud.

Hamish chuckled. "Ye're the man wi' Scotland Yard."

"Johnson must have served with them." But why only nine? He got to his feet, collected his coat and hat, and, late as it was, drove to the Yard.

Gibson was still in his little room. Rutledge had often wondered if the man had a home to go to.

He showed the sergeant the list of names. "What can you find out about these nine men?"

Gibson peered at them. "D'you think he served with them?"

"It's possible. Start there. They may be dead. Or missing."

He took the list. "Tomorrow," he said, and Rutledge knew better than to push.

The next morning, after stopping by Johnson's house and sharing his tea milk with the little cat, Rutledge reported to the Yard and went to find Gibson.

He was never sure how Gibson came by his information. Some of the other inspectors swore it was black magic.

As Rutledge strode down the passage, Hamish said, "Ye ken, the cat was put out. No' left in a house with a dead man."

"A woman? Yes, you're right, it's the sort of thing a woman might do. But the names appear to be male. A cat owner?"

When the sergeant handed him the list without comment, Rutledge saw that there were addresses for each name. Alive, then. And they were all men in the ranks of a Wiltshire regiment, and from Johnson's company.

Hamish noted, "Yon corporal lives in London."

Rutledge went to find Corporal Thomas Tomlinson in Hounslow, but he had left for his job, running a small working-man's café near Charing Cross railway station. Rutledge found it and ordered tea at the busy counter until he was satisfied that the shorter of the two men working behind it was Tomlinson.

He beckoned him over, and without identifying himself, he asked, "Do you by chance know a Sergeant Johnson? Wounded at Passchendaele in 1917? I'm looking for someone who knew him in the war."

The man went still. "And who's asking?" His gaze was steady, cold.

Rutledge told him then. About the murder. About the deck of cards. And watched the shock spread across the man's face.

"Here, you don't think I did it?" Tomlinson demanded apprehensively.

"If you didn't, you'll tell me why your name is on one of these cards." He took them out and spread them so that Tomlinson could see his.

The man hesitated, then said slowly, "It's blood money. In a way."

"What?"

Tomlinson looked over his shoulder and leaned toward Rutledge. "Lieutenant Mercer threw himself on a German grenade. If he hadn't, we'd have all been killed. As it was, three men were wounded and sent home. Johnson lost an eye. But all of us *lived*, and we felt we owed the lieutenant's widow for what he'd done. And so we get together and play a hand or two. Only we don't gamble. At the end of the evening we just pay up what we can afford to lose. A set amount. It's there, on those cards. No more, no less. Each month it's collected and sent on to her and her two children. It was Johnson who saw to that." He considered Rutledge. "My wife knows I play cards. Not why. We took an oath."

"Then who killed Johnson? It must be one of you."

"God knows." But Rutledge thought the man did—that he must be able to guess. After all, he'd served with the others.

He said, his voice grim, "Johnson was bludgeoned. He survived the war, and died in his own house at the hands of a vicious killer. Which one of the survivors wanted to stop these payments?"

"None of us. It's a *debt*," Tomlinson said earnestly. "We wouldn't touch the sergeant." And then, avoiding Rutledge's gaze, he added, "Well, there's Private Burton's wife. Since he was let go from the dockyards, she's complained about what Jimsy 'lost,' playing cards. He might have told her about the lieutenant, just to shut her up."

Hamish said, "Or himself killed Johnson, rather than face her temper."

Rutledge asked, "When did you last play cards?"

"Wednesday. This week."

Johnson was killed the next night. Rutledge thanked Tomlinson and left the café.

He stopped at Melbourne Avenue to warn Constable Turner to be on his guard, before driving on to the Burton house. And was just in time to see the constable speaking to a tall, stout woman. As Rutledge pulled to the verge, Constable Turner allowed the woman to enter the house.

He swore. She wasn't one of Johnson's neighbors, but Turner wasn't to know that. He got out and went to speak to Turner himself. "A problem, Constable?"

"No, sir. The lady from up the road came to rescue that little cat." He shook his head. "I was going to ask if I might have her for my wife. Pretty little thing. Ah, well."

Rutledge nodded and went quietly inside. Overhead he could hear someone moving about in the bedroom, trying to sift through the chaos as soundlessly as possible. Stepping into the kitchen, he saw the little cat cowering on the far side of the dresser. He silently climbed the stairs and stopped in the bedroom doorway. "No luck finding the cat?"

Startled, the woman turned toward him. Her heavy features twisted into a grimace of a smile. She stayed where she was for several seconds, collecting herself after the shock of finding him there, then took a step toward him. It was then he saw a golf club half hidden by her skirts. In the event Constable Turner got curious and came to see what was taking so long?

"She must be hiding somewhere," she said. "Such a shy creature. I expect she was frightened by the police tramping about." She kicked the golf bag aside.

"There's no money here," he said coldly. "I've searched. Johnson must have already posted it to Mercer's widow."

She stared at him. "What money?" He watched her grip on the club shift slightly as she moved again, pushing the chair he'd sat in last night out of her way.

Behind him, Hamish softly warned him to beware.

"You know very well, Mrs. Burton."

Her face flushed an ugly red. Still, the attack came so suddenly that Rutledge fell back before it, and the club slashed viciously across the doorframe where he'd been standing. "That woman won't have it," she told him in a low voice, almost a growl. "It's mine. I need it more."

They were in the passage now, and he threw up an arm to protect his head as she raised the club and brought it down again, narrowly missing his elbow as it tore through the pink cabbage roses on the wallpaper.

There was no time to shout for Turner. He needed a weapon fast, and backed away from the stairs, into the smaller bedroom. A broom lying on the floor behind him nearly tripped him up, but he managed to catch himself. Scooping up the broom handle, he held it up like a cudgel to ward off the next blow. And then, moving swiftly, he brought the bristly head of the broom around and shoved it hard into her stomach as Mrs. Burton raised her weapon again.

Off balance, she stumbled backward, crashing into the door, her surprised expression changing to one of pain as he brought the broom handle down smartly across the arm holding the golf club. It clattered to the floor just as the constable came charging up the stairs, shouting for Rutledge. He came to a sudden halt in the passage, staring from Rutledge to the woman clutching her arm.

"Help me, Constable," she cried, reaching out to him. "He's run mad!"

"What have you done to her, sir?" Constable Turner demanded in alarm.

"Stopped her from killing me as she must have killed Johnson," Rutledge said curtly, setting the broom against the wall and retrieving the club at her feet. "Take her into custody, Constable. And use your handcuffs. She's likely to attack you if you turn your back on her."

Between them, they got Mrs. Burton down the stairs, where the constable stood guard while Rutledge summoned the police van. When they'd seen the last of her, still protesting that she'd been attacked, and showing anyone who would listen the darkening bruise on her arm, the constable asked, "But what possessed her, sir?"

"Greed." He prepared to leave, then remembered. "Take the cat home to your wife, Constable."

"Thank you, sir! I will that," he answered, hurrying back into the house.

As Rutledge walked on down the street, Hamish said, "I do na' think she believed in the story her husband told her."

"No. And I find it interesting that the surviving men in that company felt obligated to help Mercer's widow."

"Guilt is a verra powerful emotion. Do you think that's truly how yon lieutenant died?"

"I don't know," Rutledge replied as he opened the door to his flat. "But it wouldn't be the first time men rid themselves of an unpopular officer and kept it quiet."

"There isna' a way you can prove it. No' now. Ye're no' in the army."

"Not unless I could make Burton confess." He paused, considering. "His wife must have got part of the truth from him. I might get the rest of it, if I'm the one who tells him she's in custody for Johnson's murder, and show him those cards. It's worth a try. If I'm wrong, no harm done."

Hamish was against it. "The army will no' like interference fra' the Yard. Besides, the war is o'er. And ye werena' there to judge those men."

That was the view of a man from the ranks. Rutledge, as an officer, saw the question differently. The men had tried to make reparations, and the army would have to take that into account. But Mercer was dead—and how he died still mattered.

He took out his watch. He must hurry. If Burton was going to break it would be now. Not later, not after he'd had time to think, and then warn the others in this conspiracy.

Hamish continued, "Ye ken, if ye're right, they'll be punished."

"Johnson kept the others in line. The Belgian cards show that. What's more, he was their sergeant. But his murder will be the excuse they need to walk away from the arrangement now. They'll perjure themselves at Mrs. Burton's trial if they have to. For their own protection. The truth will never come out."

"It willna' bring Mercer back." Hamish was still protesting as Rutledge turned and walked back to his motorcar.

The Burtons lived on the southeast outskirts of London, not far from the railway lines coming into the city from Kent. Theirs was the last house on a poor street of houses that had seen better days. Rutledge could understand why Mrs. Burton resented her husband's playing cards when they clearly needed the money themselves.

Rutledge knocked at the door, and after several minutes a slovenly man in a dirty shirt answered. "Private Burton?" he asked.

Burton looked him up and down. "And why would you be wanting him?" he asked suspiciously.

Rutledge was certain now that no one had informed him that his wife was in custody. He said, "I've come from Sergeant Johnson's house."

Suspicion vanished as alarm took its place. "Here, I don't know any Johnson."

"Your name is on one of his playing cards. And your wife has just been taken up for Johnson's murder."

The shock made him take a step backward. "No. I don't believe you. She—she left a bit ago to do the marketing."

"She left hoping to find what she's been searching for. The widow's money. Why did you kill Lieutenant Mercer? Was he that bad an officer?"

His mouth still open in shock, Burton gaped at Rutledge. "Who told you?" he whispered. *"We swore!"*

Rutledge pushed him aside and stepped into the entry. "You broke your oath when you told your wife."

"I didn't tell her—I said what we'd all agreed upon. The grenade—"

Moving on into the front room, Rutledge looked around.

Hamish said, "Ye ken, Tomlinson said he's been let go." For despite Mrs. Burton's attempt to keep a tidy house, newspapers and empty Player's packets littered the floor, while a stench of stale beer and too many cigarettes lingered in the air.

The man followed Rutledge, protesting. "I kept my word, I tell you."

He turned. "Face it, man. There *was* no grenade. What did you do, shoot Mercer in the back under cover of an advance?" When Burton didn't answer, Rutledge added harshly, "This is only the beginning. The truth *will* come out now. At the trial, or when the widow stops receiving her pittance, and asks the army why. Other wives will begin to question your 'gambling.' The army *will* learn of it. Like it or not."

"Honest to God, *there was a grenade.* The lieutenant was nearest it, and we shoved him on it—" Burton stopped, appalled, one hand clutching at the back of the nearest chair.

"And so you agreed to pay his widow. Blood money," he said, remembering Tomlinson's words.

"It wasn't as though we didn't like him. But we were all going to die, all of us. And he was right there." He began to weep. "It was terrible. Three of us were wounded by the blast. But we lived. Afterward—afterward, we agreed we'd make up for it. Make amends. Still, I haven't been able to hold a job since I got home. You don't know what it was like, Maud wigging at me, telling me I was taking food out of her mouth—I wanted to stop, but how could I? *I keep seeing him there, what was left of him.* A bloody shambles. You don't understand."

"It's no wonder the wife got Johnson's name oot o' him," Hamish said.

"Please tell me Maud didn't kill the sergeant. She has a temper, I know that, but she wouldn't kill. Not Maud." Burton went on, his voice pleading. "She just wanted—" But he could read the answer in

Rutledge's face. "Dear God." He raised his hands, clenched into fists, and jammed them into his eyes. "Oh dear God," he said again. "I wish I'd died instead of Mercer. It would be better than this."

To make certain Burton didn't try to contact the other men, Rutledge stayed with him until the police arrived to report Mrs. Burton's arrest. But as he sat there in the dingy front room with the weeping man, he felt no satisfaction. There would have to be a reckoning. Even if it meant that Mercer's widow learned the truth about her husband's death. She wouldn't welcome it. Would she resent the loss of the blood money, too?

He sighed. Justice was seldom tempered by mercy. He'd learned that long ago. The innocent suffered as well as the guilty.

Hamish said, "Ye wouldna' listen to reason."

"It isn't reason. It's what was right." He hadn't known he'd spoken aloud, until Burton answered him.

"I hope they hang me, too. It's my fault, what she did. I don't want to live." He told the constables as much when they finally arrived.

It was late when Rutledge got out of his motorcar and walked to his door. But he stopped and looked down the street toward the plane tree where he'd rescued the cat.

He said quietly, "I'd always wondered why Johnson went out of his way to avoid me. I thought it was because he was the only man from the ranks on the street. But it wasn't because I'd been an officer. It was because I was at the Yard. And he had a secret."

Hamish waited until Rutledge had shut the flat door, until there was no escape, then said, "He didna' ken you had one, too. Only it wasna' an officer you killed. It was one of your ain men. I'd have come home on my ain two feet, else."

The Violins Played Before Junshan

And now there came both mist and snow,
And it grew wondrous cold:
And ice, mast-high, came floating by,
As green as emerald.
—Samuel Taylor Coleridge,
    "The Rime of the Ancient Mariner"

San Francisco, 1859

Late in the evening, thick ribbons of fog moved like a living animal. Breathing, then thinning to vapor before revealing the shadows between the wooden barrels lining the docks. Beyond the silhouette of the opera house, oily glimmers of the bay cut through the darkness, only to be obscured again.

As Celwyn neared the docks, he heard virulent cursing, and saw a carriage driver raise a whip above his horse. He drew level with the driver, and the whip stopped on its descent to the horse's back, the tip suspended in midair. Snakelike, it shimmied out of the driver's hand. The driver backed up. The whip followed him, wrapping around his ankles and lifting him feet first into the air. His cursing echoed into screams as he disappeared into the night sky. A moment later, a splash could be heard. A satisfied smile crossed Celwyn's lips as he stepped inside Salty's.

Just inside the door sat a man in a shapeless black robe, an ornate gold cross hanging on a chain around his neck. The priest regarded

Celwyn as if he knew him, yet Celwyn would have remembered the little elfin ears, long black hair, and vaguely Asian eyes that glittered with invitation.

Curious, he settled into the chair opposite the man. The bartender rushed forward with a shot of whiskey, deposited it in front of Celwyn, and whirled to run back behind the bar.

The priest clapped. "Well trained. Like a seal at a waterfront show."

Celwyn paused, and then picked up his whiskey. He recognized that voice. The gothic architecture of St. Mark's provided excellent places to eavesdrop, such as a false wall behind the altar. This morning, the monsignor of the church and this priest had discussed some unusual incidences that had occurred during Mass.

"I do not need to know how you caused the bellowing of bulls during services," the priest said. "I only need to know that it was you who did the deed. The flute music you added probably had meaning for you, but it was in poor taste."

Celwyn finished his drink and speculated how much effort it would take to lure the priest outside and snap his neck. The man obviously couldn't appreciate the purpose of music. He also reeked of cloves.

"Your ensuing act was more violent." The bugger smiled. "The monsignor has suggested I take the matter to the police."

Celwyn rose, threw some coins on the table, and turned to go. As the priest got to his feet, Celwyn noticed he did so in a somewhat stiff manner, as if his joints needed oiling. But there was nothing slow about him as he trailed the magician out the door and into the moist embrace of the fog.

Rehearsed peals of well-paid feminine laughter emanated from the brothels lining the street. The priest did his best to keep up as Celwyn strode along. They detoured around a dapper gentleman who'd just been tossed out of one of the betting parlors and had rolled across the boards. He tried to stand, but a pair of roughs poured out of the parlor doors and set about beating him.

"Shouldn't you do something about that?" Celwyn asked, hooking a thumb at the attackers as they kicked their victim. "It's a priestly duty, I believe."

"No. I am not a priest."

How curious. Celwyn waved a hand and a strong wind arose, blowing the attackers down. They scrambled up again, only to be knocked head over heels farther down the street.

"Why not?" Celwyn asked as he rejoined him. "You're dressed like one."

They stopped in front of an alley redolent of fish and horse manure. The gaslight overhead painted his companion's face, and Celwyn noted the man's skin appeared to be the consistency of bleached leather. Like it needed a good pinching to give it some color. Celwyn straightened his cuffs. Not everyone could be as handsome as he. Nor as elegant.

They stood next to a particularly foul-smelling pile of rubbish. The man's delicate little nose didn't even twitch as he said, "Mr. Celwyn. Yes, I know your name." He eyed Celwyn as a butcher would a carcass before carving. "And about your particular talents. Your sense of right and wrong seems to be even stronger than your disagreements with the clergy."

The conversation—and the man—had become tiresome. If he knew so much about Celwyn, he would have to have known how dangerous he could be. Yet the little man again tickled the magician's displeasure.

"Murder one moment, acts of gentle kindness another. Whims."

Celwyn grabbed him by the throat and lifted him to eye-level. "Not whims." Celwyn shook him like a cat would a rat. "Evil should be punished."

A tremendous strength exploded under Celwyn's hand, and then the other man was standing a few feet away and nattering along as if the magician hadn't been about to throttle him.

"—for hundreds of years you have performed heroic acts, acts of mayhem, and then disappeared to do it all over again."

Celwyn stepped closer until their chests nearly touched. The priest stared back, not afraid at all.

"And, pray tell"—Celwyn found that phrase appropriate—"what do you think I am?"

"A supremely gifted magician. As immortal as you are amoral."

Celwyn brought his hands together, struggling for control. *"What do you want?"*

"I have a proposition for you: Help me capture a wicked man." He spoke slowly, playing his best card. "A person much worse than anyone else you've hunted and killed."

Celwyn rubbed his face. "Gad, this place smells." Next to his foot lay a half-eaten dog. "Couldn't you have asked me this at Salty's? It is a hell of a lot warmer in there."

As they began walking up Van Ness, Celwyn asked, "Who is this person you seek? For that matter, who are you?"

"Xiao Kang is a powerful criminal. He departs for China tomorrow. If we are successful, you will be rewarded, and can continue on to Singapore."

As they crossed the street, the bells of St. Mark's echoed through the briny air and into the night.

"When we reach the island of Junshan, I'll take custody of Kang and you will receive enough gold to make your stay in Singapore a long and pleasant one. It's a mysterious and beautiful city."

Payment wasn't a motivation. "Why can't you catch him yourself?"

They had reached the steps of St. Mark's and sat down. The man glanced to the side, not meeting Celwyn's gaze. "It will take all of your skills of illusion, your cunning, and more to subdue him."

Celwyn yawned. "And what will you be doing?"

"Helping, of course."

The magician regarded him. He looked skinny, peculiar, and seemed more an intellectual than capable of pummeling someone if needed. For several minutes Celwyn thought about his own level of boredom and the unknown, and wondered how depraved this Kang could be.

The other man stood and opened the church's heavy door. "You may call me Talos. Do not mention my name once we board the ship."

"Why?"

"It would only make things more difficult. You see—" He paused, and his eyes once again glittered like broken crystal in the sun. "Kang is my brother."

Celwyn felt more than knew it would soon be dawn. No hint of pink filtered through the higher panes in the rectory windows, yet faint sounds of movement could be heard in the kitchen below. In another second, he determined he was not alone in his makeshift bedchamber below the rafters. The magician had become accustomed to the rats, but found Talos's smirk as annoying as the stench of cloves that clung to the man.

"Excellent. I'm glad you have awakened." Talos jumped off a crate and beamed at Celwyn. "We must get to the docks. The *Zelda* will sail soon, and we have much to talk about along the way." He clapped his hands. "Make haste."

As Celwyn pulled on his pants, he wondered if Talos had any idea how close he had just come to flying off the church roof. But no, he chattered on.

"—voyage of several weeks." He handed Celwyn a short knife with an ornate ivory handle. "Keep that in your boot. I have sent a trunk of rather elegant clothes for you ahead to the ship. Of course, I will be the passenger with sea sickness who stays in his cabin, and out of my brother's sight."

Dawn painted the tall-masted ships of the harbor with a watery hand as sailors winched cargo aboard barques and transports. Celwyn inhaled the salty air and with it a reminder of how much he loved the sea. A moaning fog horn resounded across the bay, the sound competing with a crate of squawking chickens as it was lowered into the hold of a nearby ship. Celwyn approved: omelets.

Talos led the way toward a throng in front of a pristine barque. The *Zelda*, white with a band of blue and her three-story-high masts, would spread great expanses of freshly laundered canvas once at sea. Celwyn loved ships, especially elegant ones. He expected to discover a worthy gentleman's parlor aboard, and perhaps a decent game of poker.

Talos had wandered on ahead. Celwyn scanned the area and discovered why he had disappeared; at the rear of the crowd stood a man with elfin ears and gleaming eyes that didn't seem to rest until they encountered Celwyn's gaze. One of the most beautiful women the magician had ever seen held the man's elbow. Her hair was the color of a darkened flame, and her skin glowed with health as she murmured to Xiao Kang. He continued returning Celwyn's stare as he ushered her forward.

Celwyn presented his ticket to the purser. "I say, who is that gentleman in the beaver hat?"

The purser raised his chin and squinted. "You must mean the professor. He's sailed with us before."

A week later, Celwyn stood on the leeward deck, letting the growing wind buffet him. In the distance, thick opalescent clouds gathered near the western horizon. The magician sighed. It appeared they were about to encounter a storm. Maritime logic dictated that they would sail around the worst of the tempest, but would not sit still to let it overtake the ship.

Two of the fussier passengers clutched parasols and minced along the rail to join him in his perusal of the sea. Celwyn made a face of annoyance. Their arrival could be a social call, but he suspected that they viewed him as a wealthy prospect for the comely niece who did her best to bat her eyelashes at him while holding on to her billowing hat.

Mrs. Porter sighed. "Traveling is such a bother, is it not, Mr. Celwyn?"

"Yes ma'am, it is."

Celwyn had so far exercised a modicum of restraint with Mrs. Porter. If he wasn't careful, he'd endure hearing a repeated story of how she had found a live fish nestled in her trunk next to her flowered frocks. Maybe with a companion so it wouldn't be lonely.

He bowed to the niece. "You are looking well today, Miss Anna-belle."

"Thank you. The first officer reported that the ship will encounter a storm tonight, and we will be confined to our cabins." The niece frowned, and her perfectly formed brow crinkled. "Is this true?"

Celwyn felt a twinge of sympathy for her. Trapped with her aunt in a small cabin wouldn't be pleasant. He debated how much to say to her, but then it occurred to him that the situation could be useful. "That is one option the captain has. However," he assumed a worried expression, "I would suggest that we all stay in the salon. There are fewer than a dozen of us."

"Why?" Mrs. Porter asked. A gust of wind slammed the *Zelda* broadside, causing Mrs. Porter to lurch back to the rail and hold on with both hands.

"The salon is located in the center of the ship. It will receive less water from the waves." Celwyn stood taller. "And we can offer one another encouragement if the storm becomes too frightening."

If Mrs. Porter convinced the captain to utilize the salon, then Kang would stay there for the evening. The magician had tried for days to invent a way of getting into the man's cabin; he intended to search it and then have a conversation with him.

Luncheon was a simple affair, with the last of the fresh vegetables, an overcooked roast, and a fair claret placed before them. As he sampled the wine, Celwyn observed the other passengers. Young Mr. and Mrs. Tarryton ate like their final meal had just been served. Mrs. Tarryton nearly resorted to picking up the roast beef with her delicate fingers when she couldn't cut through it fast enough. Heavens! What about propriety and etiquette? Celwyn had heard the couple was on their way to a diplomatic posting in Hong Kong. He tapped his nose, and Mrs. Tarryton began snorting as she ate.

The magician turned his attention to the passengers at his own table, who were trying to ignore the snorting. For the first time since they'd sailed, Kang and his wife had been seated with him.

Elizabeth Kang's hand lay close enough that Celwyn could have touched the emerald she wore. He resisted the urge to do so, and continued eating his parslied potatoes. Her perfume reminded him of a lilac field nestled high in the Irish mountains.

Across the table, Kang ate with quiet efficiency. It was time Celwyn knew what the man was thinking. One of the magician's many talents, which Talos had alluded to, included the ability to invade another man's mind. While there, Celwyn could learn secrets and fears. It also made a perfect opportunity for inserting a new wisp of mystery or useful morsel of scandal.

As Celwyn turned toward Kang, the man looked him in the eye and just barely shook his head. Celwyn pushed forward. When he should have entered Kang's thoughts, nothing happened. He tried again. Nothing! Kang's lips twitched as he nibbled a roll.

Celwyn cursed, and a row of bar glasses shattered behind him. The candles across the room dimmed until he controlled his anger, and then burned even brighter than before. In the past, the magician had never failed to read another's thoughts.

It occurred to Celwyn that even if he could not read Kang's thoughts, perhaps getting to know his wife better would be just as useful. With decorum and modesty, of course. The magician had been accused of many things—some of them even true—but he'd always been a gentleman.

"Please pass the salt, Mrs. Kang."

As she handed it to him, Celwyn directed his attention to her, entering her thoughts as easily as a warm knife through butter. *"Storm . . . lifeboats . . . Mrs. Porter's double chin . . . Kang talking about his brother . . ."* Celwyn listened, and within minutes knew much more about Kang. Enough to confirm that Talos had lied to him.

Elizabeth Kang stole a look at Celwyn while silently noting how handsome she thought him. Especially the curve of his jaw. Celwyn looked away so that she wouldn't notice his look of satisfaction. He hadn't even had to suggest the thought to her!

·   ·   ·

Throughout the rest of the afternoon, the hammering of boards placed over the windows and doors rang across the deck. Barrels and other unsecured storage had been taken below. More telling, heavy crates from the cargo hold were wrestled up to the deck and tossed overboard. Celwyn hoped the passengers didn't register the significance: Dumping expensive cargo was a clear sign that extreme danger lay ahead.

When Celwyn entered his cabin, he found Talos sitting on the bunk reading a newspaper. Cloves again. He pinched his nose and crossed to the desk.

"This storm could blow us off course a great distance," Talos said without looking up.

Celwyn said nothing, but realized that with Talos so near, he had an opportunity. What more did the man know? With a deceptively blank expression, Celwyn attempted to read his thoughts.

Damnation! Celwyn gripped the desk, trying for control. Two times in one day, he had failed at such a simple undertaking. How could both brothers thwart his attempt?

"Is there something wrong?"

Celwyn waited until he could control his anger before asking, "Do you have a ship following us?"

"Yes." Talos folded the newspaper and began examining his nails. "All you must do is deliver Kang to me."

"I thought we were to do this together." Again Celwyn eyed him, wondering how much effort it would take to throttle him. Probably one hand could perform the deed.

"You should be more worried about how you will subdue Kang."

"I won't allow the passengers and crew of this ship to be hurt," Celwyn said. Played with, yes; hurt, no.

Talos stood and walked to the door. "At the right moment, attack, or cause an illusion, or whatever you do. Just be sure Kang is restrained. That is the surest way to ensure their safety." The ship dipped low and a collection of bottles beside him toppled off the dresser. "Assuming we make it through this storm."

.   .   .

Nineteen bells resonated across the deck. As the *Zelda* sailed into a wall of rain, the staccato pattering grew to a pounding cadence. The iridescent foam of the roiling waves contrasted starkly with the blackness of the night, and one by one the waves extinguished the running lamps until only the signal lamps on the bridge glowed, swinging side to side like silent death knells.

In the distance, a flicker of lightning decorated the darkness. As the first officer ushered Celwyn into the salon, a ridge of seawater topped the railing and flooded the deck.

The magician had seen livelier parties at funerals. Most of the passengers huddled on the sofas in the center of the room, except for Annabelle, who paced the room fore and aft, holding a cigarette and a full glass of wine that dribbled down her skirts with each swing of her hips. Kang and his wife sat side by side across from the Tarrytons. The magician acknowledged Kang with a nod as Mrs. Porter's voice shrilled.

"We are going to die!"

Annabelle patted her aunt's shoulder and tried to stem the flow. Celwyn crossed to the bar and poured a large quantity of sherry. When Mrs. Porter took a breath to begin another outburst, Celwyn handed her the glass. "Drink that." It wasn't a request.

She gulped and bleated, "The ship will sink!"

Another woman moaned, "I cannot swim. We will all drown!"

Celwyn frowned. A distraction was in order.

He lit the fireplace, bringing warmth and hopefully cheer. He produced a spirit board from behind the bar, where it hadn't existed before, while planting the idea in Mrs. Porter's mind that it would be entertaining to ask it when her niece would marry, what the spring fashions would bring, and a yearning for chocolate cake.

With a bit more help from Celwyn, the notion of lighting candles and summoning spirits occurred to the other passengers. He reclined against the bar and watched their conversations evolve to ignoring the noise outside: It was just a storm. Nothing to worry about. All night long, they would disregard the fury of the rain as it pounded the roof of the salon like hundreds of symphony drums.

A few minutes more and the passengers closed their eyes to con-centrate on the unnamed spirits as Celwyn shut the salon door behind him.

Seawater had stopped draining from the scuppers and sloshed star-board and back with the rhythm of the sea. It took fewer than twenty steps to reach Kang's cabin, and when the ship shifted to starboard, taking the water with it, Celwyn opened the cabin door and slammed it shut behind him. From his pocket he withdrew a stub of candle, lit it, and began to explore.

The Kangs had been assigned an excellent room. A velvet settee, a carved wooden dresser, and tall, ornate pianoforte made the space liv-able. The magician added a vase of red roses and bowl of chocolates next to the bed. As he congratulated himself on his thoughtfulness, he nearly tripped over the bedpost: An opaque eye stared back at him from atop the pianoforte.

An iridescent black bird with silver-tipped feathers sat there, twist-ing its head from side to side. Inspecting him. After a moment it soared upward with languid wings moving just fast enough to keep it aloft. As he watched, it descended and resumed its position atop the pianoforte.

Although he found the creature somewhat fascinating, considering his own predilections, Celwyn had things to do.

He began touring the room, examining various items, noting the type of shoes Mrs. Kang favored and the silk of Kang's ties. For a "professor," he appeared quite wealthy. The magician speculated what his real profession could be. His foray into Elizabeth Kang's mind confirmed Talos had lied to him: Kang wasn't a criminal. But what was he?

On top of the desk blotter, Celwyn discovered a bound collection of papers. The pages contained numbers and drawings of what ap-peared to be alchemy. On the final page Kang had written: "—*correction to Dalton's theory.*"

How interesting, the magician thought. The last line read: "*. . . suppress this discovery until such time as the world is ready for it. Until it is used for forthright purposes, not for war. I believe in the good it can do. . . .*"

Celwyn stood there for several moments, trying to understand the quixotic lists of numbers. His gifts did not extend to science; more accurately, they extended to bending the laws of science. From outside, the calls of the crew faded as the reverberation from the thunder grew louder.

What could be more perfect than nature and music together? Celwyn nodded, and the pianoforte began a tinkling baroque ballad that fit the atmosphere perfectly. He enjoyed the play between numbers and power, for that was what music and the storm represented. Even more appropriate was the contrast of elements; he produced dozens of candles and lit them.

What was keeping Kang?

It was another ten minutes before the cabin door opened and a cold gust of wind blew in along with Kang. He staggered to a halt and held out a scrap of paper. "I believe this was from you?" Kang wiggled the paper. "Inviting me to my own room?" He studied Celwyn, who lounged by the desk. "I trust you are comfortable?"

"Except for a spot of whiskey, to warm our souls." The magician rubbed his hands together and produced a bottle.

Kang asked, "Are you armed?"

"Only with the knife your brother insisted I carry," Celwyn murmured as he held an imaginary baton high, conducting the music emanating from the pianoforte.

"It is time we talked." Kang crossed the room to sit at the pianoforte. For a moment, he watched the keys as they moved and the music played. "I've surmised why you are here."

"Then you know your brother engaged me to capture you." Celwyn eyed him. "Why?"

Kang shrugged. "Because in an altercation between us, he would lose. But bring in someone such as yourself, then the odds are in his favor."

The magician poured whiskey into the two glasses and extended one to Kang. "To civilized discourse." After a few sips, he added, "You are not the supreme criminal he indicated, or fundamentally evil from what I can discover." The ship stopped swaying, and then began a slow tilt leeward. When it righted itself, he continued, "My reasons for helping your brother are dwindling."

Kang rose and began pacing the room in short, precise steps. "In 1373, the first recorded instance attributed to your magic was the images of Anubis in the clouds above Chartres. Then the khamsin in Algiers, where you turned the dust storm to water. It was only later that I learned your name."

Celwyn raised his glass in salute.

"I can appreciate the artistry in what you do, and the moral point of view that drives it." Kang stared into his glass and added, "Talos has probably asked you to . . . er . . . disable me. Is this true?"

"Yes."

"How?"

For a long moment, Celwyn thought over what he had surmised, and about the lies Talos had told him. As the American cowboys said, it was time to switch horses midstream.

The magician said, "I was to cut into your chest and find what he called 'a source of your power.' Then I was to remove it."

Kang stopped in the middle of the room and unbuttoned his shirt and undershirt. He tapped a nail on his pale, leathery chest and a distinct metal *clank* answered back.

Perhaps Celwyn was rendered speechless, although he would have denied it. Several moments passed before Kang's superior smile finally got on his nerves. "You are made of metal?" Celwyn asked.

"A type of metal, yes." Kang held out his arm and the bird swooped off the pianoforte to land on his wrist. "Many centuries ago near the Mar Maggior, the Black Sea, artificers made automats for wealthy kings and princes for their wars, and amusement. Our strength is extraordinary. We are mechanical, similar to a sophisticated clock, but with much more ability. Like a chess piece that can think on its own and has come to life. The artificers built bears, lions, and other animals, too."

"Ah." Celwyn looked at the bird, right at its diamond-like eye. "Come here."

The bird tilted its head one way, then the other, shaking itself before streaking upward in a blur. Then it plunged down again to land on the desk beside Celwyn. As it waddled closer, Celwyn tilted his head, one way and then the other, mimicking the bird. The bird hopped onto the magician's shoulder.

"Qing fancies you."

"Of course." Celwyn stroked the bird's feathers. "Why does Talos want you captured?"

"Hatred. Brotherly jealousy." Kang buttoned his shirt. "The artificers who made us are long dead."

"You can't die if you are not alive."

"Over the years, we've acquired many traits. Such as the feelings of love and the ability to grieve. That is part of living, wouldn't you say?" Kang nodded. "Talos may have also begun to feel greed. He could want an army of automatons again for war. Only this time he would want something spectacular to guarantee he would win."

"Such as your discovery?" Celwyn extended a long finger to point at the portfolio of papers on the desk. As he did so, the ship began a sickening slide toward starboard.

Kang gripped the pianoforte. The wind roared like howling devils chasing the ship, and he raised his voice above the tumult. "If you've read my study, then you know that it is a design for a weapon the world should not have right now. If ever." The wind rattled the cabin door. "For years I have had more science at my disposal than my contemporaries." Kang turned to face Celwyn. "If Talos builds a weapon from my discovery, many will be dead, or wish that they were."

The ship stilled, and the wind quieted. "Why are you traveling to Singapore when you know he hunts you? Why board this ship, knowing he is probably here?" Celwyn shook his head and stood up. "Your wife was very worried about him earlier."

"You spoke to my wife?"

"Not with words." The creaking of the ship resumed as it twisted against the wind. "*Why* are you here, sir?"

Kang stared at his hands a long time before whispering, "Because he killed my wife's father, trying to lure us back." He added even more solemnly, "He is now poisoning her mother. Slowly." Kang gripped the magician's arms. "Promise me you will protect Elizabeth," he implored Celwyn.

The man did not have to beg. Celwyn freed a hand and patted him on the back. He planned to do more than protect what was dear to Kang.

Removing a small brown object from his pocket, he offered it to Kang. "Care to partake?"

"Peyote?"

"Of the finest kind."

"On me, it would be a waste, without effect."

"True." The magician popped the disk into his mouth and began to chew.

"It would help if you knew more about Talos," Kang murmured.

Celwyn's brows rose. "Do tell."

The storm had worsened ten-fold in the last hour. As he watched Kang stagger against the squall and enter the salon, the wind stole Celwyn's hat, carrying it away into the night.

With one graceful movement, the magician gained the lowest spar of the main mast. The rain blasted the ship, bringing the first chill of arctic cold. High above, a few sailors remained in the rigging, dodging the canvasses that blew upward off the masts like enormous wings. The captain and first mate manned the bridge, holding on to the wheel as another wave swamped the ship from bow to stern and the *Zelda* dipped so low the waves licked the deck rail on the leeward side. Then she righted herself, spinning clockwise in the wind. A row of lightning arose beside the ship like an illuminated stage.

Celwyn loved the sea. Even more, he loved a fierce and flamboyant storm.

The magician raised his hands, conducting the expanse of lightning as it gyrated, dancing to an unheard melody. He bowed, and the thunder boomed directly overhead, threatening to bounce him off the spar. Celwyn laughed, relishing the display of so much beauty and power. But with a sigh, he knew it had to end. He closed his eyes and spread his arms wide, holding them steady until the winds calmed.

When he opened them again the *Zelda* floated on a hushed sea, so calm not a ripple crossed the glasslike surface. The rain continued to fall, silently turning to snow.

Under banks of low clouds, dawn bled orange and pink on the edge of the horizon. Chunks of ice as big as small boats floated in the snow surrounding the ship and a towering iceberg glimmered just off starboard. Many more icebergs loomed out of the shadows. The *Zelda* had been blown far north, where they grew as high as castles. Masses of canvas draped off the main mast and into the water, while fragile threads of ice formed a crystalline spiderweb above the bridge, where the captain and first mate began to stir.

The salon door creaked open, and the passengers stumbled out to the deck. From below, the first of the sailors poked their heads out and joined the others. The Tarrytons made their way starboard to Celwyn, and the others followed. Kang escorted his wife with a watchful eye.

With her hair undone and a general air of dishevelment, Annabelle resembled a drowned cat. She opened and shut her mouth several times before pointing at the ice. As she did so, the crew unstrapped long poles from the bulkheads. Just as they took positions at the rail, First Officer Gray arrived with a bow and reassurances.

"They will push us away from the ice. The others"—he turned and issued orders—"will get the ship ready so we can catch the first breeze out of here."

Celwyn sighed. It would take hours to get the sails set and underway. The crew would require some unexplainable help. And enough wind to set them on course again.

Mrs. Porter appeared at the magician's elbow, seemingly invigorated, or still tipsy from the night before, wobbling like a marionette even on the calm deck. She looked beyond Celwyn with the glassy-eyed stare of one of the drunks on Cannery Row.

"Officer Gray, what *is* that?"

Through lowered clouds, the shadows had darkened and become distinct against the background of soaring ice floes. Another ship drifted out of the mist, floating toward the *Zelda*.

Mrs. Porter began to scream.

The cabin door under the bridge flew open. Talos stepped out with a pistol in each hand. Without hesitation, he shot Officer Gray through the heart. Before the body hit the deck, he turned the gun on Elizabeth Kang.

Just as quickly, Kang stepped in front of her. The bullet ricocheted off him with a solid *clang*.

The *Zelda* lurched starboard as a loud rending ripped along the leeward side of the stern: Talos's ship had run into them. Kang regained his feet as the other ship floated away. A dozen deadly cannons, all capable of punching a fatal hole in the *Zelda*, became visible, and hundreds of small men with black hair and elfin ears swarmed the deck of the other ship. They chattered among themselves, identical of voice and words.

Annabelle pulled a still-screaming Mrs. Porter across the deck to join the other passengers hiding behind the bulkheads. The *Zelda*'s crew retreated to the far end of the bow, leaving Talos, the Kangs, and Celwyn alone on deck.

Kang held Elizabeth behind him as he faced his brother. Although the two of them couldn't stop glaring at each other, it was Celwyn that Talos addressed.

"Mr. Celwyn, would you be so kind as to do what we agreed upon?" His smile was triumphant. "We have reached that moment."

Celwyn's fingers flexed as he studied the other ship.

Talos growled. "*Now*, Mr. Celwyn, or my crew will blow holes through this ship and the passengers will die."

"Because it is your *brother* who is evil?" Celwyn murmured.

Talos's laugh echoed in the cold air. "You must desire bloodshed, Mr. Celwyn. That is unfortunate because——"

Celwyn breathed deeply, hands flexing, and a deluge began, a veil of rain so thick nothing could be seen. From across the water, forlorn violin music could be heard: five notes repeated softly and growing into a crescendo surrounding the *Zelda*.

As the rain cleared, five tall men encircled Talos, all of them Celwyn. The music became deafening, reverberating until the walls of ice cracked, the sound like gunshots that repeated, causing more fissures, and more immense icebergs to split open.

All of the Celwyns moved closer to Talos, circling faster and faster. Each of them moved deliberately, orchestrated to confuse, illusions designed to kill. In a swarm they covered Talos like insects. He fought them until one cut through his shirt and removed a metal disc.

As the violins grew quiet, the four illusions faded into a gray mist, dissolving into the frigid air. Celwyn handed the piece of metal to Kang.

Kang bowed. "Thank you."

"My pleasure."

The flurry of activity on the other ship increased as Talos's automatons threw lines across to the *Zelda*, ready to board her. Still others stuffed the cannons with explosives.

"Excuse me." Celwyn turned to the *Zelda*'s main mast, climbing high to the eagle's nest.

The magician faced the other ship. As if pushed by a celestial hand, Talos's ship spun away and began to move toward the ice. Celwyn concentrated his gaze on the other ship's main mast. With a tremendous roar it exploded into flames. The burning canvasses blew upward as the blazing vessel was propelled into the immense field of ice.

Celwyn shook his fists, and from the belly of the other ship came a rumble, and then its magazine detonated, the heat from the conflagration melting the nearby ice floes. In moments the ice refroze and the last of the automatons became still inside the crystal tomb of ice. The explosions echoed into the distance as great walls of ice fell into the sea.

The iridescent bird hovered above Talos's unmoving body, and then soared high, orbiting the *Zelda*, flying between the masts and streaking upward again, diamond eyes glittering.

A moment more, and the bird landed on Celwyn's shoulder as the violin music began again.

Forlornly, triumphantly, in celebration of the sea.

What Ever Happened to Lorna Winters?

LISA MORTON

For some, it's the handshake at the end of the meeting. The smile at the restaurant table that tells you the answer is "yes" before you even ask. The email that makes you laugh. The sure knowledge—the kind that's *so* sure you feel it in every fiber—that the person next to you will do something great, but only when they work with *you*.

For me, it was that moment when I realized the blonde getting murdered in the old 16mm film was Lorna Winters. I knew then that those three minutes of black-and-white footage were going to become an important scene in the story of *my* life.

The battered old steel reel holding the nearly sixty-year-old footage arrived at my workstation the way most movies arrived there: in a box with other films and the accompanying paperwork.

I'd worked for BobsConversionMagic.com for two years and an odd number of days. When I'd taken the job, I'd been stupid enough to think it was a temporary fix for my unemployment problem. Since graduating with a film degree, I'd somehow failed to set Hollywood on fire. I'd tried all the usual approaches to getting a foot in the film industry door: I'd made two short films that I'd entered into festivals (the second one, *Raw Material*, had won a runner-up prize somewhere in Michigan), I'd written three feature screenplays that I kept in the trunk of my car at all times, I'd joined a writers' group that gathered once a week for breakfast at a Westside eatery, but everyone I'd met had been other writers as desperate as I was. I wrote a blog on the history of film noir that had a few dozen followers but had yet to lead to anything else.

And I was flat broke. I was a terrible waiter, an even-worse burger-flipper, and my car was so badly in need of a paint job that signing up for some driving app just seemed useless.

So the day my old college buddy Elliott called and said he could get me a film job, I jumped at the chance.

It turned out the "film job" was actually working for a place that converted old home movies into DVDs. And the company was in San Bernardino. I wasn't thrilled with the idea of leaving Hollywood behind for the Inland Empire, but I was even less thrilled at the thought of living on ramen and friends' futons forever. The pay was decent, I figured apartments in that area would be cheaper than L.A., and maybe six months of transferring Uncle Harold's old Christmas movies to digital would be enough to finance one more short film that I thought had a great script.

And two years later, I was still pulling battered reels out of boxes and threading them through Bob's old telecine.

Bob Zale, who owned the company, had turned out to be a damned decent boss to work for. He was a guy in his forties who, like me, had walked away from a Hollywood crash-and-burn, and, also like me, he loved old movies. My college bud Elliott may have left the company not long after setting me up there (he moved back home to South Dakota, where his parents' basement beckoned to him with its siren song), but Bob and I bonded over many late-night beers and Robert Mitchum, Gloria Grahame, and Humphrey Bogart. We knew every bit player, the location of every rain-soaked street, the title of every forgotten gem.

Here's how my days usually went: I'd arrive at work around 9 A.M. (Bob didn't freak out if I was late, so long as I got through the day's work). There'd be a few boxes of movies waiting for me; they'd already been received and checked in by Joanne, who ran both Receiving and Reception at Bob's (we didn't get much walk-in; most of the business came via the website). I'd pull out a reel, load it onto spindles on a flatbed, add a take-up reel, and crank through it by hand just to inspect the film. I could do basic fixes—repair splices, simple cleaning. Then, once I'd made notes about problem areas and solved what I could, the reel was loaded onto the telecine machine. Bob had two of them, both old Marconis that were probably far from the high-tech devices most customers imagine, especially if they'd watched Blu-ray supplements about digital remastering. We weren't sitting in front of a bank of computer screens carefully watching a transfer to color-correct and paint out imperfections; instead, I perched on a wobbly wooden stool peering into a screen the size of a paperback novel, just making sure the digitization was really happening.

That day's first two transfers were typical stuff: faded footage of a backyard barbecue, and a family of wife and two girls horsing around on a deserted beach (Dad was presumably the cinematographer). In my two years working for Bob, I'd seen this stuff hundreds of times.

The next movie I threaded onto the machine from the same box was black-and-white. It seemed to be shot at night, on the back of a yacht. It opened on an empty deck, surrounded by a low metal railing. In the background, light glimmered on moving water.

After a few seconds, a woman entered the frame. Her back was to the camera, but she carried herself with such natural poise that I guessed she was beautiful before she turned. She walked to the edge, leaned on the railing, bent down to look into the water. Her long blond hair blew in the breeze caused by the boat's cruising. She wore an elegant sleeveless black dress; it must have been a warm night, because her exposed shoulders didn't huddle against any cold.

She turned to face the camera at last. It was a full shot, but even on the small telecine screen I could see I'd guessed right: She *was* beautiful.

I squinted and leaned in, trying to get a better look. Just then a man walked into the shot. The woman reacted with surprise—not the good kind—at seeing him. In fact, she backed toward the railing, her eyes narrowing.

It was that expression—the calculating coolness hiding the alarm—that confirmed who she was. It was one of her trademarks, a look that had made her one of film noir's greatest icons.

She was Lorna Winters.

I nearly stopped the transfer in disbelief. *Lorna Winters!* I watched a few more seconds to be sure, but there was no doubt. Her tall, lean figure, the long blond hair with a few streaks of light brown, and that face . . . Lorna Winters, who had slapped Richard Conte in *Rat Trap.* Lorna Winters, who had raised male temperatures across the country when she'd flirted with Sterling Hayden in *Bullet's Kiss.*

Lorna Winters, who'd made seven low-budget film noir gems, one last expensive studio production (*Midnight Gun*), and vanished without a trace in 1960.

I watched, breathless, as she argued with the man who'd entered the scene. He was a big man, wearing a suit with no tie. Lorna tried to walk around him, but he turned to block her, facing the camera. He had a classic thug's face, heavy features, slicked-back dark hair, white scar over one eye.

I'd seen him before: There'd been one shot of Dad in the backyard barbecue movie. He'd grinned, lifted his long fork, waved it in a jaunty way when a little girl ran up to him.

Now I was watching this same man pull a gun out of his jacket and level it at Lorna Winters.

Her chilled façade nearly cracked, but she forced a smile and a nod toward the gun. I didn't need sound to know she was saying, "You're not really going to use that."

His jaw clenched, he pulled the trigger. The gun went off. Lorna staggered back, grasping her chest, her mouth open in shock.

She came up against the railing, and he fired again. Her feet went out from under her on the slick deck, causing her to flip right back off the end of the boat into the sea. He calmly walked forward, leaned over the railing to search the night waves, then holstered the gun.

The film ended.

I was so stunned that I dropped the reel getting it out of the telecine. I got it wound up nice and neat again, checked the digital file, burned it to a DVD, and rushed off to my workstation. I had to see it on a decent-sized monitor. I had to be sure.

The DVD started playing. I held my breath as the woman walked into the shot, finally turning.

No question—it was Lorna Winters.

What was I watching?

It seemed logical to assume it was a scene from a movie . . . but if it was, it was a Lorna Winters movie no one had ever seen, because I'd seen her eight films enough times to know every shot, and this was definitely not in any of them. An unfinished film, maybe? It couldn't be a deleted scene, because her character hadn't died by being shot on a boat in any of her existing movies. And the man who shot her . . . he wasn't an actor in any of the movies. In fact, if he was an actor at all, I'd never seen him in anything.

And what studio would've let Lorna Winters flip off the back of a moving boat like that? They would've saved that for a stuntwoman, adroitly substituted for Lorna after a cut.

The knot in my gut told me what I'd just seen was real. The answer to one of Hollywood's greatest real mysteries: *What ever happened to Lorna Winters?*

I stopped the playback, yanked the disc out of my computer, and went to Bob's office. He was there, seated behind a desk piled high with papers and movies, the walls around him lined with crowded shelves and boxes.

He was on the phone, saying something about how "the transfers looked great" and he'd make sure we "sent a tracking number." He saw me, waved a hand indicating that I should wait, and finished the conversation. When he finally ended the call ("No problem, Mrs. Simmons, always nice to hear from you."), he shook his balding head. "That is one bored old woman. Jesus, she does this with every order—"

Bob must've seen something in my expression, because he broke off, concerned. "Hey, what's up?"

I handed him the DVD. "*This.*"

"What is it?"

"An order I just completed. You need to see it."

"Why?"

"Just watch it."

He eyed me uncertainly for a second before sliding the DVD into his own computer. I didn't even bend over to watch it with him; instead, I watched his expression. When his mouth fell open, I knew he'd gotten it. "Is that . . . ?"

"Lorna Winters. Keep watching."

He did. The film finished. Bob continued to stare at the screen. "Jesus H. Christ. Is that *real*?"

"You tell me."

He considered for a few seconds, staring at the frozen last frame on his monitor. "It's gotta be a scene from a movie—"

"The man is no actor. He's Mr. Family Guy in the other movies included with this lot."

Bob leaned forward to bring something up on his computer. I waited as he read through some text. "I'm looking at her Wikipedia entry, says she disappeared in 1960, just after finishing *Midnight Gun*. She'd been dating some mobster named Frank Linzetti, but they could never tie him to anything." He stopped reading and looked up at me. "You think that guy in the movie is Linzetti?"

I shook my head. "Google Linzetti—he was a good-looking guy. But maybe this dude worked for him."

After a long exhale, Bob pulled the DVD out of his computer. "Christ. We've got to hand this over to the police. And we'll need to talk to the customer. Who is it?"

I'd brought the order with me. "Name's Victoria Maddrey. She has an Encino address, so she probably has money." I saw Bob squirming at the thought of all this, so I added, "Let me do it."

He looked at me, surprised. "Really? Dealing with the cops?"

"I don't mind. I *want* to do it. I mean, think about it, Bob: We could be the ones to figure out what happened to Lorna Winters."

Bob smirked. "I love you, Jimmy, but you know that doesn't belong to us. We can't make a bundle selling it, at least not legally."

"I don't want to sell it. I want to work with it. I want to *know.*"

Bob tossed the disc to me. "Knock yourself out, amigo."

The next day I headed west on the 10 freeway. I had an 11 A.M. appointment with the Cold Case Homicide Special Section of LAPD's Robbery-Homicide Division, and a 3 P.M. with Victoria Maddrey at her home.

Despite traffic (how does it keep getting worse?), I made it to downtown L.A. in time, paid a ridiculous amount to park, and was waiting for Detective Dorothy Johnson at 10:55 A.M.

The detective assigned to talk to me turned out to be a tired-looking middle-aged African American. I told her who I worked for, handed her the disc, gave her the CliffsNotes version of The Lorna Winters Story, and let her take a look.

If you base your notion of cops on movies and television, you probably think they all dress in tailored suits, work closely with forensics teams in glistening blue-lit labs, and are obsessed with every case they get. But, as I waited for Detective Johnson to finish watching the movie, I realized nothing could be further from that. The truth was that her desk was a cluttered little island in a sea of other cluttered little islands, that her pantsuit was old enough to be seriously out of style, and that she was underwhelmed by what I'd brought her.

She finished watching and turned to me. "So first off, Mr. Guerrero," she said, in a tone that told me this wasn't going to go well, "we're actually talking a missing persons case, right?"

"Before yesterday, I would've agreed. But then I saw this."

"And what makes you think this is real?"

I squirmed, suddenly—irrationally—feeling as if that movie was a friend who'd just been insulted. "I know Lorna Winters's work inside and out, and that's definitely not a scene from any of her movies. And no studio would've let a star take a dive off a moving powerboat like that."

Johnson looked at me a few more seconds. In her eyes I saw a lifetime of disappointment—with people, with what they were capable of, and with what she'd never unravel. "You say this Lorna Winters disappeared in . . . what, 1960?"

I knew where this was headed. I just wanted to be out of there. "Right."

She pulled the disc from her machine. "This is a copy we can keep?"

"Yes."

She spoke as she slid the disc back into its little glassine envelope. "You have to understand that there's not much here. See these?" She tapped a stack of folders on her desk. "These are all the cases I've got actual evidence on, mostly DNA. With this case . . ."

"But you get a good look at the guy who shot her."

"And maybe he really shot her, or maybe that's just practice for a movie, or somebody's gag reel. Otherwise . . . look, if I get a break from the other cases, I'll see what I can do."

Detective Johnson would never get a break, because people had been killing one another in this city from Day One, and around 9,000 of those murders had never been solved. I got to my feet, trying to sound sympathetic. "I understand. Thank you for your time."

"We'll be in touch if we need anything."

I knew I'd never hear from her.

Fortunately, my second appointment of the day was far more productive.

Victoria Maddrey was a slim, attractive woman in her late fifties. Her house was in the foothills at the southwest end of the San Fernando Valley; even though the house was older, it was immaculate, and I could only imagine what the property taxes must've been. It was surrounded by a lush garden of hibiscus and bougainvillea, with a tall old magnolia tree dominating the front yard. Victoria was simply but tastefully dressed, with the air of a proud woman who'd put a lot of work into her life.

She took the box of films and discs that I handed her, set it aside, and invited me into a comfortable living room. I wasn't used to this kind of money, even as I realized this wasn't the high end of the wealth scale in L.A. She brought me a cup of coffee, and then we got down to business.

"Ms. Maddrey, I'd like to show you something that was on one of the films you sent us."

"Please, call me Vick."

I pulled out my iPad, which I'd already loaded with the film. I brought it up, hit *Play*, and passed it to her.

I have to say, she impressed me. Her face remained implacable as she watched, not a flicker of emotion. When it was done, she handed the iPad back to me without speaking.

"The woman," I said, "is an actress named Lorna Winters, who disappeared in 1960. Can you tell me anything about the man?"

She took a sip from her own cup, and then said, "The man is my father. Vincent Gazzo."

I had to set my coffee down before I choked. "Your father?"

For the first time her elegant surface cracked, but it was a hairline crack—all she did was look down. "My father liked to call himself a 'security consultant,' but he really worked for the Mafia. Do you know the name Frank Linzetti?"

"Yes. He was dating Lorna Winters—the woman in that film."

Another hairline crack, but this time of curiosity. "Was he? How interesting. My father worked for him."

"And your father is . . . ?"

"Dead. He died in 1990, of a heart attack. Ironic, isn't it, that he spent a lifetime hurting others and making enemies, but ended up dying because he'd eaten too many cannoli." She gestured around the perfect room. "He left me this house. I know I should've sold it at some point, but my husband and I are really quite fond of it."

"It's a beautiful house." Secretly, I wondered how much the Mafia's equivalent of a grunt made. Even sixty years ago, this would've been an expensive house.

An uncomfortable silence passed. I knew she wanted me to go, that she just wanted this painful reminder of the father she was ashamed of to be gone. "There's something you should know: We had to report this to the police. I don't think they have any intention of following up on it, but . . ."

"Of course. I understand. I'm still amazed that Father never did time for anything worse than tax evasion."

I finished the coffee—possibly the best I'd ever had—and stood. "I won't trouble you anymore. I know this must be difficult."

She stood, offering me a hand and a small smile. "You'd think I'd be used to it by now. Thank you, Jimmy. You've been very kind."

I wondered, then, what her life had been like. I realized she must have been one of the little girls I'd seen romping on the beach in one of the other movies, or the one laughing as she bit into the hot dog her daddy had just grilled for her. I imagined her growing up, as she realized who her father had really been, how she'd built a wall to protect herself from either loving him or hating him too much. And I thought about the film I'd just shown her; if it had been human, it would've just told her that Pop was a killer while we both watched her, waiting to see how she'd take it.

She and the house both looked good, but I was glad to get back onto the crowded freeway and head home.

Back in San Bernardino, I filled Bob in on both meetings. He listened, then gave me the best news I'd had all day. "Dug this stuff out of some old boxes for you."

He tossed a stack of yellowing, brittle old magazines at me. I picked up the top one: It was a 1959 movie star tabloid called *Confidential,* one of the real sleazebag rag sheets from the time. The cover had photos of celebrities looking drunk or bewildered, plastered against bright red and yellow backgrounds, while the nearby text shrieked something like *"Why Sinatra is the Tarzan of the Boudoir"* or *"James Dean Knew He Had a Date With Death!"*

In one corner was a photo of Lorna Winters, holding the hand of a young man in a suit, both looking like they wished they were anywhere else but near that camera lens. *"Lorna Winters Steps Out with Director!"* bellowed the text.

"I bookmarked the article," said Bob.

I flipped to the piece of paper he'd stuck in. It was a one-page piece on Lorna Winters and David Stander, director of *Midnight Gun*. There were two photos: the same photo of Lorna and David Stander, holding hands, turning their heads away from the photographer, and a smaller inset of Lorna and a different man—dark, handsome, with a toothy grin, who looked like a shark about to chomp. They were seated in an extravagant restaurant booth; the caption read *"Lorna and Frank Linzetti, together in happier times."*

The accompanying text speculated that Lorna had fallen for her director on *Midnight Gun* and had two-timed Linzetti, who she'd been involved with for a year.

My gut performed an acrobatic flip. "Oh my God . . ."

"Yeah," Bob said, "so she dumps her mobster beau for this director, Linzetti flips out, and sends his hired gun to take her out."

I thought for a second. "And the hired gun has to film it to prove to the boss that the job's been done."

Bob nodded.

I went home after that. Bob suggested we hit our favorite margarita joint, but I told him I was tired from the day of driving.

That was a small lie. All I really wanted to do was go home and watch the film (*my* film) again. And again.

I put it up on my television. The image quality wasn't great blown up that big—grainy, high-contrast, the result of a cheap transfer—but it made details clearer. Now I could see a life jacket hanging on the railing at the left of the frame. A white blob at the right I knew had to be the moon, probably covered by a light fog. There was Lorna . . .

I hit the DVD *Pause* when she came on so I could get up, come back with a bottle of tequila, then hit *Play* again. "What are you trying to tell me?" I muttered. "You're hiding something from me. C'mon, partners don't keep secrets from each other . . ."

Lorna . . . beautiful, young Lorna. What could she have been if she hadn't had the bad luck to hook up with a bad-tempered gangster? She'd just made her first big studio picture, and she was good in it— *damn* good. She could've been the next Kim Novak or Lauren Bacall. Hell, she was young enough that she could've been the next Jane Fonda or Faye Dunaway. She died at twenty just as the wildest decade in movie history was in pre-production.

I watched the film two, three, four times, getting progressively drunker. I watched over and over as she was shot—that look on her face, that instant of shock, that spasmodic clutch at the lethal wound, that tumble over the decking. With enough tequila in me, I kept talking to the film, urging it to spill its secrets, to stop teasing me with the promise of revelations. "You gotta tell. C'mon, baby, spill . . ."

I think I was on the fifth viewing when something pinged off the back of my sodden brain. Something *wrong.*

I wound the scene back a few seconds, to the moment when Vincent Gazzo pulled out the gun. I got off the couch, not even caring that I spilled the half-inch left in the tequila bottle, and walked up to stand closer to the television.

"Yeah, that's it . . . give it up . . ." I muttered as I hit *Play* again.

There was the shot. There was Lorna grabbing at her chest—

There was no blood.

I paused the image, trying to peer through the heavy digitized grain. Lorna's hand looked pale, spotless. She was wearing a black dress, so with the poor quality I shouldn't expect to see anything there, but . . . wouldn't her fingers have been at least a little splattered? Wouldn't blood have seeped through them?

There was something else, though, and it wasn't until I watched the movie again, from the start, at half speed, that I got it: In the beginning, the boat left a clear wake, a *V* of white water.

When Lorna was shot, the water behind the boat was still.

The boat wasn't moving.

I fell back on my ass, then, too drunk and too stunned to get to my feet. "You *fake*," I snarled at the frozen picture on my screen, stopped at the point where Lorna was halfway over the rail, her delicate high-heeled feet no longer on the deck. "God*damn* it! You were fake all along! And I went along with you!"

I stopped the player, slid the tray open, grabbed the disc, and hurled it across the room. It collided with a wall, bounced off, and hit the floor. I collapsed on the rug, wanting to howl over the betrayal. "Son of a *bitch*! How could you do this? I thought we were in this to-gether."

I felt like the noir hero who gets set up and knocked down by a dirty partner. I almost called Bob to tell him, but instead I passed out.

I woke up in bed the next morning with no memory of having dragged myself there. My head throbbed with the agony of a thousand ex-ploded blood vessels, although three glasses of water and two cups of coffee helped. A little.

I did call in, then, to tell Bob I was running late. "It's a fake," I told him, "a goddamn fake. She's not really shot, and she flips into calm water. The boat's not even moving."

"Well," Bob said, "it's still a newly discovered piece of Lorna Win-ters film. I say we talk to the owner again, see if she'll consider selling it."

I got into the shower after that. As warm water sluiced over me, easing the pain in my head, I thought. I still wanted to know what the film represented—a promo reel for a new movie? A gag? Vincent Gazzo had died a while back, so we couldn't ask him, and his daughter knew nada. Frank Linzetti had also died, in 2009, in a federal prison where he'd been serving time for money laundering. Wherever Lorna Winters was—dead or alive—remained unanswered. That left one person who'd been involved with the whole thing back in 1960: the director David Stander.

I turned off the water, wrapped a towel around myself, and practi-cally ran to get my phone. A few seconds later, I had the facts about Stander: He'd made a few more movies for Columbia, but had never really hit it big. He found more success in television, and had directed every show from *Bonanza* to *MacGyver* before retiring in 2008. He'd married his secretary, Nora Chilton, in 1962, and they lived now in the Cheviot Hills area of Los Angeles.

Bob had a friend who worked in the office at the Directors Guild; one little white lie to his friend about wanting to film an interview with David Stander got us his phone number. I called it that afternoon.

When a man answered on the first ring, I asked, "Is this David Stander?"

"Yes, it is."

"Mr. Stander," I began, hoping I sounded convincing, "my name is Jimmy Guerrero. I'm working on a documentary about Lorna Winters, and I was wondering if it might be possible to meet for a brief interview?"

"I'm sorry, no."

No explanation, no excuse . . . but he also didn't hang up, so I pressed on. "Oh, that's too bad, because we've got some newly discovered footage of Miss Winters that we were hoping you could shed some light on."

"What kind of footage?"

"Something filmed privately. It shows Ms. Winters on a boat, and . . . well, it looks like she gets shot."

There was a pause. Then Stander said, "Where did you find this footage?"

"It belonged to a man named Vincent Gazzo."

Another long beat. When Stander finally spoke again, he said, "I can meet you at 5 P.M. today."

He gave me his address. I told him I'd be there and hung up.

I got dressed, went into work, and asked Bob for the rest of the day off. When I told him why, he closed the door to his office, sat down behind his desk again, and said, "Jimmy, what if Stander watches the film and then tells you he doesn't know anything about it?"

I started to say, "So what if he does?" but I realized it would be a lie. Bob was right; David Stander was the dead end. If he couldn't—or wouldn't—supply an answer, it would hurt. Bad. "I don't know," I answered.

"I think . . ." Bob trailed off, trying to find the words. "I think you might be counting on this too much."

It was true. The film was like a living thing for me; a partner that whispered promises, who offered the reward of giving me that shot in film history I hadn't earned otherwise. I could be the one who brought one of Hollywood's greatest secrets into the light. If my own talents—or lack thereof—as a filmmaker couldn't give me fame, maybe this could.

"Maybe," I said to Bob, a guy who was me with twenty years added. "But don't tell me you don't want to know, too."

He shrugged. "'Course I do."

I left early, given traffic on the 10, and made Cheviot Hills by 4 P.M. I killed time just driving—past the massive 20th Century Fox lot, past what had once been the MGM lot, past the Westwood cemetery. I figured the last was the only one I might ever have a shot at getting into.

Finally 5 P.M. approached, and I headed to the address David Stander had provided. I negotiated my way past manicured lawns and houses that had once been middle-class but were now homes to millionaires. I pulled up and parked before a lovely two-story Tudor-style, with a rose garden leading up to the front door. It was 4:55 P.M. I took my iPad and a copy of the disc—in case he wanted to see the film on his own TV—and walked up to the door.

"Don't let me down," I whispered to the disc.

My knock was met a few seconds later by a man in his eighties who was still straight and trim, wearing casual slacks and a polo shirt. Even with thin gray hair and lines in his face, I recognized him from the tabloid photos, when he'd been holding Lorna Winters's hand.

"Mr. Stander," I said, extending a hand. "I'm Jimmy Guerrero."

He took the hand, but released it too quickly—he wasn't comfortable with any of this. "Yes, Mr. Guerrero. Come in."

David Stander had kept himself in good shape; he still moved well, with only a slight slowness to his gait as he led us to an entertainment room. But he was tense—*too* tense for this to be a casual interview. He turned to me before a large television screen and said, "May I see the footage you mentioned?"

I handed him the DVD. He put it into a player, turned it on, and stayed standing to watch.

As the scene played out, his expression changed, or should I say *opened*—he moved from anxious and guarded to noticeably shaken. As Lorna Winters fell into the sea, he collapsed into a padded armchair.

I asked, "Are you all right, Mr. Stander?"

"Yes, I . . ." He broke off and looked up at me. "What is it you really want, Mr. Guerrero?"

"Please, call me Jimmy." I told him everything then: about Bobs ConversionMagic.com, about my sad attempt at a Hollywood career, about how much I loved Lorna Winters, about what those few minutes of film meant to me.

When I finished, he nodded and rose. "Jimmy, my instincts tell me I can trust you. Besides, this has gone on long enough."

"What has, Mr. Stander?"

He turned to leave. "Excuse me a moment."

Stander was gone only a few seconds. I heard soft conversation from another part of the house; after a minute, he returned with a woman. "Jimmy, I'd like you to meet my wife, Nora."

I started to extend a hand—and froze, too shocked to move.

I was looking at Lorna Winters. Older, yes; aged, yes. But she was still beautiful, with those unmistakable high, broad cheekbones and chilled blue eyes. Her hair was silver, but she still wore it long. She reached out and grasped my hand, and when she spoke it was with Lorna Winters's husky-around-the-edges voice. "Jimmy, I'm so pleased to meet you. David tells me you've brought us something quite special."

I was speechless as David started the DVD again. She watched it silently until the onscreen Lorna flipped over the railing, and then she laughed. "I still remember how cold that water was."

David said, "Probably my finest accomplishment as a filmmaker."

"*You* made this . . . ?"

Nodding, Stander said, "You see, Frank Linzetti had gotten his nasty hooks into Lorna. He was an evil, abusive son-of-a-bitch— when she showed up for our first meeting on *Midnight Gun*, she had to wear oversized sunglasses because of a black eye."

Lorna sat down nearby. "That was because I'd just tried to leave him."

David sat on the arm of Lorna's chair and took her hand; the way she smiled at this simple motion was testament to not just their love but their *care* for each other. "We fell for each other," David said, "and Frank found out. He threatened me first, but I told him I didn't care. That was when he sent Vincent Gazzo. Fortunately, Gazzo liked Lorna, so we were able to buy him off."

I thought about that. "You bought him off . . ."

"Not with money—I didn't have enough of that. But I had my family's house. We got creative with some paperwork and made it look as if Vincent had inherited a house from an uncle, but really it was what I gave him to help us make that movie."

"His daughter still lives in that house. So you convinced Linzetti that Lorna was dead."

Stander nodded. "Then it was just a matter of getting her a new identity and keeping her out of the limelight."

"Which," Lorna said, "I was happy to do. I missed the acting, but not the rest of it." She looked at me and frowned slightly, then handed me a tissue from a box on a nearby table.

I hadn't even realized I was crying.

Because Linzetti was gone and it was safe at last, they let me reveal everything. Not long after the big news broke, the American Cinematheque held a tribute to Lorna, and she invited me as her special guest.

I know this will all fade soon, that Lorna will get her privacy back and I'll be just a guy making old movies into DVDs again. Still no Hollywood breakthrough for me, but that's okay because I've got something better.

And I've got a three-minute movie to thank for that.

Oglethorpe's Camera

CLAIRE ORTALDA

Oglethorpe is famous. He has a dedicated camera trained on the window he clambers into every night. He has his own Facebook page. He has Likes, hundreds of them. He has fans all over the world. The Dutch, especially, seem to favor him. I'm not sure why.

He's much more popular than I am. Admittedly, I don't have long white whiskers and soft brindle-and-white fur. I just don't. I'm a human, and other than the hank of reddish-brown hair the color of garden mulch on the top of my head, I'm pretty much naked under my clothes. I know Oglethorpe thinks I'm ugly, but he is a very tolerant cat.

And giving. He is a most giving cat. In he comes nightly, through the upstairs bedroom window left just ajar. He comes bearing posters, slippers, lottery tickets, box tops, leaves, advertising circulars, candy boxes. Camellia blossoms, socks, Starbucks cups. I am awakened by their soft click or muted thud as each item is deposited on my hardwood floor from the height of the window. Small paper bags, mittens, Styrofoam plates. Flags on sticks. A ketchup packet, slightly punctured. Business cards, sandpaper. More leaves. Lots of leaves. Parking tickets. A hand-printed essay on blue-lined paper. *"B-. Very interesting, Tanika, but please learn to proofread!"* A Jehovah's Witnesses pamphlet. *"Is Hell hot?"* A drooping rosebud. A knit cap soaked in blood.

I shriek from my bed. Oglethorpe, lit in the electronic glow of my alarm clock, looks up from between hunched shoulders.

I can tell he is rather miffed by my reaction. Oglethorpe selects carefully and conveys his items, sometimes for blocks, in his mouth and then must leap from car hood to fence to wisteria loggia to reach the window, never losing his grip on his treasure. It's a lot of work, it requires doggedness—excuse the expression—and discrimination. All Oglethorpe asks in return is appreciation of a positive nature.

Shrieking, screaming, flinching away, and expressions of horror are not, in his book, positive.

I switch on my lamp. My feet find my pink slippers. I extract a Kleenex from my bedside box. I advance on the horrid thing, over which Oglethorpe crouches.

"Oglethorpe," I say. "Let me see it."

Oglethorpe does not stand down. I must reach under his chin with the tissue to pull the knit cap away from him. Squatting, I examine it.

Blood. A lot of blood. The thing is saturated. Could one sustain that amount of blood loss and survive? Especially if the blood loss was from the head? Perhaps, though, the blood loss was not from a head. Perhaps the hapless victim had been carrying the cap and used it to staunch a flesh wound.

Tentatively, I lift the cap, using the tissue to protect my fingers. It feels heavy with its gruesome cargo. With it dangling from my finger-tips, I turn it around to view the other side. A hole around which there is blood turned almost black. Bits of white slivers. Other stuff. I shudder and drop the thing. There can be no doubt. The wearer of this hat has been murdered.

Oglethorpe eyes me balefully, then creeps forward to extend his chin over the stiffening cap again.

"Oglethorpe," I say. "Where did you find this?"

He fails to respond. His expression deepens to real annoyance. I imagine this is one of the heavier items he has had to convey, and this is the appreciation he gets? I stifle the urge to grab him and wash his mouth out.

I carry the tissue to the bathroom and toss it into the toilet. I wash my hands about a million times. All the while, I am thinking. Could this have occurred tonight? It must have. The blood was stiffening on the ribbed wool but had not completely dried. Yet, I had heard no sirens. Does that mean . . . ? I grab the bowl of my pedestal sink. Does that mean someone is lying out in the dark streets right now?

I emerge from the bathroom, leaving the light on, and sit on my bed, staring at Oglethorpe and . . . that thing. What can I do? Call the police and say my cat brought home a bloody cap? Go out into the night, when there is a murderer on the loose, and try to locate the body? Not likely. I wonder how far Oglethorpe ranges in a night, anyway.

I stare at my cat and he at me; both, I imagine, wondering how much we really know about the other's secret lives.

I go into the bathroom and remove the plastic bag lining my wastebasket. There are only a few tissues in the bottom. These I throw into the toilet. I find the glove I wear when dyeing my hair and put it on my right hand. In my left, I carry the bag. I advance upon my cat.

He stiffens and hunkers lower over his prize.

"Oglethorpe," I say in a firm but reasonable voice, that of parent to loved child, boss to respected employee. "I am going to take that cap."

Oglethorpe slits his eyes.

I grab for it. Oglethorpe's claw slashes out. I feel a sting on my arm above the rubber sleeve of the glove. "Ow!" He makes a low, yowling, vibrating sound. His tail switches. His eyes look mad. But the thing is in the bag.

After secreting the bag with its cargo in the antique cabinet where I keep my soaps, I grab cleanser and tissues and attack the place on the hardwood floor where the thing had lain. Oglethorpe has retreated to the windowsill where he sits with that flat, wild look in his eyes, twitching his tail, watching me. I flush the tissues down the toilet, scrub my hand with soap, first in the glove then bereft of it, and finally return to sit on the edge of the bed.

Cold air comes in through the open window. I shiver. Oglethorpe glares, seeming, somehow, to no longer be my cat, as if a wildness, even a murderousness, has invaded him. I wish he would go out the window and find me a nice camellia, something to erase this bad blood between us. But he does not go. He stares, as if remembering some past life when he was a hundred times bigger than he is now and ate my ancestor.

After a while, I fall over on my side onto the pillow. A while after that, my eyes close in that drifting reverie that precedes sleep.

The first thing I do this morning is to check to see if the bloody knit cap is still there. Absurd. Where would it have got to? Oglethorpe, skilled as he is, can't open securely closed cabinets. By the way, where is Oglethorpe?

He does not come home for breakfast. I get ready for work, drink my morning smoothie, and call Jen. Jen is my friend who set up the whole camera/Facebook thing documenting Oglethorpe's nighttime raids. I am a bit of a Luddite—well, a lot of a Luddite. She gets the raw footage from the window camera sent to her computer, where she edits the images so it looks like Oglethorpe is coming through the window with a new find every two seconds or so, raising his chin in that characteristic way so his found object clears the windowsill. Sometimes she adds commentary. Sometimes, when I am over there when she's doing the edits, I do the commentary, which consists of wry statements regarding the objects, such as "Woo! That completes the pair," if he brings in the second sock, et cetera. Not that witty, but Oglethorpe's fans, as mentioned above, are international and legion.

Incidentally, yes, there is a way to turn the camera off when I (or we, if the situation warrants, rare as that eventuality is lately) desire privacy. After all, it is mounted in my bedroom window, but pointed at the aperture itself, not toward the bed or where I dress or anything. In case you are wondering what kind of person I am.

"Jen," I say, gulping pulverized kale. "I need you to edit something out of Oglethorpe's feed."

"What?" she says. She sounds sulky this morning, not usual for her. She is the crisply competent type.

I explain in rather gruesome detail about the bloody stocking cap Oglethorpe brought home. I tend to repeat myself when I am excited so when I launch into "I mean . . . he just dragged this thing in, right over the sill, ew, I better clean that sill, I did clean the floor—"

She interrupts me. "I'm still finishing the website for my client from hell. I don't have time to be dealing with frivolous stuff like this."

"Jen," I say, slightly wounded. "You know I can't do this myself, or I would. It was your idea to do the Facebook page—"

"I do this as a favor, you know, Blaire?" she breaks in. "On my own very valuable time. I do it because you are so nuts about Oglethorpe, and I use that word in both senses. Admittedly, Oglethorpe is an outstanding cat, but maybe if you had given Hugh a fraction of the attention you pay that demon fur ball, you and he would still have a thing going, and I wouldn't have to listen to you whining about your love life or lack thereof."

"Jen!" I feel betrayed. Her portrayal of me shocks. I fancied we were exchanging female confidences and all along she's been thinking I am crazy, whiny, and a lousy love partner.

"Oh, I'll do it," she says grouchily. "We don't want people in the Lesser Antilles choking on their papayas when they see Oglethorpe's feed. Done. Don't worry. Bye."

Jen painted the situation as if Hugh had broken up with me, but in fact I had initiated the breakup, tired of his blend of passivity and aggression. I had met him right here on Delaware Street in Berkeley. He was walking his dog and I was on my way to the BART train. He told me not to get near his dog as she was "very nervous," though I had no intention of getting near his dog. As she passed, he tightly reined in the animal—a mild-looking, slightly confused black-and-tan shepherd mix—as if I might lunge at her.

He repeated this annoying act the next few times he saw me, while I tried a variety of countermeasures: First, veering way to the side of him onto a lawn when he came by and did the bunching up the leash trick. Next, brushing very close to Hugh as I passed. The third time, I squatted down and said, "Nice doggie," ignoring the man's babble about how he had found the poor beast, thin and scabby, tied to the fender of a car, how she flinched if anyone got near her. Once, the dog regarded me with eyes the color of caramels, then slowly wagged her tail.

The effect on Hugh was incredible. "She likes you!" he exclaimed. He immediately became a different person. He told me his name, a name his grandmother did not like, he explained, so she always called him Hug and gave him one when she said it, laughing at her joke. Wasn't that cute?

It was not. There was very little about this man that was, so why I had agreed to accompany him and the dog, whose name was Antigone, for coffee outside at a nearby dog-friendly café, I could not really say.

I fell, not in love, but into a kind of desultory romance with Hugh Hug. This was the way he was about sex: He would come into the room and fix me with a stare that had everything stripped away but pure, animalistic urge. It was as if he didn't speak English, as if he were some kind of primitive off an island, like the guy in that movie *Swept Away*. For some reason, this held a certain appeal for me. But after sex, he would always examine the uneven, white-rimmed flesh of his cuticles, which he didn't seem to know how to push down like everybody else, and say something like "I had a fort when I was seven that I built myself and the goddamn contractor next door shoved it over with a bulldozer. He is the only person I ever wanted to murder."

But what really made me break up with him was when, post-coitus, he started making a mental survey of my friends, one by one, and wondering aloud what it would be like to have sex with them. I told him to stop, I told him to leave, and, out of desperation, when he got to my best friend, Jen, I told him to go ahead, that she was a holy-terror bitch underneath that helpful façade, and the two of them having a relationship would be my greatest revenge for all the crap he'd put me through. I added that he should put his pants on, get out, and, not incidentally, never come back. My so-called obsession with Oglethorpe, despite Jen's theories, thus had nothing to do with the breakup, though, just for the record, Oglethorpe had not liked Hugh or Antigone and seems quite content that I sleep alone now, though I can't say that I am.

Whatever. I grab my coat and purse and head out the door.

Cops. All over the place. Sirens. A small crowd gathering around my neighbor's oleander bushes. I see some dirty tennis shoes, sprawled, connected to corduroy-clad legs. Those tennis shoes. Orange. How I had hated them.

I push past a lady with a waist-length white ponytail. Knock into a kid toying with a skateboard, pushing it forward a few inches, back. "I need . . ." I gasp, elbowing him.

Oh no. It's true. Hugh.

He is facedown, sprawled. The hair on the back of his head is dark, matted, and sticky-looking. I hunker down in a squat, my hands pressed to my lips, squashing them against my teeth. I feel silent, very silent, alone silent, but I hear little whimpering noises coming from my lips.

Something soft bumps against my chin. A black-and-tan dog, trying to crawl into a lap that isn't there, trying to fit under my chin. "Oh, Antigone!" I moan and hug her.

The cop trying to keep the gathering crowd back looks at me sharply. "You know the deceased?"

I nod miserably.

He takes out his phone. "Name?"

"Hugh Connoley."

"What's your name?"

"Blaire Elliott."

"What's your relation to the deceased?"

"He . . . a friend. He was a friend."

"Do you know his address?"

Absurdly, I point, backward, down Delaware three blocks to his apartment.

The cop enters all this info into his phone, then speaks into his shoulder radio. "Stay here, ma'am, please," he says when I stand up and grasp Antigone's dangling leash.

I wait what seems a long time. Probably forty-five minutes. Hugh is covered with a white plastic sheet. One of the cops, poking in the foliage, picks something up, shows it to another, grunts "Nine millimeter." The shell casing is bagged. More cops arrive and double-park, slowing workday traffic. There's a coroner's van and a crime unit truck.

Finally, a detective arrives, asks various questions. I am pointed out. He comes over to me and introduces himself. "I'm Kevin Lanke. I'm in the homicide unit of the Berkeley Police Department. I'd like you to come with me and give a statement at the station, if you would." His tone implies that indeed, I would.

I look down at Antigone. He does, too. "Can you take your dog home, please? I'll follow you there."

I explain that it's not my dog, it's Hugh's dog. His eyebrows raise. "I can put her in my house," I offer, "temporarily." I wonder what Oglethorpe will think of that.

The detective alerts on that. "Where do you live?"

"Right here." I gesture backward one house.

The detective ponders this, tapping his phone against his leg. "Okay," he says. "Let's do that."

The detective comes into my kitchen, where I enter through the back door. His eyes rove the house as I get Antigone a bowl of water and some dog biscuits I had bought for her when Hugh and I were an item.

"You have a dog yourself?" he asks.

"No," I say.

We go downtown—well, a mile away—to police headquarters, in his unmarked car. He does a million things while he drives: looks around, fiddles with his onboard computer, checks his phone.

Once there, he puts me in one of those windowless rooms that always make me claustrophobic when I see them on TV programs. He leaves me there. I figure I am being filmed. I think of Oglethorpe and

wonder, for the first time, if he objects to having a camera trained on
him every night. When the detective finally returns, I am feeling a little
asthmatic. He asks me if I need medical care. I say no and that I want
to get out of here quickly. He smiles.

I am in there for an hour and a half, mostly because Detective
Lanke evidently has a bad memory, ha-ha, and asks me to repeat everything a million times. I tell him how we met and about our relationship. I tell him about his grandmother hugging him. I tell him
that Hugh was a techie but consumer-oriented. I tell him he has designed software that eliminates many of the bugs present in the most
popular operating system, and was just trying to bring it to market,
but . . .

The detective pounces. When he's interested in something I am
droning on about, he kind of smiles, I have noticed as the minutes tick
by. It's not a real smile, just a baring of teeth that seem uncommonly
wet.

"But what?" he asks.

I don't really want to get into this. "Well, his investor, his friend,
was trying to get his money back, and Hugh didn't want to because he
was just about to launch, he said. Something like that. This information is two months old," I added.

"Is that when you broke up?"

"Yes."

"Why did you break up, again?"

I flap my hand sideways. "No real reason. Just got . . . tired of each
other's acts. You know."

"No. I don't know," he said, smiling wetly.

"Well, you know. People get tired of one another."

"What 'acts'?" he pursues.

I am not going to tell him about his primitive islander routine. "I
don't know," I said tiredly. "He seemed uptight all the time, and he
thought I was too devoted to my cat."

"Was this your only serious relationship, Miss Elliott?" Detective
Lanke asks, abruptly exploring new ground.

"What do you mean?" I ask. "Of course not. I am thirty-seven and, though my cat does not think so, I've been told I'm reasonably attractive."

"I meant recently. Just before or just after Hugh."

"Well, my husband was just before Hugh. Our divorce came through about three weeks after I met Hugh, but we'd been separated for almost a year before that."

"How did he feel about Hugh?"

"Oh!" Another hand flap. When had I developed this habit? "He—Joe, I mean—would come over to my house and tell me a million things wrong with me, then break into tears and beg me to come back to him. Yeah, he hated the whole *idea* of Hugh."

"Joe . . . what?" Lanke's hand is poised over a notebook.

"Oh, please. Joe didn't kill Hugh. I don't know if they ever met."

"Joe what?"

I sigh. "Joseph Ardle Smythe."

I give him the address, and he finally lets me go. He offers me a ride home, but I am sick of him. It's only a mile. I walk.

Two days later, I am served with a search warrant. First come a team of crime scene types in white overalls with shower caps over their shoes. They spend a lot of time in the bedroom and the bathroom, emerging with three evidence bags: one containing the bloody cap, one my plastic gloves, and one my sink stopper. Uh-oh.

Next come detectives with big feet. They open every drawer and paw through my papers. Then comes a two-man tech team. They take Oglethorpe's camera.

"Oh no!" I wail. I am given a receipt.

I slam the door on the last of them and go upstairs and climb on the bed. Oglethorpe appears in the window and looks at me, tail switching. He thumps down on the floor and disappears for a while. But within five minutes he is on the bed with me, pushing into my armpit with his nose, as he likes to do. I hug him. He purrs.

"I'm sorry, Oglethorpe," I whisper. I think of his fan base.

. . .

I call Jen the next day and tell her that she better put something on Oglethorpe's Facebook page telling his fans that he is on hiatus. Or something.

"Why?" she demands.

I tell her about the police taking the camera. "Hoo, boy!" she says, and chuckles.

"What's so funny?' I ask.

"Gotta go!" I can hear her laughing as she slams down the phone.

I never do this, but I go to a nearby bar, Chez Here, by myself. I sit at the bar and order a margarita. I need to think, and the atmosphere is not conducive in my own home, with the uneasy truce of Antigone and Oglethorpe and things still a mess from the police.

The first thought I have, after the agave and lime juice have engineered some rearrangement of my brain cells, is that I am a suspect. Duh. It seems so obvious now. Is that what Jen had meant by "Hoo, boy!"—that she had realized it right away? I take another swallow and lick salt off my lips. *If so, best friend, why did you laugh?*

Someone slides onto the stool next to me. He smiles. He has wet teeth like you-know-who.

"What're you drinking?" he asks, signaling the bartendress.

"Go away," I say.

He frowns. "I don't know that one." He points a finger at me. "Cointreau, pear juice, and muddled sinsemilla, am I right?"

I have to smile.

He holds out a hand. "Steve Lanke."

"Lanke!"

"You say that like you know my brother."

"Know and dislike," I say.

"That makes two of us. Police work turns you cold." He mock-shivers.

"You're a spy," I say. "You followed me here and are going to try to pump me for information because your horrible brother thinks I killed Hugh."

"Who?"

"Hugh."

"That's what I asked!" It's stupid, but we both laugh, he for the normal duration. But I go on giggling for almost a minute. Okay, I admit it. A little alcohol goes a long way with me. Especially when I'm stressed. After two more margaritas, I am convinced that Steve not only is not a spy, but that we are united in despising his cop brother, and furthermore that it would be a really good idea to brave Antigone and Oglethorpe and repair to my camera-less bedroom. We do so.

I live on orange juice and aspirin the next day at work, but after coming home and consuming most of a small cheese-and-olive pizza, I start to feel better and cognitive activity returns. I feed Antigone and Oglethorpe on opposite ends of the kitchen, then put on my coat and trudge over to Jen's.

She's not acting like a bitch tonight. She pours us two jumbo-sized glasses of zinfandel and we repair to her couch. I end up telling her about Steve. "Woo-hoo!" she says.

"I hope he's not a spy," I say, looking up at the ceiling.

"Think you'll get first degree?" Jen asks.

I drop my eyes. "That is *not* funny, Jen."

She smiles. Something evil in that smile. "Sorry."

I see something beyond her, on a side table. "Hey, that's not Oglethorpe's camera, is it? I thought the cops had it."

"Well, gee, Blaire, they made more than one, you know?"

"Yeah, but why do you have another one?"

"Jeez, Blaire, you're so suspicious. Don't you know cops keep things forever in a murder case? I was going to set up another camera for Oglethorpe. You know, a gift? And a gift of my time, too, which I don't have much of left over."

I sit forward drunkenly, set down my glass with a *clink* on the coffee table, and heave myself out of the too-soft low couch. I traverse the coffee table and lift the camera. "Will I be able to learn how to use it?"

"Sure. It's just the same as the other one. Besides, you don't have to do anything. I do everything."

"I have to know how to shut it off." I playfully look through the camera's viewfinder at her. "There's Steve now, you know."

Jen spits wine down her sweatshirt in a half-cough, half-guffaw. "Don't worry," she says when she is able. "This camera works *exactly* the way the last one did."

She installs it the next evening and that night, late, Steve comes over. I show him the camera and explain about Oglethorpe's worldwide fame and ostentatiously flip the switch on the side. "There now, privacy."

He feigns wide-eyed non-comprehension. "What do we need that for?"

I slip my robe off. "I'll show you."

I am sitting on Steve's lap when I hear a *thump* and whirl around. Oglethorpe has deposited an old flip-flop, filthy, with crumbling rubber, on the floor. He gives me a look of pure contempt, scrabbles out the window and disappears.

I am not doing such a great job at work the next day. I'm an assistant property manager at a big commercial building in the Financial District in San Francisco, and I'm supposed to "sell" the square footage and know the amenities and how much reconstruction is allowed and so on for each unit, but a lot of that keeps getting obliterated by memories of last night with Steve.

I am happy to see his number light up my cellphone. "Hey," I say.

"Got a call from Kevin today. He told me to knock off any relationship with you, that you were a murder suspect."

I freeze. I mean, I know I am a suspect, but how the hell did Detective Lanke know about Steve and my relationship? I ask Steve this pressing question. "I don't know," he says. "I haven't told a soul. Have you?"

"Well, just Jen. She's my best friend. But she wouldn't tell."

"Well, I guess she did."

My clients come back from a review of the toilets and I have to hang up. I show the rest of the space in a daze. Jen wouldn't do that. I mean, who would? Call the detective and rat on her girlfriend that she was boffing his brother? It didn't make sense, even if Jen didn't like me. And Jen did like me. She was my best friend.

Steve has some lame excuse for not coming over tonight. I curl up on my bed with a cup of hot tea, trying to figure out another person besides Jen who would have told Detective Lanke about us. I give it up. It seems petty . . . unless the detective really thinks I killed Hugh. Ridiculous. It is merely coincidence that Oglethorpe selected the bloody cap, coincidence that I knew Hugh, coincidence that he was found dead near my house, and his bloody cap was found in my house. I clutch hunks of my hair. That confluence of events does sound really bad. But not to someone who knows Oglethorpe. And the cops had been given the URL for the cat's Facebook page. Anybody who knows Oglethorpe's nightly forays, and there are thousands of people who do, knows that he just selects items at random and brings them to me.

Or does he? I sit up and swing my legs off the bed. I remember that I had thought that I really don't know what Oglethorpe does nights. Maybe it is time I find out.

Do cats have good senses of smell like dogs? I wonder, as I crouch in my own bushes in black sweats, if Oglethorpe will be able to detect me. I wait for what seems like an hour, freezing to death, my thigh muscles cramping as I squat, for the cat to return.

From my vantage point, I see someone in a hoodie across the street looking like he is casing George Dodd's MINI Cooper. I hear a *thwack* and then the tinkle of glass. The thief reaches in, opens the door, rummages within. A black SUV screeches up, and the hoodie climbs in. Off they go. Geez! I didn't know Delaware Street was such a hotbed of crime.

I change my position slightly and rub my fingers together, and then I hear it: that oh-so-familiar thump of small feet. Oglethorpe. I straighten up in time to just see his tail disappearing inside the window frame. A few minutes later, after depositing his find, presumably on my bedroom floor, he is out again, jumping from window frame to wisteria loggia to fence to car hood. He turns left on the sidewalk and disappears. I follow silently.

He trots purposefully down the street, using the sidewalk, which is convenient for me. He trots several blocks, in the direction of Hugh's house, actually. Suddenly, he cuts left into a yard. I follow but see his white butt disappearing over a tall fence I could never scale. Damn! I've lost him. I dash to the fence, which is smooth wood, and boost myself with trembling arms just so I can see over. Again, I see that familiar white butt, tail aloft. He has jumped over the fence leading into the front yard as well.

I let myself down and dash back to Delaware Street, running hard now and not caring how much noise I make. I make a left and tear down the side street to the street parallel to Delaware, Hearst Street, hang a left and thud up the sidewalk to the third house up from the corner—at least I had the good sense to count—and stop suddenly. Jen's house, and Oglethorpe scampering up the porch steps.

I drop behind a tree. I hear Oglethorpe meow. He paces the porch prettily, tail high. The door cracks open. Jen, speaking in a high, cutesy voice. "Hi, Oglethorpe. Look what I have for you! First, your treat. Yum! Your favorite! Now here's this. You take this back to your mommy. Okay? That's a good boy."

And here comes Oglethorpe trotting down the steps, with what looks like a square of paper in his mouth. I retreat up the street and hide behind a tree. I see him go to the neighbor's, bounty still between his teeth, and scale the tall fence.

I walk home, thinking. What was Jen up to?

The streetlights make the halo of shattered glass around George's

MINI Cooper sparkle. I shake my head and enter my house. I walk upstairs. Oglethorpe is grooming himself on my bed. The square of paper is on the floor. I pick it up. An instruction manual for a Sig Sauer P226 pistol. I leaf through it. I find it's a 9mm. I sink down on the bed, next to Oglethorpe. It's only then that I realize that the lens of the new camera Jen has installed is not faced outward, where Oglethorpe hops through the window, but right at me.

It takes me about forty-five minutes to work it out that night, sitting on the bed. I get on the web, too, and find a manual for the camera. I find a diagram of parts, which shows me that the button I had been pushing to "turn off the camera" when I had, ahem, nighttime visitors, did nothing of the sort. It was a "quick-zoom" function. Thanks, Jen. While I thought I was ensuring my privacy, in fact I was giving Jen, monitoring the feed the next day, a close-up.

And monitoring brought up another point. Luddite that I am, I am able to figure out that this camera has remote-control capabilities. Jen could spy on me at will.

And she had, that night I told Hugh what a bitch she was. I didn't think she was a bitch, or hadn't! It was just a way to tell Hugh to shut up! Could Jen be that obsessive and hateful to commit murder just to set me up? For one remark?

I remember now Jen's sensitiveness, the way you have to kind of flatter and nurture her while she can be abrasive and get away with it. I remember when we'd taken a magazine test about narcissism, and how Jen got the blue ribbon. We had laughed together. We had laughed.

At first Detective Lanke doesn't believe it, until he gets a search warrant for Jen's house. It's all still on her computer, all the unedited feeds and a lot more. The kind of ravings of someone who sits at home and stews over perceived slights. They also find a Sig Sauer P226.

It turns out Steve is pretty good at technical stuff. Oglethorpe's fans were getting rabid over the fact that there had been no reports on his nightly doings for almost a month. Steve installs a camera that even I can turn off, and catches Oglethorpe's fans up on the exciting news, which serves to increase his Likes and FB friends a thousandfold.

Oglethorpe still goes out nightly and brings back . . . stuff. The latest is George Dodd's insurance bill. Poor George. I return it to him with apologies.

Steve is more or less a permanent resident, and so is Antigone. Oglethorpe has taken to sparring with Antigone, bapping her with fast paws—a right, a left, a hook. Antigone can move like Floyd Mayweather though. Just a little head wiggle and the paw sails by with millimeters to spare.

We catch that on camera, too. The Dutch love it.

The Last Game

ROBERT DUGONI

Eric Applebaum awoke with a start and quickly looked about. Disoriented and confused, he felt a tight pressure low across his lap. A hand touched his shoulder. Applebaum startled a second time. The woman stood with a sympathetic smile on her pleasant face. She wore a plain blue dress—perhaps a uniform of some type, from the looks of it.

"I'm sorry," she said. "I didn't mean to startle you." She bent down and Applebaum considered her warm and inviting expression. Did he know her? "I saw you wake," she said. "I just wanted to tell you there's nothing to worry about. Everything is fine."

He sat in what looked to be the aisle seat of an airplane, a pillow behind his head. It was late at night, judging from the darkness of the cabin interior. Applebaum's seat was illuminated in a white circle of light, the only light in the entire plane. He gave the woman an understanding nod, though he understood nothing. He was more embarrassed than startled, but he never liked admitting the problem with his memory. Made him out to be a doddering old fool. It wasn't that he couldn't recall having fallen asleep; he couldn't recall getting on the airplane, and he had no idea where he was going.

"Can I get you anything?" the woman asked. "Another pillow or a blanket?"

It took Applebaum a moment to find his voice. "No, thank you," he said. "No, I'm fine."

The woman gave his shoulder another gentle squeeze, stood, and started up the aisle. Applebaum thought of a way to ask without looking like one of those old men who'd completely lost his mind. "Excuse me, miss."

The woman returned. "You have a question?"

"Yes," he said. "I'm sorry, but how long before we arrive . . ." He let the end of the sentence trail off, giving her space to fill in the blank. It was an old salesman's trick. When in doubt, let the customer finish the sentence.

"It won't be long now." The woman smiled. "We'll be there soon."

He watched her walk up the aisle, until the cabin's darkness enveloped her. Then he quickly patted the breast pockets of his jacket, where he usually kept his boarding pass, but didn't hear the crinkle of paper in either pocket. He reached inside and confirmed his pass was not there. He looked to the seat in front of him, but didn't see that he'd slid the boarding pass into the seat pocket either.

Applebaum sighed and wondered if he'd left his pass in the terminal, though he didn't recall being in a terminal. No, that couldn't be right. How could he have gotten on the plane without a pass?

He didn't want to admit it, but at seventy-seven, he was more prone to having these spells of confusion—not that his mind wasn't sound. He took great care of his mind. Always had. He finished the *New York Times* crossword puzzle each day, including Sundays, which were the most difficult. Weekdays took him about forty-five minutes, sometimes an hour. Sundays were more challenging, and usually took an hour and a half, but he finished them. Sandy, his wife, used to say he was OCD about finishing, but he didn't see it that way, not at all. It was just the way he'd been raised. His father taught him to finish what he started. That included things like the *New York Times* crossword and food on his plate. "Waste not, want not," his parents always used to say. They had both been children of the Depression who knew what real hunger felt like. Applebaum had taught his children the same way. It wasn't OCD, not at all. It was personal responsibility.

"If you start a project, you finish it," he'd told his kids, and they'd turned out okay, hadn't they?

Sadly, however, it appeared that completing the daily crossword puzzle wasn't going to stave off his bouts of confusion—not if the current circumstances were any indication. He'd forget things like turning on the stove and people's names . . . people he knew— sometimes even his own children, and of course the grandchildren.

"Sandy," he whispered, so as not to look like he was talking to himself. "Sandy was my wife's name. Thank you very much. And I have three children. Eric Junior, Rose Marie, and Denny. And eight grandchildren . . . Nine." Rose Marie had just had another child. Had it been six months? He tried to recall his grandchildren's names, but couldn't at the moment—but that was to be expected, wasn't it? Nine names?

He focused instead on a more pressing concern—where the heck was he going?

He'd spent a large portion of his life on airplanes. He'd been a salesman and traveling had been part of his job—up and down the West Coast every week, and occasionally to Arizona. He'd had to travel if he wanted to keep his job and support his family. Sandy and the kids wanted to live in Seattle. The company agreed to keep him on because he was their top salesman, had been for each of his forty years with the company. So he could live where he wanted, but that meant traveling a lot.

After he'd retired, he didn't like to travel. And who could blame him? The novelty wears off quickly when you've traveled more than 300,000 miles every year for work, even if you could fly first class, though he hadn't. Didn't see the point of that, using up all those miles he'd accumulated just to go down to San Francisco, or Los Angeles, or to Phoenix. Those were miles he was saving for his retirement. So he could take Sandy to all those places she wanted to go, though it didn't turn out that way.

Sandy had wanted him to retire five years earlier, when he'd turned sixty-eight. He'd told her he wasn't ready to retire then, wasn't ready to be "old." Old people retired. Then they spent their waning years in white sneakers, standing on the decks of cruise ships with other old people. He was certainly more productive than that. He had a good mind, and his body was in good shape. So he'd told her he wanted five more years. He promised her. He told her that in five more years his pension would be almost $300 more a month. They'd have more money to travel—not like kings, certainly, but with all the frequent flier miles he'd accumulated, not like paupers either. They could see everything she wanted to see.

But it wasn't meant to be.

Sandy got pancreatic cancer a year before he was set to retire. The doctors gave her a year. She lasted just six months, and spent most of that time too frail to travel. After he'd lost her, he'd decided to clean out the cabinets, and found the travel brochures she'd been accumulating. He spread them out from one end of the dining room table to the other. She had a brochure for a trip to the Mediterranean with stops in Greece, Italy, and Turkey. He found another for India to see the Taj Mahal, and another for a safari in Africa, a fourth for a trip to China to walk the Great Wall. She'd kept brochures for cruises, too. And she'd waited patiently for Applebaum to retire, never complaining, never pushing him. Never happened.

Applebaum sighed.

He'd disappointed her. And he'd disappointed his children. Rose Marie had never forgiven him for not taking Sandy on the trips she deserved. She'd said that her mother had been a fool to wait for him, that she should have traveled without him. Then she'd stormed out of the house. That had been how long ago? Applebaum couldn't recall. They'd never reconciled, he and Rose Marie. They were both too stubborn. Besides, it was too late to apologize to Sandy. That was the worst part. He'd let her down.

After Sandy's funeral, Applebaum didn't feel like traveling anymore. He'd traveled enough. But now here he was, traveling somewhere. But where? And why?

He sat back, trying to deduce from clues around him where he might be going, seeing his predicament as not unlike a crossword puzzle. There were tricks to solving crosswords. Get one clue right and it makes the next question a little easier. After a few more clues, the letters begin to fill themselves in, and soon the letters become words. So, what were his clues?

He considered his clothes. He was wearing his best suit, navy blue with subtle white pinstripes. And he was wearing his best tie, the one Sandy had bought for him at Macy's. No problem with the long-term memory. The tie was gold with a blue diamond pattern that matched his suit perfectly, but the price had been more than he'd wanted to spend. Sandy kept saying, "Just buy it, Eric. You can't take it with you."

But Applebaum hadn't been raised that way. You didn't just spend money on something because you wanted it. He'd told her if that type of reasoning made any sense, then he might as well buy a forty-foot yacht and cruise the Mediterranean—not that he could have afforded such a luxury. He had responsibilities—to Sandy and to his kids. It was his job to provide them a home and educations. He couldn't just spend money willy-nilly. So he'd put the tie down and walked out of the store.

Sandy, however, had other ideas. She'd gone back and bought the tie and gave it to him as a Christmas present. Well, he had to take it then, didn't he? He didn't want to look like one of those ingrates.

He wore the tie on special occasions, and even then he took great care not to spill on it. He'd worn it to each of his three children's weddings, and to his fortieth wedding anniversary, and to the funerals of friends—and to Sandy's funeral, of course. He had to wear it then, didn't he? After all, she'd bought it for him. He'd told Sandy that, when the day came, he wanted to be buried in his blue suit and gold tie, so he could be presentable when he faced his maker. But she'd gone before him and now that responsibility fell to his children, to Eric Junior, his oldest.

And that's when Applebaum had filled in enough clues in the

crossword puzzle for his brain to remember the purpose for his trip. A funeral. That was it, wasn't it? *Has to be,* he decided. He smiled as if he'd just finished the final clue to the Sunday *New York Times* crossword. All it took was a few clues.

He was flying back to San Francisco for the funeral of his grammar school baseball coach. What was his name again? *Chuck. Yes, Chuck McGuigan.* Yes, that was it. The first adult he'd ever called by his first name. His parents didn't like it. They'd taught him to use Mr. and Mrs., but Chuck had been different. "You can call me Chuck, coach, or skipper," he'd said, gathering the team for that first practice. "Mr. McGuigan is my father."

But now Chuck had died, and that was the reason for the suit and tie and the reason for being on the plane, the reason for going home. Applebaum wanted to look his best, to pay his respects.

The plane jolted again, enough to shake him from his reverie. He looked around and noticed the light across the aisle shining down on the cherubic face of a young boy, staring up at him. Applebaum didn't recall the light being on before . . . but he couldn't be sure. Not with him forgetting things.

If the boy was embarrassed to have been caught staring, he didn't show it. His parents had probably never taught him that it was impolite to stare at others. He just sat there with a vague expression on that innocent face, as if he and Applebaum knew each other. Applebaum might have just ignored the boy but, well, they'd made eye contact, hadn't they? He had no choice but to say something at that point, didn't he? It would be rude not to.

So he nodded and said, "Hello."

The boy gave a half-hearted grin.

"Are your parents sleeping?" Applebaum said. The two seats beside the young boy were pitch black.

The boy squinted in thought. Then he slowly shrugged.

"You don't know?"

Another shrug.

Seems perplexing, to say the least, Applebaum thought. "Are you traveling alone?"

This time the boy nodded.

"By yourself?" Applebaum asked, his voice rising in surprise. *Good Lord.* "How old are you?"

The boy held up the four fingers of his right hand.

"Four?" Applebaum said, now dismayed. "And you're flying alone?" Another nod.

Applebaum looked up and down the aisle, but he no longer saw the flight attendant. He assumed she was in the darkened front of the plane. This was outrageous—a child of four flying alone? What kind of parents allowed such a thing?

"Are you scared?" Applebaum asked.

The child shook his head.

"No?" *Remarkable*, Applebaum thought. But then again, the child was probably used to flying alone. His parents were likely divorced and living in different states. They shuttled the poor kid back and forth probably to comply with some court order.

"Are you meeting someone when we land?"

This time the child nodded.

"Well, that's at least something," Applebaum said. "Is it a parent? Are you meeting a parent?"

The boy smiled.

"A father?"

The boy nodded and smiled.

Applebaum was appalled—parents shipping kids back and forth like they were cargo. This seemed a bit extreme, though: a child barely old enough to talk, and who maybe didn't at all from the gist of their conversation so far. What would happen if the father was delayed and couldn't make it to the gate? Surely they wouldn't leave the child alone there, would they?

And that sparked another memory and completed another clue in the crossword puzzle. Applebaum hadn't thought of the incident in years. He'd been left alone once—at the baseball field. His mother had simply forgotten him. Everyone else had gone home. He'd been offered rides, but Applebaum had assured everyone that his mother was coming for him. She had always come for him.

He'd sat on the dugout bench and waited. It had grown dark and cold. Shadows began to creep over the field. That's when he'd become scared, when his imagination ran wild and he was certain people were on the dark infield, zombies who came out at night and ate children left in the park by their parents. He'd been just about to get up and run when headlights lit up the dugout. A moment later, he'd heard his mother's voice calling his name.

"Eric? Eric?"

He was so happy she'd come that he forgot to be upset at her for being late.

"Do you want to know where I'm going?" Applebaum asked the young boy, thinking the least he could do was entertain the lad, seeing as it appeared they were the only two awake on the entire plane.

The boy nodded.

"To a funeral, I'm afraid. I know it isn't pleasant to think about, but there it is. We have to do these things sometimes in life—the unpleasant things." Another thought came to him and Applebaum said, "Do you know what a funeral is?"

The boy shook his head.

"No. No, of course not. Why would you? Well, a funeral is held to honor someone who has passed away. It's a ceremony. You don't understand a word I'm talking about, do you?"

The boy shook his head and gave Applebaum a blank expression.

"Do you talk?" Applebaum finally asked.

The boy shook his head.

"No, no, of course you don't. Is that because you don't want to, or because you can't?"

The boy took a moment, then shrugged.

"Of course you couldn't very well answer a question like that now, could you? Not if you can't talk. No, of course not. Well, since we're both awake, and you seem intent on staring at me, I'll just go ahead and tell you my story. Would you like me to tell you a story?"

The kid nodded.

"You would?" Applebaum said, surprised. "Well, that's something anyway. Kids nowadays don't like to hear stories anymore. Not from an old man like me. When I go to visit my grandchildren, they're always on their phones or their computers. They don't want stories, and they don't want to play. Kids don't get outside and play anymore. You're all cooped up inside, playing on computers and phones. That's why we have obesity in this country. Did you know that? No. No, of course you don't. Kids are obese because they don't get outside and play games like baseball anymore. You know why all the baseball players in the major leagues are from South America nowadays?"

The kid shook his head.

"Because kids in South America can't afford computers and phones, not like here in the United States, so they go outside and play. Ironic, isn't it? I mean, here we invented the game, and American kids don't even play it anymore." Applebaum thought of something. "Would you like me to tell you a story about baseball?"

The kid didn't respond.

Applebaum looked forward, staring at the back of the seat in front of him. "The grandest game ever played, baseball," he said. "When I was a boy—a bit older than you, but still just a boy, mind you—that's what I wanted to be. I wanted to be a baseball player. That was every boy's dream back then. We didn't sit inside. We didn't even have computers when I was a boy, or phones for that matter. So we had to interact with one another, and play games like baseball, or come up with games of our own. We'd get together Saturdays and every day in the summer and we'd pick teams for games like three flies up."

Applebaum smiled at the recollection. "I know I'm not much to look at now, not with gray hair and this potbelly. Hell, I can't even play nine holes of golf, not anymore. My legs just won't hold me up for that long. But back when I was a boy, not much older than you, I was one of the best baseball players, and that was saying something back then, because back then everyone played. And I mean *everyone*. But you see, what we had then was coaching. We didn't just play. We were coached on *how* to play by the best darn baseball coach out there. And you see—"

Applebaum turned back to the seat, but the overhead light had gone out and the seat was dark. He could no longer see the child.

Now, that was the damnedest thing.

The boy certainly couldn't have reached the light. He looked up and down the aisle, curious as to whether the flight attendant had come and turned it out for him.

"Don't stop now."

Applebaum turned to his right. A young man sat in the window seat, the seat between them empty. His overhead light spotted him like an actor on a darkened stage. "Seems like you were just getting to the good part."

Applebaum considered him. The young man looked to be in his early twenties, about the age Applebaum had started as a salesman. He wore a sport coat with patches on the elbows, a bit threadbare, and a thin tie, the kind of coat and tie Applebaum had worn.

"What's that?" Applebaum said, confused.

"The story you were telling, seems like you were just getting to the good part."

"You like baseball?"

"I love baseball. That was my favorite sport growing up."

"You don't say? It was mine, too."

"So tell me about this coach. Chuck, was it?" the young man said.

"That's right," Applebaum said, though he couldn't recall having said Chuck's name out loud, but then he must have, mustn't he? Damn memory. He must have been telling the young boy and this young man had been eavesdropping. "Chuck McGuigan," he said. "Best baseball coach a young man could have."

"Sounds like it."

"Oh, we had a heck of a team, too, even if it was only grammar school. We had real talent."

"You don't say."

Applebaum felt himself getting excited again. "I do say. Okay. I'll tell you the story of Roffice."

"Roffice? What's Roffice?"

"Just listen. You see, it was the championship game. Danny O'Leary started at shortstop—which he did when he wasn't pitching. He and Billy Healy traded off those same positions, you see? Dan Burri started at catcher, and Chuck's son, Matty, he started at first because he was a lefty, and Chuck was old school, you know? If you were a lefty you played first or the outfield and that was that."

"And let me guess. You played second base?"

"That's right. How did you know?"

"I was a second baseman myself. You look like a second baseman."

"Tough position," Applebaum said. "You had to be good going to your left and your right."

"And quick enough to pivot and turn the double play," the young man said, as if reading his mind. "Did you relay pitching signals to the outfielders?"

Now, that was surprising. Not many people knew that small but important detail of the game. "You bet we did. We'd make a fist if the pitch was a fastball, and we'd wiggle our fingers if it was a breaking pitch."

"You did that?"

"Every pitch," Applebaum said. "Chuck taught us that. We were well ahead of our time, I'll tell you that."

"Chuck was a good coach, wasn't he?"

"Chuck was the best. He'd been a good enough ballplayer to get drafted by the Cincinnati Reds."

"No kidding?"

"He was a student of the game, knew it inside and out. And he was built like a brick wall, strong as an ox and fast as a gazelle. He'd drop and do twenty-five pushups and pop right back up, not even breathing heavy. He'd have played pro ball, but his father wanted more money than the Reds were willing to pay. Back then they didn't pay in the millions like they do now. So his father made the practical decision, and Chuck became an accountant."

"That's too bad."

"Not for us kids. If he was disappointed, he kept it to himself."

"I interrupted you. I think you were going to tell me about Roffice and the championship game."

"Was I?"

"I think you were just about to."

Applebaum looked about. He couldn't remember.

"I think you were going to tell me about the infield fly rule," the young man said. "About how you won the championship game because of the infield fly rule."

Applebaum's eyes lit up at the memory. "Do you know the infield fly rule? I mean, really know it?"

"Well, I—"

"The infield fly rule won us the eighth grade championship."

"No kidding."

Applebaum paused. Sandy had always told him not to talk too much, not to be one of those people who bored everyone with stories. "Would you like to hear the story?"

"I certainly would, I mean, if you're not too tired."

Applebaum smiled at that. Why, when he'd been that young man's age he could fly all night, make visits to his clients, then fly home without shutting his eyes. And the next day he'd be at work at 7 A.M. sharp.

"Okay. This was 1953. We were playing at a ballfield called Washington Park—"

"I know it," the young man said.

Applebaum perked up at this. "You do?"

"Sure. That's the field behind Burlingame High School with the wooden grandstand and bleachers and the sunken dugouts."

"It was like playing in one of the old ballparks—like Wrigley Field in Chicago, because there was ivy on the outfield fences."

"I remember," the young man said.

"Well, the team was St. Robert and they were unbeaten, just like us. The score was 1–0 in the bottom of the seventh—"

"The final inning for grammar school games," the young man said.

"That's right. And St. Robert, they had this one kid. T. J. Noonan. He threw nearly 80 miles an hour, and had a curveball that would drop off the table."

"Wow," the young man said.

"But we managed to eke out a run against him in the top of the seventh. So there we are, three outs from the championship. And then

St. Robert manages to get two players on base, first and second, with no outs, and guess who's on deck just waiting to hit?"

"T. J. Noonan?"

"That's right. It meant that even if we got the next batter out, T.J. was coming up, and he could hit as well as he could pitch."

"Doesn't sound promising."

"Sure didn't feel like it, I'll tell you that. So Billy Healy is on the mound, and he falls behind the batter, three balls and one strike. And there's T.J., calling out to all of us that he's coming up next."

"He was rattling you."

"He was trying."

"Sounds exciting."

"I'll tell you, the place was going crazy. Well, Bill, he throws a strike and the batter pops the ball up in the infield to our shortstop, Danny O."

"Did he catch it?"

"Don't rush me. This is the good part. You see, Danny starts yelling, 'Roffice! Roffice!'"

"Roffice?"

"That's right. It was Chuck's acronym, to help us remember the infield fly rule. *R* stands for runners. There have to be runners on first and second or first, second, and third with zero or one out."

"What are the two *F*s for—fair fly ball?"

"Exactly. A fair fly, in the infield."

"That's the *I*."

"Which the player can catch with reasonable effort."

"The *C* and the *E*," the young man said.

"Here's the thing," Applebaum said. "Most grown men don't know the rule, let alone eighth grade boys. But we did. See the key is: The batter is automatically out, whether the infielder catches the pop-up or not."

"That's the first out. With T.J. still coming up."

Applebaum shook his head. "That's what everyone thought. But Danny O, he gets under the ball and catches it, then he lets the ball drop at his feet."

"He dropped it?"

"He sure did," Applebaum said, smiling. "And as Chuck liked to say, 'That's when the circus comes to town, boys!'"

"What happened?"

"The runner on first takes off for second, so the runner on second takes off for third because they're both thinking they have to run because Danny dropped the ball."

"But the batter is out," the young man said.

"Exactly. So the runners don't have to run. And that's when Danny O picks up the ball and tags the runner who has left second."

"The second out of the inning."

"And then he fires the ball to me, and I tag the runner sprinting from first to second."

"Triple play," the young man said. "And T.J. never gets to come up."

"We were running off the field cheering and backslapping one another, and the kids on the other team were crying and throwing their helmets. Their coaches gathered around the umpire protesting, and the parents in the stands are hollering, but there was nothing to be done. We'd played by the rules because Chuck taught us the rules. And we were the better team for it."

Applebaum smiled and looked to the young man, about to continue, but the light was no longer on, and the young man was no longer in the seat. He wondered where the young man could have gone, and why he hadn't listened to the end of the story. The end was the best part of the story, and the young man had seemed so engaged. *Well, isn't that something? Listen to the whole story and then not find out the ending?*

Another thought came to him. "1953," he said. He'd been twelve in 1953, which would have made Chuck at least forty. He'd had seven kids. Matty was his third. But Chuck couldn't have been forty because . . . Applebaum did the math in his head. He couldn't have been forty because if Chuck had been forty then, he would now be . . . *one hundred and five?* That wasn't possible. Was it?

Applebaum scratched his head.

That *couldn't* be possible.

The plane suddenly bounced, his chest pressing against the restraint. They'd landed, but where? Applebaum was more confused than ever. There'd been no announcement by the stewardess or the pilot. And all the lights in the cabin remained out, all except for his.

The plane taxied to a stop. Applebaum unbuckled his seatbelt. The lights came on. The boy who had been seated across the aisle now stood looking at him. Applebaum turned. The young man was there also, smiling.

There was no one else on the plane.

The young boy held out his hand. Applebaum took the boy's hand, and it felt comforting. The young man put his hand on Applebaum's shoulder and they walked to the front of the plane.

Applebaum wasn't afraid or confused. When he reached the door, there she stood, waiting for him.

"Sandy?"

She smiled at him. She looked radiant, as young and as beautiful as the day they'd gotten married.

Behind her stood other familiar faces. Danny O'Leary and Billy Healy, Matty McGuigan and Dan Burri. His grammar school friends. The best friends he'd ever had. And Chuck. Chuck was there also, but the young Chuck, not the one who'd been in the casket in church that day. He wore a baseball uniform and a ball cap, a bat over his shoulder like he was on his way to play a game.

Applebaum looked down at the young boy. "Who are you?"

The boy handed Applebaum a cap and a glove with a ball in the webbing. His glove, when he'd just been a boy. And when Applebaum looked down, his blue pinstriped suit had transformed, and he was wearing a uniform.

"Welcome home," Sandy said, taking his hand. "Play your game. I don't mind waiting."

Applebaum smiled at her, and when he took her hand, his uniform changed back into his blue suit and Sandy's tie. He handed the glove and the ball back to the boy.

"I played that game already," he said. "It's just a story now. And we have some traveling to do."

NO 11 SQUATTER

ADELE POLOMSKI

The convenience store had a warm, cardboardy smell, and was crammed with things Minnie didn't want. A whole aisle of sports drinks in nonsense colors. How could anyone drink that much? Her old bladder wasn't what it used to be. Her skin wasn't anything to brag about either. When was the last time it fit without sags or bags? At least she had her eyesight.

From the register, the clerk, a man with an Indian accent, wearing a baggy gray cardigan, glowered at her. His face was as pockmarked as a pancake ready to flip. Minnie winced. She hoped she hadn't mentioned it, but then why else would he look so angry?

Minnie moved to the candy aisle, where a large bag of those foil-wrapped things that look like silver nipples sat open, spilling onto the floor, making a mess. She missed the store the way it had been when she was younger. Cheerful, more inviting, less cramped. She remembered coming here on Sundays with Sean for the newspaper and . . .

A sensation of being watched burned off the fog in Minnie's brain. She looked up into icy gray eyes, the whites marbled with red. A man across the aisle, staring. Blind terror tore through her. She'd seen that man before. A howl rushed up her throat and got stuck there. Her bladder, full of hot liquid, let go.

"Minnie?" asked a black woman with apple cheeks and hair drawn into a ponytail of bright orange dreadlocks. Grace.

"Are you all right?" she asked, her face a blend of concern and compassion.

Minnie wanted to warn Grace. The man was dangerous. They needed to call the police, but Minnie remembered wetting herself and humiliation flared, drowning her terror. She felt a rush of blood to her face and neck.

"Minnie? Tell me what's wrong. Are you sick?"

"I've peed my pants," Minnie said miserably, but when she looked down, she didn't see a dark stain. "You've got me in diapers!"

"You won't wear diapers. You insist on pads. What's happened? Why did you look so frightened?"

Minnie looked around. "A man . . ."

"What man? There's no one in the store but us and Martin."

"Well, he's gone now, but I saw him."

"It's all right," Grace said in a soothing voice. "We'll sort this man out. Have you found it?"

"Found what?"

"Your shopping list. You insisted on writing it yourself. Remember?"

Minnie took a shuddering breath. "There's something I need to tell you. It's important."

Grace waited, and Minnie looked around.

"What is it?" Grace asked.

"I can't remember!" Minnie said, furious with frustration.

Grace patted her arm. "Don't worry. You've still got lots of good qualities."

"The good are supposed to die young." Life at her age wasn't worth living. Not when you wore diapers. She looked down at her pants. At least she hadn't wet herself.

"Can I have your handbag?" Grace asked.

"Why? And why is the clerk looking at me like that?"

"Martin's a bit annoyed because last time, when you came in on your own, you nicked a can of pasta."

"I don't like canned spaghetti!"

"Then why did you steal it?" asked the clerk in a sing-song voice.

"I've never stolen anything in my life. And your store is messy."

"Can I see your list?" Grace asked.

"I don't know how you do it," the clerk said, shaking his head. "You have the patience of a martyr, I think."

Minnie unclasped her ancient handbag and a silk eyeglass case caught her eye. Was that new? She didn't need glasses. Did she? Or a hearing aid. If she could have her memory restored, she'd give up her perfect vision and hearing, and wear a diaper.

Grace shook her head. "My mother always said, 'patience is bitter, but its fruit is sweet.' Besides, I like Minnie. She's a good gig. Easy on my back. My last client weighed over two hundred pounds and left me with a herniated lumbar disc. We make a good team, don't we, Minnie?"

"You're bossy," Minnie said.

The clerk snorted, but it was true. Grace made Minnie wash and dress though she would have preferred to stay in her slippers and nightgown. She dyed Minnie's hair a nice chestnut brown, which was better than the hairdresser on Main Street, who dyed her hair a red that matched the rims of her eyes, and permed it into rows of silly sausages. Grace styled Minnie's hair smartly, making the mouse-pink skin of her scalp less conspicuous, so that was all right. Sometimes, she manicured her nails.

Minnie fingered the pearls wound around her neck. She didn't like jewelry, especially costume jewelry. Why had she worn pearls? It worried her, her mind not being as sharp as she'd like it. She hated being afraid. Afraid she'd bungle something or forget something important.

"Let's see what you've got, then," Grace said, holding out her hand.

Minnie stared at the scrap of paper she was clutching, gleaned from a bundle of scribbly notes held together with a large paper clip. Printed on it, in her spidery hand, were the words: *"NO 11 SQUATTER."*

"What does 'squatter' mean?" Minnie asked, though she knew very well what the word meant, but not why she'd made note of it. She wrote down only important things.

"Last week an old man was mugged at the beach," the clerk said. "His face smashed in with a rock. I heard a rumor it was squatters."

"Give me your bag and I'll have a look," said Grace.

Grace pulled the handbag away, and a fresh undertow of anxiety flooded Minnie's brain. "I want to go home. Now," she said, sounding as petulant as a toddler. Minnie didn't care. She wanted to feel safe, and she didn't feel safe here.

"We've come to do our shopping, haven't we?" said Grace.

"My daughter does my shopping."

"Priscilla's busy with work, isn't she?" Without asking, Grace turned out the handbag onto the counter, letting loose a flurry of paper scraps.

"Perhaps a squatter—" Grace said.

"What squatter?" Minnie asked, tuning back in to the conversation.

"A squatter crackhead who needed ocean air," said the clerk. "That poor old man was in the wrong place at the wrong time."

"Or he could have stroked out and tripped," Grace said. "Hit his head or something. We really don't know whether he was mugged, now, do we? Can't always expect the worst." She read a scrap of paper in her hand. "*Frank's place. Pale eyes, thin mouth, stubbly gray hair, tall.* You looking for love, Minnie?"

Minnie felt a stab of annoyance and then a cold ripple of apprehension. The man with the colorless eyes and stubby gray hair. "Grace, we need to go home!"

"Ah. Here's your list. Milk, apples, American cheese, ham, and a loaf of whole grain bread. Let's go shopping, Minnie," she said, handing Minnie back her handbag.

"You've mixed up my notes," Minnie said, frustrated again. "I can't remember what I need to tell you!"

"Chocolate's good for the memory," said the clerk. "Dr. Oz said that. It's in this month's *Woman's World*. Read for yourself."

A pair of untidy teenaged boys slouched into the store, and the clerk found something more interesting than Minnie to keep under surveillance.

Together Minnie and Grace gathered supplies, including a bag of barbecue potato chips for Grace.

They were waiting at the register when the clerk shouted, "You can't open a bag of chocolate without paying for it. That's stealing. Get out now!"

"Hey, chill. Wasn't us," said one of the boys while the other fooled around with his cellphone.

The boy with the cellphone nodded without looking up. "It was like that when we got here."

"Hassle us, and my parents are gonna sue your ass. My mom's a lawyer."

"We haven't eaten any of your stupid chocolate. And your store smells like piss."

The clerk turned to glare at Minnie, who felt a cold heaviness between her legs. She felt ashamed. She wasn't a child. She didn't steal cans of spaghetti. Did she?

"Come on, then," said Grace. "Let's pay for our things. We'll take that bag of candy, as well, Martin. No worries, eh?"

"And eggs," Minnie said, the idea coming to her in a flash. "We need eggs."

Grace looked surprised. "You're right."

Minnie smiled. "See, my memory's just fine. You'll have to remember to tell Priscilla."

Together, Grace and Minnie had developed a system for communicating wordlessly. Not Morse code, which would have been better. Minnie's grandfather used to blink in dots and dashes after his stroke. She thought it was nice that he didn't have to feel so lonely and could communicate with his war buddies.

Minnie and Grace didn't need anything as complicated. One blink for "yes," like a thumbs up, and two blinks for "no" did the trick.

When Priscilla came round to ask whether Minnie had eaten lunch, Grace would blink once and Minnie would say, "Yes." Had she eaten scrambled eggs? Grace would blink twice, and without looking at the sink or sniffing the air for a clue, Minnie, with a confident smile, would say, "No." To end the grilling, Minnie would sniff and say, "I'm too old to be playing twenty questions."

Then Grace would prepare tea or coffee for Priscilla, who would check the cupboards, commenting on what they did or didn't need. "Mom shouldn't be eating so much candy," she chastised Grace that afternoon.

"It's chocolate. Good for the memory," Grace said. "We saw that on Dr. Oz, didn't we, Minnie?"

Though Minnie had lost any thread of the conversation minutes ago, she looked at Grace, who blinked once, and said, "Yes, of course," in a starchy tone meant to end the discussion.

When Grace had poured tea, Priscilla said, "Can you be a dear, Grace, and run my Lexus through the car wash? The interior could use a good vacuuming, and if you can remember I have a prescription to pick up at the CVS."

"Really, Priscilla," Minnie said. "I'm tired."

"Not you, Mom. Grace can go."

"But we go everywhere together."

Priscilla held out some bills. Grace took the money and went off wordlessly to get her coat. Minnie adored going to the drugstore and said petulantly, "Grace's my partner, not yours."

"She's your aide and well compensated. I thought you said you were tired. If you're going to lie down, at least she can be useful."

"She is. I'd be lost without her." It was true. Minnie remembered getting lost coming back from the convenience store. She'd been terrified wandering the avenue, not sure which street was hers.

"So, do you want a nap?" Priscilla asked.

"I'm not tired anymore."

"Good. We need to talk."

Priscilla parked Minnie in her favorite armchair, a sea-green Barca-Lounger overlooking the street. If the wind blew the right way and the windows were open, she could hear the ocean. "You used to love the beach when you were a child," Minnie said.

"True, Mom, but the neighborhood isn't what it used to be."

Minnie surveyed the empty street. "The summer people are gone. But they always come back."

"Yes, well, I'm sure you've heard there was an attempted break-in down on the bay side. Did the police talk to you about it?"

"No."

"Are you sure?" Priscilla handed Minnie a cup of tea she didn't want.

"I think I'd remember something like that," Minnie said, though truthfully she had no idea.

"When I arrived earlier, I saw a uniformed officer knocking on a door across the street. At Frank's house."

"Frank's house. Number eleven?"

"I suppose so. Frank must be visiting his sister in Miami."

"Not Miami," Minnie said. Something nibbled at a corner of her mind, filling her with a nagging apprehension. Frank usually wintered in Florida, but this year he'd changed his mind. He'd spent a week with his sister and then had come home. She'd seen him opening his front door. She remembered that clearly. When had that been? A day or two ago?

"All right, wherever then," said Priscilla. She paused and looked at Minnie. "What's wrong?"

"I don't know," Minnie said, then shook her head. "I mean, nothing. Nothing's wrong. Not with my memory, anyway." She put down the untasted tea. She would be sick if she swallowed anything.

Priscilla looked doubtful. "Look, the point is the neighborhood's getting dangerous, and soon property values will drop."

"The crack addicts?" Minnie asked.

"Precisely. Two towns away it's an epidemic. How long before the marauding hordes infest this neighborhood?" Priscilla sat opposite Minnie on the matching ottoman. "People will rent to anyone these days. Everyone needs money."

She reached out and took Minnie's hand. Priscilla's hand felt warm and soft and comforting, and Minnie thought she hadn't felt this close to her daughter in years. Priscilla talked and talked, and Minnie couldn't keep herself from smiling, imagining Priscilla as a young girl. Sweet and sensitive. Too sensitive. Always having her feelings hurt at school.

"So, you understand where I'm going with this?"

Minnie smiled, and Priscilla let go of her hand. She had no idea what Priscilla had been going on about, only that she wished Priscilla hadn't stopped holding her hand.

"Well, look at the time," Priscilla said, standing. "Tell Grace I'll pick up the car tomorrow."

A light kiss on the cheek and Priscilla was gone.

Sometime later, Minnie was still in her chair in front of the window when the kitchen door opened. Grace announced herself, came into the living room and looked around. "What happened to Priscilla? I've got her car and she owes me five dollars. I tipped the car wash attendant." She dropped a prescription bag on the coffee table.

"You went to the drugstore without me?" Minnie loved CVS. The clean smell of detergent and the friendly pharmacists who all looked younger than the mayonnaise in her refrigerator.

"What's that you're holding?" Grace asked.

Minnie turned the brochure over in her hands. Old people, sitting around, laughing together. "I'm trying to read it, but I can't make sense of it. I think I'm tired."

The expression on Grace's face hardened, but she said gently, "Come on. A nap before dinner will do you good." Grace took Minnie by the arm and helped her shuffle to the bedroom they shared. A hospital bed for Minnie and a twin for Grace.

The telephone rang, and Grace left to answer it after tucking Minnie between the clean sheets.

Minnie drifted off to sleep thinking about her husband, Sean, and what a wonderful smile he had. No one would ever smile at her like that again. There was nothing nice about growing old.

. . .

"You remember me, don't you?"

A strange man was sitting at her kitchen table and smiling at her. Not a doctor. She was home and it was dark outside, and doctors didn't make house calls anymore. "Where's Grace?" She remembered how sad Grace had been when Minnie told her Priscilla was right. She did need to go to a home. Her memory was only getting worse. She didn't care anymore. It didn't matter. What made her feel sad was the possibility she'd never see Grace again.

Then she remembered the man sitting across from her. Something about his face looked familiar. She looked down, away from the colorless eyes. The table was littered with notes, dozens scattered about, all in her handwriting. "Where's Grace? Don't hurt her. She doesn't know anything."

"And what do you know?" the man asked genially, as though they were friends.

"How did you get in?"

"You let me in. Don't you remember?" He smiled, and she could almost believe she had invited him inside. Offered him coffee or tea, and he'd said not to bother. Young people always worried about how clean an older person kept their home. She remembered her grandmother's house. Her father wouldn't have eaten a cracker off any of her grandmother's dishes.

She looked up and met his smile. Nice teeth. But no, she hadn't let him in. She'd found him sitting at the kitchen table when she'd gotten up from her nap. It was dinnertime and Grace should have been warming up a can of soup or making a ham sandwich. Where was Grace? She should tell the man to get out, but he frightened her.

"Who are you, and why are you here?" And then she felt the blood drain slowly from her face as she remembered.

"You do remember. I can see it in your face," he said, his voice still pleasant, but somehow not human.

"At the convenience store today. You startled me." Yesterday. She'd been staring outside, wondering why the draperies stayed closed at number eleven when Frank liked them open, even at night when she could see him plain as day, dozing in front of his big screen television with a can of beer.

She'd meant to tell Grace. She'd written it down somewhere. "I want to call Grace," she said. To find out that she was okay and to warn her to stay away.

"Be my guest. Do you remember her number?"

She didn't and stared at him blankly.

"Didn't think so. Ever since smartphones came along, we don't have to remember a thing, do we?"

"I don't have a smartphone. I don't think I do anyway." She did have a flip phone but she could never find it. And it was always off. She needed it, according to Priscilla, for emergencies. This was an emergency! Where was it, and where was Grace?

"What's this supposed to mean?" He held out the scrap of paper printed with *"NO 11 SQUATTER."* The sight of his hairy hand sheathed in a latex glove sent a geyser of adrenaline through Minnie and brought back the memory in living color. His face. In the front window of Frank's home, peering at her from behind a crack in the draperies. The sun had been right and she'd seen his face, and he'd seen hers.

The door opened and Grace appeared. "Priscilla wanted her car back and——" Minnie turned, relief flooding her heart before a fresh stab of panic tore through her. Grace needed to go and get away from this latex-gloved madman who would surely kill them both. She stared at Grace, willing her to understand, blinking furiously, three dots, three dashes, three dots. *SOS*, to warn her, to tell her to get away, to go get help, but they didn't have a signal for that, or else she'd forgotten.

"Oh, you have a visitor," Grace said. "Minnie, you didn't tell me. Is this gentleman a friend?"

Minnie looked Grace squarely in the eyes and blinked twice. Then she said in a voice that wavered with alarm, "Yes, I forgot to mention he was in town. You know how forgetful I've been lately."

"Is everything all right?"

She blinked twice and said, "Of course. We're having a nice chat."

"So you know each other?"

Two blinks. "A student of mine. When I taught third grade. It's a small world, isn't it?"

"I'm Hank," the man with the stubbly gray hair and unnaturally pale eyes said without getting up or holding out his hand.

"All right then," Grace said cheerily, though Minnie could see the fear that had settled on her face. "Priscilla will have my head if I don't get her dry cleaning before the place closes. She's waiting for me at her office. You know what she'll do when I'm late. Send out the cavalry. See you in a bit, Minnie. Enjoy your visit."

The man was out of his chair faster than Minnie would have believed possible. "You're not going anywhere."

Grace screamed and the man clapped a gloved hand over her mouth. Grace struggled. The strange man was strangling her. A bolt of rage surged through Minnie. She didn't want to see Grace hurt, and for the first time in a long time, she didn't want to die.

The paring knife in the knife holder wasn't very heavy or as large as some of the others, but it was sharp and if she hit the right spot . . .

And she did.

"It's a miracle you weren't hurt, Mom."

"Nonsense," Minnie said. "Fear does amazing things for a body, even an old body." She'd said the same thing to the police when they reported finding Frank bound and gagged in his basement. His big television was gone, along with most of his furniture. The squatter hadn't sold off his stamp collection, and he'd been grateful for that.

"How is Frank?" Minnie asked.

"Dehydrated, but he should recover in a few days," the police officer said.

If she was a police officer. She wasn't wearing a uniform. Minnie couldn't remember her name. "I really should write things down," she said, looking around for a pen.

"You need a proper notebook," Grace said. "And some cognitive training wouldn't hurt, would it? Let's be honest, Minnie."

"Speaking of honesty, you understand now why you have to move," said Priscilla. "The neighborhood isn't safe."

"I'm staying put. I'm forgetful, not crazy. And I have Grace, who incidentally will not be running any more of your silly errands. Find your own assistant. We're going to be busy organizing a neighborhood watch."

The young woman, a police detective, Minnie decided, cleared her throat and thanked everyone. "As we say, if you see something, say something."

"Least of all," said Minnie, "write it down."

The young detective was about to leave when Priscilla said, "Detective, just a moment. Don't you agree? The neighborhood isn't as safe as—"

"Priscilla," Minnie said in her best elementary school teacher voice, "that's enough. Goodbye, Detective, and thank you again."

"Mom, I just want you safe."

"I do feel safe. And as Grace often says, 'We can't always expect the worst.' That's not really living, is it? And anyway, I seem to remember we have a plan." But for the life of her, she couldn't remember what it was.

Then Grace chimed in, "Neighborhood watch. Remember?"

"Of course, I remember," said Minnie, "I'll just go find my notebook and write that down."

A Cold Spell

MARK THIELMAN

The night sky above Eastham hung black, black as pitch, black as the soul of the lost. The cold air bit at Samuel's exposed face. He could not remember weather like this during his years in the Massachusetts Bay Colony. Stomping his feet to warm himself, he hurried forward; the sooner they returned to his hearth, the quicker he might feel temporary relief from this never-ending winter.

The wind pushed stinging needles at him. Though Samuel wore his linen shirt and thickest doublet beneath his cape, the cold penetrated all. Beside him, he heard a groan.

"We hath not much farther to travel, Sanaa," Samuel said.

"We already gone too far on dis night, Mr. Samuel," Sanaa replied.

Despite the cold and the circumstances of their journey, Samuel smiled. Sanaa's accent seemed more pronounced in the dead of winter, a physical reaction, he supposed, to a yearning for her native Barbados.

As they passed the graveyard, Samuel resisted the impulse to glance toward Elizabeth's and Joanna's graves. Nothing would be gained by scratching at that wound. Instead, he pressed onward.

Soon, Samuel could see a small gathering of the town elders, their steeple-crowned hats illuminated by the torches they carried. The men talked among themselves, their exhaled breaths like smoke from a dozen fires in this cold. Samuel quickened his pace. Sanaa, by contrast, slowed, allowing the distance between them to lengthen.

"Brother Samuel," a voice said, "evil treads heavily among us this night."

Samuel thought he heard excitement in Reverend Purge's tone. He nodded, acknowledging the minister.

"May God be with us all," the reverend said.

Samuel's eyes swept the gathering. In a circle stood most of the freemen of the village. As the elected constable, they waited on Samuel for direction.

"Who found this man?" he asked.

"I did."

Samuel recognized Timothy Bennett, the son of John and Good-wife. He waited to see what Timothy would volunteer.

"Mother bade me to check upon the cow we keep in our far parcel of land, the one near the Glower property. Having made my inspection, I hurried home. I stumbled here upon a log that lay across the path. When I made to remove it, I discovered it to be the leg of this man, William English."

"And this was how ye found him?"

"Aye, Brother Samuel."

Samuel studied the body, arms outstretched, the corpse's legs pressed together, loins clad only in a homespun cloth, dressed more like a savage than a Puritan.

"We must take English to better light and examine him more closely," Samuel said.

No one moved.

"Perhaps the meetinghouse?"

Reverend Purge shook his head. "We shall not invite death into our sacred place."

"Sanaa." Samuel turned. He found her huddled alongside Bethuna, Reverend Purge's house slave, who also had been brought out on this night. "Hurry to the house and clear the table."

"Yes, Master Samuel," she said and disappeared into the darkness.

Turning to the assembled men, Samuel said, "We shall take him to my home. Death has been a frequent enough visitor there. Who will help me?"

No one spoke of the fever that had taken Samuel's wife and daughter.

"The good reverend will grant us forgiveness for any handling of the body."

Reverend Purge scrunched his face into a deeper frown. Samuel chose to assign the expression to the cold.

Major Dan limped forward. "I've handled my share of bodies fighting on the frontier. I shall help, Constable." Supporting himself on his one good leg, the major grabbed the dead man's ankles.

Samuel had hoped that another, more swiftly moving fellow, might step forward. Still, help was help. He grabbed the dead man beneath the shoulders and lifted.

The assembly gasped.

"He retains the shape of our crucified Lord," Reverend Purge whispered.

Samuel looked down. Much to his surprise, the dead man's arms remained extended out to the sides.

The pace proved slow and difficult. The major's herky-jerky walk nearly pulled the corpse free from Samuel's icy hands. No other member of the party dared come close, rendering their lights ineffective. Several times, Samuel stepped off the path, his foot crunching on the frozen snow. Eventually, however, the party arrived at his house.

Samuel and the major steered the outstretched arms inside and onto the table.

The others followed, their fear overwhelmed by their curiosity and desire for warmth. Sanaa's thin frame bustled about the room as she quickly retrieved pewter mugs of warmed wine from the hob and delivered them to the major and Samuel. A third she handed to Reverend Purge.

"Thank you," Samuel said. He pressed the mug against his palms, waiting for the warmth to soak through his outer wraps.

The other men said nothing. Reverend Purge brought the cup to his lips, tasted the wine and paused, studying it.

"The wine has a bit of the nutmeg," Samuel explained. "My wife knew how I liked it, and Sanaa always paid close attention to Elizabeth. Shall we pray, Reverend?" Samuel asked.

Reverend Purge and the others bowed their heads. Purge offered up a lukewarm prayer asking that, in the unlikely event this foreigner's soul was not already consigned to Hell, God, in his mercy, take pity upon it.

"Might not Brother English deserve more intercession?" Samuel asked quietly.

"William English must make peace with whomsoever he finds himself before," the reverend answered.

"He was a freeman living here . . ."

"English was among us, but never part of us," the reverend said, facing the crowd, "born William L'Anglais, a Huguenot. The man and his wife changed their last name when they settled on the frontier. The wars with the savages forced them upon us. Perhaps your Puritan brothers in Bermuda were more accepting of false beliefs."

"Did English not participate in the community?"

"Paid his tithes, stood his watch. He attended meetings nearly every Sunday."

"And be it not true that his wife, Prudence English, earned renown for her skills as a baker?"

"I do not say that they are without merit, though I disapprove of the woman's desire for notoriety over quiet service to her husband and our Lord, but still—"

The reverend's statements were interrupted by Sanaa's gasp. She held one hand to her mouth and with the other pointed an outstretched finger at William English's arm.

"Master, de marks."

Samuel looked. The palm of English's right hand bore a round, red wound. He located similar marks on his left hand as well as both feet.

"His side showeth the mark of the spear!" the reverend cried.

The crowd pressed closer to the table. Just above the homespun on his right side, a clean gash in his flesh.

"The Devil has made a mockery of Christ through his desecration of this body," the reverend announced.

"Master, de tips of dem fingers." As Sanaa spoke, she gently touched the pads of her own fingers with her thumb.

Samuel shifted his gaze back to the hands. The fingertips of English's left hand appeared burned. He also noticed a red mark higher up on English's forearm.

"The troubles of Salem visit us," Reverend Purge said.

"Can thou be certain?" Samuel asked, his eyes flicking among the body's wounds.

"The fingertip burns are well-known among those of us who study such matters," the reverend said. "Pity you have not attended the Harvard College. Usually, such marks come from holding the flaming pen when writing your name into the Devil's book."

The circle slackened, every man distancing himself from this witch-vessel.

"Call thy families. We must pray," Reverend Purge declared.

Even Major Dan shook with fright; here was an enemy against which he had no experience. He hobbled out the door as quickly as his one good leg would carry him.

Reverend Purge left last. "I trust, Samuel, that I will see thee at the meetinghouse. Your hands touched this defiled body."

"I will be along directly, for I have no wish to fall prey to the Devil nor anyone else," Samuel said.

The Reverend, satisfied, adopted a conciliatory tone. "You have been a welcome addition to Eastham since your family sailed from Bermuda. We mourned your tragedy and supported you by electing you for office. I trust your zeal for Puritanism." He pulled open the door, sending a blast of frigid air into the room, then disappeared into the night.

When Samuel was sure they were alone, he looked at Sanaa. "What do you think?"

"I prepared de poultices for de women who burned fingertips pulling pans from de oven. De fingers look like dese. Dis is a burn, but de reverend may be hasty about de source."

"And the other wounds, do you notice anything about them?"

"The Christ marks show where de Bible says," Sanaa answered.

He looked again and nodded. "I should never have taught you to read," he said, a faint smile on his face.

"Pity you had no opportunity to study at de Harvard College. Imagine what I know den."

Samuel grunted. "What else do you see about the wounds?"

Sanaa studied them quietly. "Not'ing."

"No blood," he said. "Nor was there any spilt where the body lay. We shall confirm this on our walk to the meetinghouse."

This time Sanaa grunted. "I just thawed from de last walk."

"Help me carry English's body to the barn. The cold is like the sunshine in Barbados. Continual exposure will lessen your sensitivity." Samuel slid into his cape, adjusted his hat, and then opened the door to the outside. A blast of arctic air punched them both. Samuel slammed shut the door.

"The master, he know best about de sensitivity," Sanaa said.

Wrapped tightly, Samuel looked to her. She reluctantly nodded and bent down to clasp English's feet. Samuel again slid his arms down to the shoulders. His hand brushed against the back of the dead man's head.

"Sanaa, come here."

She joined him at the head.

Taking her wrist, he guided her hand behind the man's head.

Her eyes widened.

Together, they carried the body to the barn, then set out for the meetinghouse, pausing only briefly at the spot where English's body had lain.

"No blood, Samuel," Sanaa confirmed through chattering teeth.

They hurried to the gathering place.

Inside, a nervous crowd had assembled. Prudence English and her daughter were already in their seats, red-eyed, crying softly, surrounded by supportive women, many the wives of the men who had fled Samuel's house. He slid into his assigned seat while Sanaa moved to her spot in the very back corner of the building.

As Reverend Purge climbed the high pulpit, the low rumble of conversation fell away. He had dressed tonight in full ministerial robe, black with only the white Geneva bands providing contrast. Against this backdrop, his bald head and silver beard shone. His glowering eyes, framed by wrinkles of wisdom and experience, focused slowly on everyone in the room. Occasional sniffles could be heard from Prudence and Eden, her daughter.

"Bow your heads," the reverend commanded.

Purge prayed with far more zeal than he had earlier. The Devil, he began, attacked most strongly his harshest foes, and this night fiendishly had visited Eastham, their utopia of godliness. But, he prayed, we believers would not falter, but rather unite to uncover the witch among us. We pray there is but one, he added.

When he finished, only the wind could be heard, battling the walls of the meetinghouse, probing for chinks in the wooden exterior, the penetrating cold searching for a way inside.

Reverend Purge lifted his face, glistening with perspiration from the force of his entreaties. "We must pursue this matter," he declared. "Prudence English, come forward, that you might answer questions about your husband's death."

Prudence lifted her head, and although Samuel would not have thought it possible, her complexion, already ashen, seemed to pale. Red-rimmed eyes looked weakly to the pulpit.

Samuel stood. "Reverend, the woman has just learned of her husband's death. Let us show charity." Samuel heard murmurings among the gathered, although he could not tell whether they supported or opposed his suggestion.

"As we have seen, the Devil shows no pity. We must proceed."

No one else challenged Purge.

With a woman supporting each elbow, Prudence English shuffled toward the front of the room.

"Goody English, pray tell when you last ate?" Samuel asked.

"I made rye cakes earlier. My daughter ate, but I have not yet taken a meal."

"We must at least allow Goody English to eat before examining her," Samuel said.

"She has no need of earthly food. Though she walks through the valley of the shadow of death, the rod and staff shall support her in this necessary task," the reverend answered.

The women assisting her hurried back to the safety of their seats. Prudence English stood before the assembled townsfolk, quaking. Reverend Purge climbed down from the pulpit, heavy footfalls echoing in the silent room. He lovingly laid the Bible upon the unadorned communion table, the only other piece of furniture within the simple room.

"Come to me, Goodwife English."

Haltingly, she moved forward.

"Lay your hand upon the Bible."

Her shaky hand touched the Scriptures.

"What do you know of your husband's last hours?"

Prudence said nothing; her arm shook and her teeth chewed upon her lower lip.

"Speak," the reverend commanded.

Everyone in the pews pressed forward to hear.

"We escaped the frontier with little," she began, "and have tried to rebuild. With limited land, we survive as shopkeepers. We sell the wheat bread I bake and live upon the rye. We churn butter from excess milk God grants us. Goodman English sometimes finds items within the community from which we profit. God blessed us, and we began to prosper. William left this afternoon. He was to meet another and to tend the cow. I expected him home to sup. Several townsfolk came by seeking to do business. I recall your servant, Bethuna, as well as Widow Glower. When he did not return, I became worried. And then . . ." She fell silent, her shoulders shaking.

"And pray tell us, whom did he meet?" the reverend asked.

"I do not know."

Outside, the howling wind rattled the clapboards.

Then, Eden English laughed hysterically and fell to the floor of the meetinghouse writhing, her legs spasmodically kicking the pew.

Moving quickly from the men's side of the room, two freemen pulled Eden upright. They carried her backward to the front of the church, heels dragging. At the communion table, they turned her to face Reverend Purge and Prudence English.

The girl's head lolled to the right side and her hands danced as if unconnected to her arms. "I see Father," she said. "Father surrounded by light. He points his arm at you, Mother. He doth speak, but I cannot hear what he is saying."

"Try, child, try," the reverend begged.

"His lips form a letter. I cannot hear the word. Wha . . . wha."

"Witch," the crowd cried, a contagion of fear sweeping them.

Prudence English collapsed.

The major, acting as beadle, secured English behind the heavy oak door of the jail. At Reverend Purge's insistence, she was also chained to prevent the Devil from rescuing his servant.

The next day, the evidence mounted. Witch cakes were prepared, the rye flour mixed with Prudence English's urine, and fed to three dogs. Each animal became possessed, barking wildly at invisible foes while stumbling as if lame. Eden had been carried to Goody Towns's home and put to bed. Upon awakening, she claimed no memory of her declarations. This was of little consequence, as the entire community had witnessed her spectral testimony.

Finally, Bethuna came forward and revealed that upon visiting the English household, she had heard Prudence English mumbling unrecognizable words while standing over a figurine made of sticks and dried grass. Prudence threw the homemade doll into the fire and cackled. The sight had caused Bethuna to run back to the Purge household. The episode had been so frightening, so un-Christian, that Bethuna had blotted the scene from her memory until Reverend Purge's interview with her brought it back in vivid detail.

Prudence English sat quietly. As each damning bit of evidence fell, her face remained blank. The reports, the congregants whispered, told her nothing she did not already know. And so, it came as no surprise that when Reverend Purge called upon her to confess, she admitted being in league with the Devil, her tone flat, as if she were reciting the mixing instructions for her prized cakes.

At the end of the evidence, the reverend and the beadle met briefly before announcing that Prudence L'Anglais would be bound over to the Court of Oyer and Terminer on the charge of witchcraft. Major Dan returned her to jail, and every citizen of Eastham went to their house feeling a little more secure. A witch had been rooted out of town, and the only casualty had been her own husband.

"What say you, Sanaa?" Samuel asked when they were safely shuttered in his home, in front of the fireplace. The blustery wind muted their voices from anyone who might be outside.

"I am troubled, Samuel."

"Witches are a troubling thing."

She leaned closer to him, her coif nearly resting against his shoulder. "In Barbados, we accept de witches. Dey are part of de world around us, like angels. We do not fear dem, but rather we respect dem."

Samuel looked to the door and windows.

"We do not see dem acting like dis."

"But Goody English confessed," Samuel reminded her.

"As would we all if we had been treated so."

Samuel stared at the dancing flames. He steepled his index fingers and pressed them to his lips. "I believe you are correct," he said finally.

"As constable, you can stop dis."

"Witchcraft is both a religious and civil crime," he answered. "I cannot act alone."

Her hickory-colored eyes watched him.

Samuel stared back into the fire, thinking. Then, he slapped his thigh with his hand. "We must move quickly, before the trial condemns her. I will go to the jail tomorrow and interview her and then the child, Eden."

"Both Prudence English and Eden feel alone," Sanaa said. "Dey may not speak freely to a man." Here, she paused momentarily. "Let

dem speak wit another of de outsiders in dis community. Dey will be
fah mo' likely to speak de truth."

"And what shall I do?"

"Master Samuel, discover who did do dis murder. Let Sanaa discover who did not."

His lips spread into a small smile. "Then *dat* is what we shall do."

She smiled back.

Early the next morning, beneath a sullen sky, Samuel knocked at the
reverend's house. Elizabeth, Purge's wife, opened the door and, wordlessly, pointed to the table. The minister, still in his nightshirt, sat
yawning and rubbing his eyes. Bethuna moved slowly about the room.
Even the children seemed subdued.

"It has been a long few days, Reverend," Samuel began.

"You speak truly," he replied. "The trial shall be soon. Then we
will be rid of this scourge."

"Assuming Goody English be found guilty."

Purge's eyes flared for a moment before recovering. "Of course."

"This entire affair saddens our community."

Reverend Purge nodded.

"I should like to propose a contest to lift the village's spirits."

The reverend raised an eyebrow.

"Goody English has been recognized as Eastham's finest baker. I
thought a cake competition would give thy flock something else upon
which to focus."

"Contests lead to pride, and pride is a sin," the reverend reminded.

"Though it would reveal the premier baker when she walks to the
gallows."

"Assuming Goody English be found guilty."

"Assuming so, Reverend."

Reverend Purge drummed the table with his fingers. "An excellent
idea. We need a distraction, and this weather proves too cold for anything out of doors."

"As the community's leader, the townsfolk will look to you, Reverend. Might you send Bethuna down to assist Sanaa in preparing and delivering competition packages?"

The reverend cocked his head.

"Common ingredients make the contest fair. They reveal the superior hands."

The reverend nodded. "Bethuna, please go to Master Samuel's house and assist Sanaa."

The slave nodded and began wrapping herself.

"Exactly what we need," the reverend said, his face pleased.

"I recommend you rest, Reverend. I will spread word of the contest," Samuel said.

Samuel walked along a trod footpath. Stepping over the reverend's fence, he entered onto the English property. The small parcel had few trees to serve as a windbreak. The cold bit through Samuel's cape. He shoved his hands deeply into his pockets, fingering the smooth silver coins he carried. Samuel tried to distract himself by remembering the land in springtime, when the absence of shade made the grass grow thick and lush. It did not work. Instead, he ducked his head and pressed forward.

He knocked at the Bennetts' door. Timothy answered and ushered him inside. Samuel grasped Timothy's hand in greeting, but the young man quickly pulled away. Samuel put his palm beneath his cape and touched his forearm.

"I apologize for the chill of my handshake. Is your mother here?"

Goodwife Bennett appeared from the back room. She wore a simple brown dress of fine material held out by petticoats.

"Mistress Bennett, I bring news."

"Not more witches?"

"No, Mistress, the reverend has called for a cake-baking contest to distract our minds from the horrible situation of these last few days."

Samuel saw her tongue delicately touch her top lip. She unconsciously glanced at the new copper pots hanging near the fireplace. Whisperings said that Mistress Bennett always had considered herself a superior baker to Prudence.

"The reverend is wise. This challenge may be exactly what the community requires."

Asking her to spread word about the contest, Samuel took his leave. He walked through the cold morning air toward Major Dan's house. He caught up with the man dragging his leg through the snow.

"Good morrow, Major," Samuel said.

"Little good is to be had," he replied. "I have returned from the prisoner."

"Troubles?" Samuel asked.

"The reverend insists I call her L'Anglais, but by any name, the same. She sits, does not quarrel, barely lifts a finger. She does not eat. Chaining her like a bear in a pit seems unnecessary."

"Perhaps Sanaa may persuade her to take food. It would not do to have her die before she might be hanged."

The major consented. Samuel then stretched his legs, heading toward Widow Glower's small house.

Knocking, he announced his arrival. "Widow Glower, this is Sam—"

"Go away!" she screamed.

Removing his hat, Samuel put his ear to the frozen wooden door. Inside, he could hear only sobbing. Unsure of what to say, he returned home and waited for Sanaa. Later that afternoon, she accompanied him back across the frozen ground to the Glower house.

They discussed their separate journeys.

"I spoke wit Eden," she reported. "She cries mightily at de thought dat she named her mother. No memory has she. Prudence English has no will left. De news of her husband along wit de chains and de lonely have broken her. She'd confess to being Queen Mary."

"Watching her in the meetinghouse, I suspected as much," Samuel said.

"Bethuna fears de reverend. She will say what she thinks makes him happy."

"And she condemns a woman for it."

"She de slave. She is far from home with no place to go."

Samuel heard the implicit accusation.

"And I fear he beats her," Sanaa continued.

They had arrived at the Glower house.

Samuel raised his hand to knock but Sanaa stayed it with a finger. He stepped back. "Widda Glower," she shouted. "Dis is Sanaa, wit a message. You all right in dere, Widda Glower?"

Nothing happened. Samuel stepped forward, prepared to pound upon the door when it cracked open.

"Who's there?" the voice inside asked.

"Sanaa. I'm here wit my master Samuel."

The door pushed open a bit wider.

They stepped inside and Widow Glower quickly shut the door.

Samuel and Sanaa looked at her wordlessly. She had handkerchiefs stuffed in both ears, the tails drooped.

"Why have you come?" the widow shouted.

"We had concerns about your welfare," Samuel said.

The old lady did not reply.

Sanaa reached forward slowly with her hand and pulled the handkerchiefs free. She handed them to Widow Glower. "We fear dat you do not fare so good," Sanaa said, remaining close to the woman.

The widow's eyes flicked from Samuel to the ground and back.

"You may trust dis one," Sanaa said. "He will tell no tales."

Glower's eyes flicked back to Samuel.

"The Devil comes for me," she said and then shivered. "He wants to put my name into his book."

"Why do you think dis way?"

"He lurks outside. I have smelled his brimstone, heard his unholy hammer. I have seen the flickering dance of his minions. He comes for me, I know it. Earlier today, he knocked at my door, called me by name, introduced himself, polite as could be. 'Widow Glower, this is Satan,' he said. I heard him with mine own ears."

Sanaa convinced her to take some food and to rest, promising to pray and to make a holy mark upon the door. The exhausted woman fell into a deep sleep before they had crossed the threshold.

Leaving the Glower house, they passed by the Bennetts' small thatched-roof cowshed. The thick fireplace and sturdy bellows could readily be seen at the backside of the stall. *Makes sense,* Samuel thought, *to keep the smithy out here and not at the house, where an errant ember would endanger the entire community.* Samuel wished they were doing some forging now, for he dearly would have loved to feel the heat off the forge. As they passed, he placed his hand against the thick bricks and felt, at least in his mind, the remembered warmth.

Samuel and Sanaa walked along, neither speaking. Samuel, his arms tucked inside his cape, fondled the smooth coins inside the pocket of his doublet. He sought to untangle the twisted thoughts spinning inside his head.

Sanaa turned to him nearly as soon as they entered his house. "De governor will convene de Court of Oyer and Terminer de day after tomorrow. She will be hanged unless we act."

"Pointing out difficulties with the evidence will not change the outcome. It will only make the citizens of this town angry at us. There is a dead man who must be accounted for. If we cannot give them another, we must remain quiet for our own sakes."

"But—" Sanaa began.

"No more," Samuel said. "I forbid it. We will consider this afresh on the morrow."

The next morning when he awoke, Samuel felt the quiet in the house like an extra layer of cold air. He dressed and ate quickly. "Come," he said, "let us do what we can."

Sanaa followed behind him as he walked. Their mood and the dull light of the leaden sky were offset by the excitement of the community. The anticipation in the air was palpable and only increased as they neared the meetinghouse.

Inside, the eagerness crested. Five women stood with cakes arranged on plates. Each eyed the others. Samuel and Sanaa collected the plates.

"And who doth be the judge?" Mistress Bennett asked as Samuel received her baked offering.

"I am the collector," he said. "The judge will remain secret until after the decision has been made."

Mistress Bennett pursed her lips and squinted her eyes. She turned and looked at Reverend Purge, who gave the smallest shrug.

"I shall pray he has taste buds," she said, "though using this crude flour hardly made for a fair contest."

Some of the other women nodded in agreement.

"All began with the same supplies. This seemed the truest judge of talent. We will know when I come back at the meridian," Samuel said.

Nearly the entire village had gathered in the meetinghouse when Samuel returned just before noon. The nervous chatter within the room fell away, and a hush settled as he walked inside. Although his face was set in a grim expression, his eyes were alive, roaming the crowd. The five contestants sat on the women's side of the room at the front of the meetinghouse.

"Have they been judged, Constable?" Reverend Purge asked.

"In a manner of speaking," Samuel said.

The answer served to provoke the nervous chatter again. Samuel raised his hands to quiet the crowd.

"Before I announce the judge's results, I have a few questions for the contestants," he began. "Did each of you use the rye flour I provided?"

Each woman nodded.

"Did anyone use special ingredients?"

Every contestant declared she had not.

"I take it, therefore, no one prepared their breads using Goody English's urine."

The congregants erupted. Reverend Purge silenced the crowd, shouting, "What is the meaning of this?"

"The rye flour came from the stores of Goody English, the same flour used to make the witch cakes. See what the judges think of your handiwork." Samuel quickly strode to the back of the meetinghouse and threw open the doors. Outside, dogs chased their tails in the street, howled without reason, and in every respect behaved exactly as the beasts that were used to damn Goody English as a witch.

Samuel shouted to be heard over the din of excitement within the room. "'Twas not her urine which spoiled the cakes, but rather the rye. It is diseased." He turned his head momentarily to where the rest of the Bennetts sat. "Timothy, would you close the doors, please? We have seen enough."

"Thou hast tricked us!" Mistress Bennett cried.

"They were judged by the beasts and found to be contaminated." Samuel reached into a bag hanging from his belt. "Gladly, I will share a cake with anyone willing to eat it."

No one accepted Samuel's offer.

"This means nothing," the reverend declared. "There is the confession and the spectral evidence of her daughter."

"Her daughter who ate the cake," Samuel reminded, "and the statement of a woman chained and accused of the most horrible of crimes on the day she learned of her husband's brutal murder."

"Bethuna was a witness," the reverend retorted.

"Bethuna wishes to please her master. She knows you hunt witches, and she fears to be disobedient." As Samuel spoke, he walked to where Bethuna stood. Her eyes widened as he drew closer. Samuel laid his hand high up on her back. The woman flinched noticeably. "You were beaten?" Samuel asked softly.

Bethuna's head bobbed.

"I questioned her forcefully," the reverend said.

"Forceful questioning with your fist?"

"A switch," Purge answered, voice slightly subdued.

"Only thus did she make her claims about Prudence English?"

"The Devil does not readily reveal his handmaidens."

Samuel turned to face the meetinghouse. He could feel the crowd coming to his side.

Reverend Purge could feel it too. "I have no reason to declare her a witch without cause."

"Not intentionally, but, nonetheless, I fear you have done so," Samuel answered, his voice calm, tinged with sadness.

The reverend's eyes grew wide.

Samuel pressed forward into the momentary silence. "Reverend, you wish to protect our town, so you are alert for witches. You think and read about them; witches consume your thoughts. Your fellow ministers are lauded for purging their towns. Pride is insidious, like winter cold. It comes in through the tiniest of chinks. That is why it is a sin. Pride and desire."

A collective gasp rolled through the crowd.

"The English property sits alongside your own parcel of land. Their small pasture is the best grazing land in the village. Their cow outperforms all other beasts for milk production. That is why they have butter to sell. I fear you covet their property." Samuel quickly held up his hand to finish his statement before the reverend's expected outburst. "You are a good man who means well. I do not claim that you declared Goody English a witch to take her property, only that prideful and covetous blindness have clouded your eyes to the true facts."

Reverend Purge staggered backward before grabbing the pulpit for support. He stood silent for nearly a minute, his head turning slowly, face contorting. Then, in front of the assembled community, he fell to his knees, clasped his hands, and began praying, squeezing his hands together so tightly the knuckles whitened.

The prayer was short by Reverend Purge's standards. When his head rose, his face had relaxed.

"Beadle," he said, "might you bring Goody English to the meeting-house? I wish to beg her forgiveness."

The major rose from his seat and limped off to get the frail woman.

The reverend's eyes suddenly widened. "Granting what you say means we still have a witch who stole William English's life and made a mockery of our Lord."

"I have prayed for discernment," Samuel began. "The clothes were stripped and the marks added after he had been clubbed down," he said, looking to the faces of the men who had been called out that first night. "Remember what you saw. There was no blood on the snow nor had the wounds bled. They served as a ruse to distract."

He saw the nods of the men among the original party.

"The Widow Glower will not leave her home, for fear she will be taken by the Devil," Samuel continued. "She sees his flickering lights and smells brimstone. These are not of the Devil. They come from the Bennetts' cowshed. Timothy, you reported finding English's body upon your return from the cowshed, did ye not?"

"That is where I found him," Timothy said, still standing near the meetinghouse doors. Sanaa, Samuel noticed, stood on the opposite side of the doorway, barely on the women's side.

Samuel turned his attention away from Timothy and to the crowd of men. "Who among you has shillings? Take them out."

Samuel waited until the rustle of clothing and the clink of money pouches had died down.

"Whose coins, like mine, have smooth edges?"

Around the room, hands were raised.

"Left without the means to support his family, English shaved coins. Collecting the silver scrapings, he melted them down and mixed in bits of lead. Coin shaving debases our currency, and is a crime punishable by death. Thus, English performed this work at the far cowshed. If you travel there, you will find the furnace still warm. He thereby doubled his coins and helped to preserve his family."

Samuel paused, his eyes sweeping the congregation. "Had we proved more welcoming, none of this may have occurred. We share blame for English's sinful crime." Samuel allowed the silence to linger for a moment before continuing. "Melting silver and counterfeiting are hard work. He would need an associate. The work would also require ready access to the Bennetts' property. His accomplice, I fear, motivated solely by greed, struck him down in a dispute."

Samuel turned to Timothy. "Your chores include caring for the cow, do they not?" Before the young man could answer, Samuel continued, "Yesterday, I was in your home. The Bennett family has recently been blessed with financial success. How do you profit during winter?"

"I know nothing of what you speak," Timothy answered in a reedy voice.

Samuel's eyes returned to the crowd. "You men remember the burns on English's fingertips. Young Timothy has them also."

In a room silent as a tomb, silver coins hitting the wood floor made a sound heard by everyone.

Timothy Bennett grabbed at the coins that had fallen from beneath his cape, snatching them before they rolled away. Suddenly aware of the eyes upon him, he stood up and looked around the room. "Those aren't mine," he said. He then threw open the meetinghouse door and dashed outside, running straight into Major Dan. They both fell onto the snow, entangled in each other.

After all the confusion had settled down, Samuel sat at his dining table and massaged his temples. Sanaa moved behind him and kneaded his shoulders with her powerful hands.

"Fortunate coincidence that Timothy's secret purse split at that moment," Samuel said.

"A spirit revealed him," Sanaa said.

Samuel arched his neck slightly to see her better. "We should not make light of such matters." He reached his thumb and forefinger slightly up the sleeve of her blue dress and withdrew the fine penknife he knew her to carry. "We should not make light, especially when we know that witchcraft was not involved."

"A spirit revealed him," Sanaa insisted, "but sometimes spirits, both good and evil, still need de help."

What Would Nora Do?

GEORGIA JEFFRIES

Justyce Joyce Underwood was convicted of attempted murder in the second degree and sentenced to seven years' incarceration at the California Institution for Women in Corona by Judge Stanton Kriskieger. Ms. Underwood, headmistress of the Eastlake Academy, graduated Wellesley summa cum laude, and became the first Eastlake alumna to lead her alma mater. This was the third trial for the former Rose Bowl Princess and goodwill ambassador of the Tournament of Roses, the previous trials having ended in hung juries. Each time Ms. Underwood pleaded not guilty by reason of temporary insanity.

—*Pasadena Independent*, July 23, 2010

JJ smiled. The words were coming again, the secret words no one else could hear.

One of the things people always say to you if you get upset is, don't take it personally. Please, I beg you, take it personally.

JJ did as she was told. Because that was what her partner in crime advised she must do from the first moment she discovered her husband's betrayal. Yes, the words were coming again, calling her to rectify a wrong still unpunished.

"JJ?"

Her brother's eyes followed her as she carried the breakfast cereal bowls to the sink then returned to brush burnt crumbs from the table into her cupped hand.

"Today at twelve noon, okay?"

"Today?"

"You forgot yesterday's appointment."

"Did I?"

"Not everybody gets free rent *and* free dental care!" Robert tittered, speaking in exclamation points as he often did when her distant moods spooked his equilibrium.

JJ and her mentor, silent now, did not respond.

"I've got to do a root canal at ten thirty. Noon is the only time I can squeeze you in."

Robert's rules of order resonated in her unquiet mind.

"No need to worry about the procedure. It'll be painless!"

JJ frowned. Unconvinced. First the dental implant to replace her back molar, then the headaches. The same temple-throbbers that foreshadowed her previous disturbance.

"You were up late last night."

"I was reading."

"Anything interesting?" The last of his milky Earl Grey cooled.

"'A Good Man Is Hard to Find.'"

Her brother lifted a concerned eyebrow. "Don't you think something lighter would be—"

"What, Robert?"

A quick gulp of tea caught in his clenched throat. "Better for your spirits?"

"I'm not Mother."

"All I meant was . . . well, books can be hard on the eyes!"

"I hadn't noticed."

"Videotheque on Mission has stacks of great old comedy DVDs. *Some Like It Hot, Bringing Up Baby,* all those Nora Ephron rom-coms from the '90s. You always liked those."

"If you say so." JJ lowered her eyelids.

"Wasn't Ephron one of your commencement speakers at Wellesley?"

Her beloved's words rang through time and space, —*your education is a dress rehearsal for the life that is yours to lead*— but JJ did not speak them aloud.

"Yes, I remember. You wanted me to take a picture of the two of you after her speech. I bet it's still in your college album."

JJ did not answer. Some memories were too precious to share. Instead she peered over Robert's shoulder at the dry arroyo below. Such lovely thin glass walls in his midcentury house. Gazing at the wildflowers thirsting for next season's rain, she heard a duet sung low and sweet. A pair of mourning doves. Mated for life.

"You know . . ." Robert hesitated, then forged ahead. ". . . I'm sure you know, Ephron's husband cheated on her, too. But that didn't take the wind out of her sails."

"No, you're right about that."

"The point is she moved on. Kept her sense of humor. Made herself useful."

JJ did want to be useful again. Especially to family. And the prison chaplain had taught her that all humankind counted as family. Even her son-of-a-bitch ex-husband.

"No crying over spilled milk! I give the lady credit."

JJ's head tightened. Despite the 600 mg dose of Motrin and a heavy swig of Robert's cache of Christmas brandy, her prefrontal cortex was rebelling with a mind of its own.

"Noon sharp." His chair scraped the polished concrete flooring as he stood. "And no detours. Promise?"

She knew he was referring to the restraining order. Her ex-husband's overreaction to a casual visit to his house after she left church last Sunday.

"I'm not a child, Robert."

"What do they say? Living well is the best revenge!"

JJ had lost her marriage, her job, her reputation, her friends, and her freedom for seven years. Yes, the time of living well was overdue.

Rushing toward the door, her brother turned to have the last word. Four actually, punching each one with conviction.

"What would Nora do?"

"What would Nora do?" she repeated.

Her dear brother was wiser than he looked.

"Yes!"

Nora would dry her tears over a truffled lobster feast at Le Bernardin and slay every dragon that threatened to immolate her queendom. But JJ lived 3,000 miles west of the Big Apple, so Le Bernardin was not an option this morning. For the best perhaps. At least she was spared the sight of towering skyscrapers that looked like giant penises frozen in rigor mortis. Restitution perched just around the corner under the blinding, blue California sky. Ready to strike when the time was right, as Nora ordained. All her favorite student had to do was listen for direction. Listen hard.

"It's going to get better, JJ!"

He flashed one final Gromit-like grin of encouragement, whitened teeth even and perfect. JJ half smiled back, twisting her lower lip until the bottom half of her jawline looked like a neck lift gone bad. The least she could do in exchange for free rent and dental care.

JJ plunged her hands into the hot soapy water soaking the dirty dishes in the sink. Nerve endings tap danced underneath her scalp. She rinsed the china plates abandoned by their mother. Caressed the old family utility knife Robert used to cut his morning strawberries. Worn with the years, it needed a good sharpening. Perhaps she'd do that today on the way to her dental appointment: a gift to her brother. The prison chaplain had always advised considering others' needs first. Such a lovely man, with kind eyes that baptized his brethren in pools of hazel.

"I'm innocent," she confessed to the good father. "My husband is the guilty one."

"Jesus taught us to love our enemies."

"Even when they betray us?"

"Have we not all sinned against one another? We must learn to forgive."

Yes, forgiveness was the answer.

Scooping up her brother's used teabag, she bent over to discard it along with the rest of the morning's refuse. An unexpected complication derailed her best intentions.

The butterfly pop-up lid on the Simplehuman wastebasket refused to pop.

Why on earth a malfunctioning $89.99 garbage container should bring JJ to tears was beyond her. She stepped on the foot pedal a second time. Then a third effort, a fourth, even a fifth. All failures. The broken lid refused to budge.

Surprises are good for you.

JJ listened to Nora's voice purring in her ear and examined the soggy Earl Grey pouch. Robert never used his teabag more than once and never bothered to throw it away after he was finished. Another token of disrespect from the men in her life. Somehow it didn't seem fair. Unlike her brother, JJ drank coffee. Strong black coffee with multiple refills.

On the rare occasion they shared cups of tea together, she saved every single one of her used teabags in a crystal dish shaped like a teapot. Only after the very last drop of tea had been leached on the third day could she toss the shriveled bag and begin anew. Last week on her forty-fourth birthday she made a rare exception and brewed a fresh cup from a teabag not yet squeezed to its limit. A survival perk like one of those American Legion ribbons given to battle-scarred veterans, many of them former prisoners of war like herself.

Ding dong!

The doorbell chimed its annoying chime. Louder than usual for some reason. *Ding dong, the witch is dead.* JJ twisted her head to check the happy plastic hands on the starburst clock above the stove.

8:57.

This was no time to be distracted by Mormon missionaries. One lonely ninety-degree morning during the last heat wave, she invited them inside because they were sweating through their white shirts. After they had lapped up an entire pitcher of ice water to lubricate their sales pitch, she realized she'd made a mistake. Their certitude about her family's destined togetherness in the hereafter would be hell in heaven.

JJ fixed once again on the crumpled teabag. The trashcan outside the kitchen door held recyclables only. As long as the lid refused to open, she, too, was stuck.

Ring! Ring! Ring!

Shockwaves slammed across the back of JJ's skull. No doubt her father calling from the racetrack at Santa Anita. Win, place, or show? That's the only reason he called her. To pick his ponies. She brought him luck, he said. But what did he bring her?

The last time she'd gone to the racetrack she was two months pregnant and had taken her father at his word that he was on the wagon. He had escorted her to lunch at the restaurant with a million-dollar view of Thoroughbreds running their paces on command. A family outing, just like the good old days. Before her mother slit her wrists in the bathtub one bitter November night.

Her father had ordered a porterhouse smothered in béarnaise and knocked back a whiskey neat to celebrate. Just one, he promised JJ, to toast his grandchild-to-be. And so began another afternoon's wet slide into oblivion. She had excused herself before dessert. That night she miscarried her first and only child.

Of course, she forgave her drunken philandering father. Her bastard husband, too. Even her devoted secretary who stole the man who had sworn to stay with JJ through sickness and health. Compassion transforms all God's children, the prison chaplain promised. Grow in the narrow places and you, too, can grasp the keys to paradise on earth.

9:23.

The phone was still jangling. Her head split into jagged pieces of igneous rock, tumbling into a crater with no end.

What would Nora do?

The first of the morning's epiphanies struck like a lightning flash over Niagara Falls. A wrong number. Yes, she remembered now. Her father had died in a drunk driving accident the day she was released from prison. Welcome home, daughter. The phone went silent.

JJ could breathe again. The past had passed. The present, chock full of demanding deadlines, snapped its whip. First things first.

Sharpen the family utility knife and repair the broken mother-of-pearl handle on the ice pick that had missed its mark.

Such a lovely wedding gift, that ice pick. A favorite of her husband's. Which was why she had chosen it to deliver her message when he was walking out the door to move in with his mistress. Perhaps she should have emptied a hot pot of linguini with clams on his lap instead. A scalded groin might have appeared to be a silly accident. Not so the almost mortal wound spurting blood two inches above her husband's lying heart. Ex-husband. He and his new wife were very happy together, according to an ex-friend who no longer returned her calls. So many exes.

That sound. What was that sound? *The toilet in the guest bathroom is running again.* For weeks Robert had promised to call the plumber. One miraculous day when she happened to be feeling human, JJ offered to make the call herself, but her brother insisted he would get to it. Better if she put a cap on her nerves and a smile on her face. Of course, she understood. All those patients, such a busy man. Her brother, that is. The plumber, too. Not that she could complain. Babies were dying in Darfur and bombs were exploding in Kabul.

9:59.

JJ marched to the bathroom to do her duty. Falling to her knees, she lifted the lid off the tank and gave the rusted chain a fierce twist. Still, the toilet continued to run with impunity. She tugged and jiggled and pushed. Angry boils of sweat drenched the binding straps encasing her heaving breasts.

The WonderBra is not a step forward for women. Nothing that hurts that much is a step forward for women.

JJ laughed out loud at her partner's wit and fell back against the wall, just missing the trap set by a shiny spider weaving her heart-shaped web from toilet to ceiling. A black widow lurked behind the crapper, with no white knight in sight.

What would Nora do?

Striding into the kitchen, her head lighter now, her thoughts clearer, JJ assembled a cornucopia of ingredients essential for a culinary triumph. Flour. Sugar. Salt. And, *la pièce de résistance*, French bourbon vanilla!

But wait, the butter was missing. So were the eggs. And what happened to the chilled jar of brandied cherries she'd bought at Gelson's to garnish the key lime pie for Saturday's dinner party? All missing. Where had they gone? JJ scanned the barren refrigerator shelves. Moved the pickles. Slid the aging olives to the back corner. Hauled out the Tupperware of chunky salsa festering in mold. Yes, the butter was definitely missing.

10:22.

No time to go to the market. Perhaps pork chops *à la moutarde* instead? She swung open the freezer door, eyeballing a lone package of center-cut beauties. Once a pig, squealing with all its fleshy might, now six slabs of dead meat carved without pity. Dead, dead, dead. She became overwhelmed by the existential futility of life. Hope rang as hollow as a bad joke with no punch line.

Worst of all her ex-husband showed no remorse for his sins. He lived like a king with his new queen in the home that should have been hers.

So what are you going to do?

JJ kicked the freezer door shut and attacked the broken wastebasket, trying once again to correct its failure. But no. No go. Her throat tightened, her eyes glistened, her gut churned.

So what are you going to do? Nora demanded again.

JJ emptied the Simplehuman of its spoiled contents and dropped the family utility knife inside for future use.

11:13.

She maneuvered her brother's precertified Prius with the WAR IS NOT THE ANSWER bumper sticker into a handicapped parking place on Marengo Avenue. After a quick check in the rearview mirror, she reapplied her seashell-pink lipstick, yanked the recalcitrant wastebasket from the back seat and embarked on a mission of restitution.

The Container Store of Old Pasadena, just a stone's throw from the police station, welcomed her with open arms. Cheerful signs proclaiming the SUPER THANKSGIVING SALE were plastered across the windows. Fierce and feisty, JJ darted between the customers trotting out of the store with their overstuffed bags. She had come to get hers and she meant business. This time she would not, could not, fail. Other wronged women were depending on her.

JJ marched in to Customer Service and made her case. The twenty-something clerk, a pretty gatekeeper with luminous dark hair worn in the exact style as JJ's former secretary, denied her request.

"This model was phased out, ma'am."

"That's hard to believe." JJ's eyes narrowed. The bitch was playing her.

"Lack of customer interest."

JJ demanded to see the manager.

Ordered, yes, *ordered* to wait, without so much as a please or thank you, JJ cast an iron glare toward the man in charge. When the manager did not return her mano a mano greeting, she was struck by his strong physical resemblance to her ex-husband.

Planting herself in plain sight against the counter, JJ rocked the wastebasket like a newborn, the clanging utility knife sliding to and fro inside. Then she leaned closer to study the clerk's smooth, unscarred brow.

"Can you move aside?" the unnerved clerk asked. "We have other customers to serve."

"How much longer do you expect me to wait?"

"Maybe you'd like to do some shopping until he's free?"

"Tell him JJ Underwood has his number. If he's not here in five minutes, I'm calling the Consumer Financial Protection Bureau to file a complaint."

The clerk reacted, making eye contact with her boss.

JJ powered down the aisles looking for comfort. There were poor substitutes, lined up like relatives offering tuna casseroles at a funeral, and she ripped through them all. Three-bin laundry sorters. Heavy-duty triple-storage pails. Dual-purpose dish racks. Soft-tip bottle brushes. Collapsible strainers. Closet organizers with matching shoeboxes. All featured in the Thanksgiving Sale along with the Snapware collection. But Snapware was not dishwasher safe. She had learned this, like so much in her life, the hard way.

"Ma'am, may I help you?"

A young box boy yammered in her ear, but JJ refused to pay him any mind. Wasn't it obvious she didn't need any help? Before perhaps, when she had entered the store. Or seven years ago when the shit hit the fan. That would have been the time to offer a scrap of compassion. But nobody was listening then, were they? No. Nobody was listening despite her Herculean effort to expose the truth and make wrong right. So she took matters into her own hands with the guidance of dear, dear Nora.

"Ma'am, please?"

JJ flipped the kid off, then hustled back to the Customer Service counter and thumped the manager on his cold shoulder. Irritated and impatient, the man finally faced her. JJ noted he did not apologize for his inexcusable behavior. When she demanded restitution for his store's shoddy merchandise, he waved her off, suggesting that she just buy a new one.

"Are you telling me you're refusing to give me the replacement I deserve?"

JJ's gaze riveted on the display just over the manager's right shoulder. Stainless steel ice buckets with matching tongs. Ice picks, too.

"Excuse me." His dismissal was withering. "I have other guests waiting."

"'Guests'?"

That ridiculous corporate euphemism would not work, no sir. Her face hardening into a brittle bruise, JJ edified the manager about the just and proper thing to do. In exchange for the money spent on this very wastebasket only six months ago (she remembered the exact date because it was the first Tuesday afternoon she'd met with her probation officer), The Container Store needed to replace the damaged item.

"Give me a break. It's not the store's fault that *you* broke the wastebasket."

She did *not* break it. Ask her brother, a medical professional incapable of lying, unlike her father and husband. She simply wanted her Simplehuman wastebasket with the pop up top to work the way it was designed.

"*Butterfly* pop-up top," the condescending manager corrected her. "Model X 118. The company discontinued that line in April, so we couldn't replace this item even if it was our responsibility, which it isn't. Next guest!"

A snaking line of customers behind JJ muttered and moaned.

"Move it, lady! What the hell's wrong with you?"

JJ spun around. Wrong? With her? *He* was the asshole! Her thoughts raced. When the going gets tough, the tough get going, no use crying over spilled milk, where there is a will, there is a way.

I hope that you choose not to be a lady. I hope that you will find some way to break the rules and make a little trouble out there.

Her partner's words were coming faster now. Stronger and louder.

JJ pulled out the unsharpened utility knife and slammed the broken wastebasket against a HOLIDAY HELPMATES FOR THE HOSTESS display. Her weapon of defense held high, she raced toward the terrified manager. Yelling for help, he ran in the opposite direction, knocking down a stack of Snapware as he skidded 'round the corner.

"Buyer beware!" she screamed. "Buyer be aware!"

Fish-eyed customers dashed out of her way. JJ worried for an instant that her seashell-pink lipstick, the same perfect shade worn on her wedding day, might be smeared. No matter. She vaulted down the next aisle with a new surge of energy. This was no place for a moment of vanity. Insanity, perhaps, but not vanity. She snickered at her clever wordplay. Ignored, insulted, and inconvenienced, she could still access a sturdy sense of humor. Wouldn't Nora be amused?

And then JJ froze at the vision in her path.

A Simplehuman display mounted on a giant red triangle next to the service elevator!

Tears of gratitude stung JJ's eyes. She did not hear the police sirens wailing in the distance. Her handy utility knife at the ready, she rushed over to slash open one cardboard box after another, looking for just the right Simplehuman to take home. Industrial strength staples shredded her cuticles but for the first time she could remember, she felt no pain. JJ moved forward with passion and purpose, leaving no box unopened.

"God, please, no!"

The hyperventilating manager, now exposed from his hiding place behind the giant red triangle, collapsed to his knees.

In a rage of righteousness JJ pointed to the display. "You lied to me."

"No."

"Yes, you did."

"I'm sorry, I'm sorry, I'm so sorry."

"Are you?"

"Yes, yes, I swear! Please don't kill me."

Why would she? The man apologized.

Above all, be the heroine in your own life, not the victim.

Her right hand still holding the knife, JJ extended her left to the repentant manager. He recoiled, still terrified. She wiggled her fingers, motioning him toward her.

"I won't hurt you."

"You won't?"

JJ shook her head, her fingers spread wide. Beckoning him closer.

The manager stumbled up, his knees shaking.

Just as he stood, a nervous security guard advanced behind them. His revolver was drawn and aimed at the weapon-wielding crazy woman.

The guard did not see the cardboard debris in his path. He tripped. His gun discharged. The bullet tore into the manager's belly.

The wounded man fell forward onto JJ. Red pumped through his shirt, his blood saturating them both.

JJ dropped her knife and lowered his body to the floor. She cradled his head in her waiting lap.

"It's not too late, is it?"

Nora's rom-coms always ended with a kiss. Not a slap. Not a slash. Not a vengeful accusation.

"Sweetheart?"

JJ pressed her mouth to his, shooting her tongue between his fleshy lips. Into a warm wet vise of memory . . .

Witnesses to the shooting at The Container Store gave conflicting reports to police officers. Several customers said a disturbed woman tried to knife the manager after a price dispute. Others credit her as the Good Samaritan who gave the critically injured man mouth-to-mouth resuscitation and saved his life. . . .

—*Pasadena Independent,* November 28, 2017

Hector's Bees

AMANDA WITT

A moment of forgetfulness saved Estelle's life. That, and a penchant for margaritas.

She lived in a small cabin built by her husband on a gated gravel road that curved up the eastern side of the Sangre de Cristo Mountains. Hector was six months dead, but alive he had been a gifted craftsman, in great demand among locals and summer tourists alike. The locals hired him for skilled carpentry, for bookshelves and cedar chests, baby cradles and rocking chairs. The tourists hired him to lay bridges across streams, assemble benches in picturesque spots, and build enormous structures they called, without irony, "cabins." They then labeled Hector's creations with kitschy wooden signs: NINA'S NOOK, MIKE'S MEDITATION, KAREN'S KABIN, BAILEY'S BLESSING.

Thinking of it, Estelle rolled her eyes.

No one saw her. She lived alone, the nearest house a quarter of a mile away, well hidden by pines and the contour of the land. And besides, she was in the bath.

It was an inviolable part of her new-widow routine. Each day she rose before dawn and briskly set about tending their five acres, cleaning their cabin—theirs truly was a cabin—and replenishing her stock of Authentic Handmade Mexican Jewelry. She worked hard, because Hector would have frowned to see her bow before the black depression that stalked her day by day. She worked hard because sweat staved off despair.

But at five o'clock, Estelle mourned. She mixed a pitcher of margaritas, stripped off her clothes, and slid into a warm unscented bath, where she remained throughout the long mountain dusk, until night fell and she could prepare a small supper, conclude the day's chores, and tumble into night's oblivion. It was, she thought, as good a routine as any for salving a broken heart.

Especially the margaritas.

Above her head, the curtains on the window fluttered in a breeze replete with the distinctive scent of the New Mexico mountains—pine, dust, sunbaked ancient rock. From the amplified iPhone charging dock on the windowsill, Rimsky-Korsakov's "Flight of the Bumblebee" blasted on repeat, a grim whimsy, the soaring and dipping violins evoking the honeybee's clumsy cousin. And Estelle after five o'clock, bumbling through her evenings half drunk.

The bath, the breeze, the margaritas, the music. And beneath the music, unheard but always humming in her bones, ran the hypnotic buzz of Hector's bees.

Hector. His teeth flashing white when he laughed, his hands firm and sure with hammer and chisel, saw and lathe. His body, broken and bleeding in the creek at the bottom of a rocky 30-foot drop.

Estelle flinched. The water in the tub eddied around her body, much as the water in the creek had eddied around his.

Thus ran her thoughts. Once, she might have lain in the bath studying her smooth legs, the slight rise of her belly, the swell of her breasts, trying to see herself through Hector's eyes. Now she was forty-five years old, too young to be a widow, perhaps too old to attract another man or to want him if she did. She wanted only Hector, and he was gone. Murdered.

The sheriff and the neighbors disagreed. They avoided her eyes when they ran into her at the postal boxes down at the base of the

mountain; they mumbled greetings, their faces averted in embarrassment. They blamed Hector. They blamed Blue Canyon Road.

It was a bad road, one lane that curved, rose, fell. Trees bent over it,
underbrush crawled into it, giant boulders marked its every zig and
zag. People drove too quickly, took blind turns fast because they took
them every day. But there were safety precautions. Locals and summer
people alike knew to keep their windows rolled down, their radios off;
to tap their horns before descending Red Flag Hill; and, if walking, to
step off the road at the faintest distant growl of an engine.

As Hector must have done; as Hector always did.

Yet he died. And the driver did not stop.

Outside the window, the mood of the bees shifted. Even through
the haze of warm water, the depths of her grief, the music, Estelle felt
their gentle drone sharpen.

Sliding deeper into the water, she closed her eyes.

Bees didn't like strong odors, so she bathed without scent. They
didn't like dark colors, so her wardrobe leaned to light. They loved
flowers, so for them Hector and Estelle had planted lavender, raspberries, fireweed. And then there were the rain barrels—bees preferred
slightly stagnant water—and the 8-foot-tall fence, painstakingly built
with metal posts set in concrete, 12 inches apart, lined with half-inch
19-gauge chicken wire. The fence discouraged bears, raccoons, skunks,
anything that might threaten the hives, and Estelle had planted vines
on it, green tendrils dripping with pale blossoms that opened at dusk.

The bees were not ungrateful. They provided ample supplies of
golden honey, which Hector and Estelle sold in the square in Santa Fe,
along with the jewelry. The bees were their children, Hector's passion.
When Hector died, she had told the bees the bad news and hung their
hives with black.

Above her head, a single bee drifted in through the window, drifted
back out again.

Hector had loved to articulate the moods of the bees. *They're finding
the weather too warm*, he'd say when they were lined up at the entrances to
their hives, fanning madly with their tiny wings. *They're having a street*

party meant they were bearding, hanging off the front of the hives in squirming, buzzing curtains. *They're calling the children home*—that was Estelle's favorite—when the bees fanned hard, their little bottoms sticking up in the air to expose their Nasonov glands, releasing pheromones in a lemony scent that acted like a trail of breadcrumbs for their wandering progeny.

Tonight, the bees were angry.

So was she.

The musical bumblebee bumbled in its flight, violins swooping and bobbing from the phone on the windowsill. Eyes still closed, Estelle reached for her margarita, but her hand found only cold porcelain.

She opened her eyes.

She had erred. Her towel lay within easy reach, draped discreetly over her security blanket—Hector's .357 Magnum—but the frosted glass and full pitcher sat on the vanity cabinet, on the other side of the sink.

Estelle got to her feet, water streaming down her legs. She didn't lean or stretch. Better two extra steps and some water on the floor than a slip and a fall. She was alone in the world. If she knocked herself out, she might lie there all night. On the cold tiles, as the temperature dropped, there at 8,000 feet above sea level. With the window open and the front door unlocked. Unconscious, wet, exposed, she could die before morning. And she wasn't ready yet to die. Not with Hector's killer still unidentified, still free.

So she stepped out of the tub onto the small worn mat. She was reaching for the margarita, already tasting it on her tongue, salt and lime, already feeling the loosening warmth of tequila trickling through her veins, when a loud *pop* made her jump and turn.

From the window, a hand withdrew. In the water, the music died in a spray of blue sparks, an angry hissing sizzle. Then, with an echoing bang, the transformer halfway up the mountain blew.

The shock held her motionless for one heartbeat, two. Someone had knocked her phone setup into the tub. Who, she didn't know. She had caught but a glimpse, the curtains blocking her view. And she couldn't look out the window—that would require she step into water still swimming with the death spasms of her ruined phone.

So she ran. Opening the bathroom door, she raced for the front of the house, for the exterior door, trailing streams of water as she went, tracking wet footprints across the wooden planks. The bathroom window was inside the fenced-in hive area; the intruder would exit through the apiary gate. She had to get there first.

Snatching her shotgun off its hooks, she shoved open the front door.

The evening air hit her wet body, raising goosebumps. Racking the shotgun, Estelle stepped out onto the raised wooden porch and turned left, toward the apiary gate. It moved gently, swinging shut.

Estelle strode down the three steps, shotgun raised and ready. Her heart pounded in her ears. Hector's killer had come for her; that was proof. He had been stolen, not lost through random accident or indifferent hap. His death was deliberate, done with design.

Now she would know who. Now she would get her revenge.

The ground, rough with pinecones and rocks, bruised her bare feet. She strode forward nonetheless, head high, surveying the gloaming, listening. Waiting for the woods to tell her their secrets. The woods always knew when someone passed—ferns waved at passersby, birds startled into flight, frogs fell reverentially silent. Small creatures scurried into the undergrowth, fled up the pale trunks of aspens, set evergreen branches swaying.

Nothing.

Estelle scanned again, noted still no sign of human passage. A squirrel ran along a high branch; she drew a bead on it, briefly and pointlessly, thinking there was no use in going further—too many trees, too many directions the intruder could have gone. Too many boulders to hide behind, too many rises and falls.

Or the intruder might still be in her apiary. Perhaps the swinging gate had been a misdirection.

Carefully, aware of her body gleaming pale and noticeable in the deepening twilight, Estelle backtracked and approached the gate. It fastened with a simple drop bar, and she held the gun steady with her left hand, letting go with her right just long enough to open the latch.

Using her hip, she nudged the gate open. It gave a faint creak, a quiet noise but one that would have warned her as she lay in her bath, had the sound not been masked by "Flight of the Bumblebee."

Who knew she played that music every evening, who knew she bathed with the iPhone on the sill of the open window so the bees could hear the music, too? Anyone regularly passing by, that was who. Anyone on foot, anyone driving—as people ought—with their windows down to catch the mountain breeze, to listen for other traffic. To stay alert for pedestrians.

Through the vine-draped fence she could hear the angry buzz of Hector's bees. They were Italian bees originally, unaggressive and tractable, but with each generation their genetics shifted as queens mated with local rabble. "Africanized" was not a yes/no proposition, but a spectrum, and Hector's bees had grown, over the years, a little hot. This wasn't all bad; it increased their resistance to the mites decimating other bee populations. But hot bees liked their privacy and their routines. They didn't like strangers, especially at night.

Estelle was no stranger, but it wasn't wise to assume such bees would always observe social courtesies. If the intruder still lurked in the apiary and Estelle caught and confronted him, the bees might well attack. And she was naked.

She backed up, glanced around.

There. The clothesline.

She set the shotgun on the ground within quick reach. The clothesline was easy to undo because Hector had tied it in a slipknot, or maybe it was a running knot, she didn't know. As she pulled it free another piece of her heart crumbled, at this undoing of the work of Hector's hands. But there was no help for it; she had to catch his killer.

Winding the rope through the bars of the gate, she wished she had let him teach her better knots. Hers wouldn't trap the intruder, if he still lurked inside, but at least it would slow his escape if he went by the gate rather than over the high fence.

Snatching up the shotgun, she hurried back up the steps and into the cabin, going straight to the landline phone, dialing a number. While it rang, she stretched the cord as far as it would go, toward the living room window. She couldn't quite see the apiary gate, but she could almost see it. If anyone passed through, she'd at least catch a glimpse.

In her ear, a voice grunted an unintelligible greeting.

"Abe," she said.

"Yeah." He didn't ask who it was; they'd known each other twenty years, ever since a newly wedded Hector and Estelle had moved to Blue Canyon Road.

"Look out your kitchen window," she said. "The gate across the road. Is it closed?"

There was a pause. "Yeah."

"Can you tell if it's locked?" If the intruder had come from outside that gate, Estelle doubted he would bother shutting it, much less take time to thread the padlock back through the chain and lock it. Why slow his escape? If the gate were shut and locked, Estelle bet it was because the intruder hadn't come through it. Hadn't needed to, because he lived in Blue Canyon. They were ten miles from the main road, twenty-four miles from town. No one entered or left Blue Canyon on foot, except perhaps to hike across to the Tecolote, and that canyon was also gated.

"Yeah," Abe said.

"Yeah, you can tell, or yeah, the gate's locked?"

"Both."

Okay. That was good. "Abe?"

"Yeah."

"Call the sheriff. Tell him someone just tried to kill me. And keep an eye on that gate."

Stentorian breathing, the rasp of it sudden and frightened. She could picture the old man clutching his chest, faded eyes fixed on some unseen horizon.

"Take your pill," she said hurriedly. "I have to go. Will you call?"

He sucked in a gust of air. "Course," he said. "Be careful, girlie."

Even if the sheriff jumped straight into his cruiser, he wouldn't reach her for another thirty minutes, minimum. And he might not jump straight into his cruiser. He might chalk the whole thing up as a foiled burglary, reported by a woman he already had pegged as borderline paranoid. He had Friday-night emergencies, a limited staff. Estelle would be lucky to see the sheriff before midnight.

For a heartbeat she stood still, indecisive. She wanted to get dressed and check the apiary—but no. Phone calls first. Because if the intruder had escaped before she'd tied the apiary gate closed, she had only a tiny window of time to narrow down who he might be.

The mountains had no cell reception, none for five miles of winding gravel road, none for another fifteen miles of paved—across the wide meadows, through the cut in the rocks, past the HITCHHIKERS MAY BE ESCAPING CONVICTS road sign, all the way to the New Mexico Correctional Facility. Only there did reception kick in.

So if someone answered his landline, then he was home, not creeping through the woods having recently attempted cold-blooded murder.

His second cold-blooded murder.

The two closest cabins, Estelle figured, were a wash. Her attacker would have had time to get home already, if he lived in one of them.

She dialed the next farthest cabin.

"Hello?"

Linda. Before Estelle could ask for her husband, to rule Tim out as well, she heard his familiar voice reprimanding their unruly Labrador in the background.

Without a word, she hung up.

Already it had grown too dark to see the numbers on the phone. She took a few precious seconds to light the emergency candles that always stood on the end table, her hands trembling, the flame wavering and smoking before the wicks caught. How many calls could she make before the relevant window of time closed? The farthest house from her own was Harry Garcia's, way back almost to the Santa Fe National Forest. Estelle could walk it in twenty minutes, run it in less. Between Harry's house and her own lay, what, ten or twelve other houses?

She needed a pencil. She should document as much as she could, for the next—she chose a random number—six minutes. Then she would check the apiary.

A noise made her pause.

A squeak, a creak. Had she imagined it?

No. It came again.

It could be a raccoon, a possum, any number of woodland creatures. Or simply the wind. Or it could be a killer letting himself out the apiary gate, climbing the three creaky wooden steps to her porch.

She picked up the shotgun.

Around her, candlelight flickered warm and mellow, hateful. It called up memories of Hector's face in the dancing light, Hector's hands as they trimmed the kerosene lamp, Hector building a fire in the wood-burning stove. It reminded her she was alone.

It lit her clearly, as on a stage, for the dark form that might be standing outside her window.

And she was naked.

She hadn't cared before, in that initial burst of adrenaline. Racing outside with her gun in pursuit of Hector's killer. Now it felt different. Now she was a woman boxed in, alone and lit by flickering candlelight, the windows blinking light back at her so she couldn't see who stood upon her porch, watching her like a movie, like a fish in a bowl.

Dashing into her bedroom, she jerked on jeans, boots, a flannel shirt, the closest things to hand. As she fumbled a button closed, a loud knock made her heart lurch. A knock at the front door—*rat-a-tat-tat*—insistent, aggressive.

For an instant she considering hunkering down, hiding. Hoping he would go away. But there was no point; her cabin wasn't a fortress. Better to deal with this head on, with dignity, on her own terms.

Though not the terms she originally had set.

Cautiously Estelle edged toward the living room, raising the gun. The cuff of her flannel shirt hung loose, impeding her trigger finger. She shook it back, eased forward another few feet.

Even the best laid plans go astray, and Estelle hadn't so much planned as hoped, announcing her daily spell of vulnerability with bumblebee music, buying copious amounts of tequila from the gossipiest storekeeper, in hope—not expectation, merely hope—that Hector's killer would show himself. He would come to drown her, to make it look as if she'd fallen and hit her head, perhaps slipped beneath the surface in a drunken haze. Another accident. Another needless death. Hector and Estelle, so careless. But when he burst into the bathroom believing he was the predator, she the weakened prey, Estelle would rise up out of the water and raise the .357 from beneath the crumpled bath towel and blow him to kingdom come, where he would never meet Hector—residing with the angels—but would burn in hell for all eternity, contemplating his depravity.

That had been her plan. Such as it was.

Attempted electrocution by iPhone, attack by way of a window guarded by Hector's bees while the front door waited invitingly unlocked—the possibility had never crossed her mind.

She felt very stupid about that.

The pounding on the door came again. *Rat-a-tat-tat.*

At least he had come, whoever he was. That was the important thing. She was so tired of wondering and waiting.

"Estelle!"

A man's voice; she thought she recognized it.

"Estelle, I know you're in there. Open up."

Tears filled her eyes.

No. Not Harry.

A loner with some sort of military background—or maybe just a liking for army surplus stores—Harry Garcia earned a meager living doing unskilled work such as winterizing cabins and opening them up in the spring, meanwhile learning carpentry from Hector. Basically, he was Hector's apprentice, and—she had thought—his friend.

But essentially he was Hector's business rival, it occurred to her now. He did menial work, grunt-work, while aspiring to Hector's better jobs. Money was at the root of most murders, wasn't that what statistics said?

"Estelle," Harry called again. "Open up. I need to know you're okay."

Sure he did.

Harry had motive to kill Hector, but what did he have against her? Estelle was no carpenter. She wielded a hammer only to hang pictures.

It didn't matter; she didn't have to understand his motives. He had killed Hector, and in return she'd kill him. Even if she couldn't prove what he had done, no one would blame her—a woman alone, in the dark, moments after placing a frantic call for the sheriff.

Blinking away angry tears, she strode across her living room and flung open her front door.

On the porch, Harry Garcia took one look at her gun and raised his hands shoulder high.

He wasn't alone. The woman beside him gave a small shriek, her eyes going wide.

Ashley Swanson looked, as usual, like an Eddie Bauer model. She was dressed in brand-new hiking pants with zippers in implausible places, and a navy jacket done up to her chin. A lavender Fitbit peeked out from one cuff. A few strands of salon-streaked hair had escaped her artfully messy bun and curled coyly, damp with perspiration, around her pretty face. She smelled of something fruity and expensive.

Beside her Harry looked particularly uncouth. The dark stubble on his cheeks went far beyond the point of fashion; his army surplus fatigues featured a rip mended with duct tape; his gray T-shirt and unbuttoned flannel shirt had worn thin to the point of disintegration; and his work boots looked like something pulled off a casualty of the Bataan death march. As always, he smelled like sweaty male. Estelle had heard women speculate that Harry might clean up well, but this was pure supposition. No such Harry had ever been spotted.

Ashley and Harry were about the same age—mid-thirties—but beyond that, a more unlikely pair Estelle could not imagine. And it wasn't just their clashing fashion choices. Harry, a year-round resident, lived mostly off the grid and mostly off the land. Ashley and her husband were summer people, do-gooders who wanted to improve local schools, pave roads, change zoning ordinances, regulate this, deregulate that, and talk the local grocer into carrying certified-organic free-range non-GMO everything.

Maybe Ashley was slumming?

Maybe Harry was slumming.

The breeze from the apiary carried the scent of raspberries; the blossoms on the fence nodded their heads. The gate stood ajar, clothesline dangling loose.

Harry or Ashley. Harry *and* Ashley.

Estelle's blood pulsed painfully in her ears.

"Do you have a license for that thing?" Ashley said, pointing at the shotgun.

"Permit," Harry said. "And she doesn't need one." His hands were still raised, but he didn't look unduly alarmed to be held at gunpoint by a damp and wild-eyed woman. He seemed to be contemplating nothing more concerning than Ashley's ignorance of New Mexico gun laws.

"Are you two together?" Estelle said.

"What? No!" Ashley recoiled. "I'm a happily married woman."

Estelle looked at Harry. His expression said *High-maintenance city girl? Not likely.*

One or the other. A killer and—unfortunately—a bystander.

Estelle shifted, covering them both with the shotgun. "Which of you just tried to electrocute me in the bath?"

Ashley gasped; Harry's eyes went suddenly alert.

"You—" Estelle jabbed the gun at Ashley. "Why are you here?"

Ashley blinked. "Um, neighborly kindness? I was out for a walk and heard the power go. I thought you might want company, given your situation."

"My situation." Estelle kept her tone even.

Ashley's blue eyes clouded with sympathy. "Recently bereaved," she said in a stage whisper, as if the words were too awful to say aloud. Then, in a normal tone: "The power went out. I thought it might make you nervous."

Estelle contemplated the younger woman. "No," she said. "Nervous is not what it makes me."

She switched her gaze to Harry in time to see his lips twitch with a suppressed smile.

"Talk," she said, eyeing him coldly.

His gaze flicked away. "I was up behind your cabin, on the ridge"—he gestured with his chin—"tracking a nuisance bear. The one that's been tearing up trash bins at the youth camp."

He wasn't making eye contact, but his story was credible. There had in fact been a bear poking around, and though camp sessions had ended for the year, they brought in weekend groups through October. It was a dangerous combination, hordes of city people and a bear that no longer feared humans.

"Where's your rifle?"

"At home." Hands still raised, he slowly turned around, showing her his back. Through his shirt she could see the bulge of a handgun.

"Lift the shirt."

He did. "Smith & Wesson 500," he said.

That would take down a bear, all right.

"You people." Ashley snugged her zipper more tightly beneath her chin. "Guns don't solve anything."

Except rogue bears. And attempted murders. And rattlesnakes, rabid raccoons, large rats with boundary issues . . .

Harry turned back around, slowly, hands still up. His nose was twitching. "Estelle," he said. "I might sneeze. Don't get startled and shoot me."

He sounded just like he always did. He looked just like he always did. Unkempt, but not entirely unattractive. And Hector had liked him; she knew he had.

"Grief makes people crazy," Ashley said, her tone so earnest it set Estelle's teeth on edge. "But you can't go around making wild accusations. Someone might sue. And you know it was a squirrel on the line—that's what it always is. Nobody tried to electrocute you."

The pity in her face made Estelle want to pull the trigger.

Instead she swung the gun toward Harry. He leaned back, as if that would make a difference. Not completely nonchalant, not anymore. Probably wondering what sort of load the shotgun carried, slug or shot, though either would do the job at this range.

"If you were tracking bear on the ridge," she said, "what brought you here?"

He answered in a carefully steady voice, as if she were a wild animal. "It was getting dark, and I'd lost his trail," he said. "So I was heading for the road. Easier walking back that way than going cross-country."

"Harry came around the far side of your house just as I got here," Ashley said helpfully. "I came up the steps on this side, and he came up the steps on that side."

Harry cleared his throat.

Ashley frowned at him. "Maybe you got to the porch a step or two ahead of me, but that's all."

"Actually"—Harry drew out the word—"I was here before. Well before."

There was a glint in his eye.

"Oh, for Pete's sake." Estelle went prickly with annoyance.

"What?" Ashley looked from one to the other.

Estelle stared Harry straight in the face, simply to prove she still could. "He's a Peeping Tom."

Harry might have blushed—hard to tell through all that stubble. "No peeping involved," he said. "Staring openly, yeah. Guilty as charged."

Estelle didn't blush; calculations were running through her mind. "What exactly did you see?"

Harry raised his eyebrows, incredulous.

Estelle raised hers. Waiting.

Harry's gaze drifted over the shotgun—still leveled at his center mass—to Estelle's wet hair, and then to the power line stretching away from the cabin roofline.

"You came blasting out your door," he said. "Buck naked. Dripping wet. You went to the edge of the woods, gun up, and sighted on something. I backed off, went up the hill behind your cabin. Gave you time to get back inside." His eyes met hers. "I didn't want to embarrass you."

The apiary fence was 8 feet tall, impenetrable with vines. No one inside could have seen her draw a bead on that squirrel.

Harry glanced at the apiary gate, swinging gently ajar. "Ashley could have come from there. I didn't see her until she started up the porch. I was keeping my eyes on the ground, in case you were still out here. To give you a chance to see me first and get inside."

"I would never go in that place." Ashley gave an exaggerated shiver. "She keeps *bees* in there." Her profile, washed in the candlelight pouring from the open door, showed flaws that were unnoticeable straight on—a peevish set to her mouth, a few bumps marring her otherwise lovely complexion.

Estelle took more pleasure in that than she should have; she'd have to work on keeping her cattiness under control. Nobody liked bitter middle-aged women.

"Bees are dangerous," Ashley said. "I can't believe the government lets just anybody keep them any old place."

In this case, though, Estelle would give herself a pass. Her finger, curled against the trigger, tightened slightly.

Harry looked back and forth between the two women. "Honey's good for you," he said. "It helps coughs, insomnia, acid reflux, sinus problems, acne, dandruff, eczema, yeast infections, herpes."

Ashley grimaced.

"It boosts energy, memory, and sexual function. It can be used to treat hangovers, gum disease, high cholesterol. It has antioxidants."

It was as if he'd become an idiot savant.

"It's a good antiseptic and has antibacterial properties. It can be used to build up immunity to local allergens."

"Bees *are* the local allergens," Ashley said. "My husband's allergic. One bee sting and he could die."

"Did you tell Hector that?" Harry's voice was deceptively casual.

"Of course I did." Ashley looked at Estelle, spoke precisely. Carefully. No more, and no less. "I told him."

A lump rose in Estelle's throat.

Harry lowered his hands.

The shotgun, grown heavy and pointless, sagged in Estelle's arms. Around her the wind gusted, shifting directions, rattling the leaves of the aspens and carrying away the scent of raspberries Hector would never taste. *Oh, Hector,* she thought. *All I wanted was to know who took you away from me. Now I know, but I can't prove it.*

"Hector used to talk about honey all the time," Harry said. It was a eulogy, a conclusion. An acknowledgment that he had tried and failed. "He sure loved those bees."

The moon had begun its slow rise over the treetops, casting black streaking shadows, its blue-washed glow a cool contrast to the yellow flickering candlelight. A single bee hummed across Estelle's line of sight, fighting its way out of the apiary, against the wind.

Ashley eyed it warily. "Well," she said. "Guess I'll head on home."

"No." Estelle raised the shotgun to her shoulder.

"Estelle," Harry said.

She ignored him.

"You got stung," she said to Ashley. "That's why you're zipped up. You're hiding bee stings, but you can't hide the ones on your face."

The other woman shrugged. "I told you, bees are dangerous." She smiled. "And there's no law against zipping. Unzipping, though. Public exposure. There are rules against that."

"Not here," Harry said.

Two more bees joined the first. They circled around the porch, dancing their wavering airborne dance.

Estelle sighted down the barrel, drew a bead on Ashley's forehead. "You ran Hector over, and you tried to electrocute me."

Ashley stopped smiling. "She's threatening me with a firearm, Harry. You're my witness. As soon as I get home I'm calling the sheriff."

Harry said nothing. Pointedly, he turned away.

Ashley gaped at his retreating back. "You can't just let her shoot me!" Then, to Estelle, "You can't shoot me. You'll get sent to prison. Is that what Hector would want?"

Three more bees arrived.

For the first time in six months, Estelle felt a smile on her lips.

"Don't say my husband's name," she said, imagining the slug's trajectory, the efficiency with which it would wipe out every thought and memory—the sound of Hector's body tossed and broken, the sight of his soul leaving his flesh.

"You should have used the front door," she said. "Bees don't like intruders in their home."

"Neither do I!" Ashley jerked her head as a bee tried to land on her face. "They're always over at our place, zooming around, looking for someone to sting."

"They pollinate," Estelle said. "It's a public service. We'd have precious few crops if they didn't. And they don't sting if left alone."

Ashley's hands finally were up, her expression pleading. "They could kill my husband."

"So you decided to kill the beekeepers."

"I didn't say that. You're putting words in my mouth."

"Not me," Estelle said, and her heart was humming and soaring. "The bees."

"Bees can't talk."

Harry raised his arm, pointed.

Over the vine-draped apiary fence a stream of bees rose, forming a black boiling cloud that sparkled silver and gold in the light of the cresting moon. Hundreds of bees. Thousands of bees. A churning, buzzing, vengeful mass.

Ashley blanched. She lunged for the candlelit doorway, but Estelle slammed the door and blocked it with her body as the cloud began to descend, angry, implacable, buzzing with a thousand tiny wings.

Moving slowly, carefully, Harry pressed his back against the cabin wall.

The cloud poured onto the porch, shifting and roiling, and found its target.

Ashley shrieked. She batted at the bees, slapping them on her arms, her face, dancing and dodging. They landed on her neck, her ears, tangled in her hair.

"They know," Estelle said, raising her voice to be heard. "They remember."

Bees landed on Ashley's arms and back, stinging through the fabric of her jacket, crawling under the neckline, testing the density of her boots, climbing up her shoelaces into the legs of her pants. "Help me!" she cried, flailing, frantic. "Make them stop!"

Briefly, Estelle closed her eyes. She knew what Hector would say.

"Get to the creek," she said. "Get under the water."

Hector had never been a vengeful man.

Ashley stumbled down the steps, making—it had to be said—a beeline for the creek. So did the bees.

Estelle watched her husband's killer stagger down the slope and plunge into the icy water. Ashley wasn't broken and bleeding, as Hector had been when Estelle found him in that creek; she wasn't dead.

But she probably wished she were.

Still the bees didn't disperse. They hovered over the water in a shifting, living cloud, their fury audible, electrifying. More bees joined them there, streaming from Estelle's apiary, from the woods, from wild hives in the pine trees, from the paths Hector had walked and the mountains he had loved.

"They're waiting for her to surface," Harry said. He sounded almost reverent.

Estelle smiled. Africanized bees would wait for hours, would chase an enemy miles. These were only hybrids, but they'd keep Ashley pinned until the sheriff arrived. Already Estelle could hear the crunch of tires, the squeal of brakes at the hairpin curve that topped Red Flag Hill.

"What exactly just happened?" Harry asked. "And don't say *the bees remember.*"

"But they do, in a way." Estelle glanced at the apiary, at the blossoms pale with moonlight. "When bees sting, they release an alarm pheromone from their Koschevnikov glands. It clings to the site of the sting. It's very persistent."

Harry's gaze was drifting downward.

"I smelled it on her as soon as I opened the door." Estelle fastened another button on her hastily donned shirt. "It smells like bananas. I was being dense and didn't realize what it was, but the bees knew. When the wind shifted, they smelled their call to arms. Harry, stop staring. I'm far too old for you."

He grinned. "There's a word for older women who—"

"Yeah. *Disgusting.*"

He laughed. "You know," he said, "next summer you could head over to Santa Fe, join the Nearly Nude Bike Ride. Unless that's too tame for you."

Estelle smiled, kept buttoning. In the distance, through the trees, red and blue lights flickered.

"Estelle," Harry said softly, and his voice had grown serious. "I'm sorry about Hector. I really am."

"I know," she said. "So am I."

And she stood on her porch, a little less alone, and gazed fondly at the teeming cloud clustered over the creek. Her allies. Her detectives. Her agents of judgment and of wrath.

Hector's bees.

Georgia in the Wind

WILLIAM FRANK

Tommy McNaul squinted through his grimy office window as the cleanest car in Santa Fe veered toward the curb in front of the McNaul Brothers Detective Agency. The March norther was howling into its third day, and all the other surfaces in The City Different, including Tom's molars, were coated with fine grit.

The shiny Toyota Corolla eased to a stop and a slender, twitchy man in veteran jeans and a windbreaker emerged from the driver's door. He pinched his face against the wind like a preacher staring into a bar and scurried up the sidewalk toward the office.

Tom lurched to his feet and headed for the front door. He jerked it open as the driver's fist was descending to knock for the second time. The man winced as his knuckles scraped the rough wood, but he shook it off and looked hopeful.

"Mr. McNaul?"

"Tom McNaul. My big brother, Willie, is out hunting rustlers. Will I do?"

"Yes, you're the man I'm looking for. May I come in?"

"Please do." Tom shook a boney but firm hand and led the caller into the inner room. The fellow didn't seem to notice the battered furniture as his eyes flitted about. He shuffled to Tom's desk and settled tentatively into a wooden chair with loose armrests. Tom plopped down opposite and leaned forward on his elbows. "Sorry, I didn't catch your name."

"Marty. Marty Corbin."

Tom gave a deferential nod. "Nice to meet you, Marty. You an Uber driver?"

"Uh yes, how did you know?"

"Clean, older four-door in a dust storm. Never mind that, what can I do for you? I should mention that my brother provides most of the normal detective services. I specialize in art theft."

Marty nodded vigorously. "Yes, I know that. That's why I'm here. I'm hoping you can help me find a stolen painting."

Tom tried to hide his surprise. "Okay, that's my line. Just what sort of painting are we talking about?"

"A fairly large one." Marty spread his arms about four feet. "It's a picture of some flowers with an animal skull next to them. A buffalo, I think."

"Uh-huh." Tom made a point of arching his right eyebrow. "Are we talking an original oil, a print, or maybe a nicely framed poster?"

"Oh, it's an original, Mr. McNaul."

"Tom. That's fine, but who's the artist? Someone here in town?"

"Well, once, maybe. But not anymore." Marty's eyes were beginning to shine, and he leaned forward. "It's by Georgia O'Keeffe. Maybe you've heard about it. It was stolen last summer from the home of an actress who lives up near Taos. I think she was famous once—the actress, I mean."

Tom tried not to look as dumb as he felt. "An O'Keeffe, you say. Well, that would certainly be worth a lot of money. I should tell you that I work on commission, twenty-percent finder's fee plus expenses."

"I'm not in this for the money, Mr. McNaul."

"A lot of folks say that, but it happens that I am. Suppose you tell me just how you fit into this quest? I know the case. In fact, I read about it in the paper two days ago. 'Hollyhocks and Buffalo,' or something like that. The theft occurred nine months ago, but the insurance company just settled the claim. By the way, the actress was Maureen Littleton. She won a couple of Oscars back in the '60s, or maybe it was earlier, but I digress. If it's Ms. Littleton's painting, why are you here? Did she hire you?"

"No, I'm here on my own. Look, I don't have any money for your expenses, and I don't own the painting. But I need to find it. Can you help me? We can work together, and maybe you could make some money if we get it back."

"Maybe, but again, just what's your stake in this painting?"

Marty's face began gyrating, but he finally clenched his teeth and sighed. "I'm the guy who stole it."

Tom's lips parted, and he stared at Marty for several seconds before he snapped to. "Well, this should be a quick one." He leaned back, pulled open the top right desk drawer, and whipped out a pair of handcuffs. "Please extend your arms, hands close together. We'll get this one wrapped up, and you can be on your way—that would be downtown."

Marty frowned. "Don't make fun of me. This is serious, and there's more."

"Like?"

"Like my life is in danger."

"You sandbagged me. Explain."

"That article in the paper, the one about the insurance payment on the painting. I thought that might mean me and my cousin, Alex, were in the clear. So I called Alex. He was scared shitless. Someone broke into his house the same day the story came out. He was away, down in Las Cruces, but he could tell someone had jimmied the door when he got home. So he took off. He told me to lay low for a while. Stay away from home. Said he'd slipped up and let the guy who hired him know there were two of us."

Tom realized he was still holding the handcuffs. He dropped them back into the drawer next to his .38 Special and left the drawer open. Just in case. "Any idea where your cousin went?"

Marty was working his lips at a furious pace. He shook his head.

"Not for sure, but he has a place near Los Cerrillos. It's just an old trailer on a piece of land his dad left him. He goes there sometimes."

"You try calling him?"

"Yeah, but his phone's been off. He figures someone could track him if he kept it turned on."

"Uh-huh." Tom leaned back with his hands clasped behind his head and stared at the ceiling above Marty's head. "Probably nothing, but what say you and I run out to this trailer and have a look? In my profession, such as it is, it doesn't pay to ignore a coincidence."

"I don't like them either, Mr. McNaul. Uh, Tom."

"Let's go. We'll take my truck." As Marty turned away, Tom slipped the .38 into his right jacket pocket.

Fifteen minutes later, Tom steered his Tacoma past the last of the Santa Fe traffic and turned onto the Turquoise Trail, aka NM Highway 14. Marty hadn't spoken since they left the office. "We've got a quiet stretch here. Suppose you fill me in on the story."

Marty didn't look too confident, but he nodded and clasped his hands on his lap. "I lost my job about a year ago, and my cash had run out. I tried to tap Alex for a loan—just for a couple of months—but he said he was short, too. Then, a few days later, he called and said he could use some help on a job. Alex does some pretty shady stuff, and I wasn't keen, but I told him maybe. He said he could give me two grand if I'd help him pull a snatch up near Taos. No danger—a rich old lady with a painting, just in and out and disappear. I didn't like it, but two grand would pay the back rent."

Tom sighed. "An old story."

"Well, I was desperate, so I said yeah. But he called me a couple of days later and said the job had to be postponed for three months. Said the painting was being moved to Denver, to some big art museum there. We had to wait until the lady got it back." Marty shuffled his feet. "Alex told the guy he could snatch the piece when it was on the road, but he said that wouldn't do. So we waited. It was an easy job. Turned out the old lady wasn't home, and we were in and out in ten minutes. The alarm went off, but the house is out in the middle of serious nowhere."

Marty paused and looked at Tom as if expecting a question, but Tom just stared down the road. "Well, anyway, Alex took the painting, and we split up. Two days later he dropped by my place with two grand, and then he drove off. I've been sweating ever since."

"Not surprising. Any more?"

"Well, nothing happened. I got the job with Uber, and I do some part-time at Walmart. Months passed, and I figured I was in the clear. But on Tuesday I saw that article, and I called Alex."

"Did Alex keep the painting at his place?"

"Nope. He said he handed it over to the boss guy right away. Said I shouldn't worry, 'cause he didn't tell him he'd hired me to help with the grab."

"But that wasn't true."

Marty looked at his shoes. "No, I guess not."

Just past the turnoff to Los Cerrillos, Marty steered Tom onto a rough dirt track through some scrub junipers and piñon. They crossed an arroyo and made a sharp right into a meadow of sorts, though the occasional blades of grass had few neighbors. A rusted, white single-wide trailer sagged on cement blocks at the far end. The shades were closed.

Marty pointed at a battered white Ford F-150 with a long crack traversing the windshield. "That's his." He led Tom up the steps. The front door wasn't latched, and it swung inward with his first knock. "Hey, Alex. You in there?"

Marty fidgeted for a few seconds in the silence. Tom could smell death as he stepped through the door. Alex lay on the living room rug next to the sprung sofa. His empty eyes were aimed at the greasy ceiling, but they hadn't seen anything for at least two days.

Tom pulled a pair of latex gloves from his pocket and knelt beside the corpse. Cause of death was obvious from the round hole in the forehead. He glanced back at Marty. "You okay? Best you go wait by the car. This is a murder scene."

Marty stumbled back out the door without a word. Tom quickly searched the body. Alex had twenty-five bucks in his wallet along with his driver's license and a couple of credit cards. No notes or other ID. Car keys in the right pants pocket but no phone on the body. Tom made a quick survey of the usual spots a man would leave one, but came up empty.

He stepped outside and made a quick search of the truck. Still no trace of Alex's phone. He took out his own and placed a call to Eddie Romero, who worked homicide for the Santa Fe police. This wasn't in Santa Fe's jurisdiction, but Tom and Eddie went back to high school in Albuquerque, and Eddie would make the right connections. Eddie didn't pick up, so Tom left a short message and escorted Marty back to the Tacoma. "We'd best get out of here. I'll figure out the story later."

They rode in silence. The dust storm upped the ante as they approached downtown Santa Fe. Tom bypassed the office and took Marty to his little condo on a ridge overlooking downtown.

He shoved Marty down on the sofa next to Stella, his wary corgi, and poured two doubles of Bushmills on the rocks. Tom sat in a purple stuffed chair, leaned over the coffee table, and clinked glasses. "Drink it all, and then we need to get busy."

Marty looked as dead as his cousin, but he knocked the Black Bush down like a pro. Tom poured him a refill, but set his own glass on the table. "Okay, Marty. I'm beginning to take your plight seriously. You got any idea who gunned down your cousin? A name, his job, any description at all?"

"Sorry. Not a clue." Marty stared at the floor. "I think Alex wanted to protect me by keeping me in the dark. Figured I wouldn't spill anything mouthing off."

"You're probably right, but he must have spilled it himself." Tom shook his head. "Okay, here's the deal. As I said earlier, I make my living on commission. But in this case, I'm not likely to get anything, since you—I'll try to put this delicately—have no money. Still, if we recover the painting, we might get a reward from the owner, and you might keep on living. So let's do this as partners. You pay me nothing, but I get the reward. If it's big enough, I'll cut you in for something. If not, at least you survive."

Marty didn't hesitate. "That's all I want, Tom. To put this behind me. I don't deserve any share in the reward anyway."

"Okay. I have a plan. Fortunately, this is Thursday, so I'll only need a week or so to set things up. Meanwhile, we'll make a trip to visit Ms. Littleton. I've got a hunch about what's going on here, but I need to talk to her to confirm it. That sound good?"

"I guess so, but I don't want to face her."

"Fine, but you ride along to show me the way. You can hide behind a juniper when we get close. Meanwhile, I'll drop you off at Willie's place. It's secure and inconveniently located in case of snoopers. And don't fret about losing your Uber fares. Trust me, you can't be out there trolling for bullets this week. Willie will comp you room and board if you help feed the horses."

At nine on Friday morning, Tom strolled into the office of the *Santa Fe New Mexican*. It cost him two hundred bucks, but he managed to place a small ad with a photo in the *Pasatiempo*, the paper's weekly magazine of all things Santa Fe, advertising a book signing. Marty's name was prominent, as was the fake title, "I Stole an O'Keeffe." The bogus signing would be at a small coffee shop on Guadalupe Street. Tony Milan, the owner of Espresso Junction, owed Tom a favor for keeping quiet about his daughter snitching some jewelry from her employer. The date was set for Saturday, eight days hence. He chose the afternoon to keep the crowd down. He phoned in smaller ads to a local weekly and to the *Albuquerque Journal* calendar page.

Next, Tom began the search for Maureen Littleton's phone number. It would be unlisted, but he knew a lot of folks in Taos. He eventually found a contractor who had redone her roof recently and who was willing to cough up her number for a hundred bucks. A woman with an old but firm voice answered on the seventh ring. "Yes?"

"My name is Tom McNaul, and I'm trying to reach Ms. Maureen Littleton on behalf of my client. Is she available?"

"I'm Maureen, but I don't take unsolicited calls. How did you get this number?"

"I'm sorry to bother you, ma'am, but I have received information that could lead to the recovery of a painting stolen from you this past year. I understand it was by Georgia O'Keeffe. I would like to ask you a few questions."

"I'm not willing to talk about such things with a stranger on the phone. I've been bothered enough by the press checking to see if I'm dead yet. I'll give you my lawyer's number, and you can talk with him."

"Please, Ms. Littleton, this is for real. Could we meet at your lawyer's office early next week? I'm a licensed private investigator in Santa Fe, and your lawyer can check me out before we meet."

She hesitated long enough to worry Tom, but he finally heard a resigned exhale. "I'll call my lawyer, and he'll get back to you. Goodbye, Mr. McNeal."

"That's McNaul, Ms. Littleton." He heard the phone go dead.

Tom and Stella were halfway around their second lap of the plaza when his cell sounded. The number was unfamiliar, but he answered and recognized the voice of Maureen Littleton.

"Thanks for getting back to me, Ms. Littleton. I'm down at the plaza walking my dog. She likes to bum for treats before dinner. Pretty good at it."

"That speaks well to your character, Mr. McNaul. I don't trust a man who doesn't have a dog. More to the point, I discussed you with my lawyer. He expressed a few caveats, but he did vouch for you. He said you are the best art detective west of Chicago. Is that true?"

"My mom thought so, but I don't actually know of any good ones in Chicago. If you'd like another reference, I could refer you to Agent Kate Bacon of the FBI Art Crime Team, in Washington. I used to be her partner."

"I've already spoken with her. I'm afraid I treated you somewhat rudely before, but you did surprise me. Are you free tonight? Why don't you come see me after dinner? Say, nine? Just one rule—no film talk."

Tom felt his back stiffen. "That would be okay, Ms. Littleton. How do I find you?"

Maureen swore him to secrecy, passed on directions and the code for her gate, and hung up. Tom and Stella scurried up the hill to his condo, where he nuked some leftover pasta and chewed on a few lettuce leaves.

By seven-thirty, Tom and Marty were on the low road to Taos. They passed through the town, still heading north, just before nine.

The turnoff to the Littleton estate was not marked, but Marty recognized the turn onto a rugged dirt track. A hundred yards later they cleared the gate. As they rounded the third hill, Tom stopped and examined a long, low adobe structure carved into the side of a ridge and lit by spotlights. It faced east, toward the mountains. In daylight it would have quite a view.

Marty hopped out carrying his flashlight, a water bottle, and a nearly empty gym bag. He waved to Tom and slipped behind a dense juniper. The drive up sported two switchbacks and ended in a circular drive in front of massive twin doors of dark, carved wood.

Tom knocked. He didn't hear footsteps, but after at least two minutes there was a shuffling noise, and one of the doors swung inward into a dark entryway.

In the shadows stood a magnificent lady—tall, slender, and clearly in her eighties. Her face was side-lit by a floodlight near the door. It reminded Tom of a scene from *Casablanca*. He was sure the veteran actress had planned the entry lighting herself. "Please come in, Mr. McNaul."

"Tom, please. And thank you."

"Tom, then. Feel free to call me Maureen. I'm long past acting like I'm somebody of importance."

They walked in silence down a dark corridor to a dimly lit living room with broad windows and seating facing the mountains. She settled into a mission-style recliner and guided Tom onto the near end of a dark leather love seat. He guessed both were original Stickley pieces. Light from an art deco floor lamp bathed their faces in a dim amber glow. "Now then, would you like a drink? Agent Bacon said you were somewhat fond of Irish whiskey."

"Kate gives out a lot of information for an FBI agent, but yes, I do have some taste for the juice of the barley."

"Then please help yourself." Maureen flicked her hand toward a bar built into the far wall. "And bring me a drop of the Redbreast, if you would. Just half a finger. For memory's sake. I'm from County Tipperary, you know."

Tom didn't know, but he fetched the drinks. They clinked the crystal glasses before taking silent sips. As Maureen leaned forward to set hers on the coffee table, he caught a whiff of her perfume. He had no clue what it might be, but assumed it was expensive.

She leaned back in the recliner and stared at him, her head turned slightly to her left. Once again, her face was lit like a studio still shot.

Tom heard a thump from the far end of the house and turned his head. Maureen laughed. "Just my kitty. She stays out in the guest room when I have visitors." Tom figured it sounded like a pretty fat cat.

"Now, Tom. What do you want to ask me? Agent Bacon told me you're excellent at finding stolen art, but isn't it a little late for that?" Maureen drew her feet up onto her chair. "My lawyer says the painting, should it be recovered, now belongs to the insurance company. They paid me for the loss just last week. Perhaps you should be helping them find it."

"Your lawyer is correct." Tom chewed his upper lip for a moment. "I think I only have one question to ask you. It's a bit personal, but I assure you I'll keep the information in confidence."

Maureen gave a practiced flick of her eyebrows followed by a wry smile. "Sounds intriguing. Ask away."

"How much did they pay you?"

She looked puzzled. "That's all?"

"Uh-huh."

Maureen shrugged and stared toward the dark windows. After a few seconds, she shook her head and turned back to Tom. "Just under a million dollars. It must be worth far more, but that's what it was insured for. You see, I bought that painting at least fifty years ago. I did raise the insured value once, but that was probably, oh, thirty years back."

"I assume you know it's worth ten or twenty times that now?"

"Is it? Well, I'm a big girl. I don't need the money, and I was never planning to sell it anyway." She shrugged and tried to look nonchalant, but finished off her whiskey in a single pull.

"Still, I'm sorry you didn't get more." Tom glanced longingly at the rest of his Redbreast, but felt it would be poor form to drain it. "I'll leave you in peace. Thank you for agreeing to see me."

He stood up, and she escorted him to the door. As he turned to say goodbye, Maureen leaned forward, her flowing hair brushing his nose, and kissed his cheek so softly he wasn't sure they'd actually made contact. She gave a faint smile, turned away, and disappeared into the dark hallway.

As Tom reached the bottom of her steep driveway, Marty stepped out from behind the juniper. He had removed his jacket and must have stuffed it into the gym bag. Seemed odd given the cold night, but Tom shrugged it off.

Late Saturday morning, Willie drove Marty to the Staab Street office. As they entered, Tom greeted them with a fresh pot of coffee. "Well, boys, things are coming along nicely."

Willie shook his ragged mane and snorted. "Seems kind of dull so far. Glad I'm not part of this case, little brother."

"Oh, but you are. I need you to hang out in Espresso Junction next Saturday afternoon. Armed and dangerous, in case things get sticky."

"Well, now. You've got my interest."

Marty looked startled. "What are you talking about? Guns? Next week? What's going on? Aren't we heading out to find the painting?"

"Simmer down. We're not going to search for the painting because I have no idea where it's hidden. Nor am I sure who is trying to do you in." Tom leaned forward and crossed his arms on his desk. "I'll need to search some public records, and government offices aren't open in Santa Fe on weekends."

Marty clenched his teeth and snorted. "Surely you can tell me more than that. Who do you suspect?"

"Don't have a name yet. I'll tell you if I find out. Meanwhile, you stay out of sight at Willie's place. Next Saturday we'll take you to a coffee shop on Guadalupe Street for a book signing. You're going to stand up and discuss your new book titled *I Stole an O'Keeffe*."

"My what?" Marty's voice went up an octave and he appeared close to hysteria. "I haven't written any book. Are you nuts?"

"We'll debate that later. No, there isn't a book, but I advertised the signing. I'm figuring it might draw out the man who's trying to kill you. If not, I'll think of something else."

"But how can I talk about a book that doesn't exist?"

"I'm betting that you won't have to say much. For now, leave the details to me."

Marty twitched and whined for another ten minutes, but Tom just folded his arms and shook his head. Willie grabbed Marty's arm and steered him outside to his aging pickup. Tom watched the trail of oil smoke as Willie and his houseguest roared off.

Tom ran into the usual bureaucratic delays, New Mexico style. He eventually discovered that Kokopelli Insurance, a regional company headquartered in Albuquerque, had paid out for the stolen O'Keeffe. The local officials in Santa Fe knew only that it was a small private company licensed to do business in New Mexico, Arizona, and Colorado. The owner was listed as Raymond Schubert, and their only office was in Albuquerque.

Tom returned to his office and called Kate Bacon. The FBI Art Crime Team maintained detailed records of major art thefts in the United States and abroad.

Kate picked up on the first ring. "Tommy, my man. Long time. What's up?"

"Art theft and murder."

"This about the O'Keeffe? I got a call from Maureen Littleton a few days ago."

"Yeah. Stolen from her home near Taos. Kokopelli Insurance just paid off the claim."

"I heard. Tough luck. The payout was only about five percent of what it would go for at auction. What about it?"

"What can you tell me about Kokopelli? Anything about their finances?"

"Mmm. Seems to me their name came up a few times this past year. Let me run a quick search and call you back."

Kate was back on the line in twenty minutes. "Interesting company. It's a small family business, but they've paid out on three major claims in the past year. The big one was a burglary up in Aspen. Someone lifted a collection of Warhols—a portrait of Marilyn Monroe being the main attraction. That cost them twenty million. If you're asking, I wouldn't buy stock in them."

"They're not a public company, but thanks for the advice. They've gotta be hurting big-time."

"I'd say so. What's your interest in the O'Keeffe?"

"I've got a client who claims to be the thief, and someone's trying to kill him. Thinks it's related. You know I can't tell you more."

"You're always such a tease. When you coming to see me?"

"Soon, toots. See ya."

The book signing was scheduled for two-thirty on Saturday. At one, Tom watched from the window of his Staab Street office as Willie and Marty climbed out of Willie's truck. Moments later Marty burst through the door looking like a jackrabbit in a coyote den. Willie suppressed a grin as he brought up the rear. Tom waved the newcomers toward chairs and leaned back in his own. "Welcome, comrades. It's almost curtain time."

Marty clenched his fists and jaw as he summoned an admirable amount of courage. "I'm not going through with this charade unless you tell me everything you know. I feel like I'm being set up for target practice, and we're supposed to be partners. You must know more than you're letting on."

Tom frowned. "You're right. That's only fair. Have a seat."

Marty hesitated, then plopped down on a battered oak side chair, crossed his arms, and glared. Willie eased himself onto the sofa a few feet behind Marty.

Tom stood up and began to pace around the room while staring at Marty. "Parts of this case were evident as soon as you finished your story of the theft. First, the person bankrolling the heist didn't want the painting stolen while it was in transit. He insisted it be taken from Maureen Littleton's home."

Marty squinted. "Why does that matter?"

"I'll get to that. Second, the boss didn't kill your brother for nine months after the theft, then shot him as soon as Kokopelli Insurance paid off Maureen Littleton. Very suspicious. I was pretty sure I knew what was going on, but I needed some information from Ms. Littleton."

Willie was getting interested and sat up straight. "What kind of info, bro?"

"The amount of the payout. That wasn't released to the public." Willie and Marty just blinked. "The O'Keeffe was only insured for about a nickel on the dollar, maybe less. But if the painting had been stolen when it was in the possession of the museum, or during its transfer back to Maureen Littleton's house, the museum's insurance would have covered it at more or less current value."

Tom paused, but the others only blinked at him. "Okay, final point. Whoever pays off the insurance claim then owns the painting. They can do what they want with it. So, Kokopelli Insurance, owned by Raymond Schubert, now owns it. You can bet the farm that in a very short time, that painting will mysteriously reappear with a cover story about having turned up in a garage sale or something. Raymond Schubert will get his photo in the papers as he trots over to Sotheby's, auctions it off for ten or twenty million, and what do you know? His

business is solvent again, probably with a few million to spare. Understand now?"

The blinking ceased, and Marty even grinned.

Fifteen minutes later, Tom led his small team into Espresso Junction.
Tony was none too happy about a potential shootout in his coffee
shop. "Not to worry, Tony. I don't figure the bullets will fly. We just
need to scare this asshole enough that he bolts. I figure we can pressure
him into a confession before the cops show up. You can be a witness."

Tony snorted. "I won't witness much from the floor behind the
counter. You'll owe me after this one."

"Fair enough. I'll buy all my coffee beans exclusively from you."

"You already do."

Three rows of folding chairs faced a microphone in the shop's left
rear corner. The walls were lined with local art for sale. A small table
to the left of the mike sported a stack of about a dozen books with
matching covers. They were copies of a new southwestern mystery by
a local writer, but Tom rotated the stack until the spines faced away
from the seating. He placed a couple of menus atop the pile to hide
the front cover.

The crowd was sparse, as planned. By two-thirty there were eight
people scattered among the chairs. Two silver-haired ladies in jeans
and hiking shirts were chatting in the front row. A kid in black with
multiple piercings and earbuds was furiously working a phone with
his thumbs. One of the baristas took a seat in the back row next to
Tony, and two men Tom recognized as regular coffee hounds folded
their newspapers and grabbed seats toward stage left.

The eighth person was a man who looked about fifty, and wore a
leather jacket over a checked dress shirt. He sat in the last row in the
seat closest to the front door and had a small satchel on his lap. Had
to be Schubert. Tom figured Schubert would leave right after the signing and then tail Marty to a lonely spot for the hit.

Willie was leaning against the wall near the door. He flipped his right index finger at the man in the leather jacket. Tom gave a single nod and walked to the mike.

"Thanks for coming, everyone. I'd like to introduce our visiting author, Mr. Martin Corbin." He extended his left arm in the general direction of Marty. Two or three people clapped. Tom's right hand was wrapped around the handle of the revolver in the pocket of his windbreaker. "There has been a slight change in the program this afternoon. The theft of Georgia O'Keeffe's beautiful painting caused quite a sensation in these parts. Rather than have Mr. Corbin simply describe the events, we've arranged to have a representative of the FBI Art Crime Team preside over a genuine sting operation. That would be me." Tom flashed a realistic, but phony, copy of his old FBI badge. "Everyone please move calmly to the sides of the room while I take Mr. Schubert into custody."

Schubert bolted from his chair like a cat exiting a hot griddle, but as he spun for the door, Willie felled him with a short right to the solar plexus. Schubert collapsed and rolled onto his back. Willie knelt beside the gasping insurance man and held a blunt combat knife to his throat. Nobody screamed. Four of the other attendees were frantically taking pictures with their phones. The first cop car arrived in five minutes.

Another half hour passed before Tom could cool off the cops, wave goodbye to Mr. Schubert, and lead his two comrades back to the office. He poured a round of Jameson doubles. Willie lurched to his feet and proposed a toast. "To a long life, Marty."

Marty sank into a sad smile. "A longer one, at least. But what happens now?" He turned to Tom.

"Not sure, but here's a guess. Schubert is facing a first-degree-murder rap, but he'll weasel his way into a plea bargain. I don't know where he's got the O'Keeffe stashed, but if it's hidden well enough, he can toss in that chip to try and sweeten his deal. Besides, murder trials are expensive, and this is a poor state. So maybe his lawyer will try to get him murder two."

Tom paused and scratched the side of his head. "As for the painting, once Schubert confesses to the theft, he won't own it anymore. Ownership will revert to Maureen Littleton, so it will return to a wall in her beautiful house. Kokopelli Insurance will belly up, and nobody will care." Tom frowned. "Of course, this means we'll get no commission. Maureen didn't hire us, after all."

"What will happen to me?" Marty was sagging in his chair and staring into his still-full glass.

Tom felt a twinge of guilt. "Sorry. No cash for you either. But there's a bright side."

"How could there be?" Marty sounded forlorn, but he couldn't hide a twinge of hope.

"There isn't any hard evidence that you participated in the theft of the painting. Schubert didn't hire you and had never met you until today. He only suspected you because of a comment made by your late cousin, Alex. So, Maureen has her painting. The cops have their murderer, but no case against you. They may drop by your house a couple of times and growl, but you'll walk."

Tom stood up, walked over to Marty, and stuck out his hand. "Good working with you, Marty. If you get tired of Uber, give me a call. Though I warn you, we miss a lot of paydays."

Marty stood and took Tom's hand. "I could do worse. And don't worry about me. I'll get by. It's good to feel like an almost honest man again." He nodded at Willie as he left.

One week later, a long, rectangular package arrived at the McNaul Brothers office. Tom opened it carefully. The box contained a dozen long-stemmed roses and a note in an envelope. He searched the package and envelope, but found no check. The note was from Maureen Littleton: *"Tom, darling, I'm eternally grateful for your help in recovering my gorgeous painting, and I'd like to thank you. Please join me for dinner at my home tomorrow evening. Shall we say eight? Don't worry. It will be catered.*

"By the way, I may need your services. I seem to be missing a small piece of art from my guest bedroom. I had a small sketch by O'Keeffe on the wall above the bookcase. I'm sure it was there a couple of weeks ago."

From Four till Late

A Nick Travers Story

ACE ATKINS

"Sorry about the hour, Nick," Luther Jones said. "Considering the situation, the police couldn't do much but nod and act like they give a damn."

"You don't think they give a damn?"

"In New Orleans?" Jones said. "Shit. When's that ever happened?"

Nick shrugged, standing in the lobby of The Roosevelt hotel with Jones, head of hotel security, right by the old "mystery clock." The marble clock stood ten feet high, with an onyx base and a bronze woman holding a scepter in her hand. The scepter swung in a continuous circular motion, seemingly without effort. A plaque at the base read it had been displayed at the Paris Exhibition in 1867.

"Where's the girl's mother?" Nick said.

"In her room," Jones said. "The father was drunk as hell and passed right out."

Jones had on a size 50 Long blue blazer with a silver security pin. He was big and black and had a deep voice that sounded a lot like the guy on the Arby's commercials who advertised that they *Have the Meats*.

When he and Nick had played for the Saints, Jones made up a key part of the defensive line, an almost impenetrable front.

"How old is the girl?"

"Seventeen," Jones said. "Met up with some friends and never got home. Momma called those friends and they said she left them in a bar in the Quarter after midnight."

Nick had known Luther Jones for almost twenty-five years. They'd been through two-a-days, three seasons with fans wearing paper sacks on their heads, and a rough transition into regular life after pro ball. Jones had gone into work for a security firm and Nick had gone back to school, a master's in Southern Studies and now some teaching at Tulane. Sometimes he ran favors for friends, tracking down lost items and lost people. Jones called him from time to time for important guests. Pretty much all VIPs.

"I'll call her mother," Jones said. "Her name is Kendall Bogardus."

"That's mighty Southern of her."

"High-dollar folks from Oxford, Mississippi," Jones said. "Rolled into town Friday and checked in to one of the Astoria suites. Little girl's name is Kaitlyn. Also with a *K*. Just watched the security footage of her leaving the hotel. Looks as if the young lady changed her attire after dinner with her parents. Wearing a dress about as big as a cocktail napkin."

Jones walked to the valet desk and picked up the house phone. Nick wandered deeper into the long, wide-open expanse of marble and brass. The floors displayed intricate patterns of marble inlay, mosaics of bright colors. He felt a little shabby in his threadbare Levi's, white T, black leather jacket, and black cowboy boots. He hadn't had time to shave or comb his long, graying hair, a little Jack Daniel's still on his breath after playing a gig at the Maple Leaf.

"Mrs. Bogardus will be right down," Jones said. "The daddy's a pudgy dude with beady little eyes and no chin. The kind that wears a seersucker suit and a bow tie. Has a lot of money and wants you to damn-well know it."

"One of those," Nick said.

"Yeah," Jones said. "You know all those motherfuckers."

"Sure," Nick said. "Wish I didn't."

"The girl posted some stuff on Instagram at a karaoke bar on Bourbon. Left her friends after midnight. Said she was walking back to the hotel."

"Maybe she met a new friend?"

"The girl's friends are in contact with Momma," Jones said. "They say that ain't the case. She was alone."

"Shit."

"Yep," Jones said. "The Roosevelt would be mighty grateful if you'd go and do your thing, man."

"Sure," Nick said, looking at his watch. "Just remind me what I do again?"

"Stir up shit," Jones said. "Find folks."

"Oh yeah," Nick said. "That's right."

Kendall Bogardus was a tallish woman with blond bobbed hair, lots of makeup especially thick around the eyes, and long fingernails painted bright red. She wore a short black silk romper, cut low to show off a lot of cleavage and riding high to show off a pair of muscular legs. Her calf muscles flexed as she walked in some incredibly high black suede shoes, smelling like the inside of Neiman Marcus and wearing enough gold and diamonds to fill a jeweler's window. The clothes, the hair, the shoes seemed to be more suited for a woman half her age. But what the hell did Nick know? His Levi's were older than the missing girl.

"This makes me so damn mad," Kendall said, following Nick down Bourbon Street, neon shimmering in the puddles. Strippers stood outside clubs in kimonos, smoking cigarettes and looking tired. "This was supposed to be a relaxing family weekend. Dinner at Commander's, shopping at Canal Place, and then we finally got reservations at Pêche. Do you have any idea how hard it is to get reservations there?"

"About as fancy as I go is a crawfish po'boy at Domilise's."

"Well, it's hard," she said. "We had a wonderful dinner until Brantley had one too many cocktails and made an ass of himself. Kept sending back the fish. And there was nothing wrong with the fish. The fish was fucking perfection. That's what really got us off the rails. Kaitlyn hates when he drinks. He gets so damn cocky. She'd about had enough of his bullshit, and took an Uber to meet friends."

"When was that?"

"About eight. I'm so embarrassed about this I could just spit," she said. "Having to call down to the concierge and ask for help finding our daughter. This isn't like leaving my purse at some restaurant or getting tickets to a Pelicans game. That big black man called the police, and they made me feel so silly."

"Luther Jones," Nick said. "His name is Luther Jones."

"Oh yes," she said. "Of course. The police told me that young people often get into mischief in the Quarter, implying that Kaitlyn shacked up with some boy she just met."

"That does happen," Nick said. "Occasionally."

"Oh no," she said. "Not my daughter. And if she'd decided to stay out late, she would've texted me. *Oh God.* What am I doing? Walking down Bourbon Street in the darkest part of the night with some strange man I just met."

"I'm not that strange," he said. "Odd. But never strange."

"This is such a damn nightmare," she said, taking long strides in those high shoes. "This place is so horrible. I haven't been down here since college."

"I haven't been on Bourbon Street since before Katrina," Nick said. "Only reason I come to the Quarter is to visit a little blues bar on Conti."

"Have you lived here long?"

"Most of my life."

"And you were here for the storm?"

"Of course."

"And?"

"It was worse than you heard," Nick said. "Although this part was high and dry."

"My husband loves New Orleans," she said. "He comes down here all the time on business. He says he loves the food, the bars, and the casinos. Loves the Saints and the Pelicans. He entertains a lot of clients."

"And what does your husband do?"

"Medical supplies," she said. "Don't ask me any more than that. I really don't know. Brantley makes money. That's what he's good at. The only thing he's good at. I really don't ask a lot of questions. We moved to Oxford last year from Jackson. Better schools and less crime. Jackson has become way too urban. Kaitlyn had a tough time readjusting. I was hoping seeing some old friends would help her."

"She knows people down here?"

"Friends on spring break."

They weaved in and out of the Bourbon Street scene, through the drunks and cigarette smoke and flashing neon and pounding dance music. Strip clubs, puke bars, and dirty little dance clubs. Larry Flynt's Hustler Club, Barely Legal, Déjà Vu, Crawdaddy's, Chris Owens Club, Pat O'Brien's. People were dancing, fighting, screaming, and laughing. Every bit of human emotion could be found in a single block at any point in time.

"When was the last time you heard from Kaitlyn?" he said.

"A little after eleven," she said. "I thought she was coming home early. She said she was tired and bored out of her skull. We were supposed to have breakfast at Brennan's tomorrow. She adores the bananas foster. But that's all shot to hell now. My husband is catatonic, my teen daughter is missing, and I'm about to break my neck walking in these damn heels."

"I'd be happy to carry you on my back."

Kendall smiled at him. She had little crow's feet around her eyes and would probably be much prettier when she scrubbed all that makeup off.

A skinny black man wearing no shirt and missing most of his front teeth tried to whistle at her but only made a whooshing sound from his open mouth. "Damn, Momma," he said. "You got some of dat junk in dat trunk."

He offered her a hit from a pint bottle of Aristocrat Vodka. They walked past, Nick pointing ahead to the karaoke bar where Kaitlyn's friends had last seen her. He checked his watch.

It was a quarter after four and the party was still going strong.

Nick showed the bar's bouncer a pic of Kaitlyn from her mother's iPhone.

"Yeah," the bouncer said. "She was here. Hard to miss that little bitty dress, showing all that skin."

Kendall shot the bouncer a hard look and then turned back to Nick. The bouncer was slightly larger than Luther, with biceps larger than Nick's thighs. His shirt read SECURITY, as if there was any question about it.

"Damn good body," the bouncer said. "She was singing 'Party in the U.S.A.' with some friends. You know that old Miley joint? They were hot as hell. Some dude was doing body shots off her tits."

Kendall walked up to the big man and tried to shove him. She would've had a better chance trying to move the Superdome. Nick tilted his head toward her and looked up at the bouncer. "The girl's mother."

"And she's seventeen," Kendall said.

"Looked eighteen to me," the bouncer said, smirking.

"Did you see her leave?" Nick asked.

The bouncer shook his head. "Nope," he said. "I didn't see nothing."

"Okay," Nick said. "We can ask the police to review the video. Might make a difference, you letting a minor in and all."

"Come on, dude," he said. "Why you got to be like that?"

"I only know one way to be," Nick said. "How about you?"

"Fuck me," he said. "Okay. *Okay.* She left with Matt."

"And who the hell is Matt?" Kendall asked.

"One of our bartenders," he said. "They said they were headed to the Marigny to get a tattoo."

"Perfect," Kendall said. "Just goddamn perfect."

The bartender shrugged and held out his hand in the tip-me gesture that seemed like a natural reflex. Nick kept on moving right past
him, Kendall following, complaining of blisters wearing on her heels.
"Six hundred dollars," she said. "Jimmy Choos. Italian leather. Can
you believe that?"

"You want me to call you a cab?" he said. "I'll call you when I find
her."

"Not a chance," she said. "About time I do one thing right."

"What all did you do wrong?"

"Since college?"

Nick nodded, hands in his jacket as they kept walking toward Esplanade.

"How 'bout everything?"

There was only one tattoo shop that catered to all-night walk-ins in
the Marigny. Kaitlyn had been there, a fresh Polaroid of the girl and
her new tattoo pinned on a wall of thousands. The artist, a heavyset
woman with sleeve tats and short hair dyed blue, said she'd left two
hours back.

"Who was with her?"

"Some bartender," she said. "Can't remember his name. Real sleaze.
He does work for some real creeps in the Quarter."

"Who?"

"Oh," she said. "I don't know names, but you know . . . drug deal-
ers, pimps, and bookies."

Kendall's face seemed to drain of color, her mouth hanging open,
not sure what to say. The room was dark and smelled of weed and
incense. Thick look-books of tattoo designs sat atop a long counter.

"What is that?" Kendall asked, ripping the Polaroid from the wall.
"What did you scrawl on her rib cage?"

The tattoo artist leaned back into a worn-out sofa, smoking a
cigarette. She grinned. *"Nolite te bastardes carborundorum."*

"What the hell does that mean?" Kendall asked, arms crossed over
her chest.

"Don't let the bastards grind you down," Nick said.

The artist grinned wider, nodding, and pointed the lit end of her cigarette at him.

"Great," Kendall said. "Just fucking great."

Nick looked down at the worn checkerboard floor and up at the tattoo artist. "You don't happen to know where they went next?"

"No," the woman said. "But I saw how they left."

"Do you think that woman was lying?" Kendall asked. "A candy van? That sounds almost made up. Like an evil Willy Wonka. I've never heard of such a thing."

"I have," Nick said. "They're all over the Quarter. They sell weed in lollypops and cookies. They claim they don't have THC, but they get busted by the cops all the damn time. It's just a mobile front for selling dope. Sometimes it's real dope, and sometimes it's just candy."

"I am a parental failure," she said. "My daughter got into a stranger's van for candy."

"Weed candy."

"And how does that make it better?"

"Weed isn't heroin," Nick said. "And weed does have some medicinal benefits."

"Did you miss the part about a stranger in New Orleans," she said. "At what time?"

"Nearly three."

"And what time is it now?"

"About five," Nick said.

"Jesus," she said. "Can we sit down? My feet are killing me."

They found a little bench outside The Spotted Cat. The jazz bar was closed now, just a smattering of cabs and Ubers running down Frenchman Street. A few clubs still playing music, people dancing or walking crooked down the sidewalks. The Marigny before The Storm had been a quiet little pocket of good clubs and bars away from the Quarter. Now the Marigny was worse than the Quarter, loud and obnoxious with the chug-and-vomit crowd. He wished they'd all just stayed on Bourbon Street where they belonged.

"So," she said. "This can't be it? This can't be your job."

"No," he said. "I'm in a band called The Revelators, and I have a prewar blues radio show on WWOZ."

"I mean a real job," she said. "What do you really do?"

"I loaf," Nick said. "I pick up some money when I need it. I like to play music. I like to relax. I like to have a good time."

"You're kidding."

"Not at all."

"Do you have a trust fund?"

Nick laughed and pulled out a pack of Marlboros, firing up a smoke. He liked New Orleans best early in the morning, just before dawn, when everything was starting to grow still and quiet. He remembered being here a few days after the city flooded while everyone was evacuated. You could stand on Rampart Street and hear the wind shooting down the streets and around the buildings. As still as it had been since the city began three hundred years ago.

"Are you married?"

"Nope."

"Divorced?"

"Nope."

"Gay?"

"You mean extremely happy?"

"Are you a homosexual?" she asked.

"Is it the boots?" he said. "Too Village People?"

"No," she said. "Where I'm from, there aren't too many unmarried straight men. Unless they've been divorced. I got married at twenty-two. I had fourteen fucking bridesmaids. Brantley was Colonel Reb at Ole Miss. So much fun. The life of the party."

"I got my master's in Southern Studies at Ole Miss," Nick said. "My thesis was on Sonny Boy Williamson."

"I don't know who that is."

"His real name was Alex Miller," Nick said. "Recorded for Chess Records in the '50s. You know the song 'Nine Below Zero'?"

She shrugged. "You probably didn't attend too many Greek philanthropy events."

Nick shook his head, tapping the ash from the cigarette on his boot heel. "What's your husband like now?"

"Still the life of the party."

"Where's the party?"

"I'm not sure," she said. "It seems to have ended several years ago. The dumb bastard didn't get the memo."

Nick smoked the cigarette, watching a man and woman leaving a corner bar. They walked hand-in-hand back toward Esplanade as the light just started to go from black to gray. The girl's shoulder blades looked sharp and dangerous, bony as hell under an open-back silk top. Nick leaned back on the bench and stretched his arms out wide, the old football injuries cracking and popping under his jacket.

"My tattooed daughter is lost in a weed van."

Nick looked down at his cellphone, scrolling through some numbers, endless contacts and names and addresses. He knew some folks who knew some folks who knew where those weed drivers set up shop.

"So, what now . . . we just wait?" Kendall asked.

"How are your feet?"

"They hurt like hell."

"Can you go one more mile?"

Kendall leaned down and unstrapped her heels, standing up and tossing them into the nearby garbage. Nick watched her and tossed his spent cigarette down to the sidewalk, crushing it under his boot. He recalled a night a long time ago, maybe twenty years back, watching the sunrise through the windows at Café Brasil as the Iguanas played an endless set. Full of Dixie with a young girl at his side. Now the bar was gone, the girl was married, and the Iguanas had all but broken up.

"I admire your style," he said. "But around here, you better watch where you step."

"What is she trying to do?" Kendall asked. "What is she trying to prove?"

"She's a teenager," Nick said. "What were you trying to prove as a teenager?"

"I knew you'd ask that," Kendall said. "Damn you. My daughter is nothing like me."

They'd followed Royal Street back the way they'd come, all the way to Canal Street, where Nick spotted the van painted up in a tableau of tokers: Cheech and Chong, Willie Nelson, Bob Marley, Shaggy and Scooby.

A bone-skinny white dude with dreads sat behind the wheel listening to some Peter Tosh, dark sunglasses on, looking as if he might be asleep. Nick tapped the window and the man let down the glass. "Yeah?"

"You pick up some parties in the Marigny a few hours ago?"

"Maybe I did and maybe I didn't."

Nick looked both ways on Canal, the street empty besides some homeless folks lying against the storefronts. He grabbed the man's hair and knocked his face against the wheel, honking it twice. The stoner's sunglasses cracked and remained crazy across his sweating face.

"You want to get killed?" the man said.

"By a guy who sells candy to kids?"

"You know who I am?" he said, trying to look tough.

Nick reached through the window and took off the man's busted sunglasses and tossed them to the pavement. He held out his hand for Kendall's phone and she handed it to him. He showed the lollypop man the pic. "You know her?"

"That girl was wild," he said. "Making out with her boyfriend in the van, doing a little striptease for the rest of the kiddies."

"Where is she?"

"She paid," he said. "And I put her ass out."

"Where?"

"Go fuck yourself."

Nick snatched up the man's dreads and opened up the door to drag him out. He put his hands to his face and said, "Rampart Street."

"Where?" Nick said, looking up at Kendall as he dragged the man half out of the van.

As Nick got him down on the pavement, the stoner gave him the cross streets, near Conti, and right near the St. Louis Cemetery No. 1.

"I should kick you right in the tail bone," Nick said.

"I never touched her."

"Maybe not." Nick pointed to the tableau on the side of the van and the drawing of a red-eyed Shaggy and Scooby. "But you just ruined my childhood."

They stood on the corner of Conti and Rampart, nothing around them. Nick picked up a pair of flip-flops for Kendall at an all-night grocery on Canal. She'd pulled her hair back into a ponytail and stood, arms akimbo, by the steps of Our Lady of Guadalupe Chapel. She'd washed her face in a bathroom, and looked much younger in the first light.

"What now?"

"Maybe she's trying to make Sunday Mass," Nick said.

Kendall didn't laugh. She looked down at the phone, a few cars passing along Rampart and over on Basin Street. Rampart had cleaned up a good bit in the last few years, nice iron streetlamps, streetcars running, a few boutique hotels. Back in the day, this had been crack alley central. You didn't get down this way unless you planned on getting mugged or stabbed. Many of the decrepit buildings and drug dens had been cleared, replaced by neat vacant lots and big commercial real estate signs. New condos and gas stations all around the side streets leading up to the old above-ground cemetery. Nick kind of missed the old sleaze. The sleaze had character.

"What did that woman mean by creeps?" she asked. "Are these some really bad people?"

"Maybe," Nick said. "Maybe not. In the Quarter, being a creep is a kind of profession. Don't take it too literally."

Kendall's phone rang. She snatched it from her purse and turned from Nick, talking in hushed tones. Nick stood by, watching the street, looking on at all the changes, trying to imagine what it had looked like back in Louis Armstrong's time: jazz clubs, brothels, all-night gambling houses in the red-light district.

"That was Brantley."

"She's back at The Roosevelt?" Nick said.

"No," Kendall said, her face drained of color. "Someone has Kaitlyn and they want us to pay to get her back. They want to meet."

Nick nodded. "Okay," he said. "Just tell me where."

Brantley was even worse than Luther Jones promised, a weak-chinned, schlubby-looking dude in a wrinkled Polo shirt that stretched down low over a pair of khaki shorts embroidered with little blue whales. He wore a pair of Docksiders on his little feet.

When he saw them, Brantley bowed up his chest and tried to suck in his gut, hands on hips, trying to look like a man in charge. His eyes were red and pouchy, and he was in bad need of a shave and shower.

"So glad you decided to join us, Brantley," Kendall said. "Now that you've slept it off."

They'd met up at the Riverwalk by the Aquarium. It was past six, the sun rising over the city, casting the concrete paths and the Mississippi River in a cool, gray light.

"Who the hell is this?" Brantley asked.

"This is Mr. Travers," Kendall said. "The hotel asked for him to help us."

"Doesn't look like a security guard to me," he said, eyeing Nick. "What exactly are you?"

"A sentient being," Nick said. "With an occasional mean streak."

Brantley snorted. Nick noticed the pockets of his shorts bulged from his bony legs. Brantley noticed the staring and turned to Kendall. "I did exactly as they asked," he said. "Five thousand dollars. The hotel got it for me this morning. They wanted to involve the police and I told them no thanks. This isn't the first shakedown I've gone through. This fucking place. Everyone with their goddamn hand out.

I expect after all this is over, this guy will want something, too. Won't you?"

"My deal is with the hotel," Nick said. "I keep the tip jar in my underwear."

"He's making jokes," Brantley said. "Everything is funny when it's not your goddamn daughter."

A cool iron-smelling wind blew up off the rocks along the waterfront. The big paddle wheelers were moored along the docks, lightly rocking against the pilings, a few early morning joggers starting to run past. Nick was starting to feel the lack of sleep, stomach rumbling, knowing that somewhere nearby, someone was frying beignets and making hot coffee.

"What did this guy say?" Nick asked.

"He said 'we want five thousand bucks,'" Brantley said.

"Or what?"

"Or they'd keep Kaitlyn."

"Did they say they'd hurt her?" Kendall said. "God."

"No," Brantley said. "It was strange. The whole thing was weird as hell."

Nick waited, wind ruffling his hair, standing there searching for the last cigarette in his jacket. He looked over at Kendall as she stared at her husband, hands still on his hips, pockets bulging with cash.

"It was like the guy couldn't stop laughing," Brantley said. "Acting like me and him were friends or something."

They showed twenty minutes later. A young girl in a green flowery crop top, matching short skirt, and very tall white heels and a young guy, who didn't look much older, in a black T-shirt and jeans. Kaitlyn looked a lot like her mother, thankfully, but shorter and thinner, with an upturned nose and a pixie haircut. The boy had a buzz cut and a lot of tattoos on his skinny arms. He kept his hand on Kaitlyn's back and nodded at Brantley, which threw the man a bit. Brantley, his puffy face drawn and haggard, let his arms drop to his sides. He kept eye contact and nodded at the younger man.

"What's all this shit?" the kid asked. "This looks like a party."

"This is my wife," Brantley said. "I don't know this other man. He wasn't invited."

The kid looked up at Nick, smirking, and shrugged a little. "Tell him to get the fuck out of here."

"Or," Nick said. "How about I pick you up and toss your narrow little ass into the river?"

"Do I look stupid?" the kid asked.

Nick looked to Kendall and he saw a slight smile on her face. She'd moved up to her daughter and reached out and offered her hand. The daughter, who didn't seem scared or worried, didn't take it. She just clenched her jaw and stared at her parents.

"I don't know," Nick said. "You look a little stupid. And you're not getting a dime from these people."

"I may be young, but I got friends," he said. "See that guy standing on the levee? You want to fuck with him?"

Nick looked at the long, grassy levee and saw a fat white guy in a tank top. He had on blocky jean shorts and sunglasses. He looked about as scary as a toothless bulldog.

"Sure," Nick said. "Why not?"

Brantley hadn't said a word. He just stood there, not making a move to grab his daughter or confront the man. The kid and the older man just stared at each other, wordless, seeming a hell of a lot like two people who'd met before.

"Pay up, Brantley," the kid said. "We tried to be nice about it."

"Sure, sure," Brantley said, reaching into his pockets, pulling out bundles of bills right there on the Riverwalk. Nick wondered if all of them wouldn't be mugged by someone else before the transaction was over.

"You son of a bitch," Kendall said.

"What is this, Matt?" Kaitlyn said, looking over at the kid. "What's going on?"

"Your dad is a loser," he said. "Just like you said. What kind of moron always bets on the fucking Saints? Those guys are all heart, but they let you down every damn time."

"Not every time," Nick said.

Kaitlyn pulled away from the kid and moved closer to her mother for a moment, Brantley looking around as he started handing over bundles of bills from his ridiculous preppy shorts to Matt. Nick watched, noticing Matt had a crudely drawn tattoo of the Monster Energy Drink logo on his forearm. His ear was pierced, and he had some kind of Asian characters on his left hand. Nick was pretty sure it read "Dip Shit" in Japanese.

"I'm done," Kendall said to her husband. "I'm so fucking done."

Nick looked up the levee at the fat dude in the shades and offered him a friendly wave. The man pretended not to notice.

"Was all this bullshit?" Kaitlyn said. "Tonight? Everything you said to me and promised? Everything was just to get your stupid money my dad owes you."

The kid, Matt, shook his head, and placed his hand on Kaitlyn's elbow. "When we met at the hotel and I told you to meet me out, I meant it," he said. "You're so damn beautiful. So goddamn smart and classy."

"Shut up, Matt," Nick said. "Or I'll puke. Give him the rest of the money, Brantley."

Brantley did as Nick said, looking down at his Docksiders. A cold, brackish wind kicked up off the river and filled the early morning silence.

"I'm not coming home," Kaitlyn said. "All of you just leave me the hell alone. I'm tired of it. Everything is so fake and boring and stupid. And I hate it. I hate you all."

She shook off the kid's grip and walked toward the Aquarium, a big banner flapping in the wind that read REEF RESCUE. A FAMILY-FRIENDLY EXHIBIT.

No one made a move to follow Kaitlyn but the kid. Brantley looked up from his feet and stared at Nick. He belched into his fist and said, "What are you looking at?"

Nick tilted his head and said, "You know? I'm really not sure."

"Screw it," Brantley said. "I'm going to drink a Bloody Mary and go back to sleep. Give me a call when it's time to eat."

Nick stood with Kendall and watched him walk away, disappearing around the edge of the Aquarium, heading back to Canal Street in the direction of The Roosevelt hotel. It was morning now, bright and full of energy, ice cream carts and little art kiosks setting up along the Mississippi. Nick looked at his watch, smiling up at Kendall.

Kendall seemed to shiver, wrapping her arms over her chest. Nick took off his leather jacket and handed it to her.

"We should go after her," she said.

Nick nodded. "We will."

"Everything is a mess."

Nick shook his head. "Maybe not everything."

"I've never been good at decisions," she said. Her hands were balled into fists so tight her knuckles turned white. "And I'm goddamn sick of it."

"Let's start with Kaitlyn," Nick said. "You go get her back. Maybe I'll kick that street rat's ass while we're at it. Then, breakfast. Café Du Monde is right around the corner."

"I do think better on a full stomach," said Kendall, and she straightened her shoulders and tossed her hair back, already walking away from the river and toward her daughter.

"Sounds like a plan."

"Breakfast would be nice," she said, smiling sideways at him. The subtle lines in her face quite pleasant. "I would like that a lot."

Bite Out of Crime

ALLISON BRENNAN

I

Jamie Blair first saw the mutt eating out of a Dumpster behind the barbecue restaurant on Folsom Boulevard near the freeway.

It was after eleven that night, when Jamie was on her way home after robbing a couple of houses on 49th Street. Rich neighborhood with lots of targets, but she was good at her trade: She'd never been caught. After all, someone had to take care of her deadbeat parents. Pay the rent, buy food, put gas in her mom's beat-up car that Jamie still wasn't old enough to drive.

"Ignore him," she mumbled to herself. Problem was, she liked dogs—primarily because they weren't people. That the poor dog was digging through garbage for a meal made her angry. Well, a lot of things made her angry these days.

She slowly approached. He appeared mostly German shepherd, but a mutt because he was too small for the breed. And he didn't look like he'd been on the streets long—a little dirty, but not too skinny.

He looked at her and there was something in his sad eyes. Fear. Apprehension.

Hope.

She pulled a half-empty bottle of water from her backpack, then squatted down as the dog came over. She poured the water out slowly, and he lapped it up. Poor thing—it had been a hot day, though when the sun went down so did the temperatures. Such was autumn in Sacramento.

When the water was gone, she tossed the bottle into the Dumpster and started to walk away.

The dog followed.

"You can't come home with me," she said.

Her mother would have a shit fit if she brought a dog home. But she couldn't just leave him here. If animal control got him, they'd kill him if they couldn't find his owner. And what if he'd been abandoned? He didn't look like he'd been on the streets for long, but she'd never forget when her neighbors across the street moved and left their cat behind. That poor animal waited for them to come home, losing weight every week. Jamie had fed it until her mother whacked her up-side the head for giving their food to "a filthy feline." A month later Jamie found the cat dead in the gutter, victim of a hit and run.

She couldn't let that happen to this mutt. It just wasn't fair.

Jamie squatted again, and the dog came right up to her and licked her hand. He wore a collar and she looked at the tag.

His name was Duke. There was a phone number.

"One night, Duke," she said. "Then I'll call your owner."

She almost didn't expect him to follow. She resumed walking through the parking lot to the hole in the fence that cut off a good quarter-mile of her trek home.

Duke followed.

Twenty minutes later she was at her house, the small side of a corner duplex surrounded by duplexes up and down the street. Her mother was passed out on the couch; the huge flat-screen television played some sitcom with a fake laugh track.

Duke growled softly.

"Quiet," she told him, not knowing if he could understand her.

He still growled. Great. Duke didn't like her house. Her mom did nothing all day—she watched soap operas, drank beer, and smoked pot. Maybe that was the problem. He didn't like the smell. She wrinkled her nose. She didn't like it much either.

"Stay," she ordered. He sat like a sentry at the front door.

Jamie didn't dare turn off the television—that was the fastest way to wake up her mom. She went to the kitchen, since she'd just gone to the store the other day and there was fresh food. Cooked two hamburgers on the stove as quietly as possible. She put American cheese on both, then mustard and ketchup and pickles on hers, and left Duke's plain. She figured dogs didn't much care for the extras.

She cut Duke's hamburger into quarters, and hers in half, then took them to her bedroom along with another liter of water and a plastic bowl.

Duke was still sitting by the door, right where she told him.

She motioned for him to follow, and he did. She unlocked her door—if she didn't lock it, her mom would toss her room until she found all her cash and then buy hard drugs. Pot didn't make her mother mean, but if she started using the serious shit again, she'd become unpredictable.

Jamie turned on her fan and opened her window. She put water in a bowl for Duke, then gave him the plate of hamburger. She ate hers slower than the dog, watching him. In the light, he actually looked pretty clean and healthy, though his paws were dirty and two of his claws were torn off. Maybe he'd gotten lost. Jumped his fence or something. Could have walked a long way, that's how he hurt his feet.

She ate half her burger, gave Duke the other half, guzzled some of the water, then emptied her backpack.

Tonight had been a good score.

She'd hit three houses—three was her lucky number, so she always robbed three houses a month, usually on the same night. She staked out her territory for weeks—sometimes months—before she picked the marks. She had to make sure they didn't have security systems, no dogs, no nosy neighbors, and confirm that they'd be out for the evening.

She scratched Duke behind the ears, and he put his head on her lap.

Jamie never took anything that couldn't fit in her backpack, which made it even better because most of the time, the people didn't even know they'd been robbed, and if they figured it out, they really couldn't remember when. Five credit cards—those would go to a fence she worked with for a hundred dollars a pop. Some jewelry—those would go to another guy she knew. He always shortchanged her, but she could usually get a few hundred from him for anything she brought. He'd taught her the difference between real and fake. Diamonds and gold moved well. And, of course, cash. People left cash all over the place, and she knew the best hiding places, but rich people didn't hide their money. If they didn't have a safe, they put cash in jewelry boxes, desk drawers, and with their underwear. Weird. She taped her stash to the bottom of her bed or in the vent behind her desk. Sometimes rolled up in her old Converse if she knew her mother was snooping around.

Tonight she'd walked away with over a thousand bucks, most of it from the Tudor house three down from the corner whose owners were at the Community Center Theater.

She didn't particularly like stealing from people, but it was better than living on the street, and she only targeted people she figured could afford to lose a few bucks. She couldn't wait until she graduated high school and could leave. Maybe go to college. Not a big college, but a community college. She could probably go for free because her parents were deadbeats. She didn't know what would happen to her mom in three years when she walked away—the woman couldn't take care of herself, and her dad was in and out so much he might as well be gone for good. But she didn't feel guilty at the thought that she would someday leave and never look back. Maybe she'd get a dog. Like Duke. Someone to keep her company. Because dogs didn't lie to you, they didn't steal your shit, and they didn't smoke so much dope they couldn't hold down a job.

"Down, Duke," she said, feeling bad for kicking the dog off her bed. Still, there wasn't a lot of room and he wasn't exactly clean. She put a blanket on the floor and he curled up on it. She was about to turn off the lights when she saw something written on his blue collar.

1414 48th St.

The address was written in permanent marker, but it was so faded that she hadn't noticed it until it was under the light just right. She knew that address—it was directly behind one of the houses she'd robbed that night. She'd targeted 48th Street last month, though not that house, for two reasons. First and foremost? She'd heard a dog in the backyard. She never targeted houses with dogs. And second? The old woman who lived there was nice. She was always out on the small porch sitting and drinking tea, or watering the gazillion flowers that bloomed along the perimeter. She waved at Jamie when she walked by with her backpack—probably thinking Jamie was going to or from school or a friend's house. Never thinking that Jamie was staking out the neighborhood. Never thinking that Jamie had robbed her neighbors.

Terrific, she thought. She avoided any street she hit for months because she didn't want anyone to notice her. It's what had kept her under the radar for the three years she'd been a thief.

But Duke wasn't her dog, and her mother would never let her keep him, so she didn't have much of a choice. Maybe when she called in the morning, the owner would meet her somewhere. Maybe there was even a reward.

She didn't want money for Duke, she realized. She wanted to keep the dog. But that wouldn't happen.

Jamie hid the cash, put the cards and jewels in separate envelopes and back into her backpack, locked her door, and slept.

II

"What the hell, Jamie?" her mother said that morning as she was leaving. Her mother was drinking coffee and eating cereal from the box, one eye on the game show blaring from the TV. "You brought a dog into my house? What if he shit on the carpet? Am I supposed to clean up after him?"

"He followed me home last night. He has a collar. I'm taking him back to his owner."

"You shouldn't have brought him inside. Really, Jamie, you're so irresponsible I don't know what to do with you."

"Pot, kettle," she said.

Her mother teared up. "I don't know what I ever did to deserve that."

A long list immediately sprang to mind, but Jamie ignored it. "Mom, I'll be home tonight."

"We're out of food."

"I went to the store three days ago."

"I just need a little money."

Of course she did. It was four days before her disability check hit her bank account, and she was out of beer.

"I don't have a lot."

"Just forty, fifty dollars?"

"I can stop at the store on my way home."

"I'll go."

Jamie didn't want to fight. She was so tired of being the mother in the house. She pulled two twenties from her pocket and put them on the kitchen table. "That's all I have."

"Thanks, baby. And the dog isn't that bad. If you can't find his owner, you can bring him back—but he has to stay outside."

"Okay. Thanks, Mom," she mumbled.

Her mother never asked her where she got the money. On the first of the month when her mother fretted because she was a hundred dollars short on the rent and Jamie gave her five twenties. Or when they were at the grocery store and her food card went tilt and Jamie pulled forty dollars from her pocket to cover the difference. Never once. What did she think?

Jamie didn't care. Three years—less than three years—and she'd graduate from high school and leave. Never look back.

First stop, she sold the credit cards to her guy Milo. Five hundred bucks, crisp and folded, rested in her back pocket as she walked ten blocks from his apartment to 48th Street, where she would have to turn Duke over to his owner. She'd tried the number earlier, but there had been no answer.

The whole time, Duke stayed with her. Not even on a leash, yet he stayed within two feet during their walk. She could get used to a dog like Duke.

As soon as they turned onto 48th Street, Duke knew he was almost home. But his reaction surprised Jamie—he tensed, walked slower, and practically tripped her several times, as if he didn't want to go home.

"What's going on, Duke?" she asked. Like he could answer her.

The address 1414 was in the middle of the block. It was one of the smaller houses, but just as well-maintained and stately as all the others. This was the edge of the so-called Fabulous Forties, a section of East Sacramento that boasted some of the oldest and most beautiful homes in town. Wide, tree-lined streets. Large yards set back from the road. Rich people with expensive toys. It's why Jamie targeted the area—she figured they wouldn't miss what she took. And no one looked at a white teen girl in clean clothes with any real suspicion.

Jamie knew the routines of every household in the area—that's how she didn't get caught. She didn't remember names, but she remembered numbers, cars, and faces. Addresses, times. The married couple north of 1414 both worked; they were doctors and kept odd hours. He drove an older Mercedes, she drove a Prius. The family on the south side had two teenagers—jerks. She knew them, vaguely— had seen them around. Not from her school, but in her neighborhood buying drugs. *Troublemakers*, she thought. Why did they need drugs when they lived in a place like this? When they had everything they could ever want? The oldest even had a car—she remembered when he got it for his birthday last year. At least, that's what she assumed when she saw the new wheels—a big-ass, brand-new red truck, and he was still in high school.

Behind 1414 was the house Jamie had hit last night. A lawyer who drove a new BMW and went to work from eight to six every day. His wife didn't actually work. She volunteered for charities. Jamie wouldn't have hit the house at all because volunteering was actually a good thing to do for people—but then she learned the wife was having an affair. A muscular guy who drove a small but tricked-out black Dodge truck. The guy came by several days a week, usually in the morning. He'd been there Thursday, but not yesterday—at least not when Jamie walked by, at ten and again at two.

It was because of that affair that Jamie decided they were on her list. They didn't have an alarm, they didn't have a dog, and the locks—though good—wouldn't give her too much trouble.

Jamie walked up to the front door of the old woman's house. Duke started whimpering.

Something was wrong. She knew it, but still she rang the bell. Silence. She knocked. Still no answer.

Jamie walked around to the back of the house. Her heart raced. Her heart never beat this fast when she was breaking into a place—why was it thumping so hard when she wasn't doing anything wrong?

The garage was detached and behind the house. She looked in through the lone window. An old sedan was parked there. She knew from her previous surveillance that the old woman had only the one car.

So she was home. Or on a walk.

Really, a walk, Jamie? She's like eighty! How far could she go?

Vacation? Maybe that was it. She was on a vacation, and the people who were supposed to be watching Duke screwed up.

Then why was Duke acting so weird?

She turned, and the dog was lying down, his head on the ground, his legs in front of him. He whimpered. Then she noticed a big hole under the fence that separated the driveway from the backyard. It looked new. That's how Duke got out, she figured.

"Did something happen to your owner?" she asked.

She didn't want to call the police. She didn't want to do anything but leave, but Duke wasn't her dog.

Jamie walked next door to where the doctors lived. The Prius was there, which meant the wife was home. She rang the bell. No answer. *Maybe she went to work with her husband. Great.* She rang again, then knocked.

She heard movement, then the door opened. A tired woman stood there wearing pajama bottoms and a tank top. "It says no solicitors for a reason," she snapped.

"I'm sorry," Jamie said. "I found this dog and, um, he has a collar that says he belongs next door, but no one's answering."

The doctor looked over Jamie's shoulder and clearly recognized Duke. "Oh. That's Duke. Where'd you find him?"

"At the barbecue restaurant off Folsom."

"That far down? I've never known Duke to stray. Just put him in the backyard. Emily is probably at the store."

"I was going to put him in the yard, but I saw a car in the garage." Jamie lied smoothly. She had to be a good liar in her line of work. "I walk down this street all the time because my best friend lives over on H Street, and I know the woman who lives there is really old, and I just thought maybe . . . something might have happened. She loves her dog. I think she would have been looking for him. I found him last night."

"Oh dear. Just hold on a minute, I'll go over with you."

"Maybe you can just take Duke?" Jamie didn't want to get in the middle of this. She just wanted to return the dog.

The doctor shook her head. "My husband is allergic. Just hold on, we'll check on Emily."

She walked away for a couple minutes and Jamie almost left. She glanced down at Duke. He was watching her, as if to say, *Don't leave me.*

He didn't, of course. She was projecting.

The doctor returned wearing flip-flops and carrying a key ring. "Emily gave us a set of keys when we moved here, in case of an emergency. I hope nothing is wrong. What's your name?"

"Jamie."

"I'm Teresa Linn. It was very nice of you to bring Duke back."

"He kinda followed me."

"He doesn't like most people, you should feel lucky."

Jamie glanced at Duke with a half-smile. She knew they were kindred spirits.

Dr. Linn rang the bell and knocked. "Emily? It's Teresa. Are you okay?"

There was no answer.

"Emily, I'm using the key to come in, okay?" She unlocked the door. "Jamie, wait here for a second, okay?"

Jamie had no intention of going inside.

Dr. Linn opened the door and a foul smell rushed out of the stuffy house. Jamie gagged, and Dr. Linn paled. "Oh no." She ran into the house. Duke ran after her.

"Duke!" Jamie yelled. "Stay, Duke!"

Dr. Linn screamed, and Duke started barking. Jamie wanted to run far away, but she didn't. She followed the dog and found him and Dr. Linn in the kitchen.

Emily, the kind old woman, was lying on the floor. She was very dead, her face swollen, and she had bruises all over her neck.

Jamie sucked in her breath, then felt nauseous because of the smell.

Dr. Linn turned around and pushed Jamie out of the house. Duke started to howl, an intensely mournful sound.

"Duke!" Dr. Linn shouted. "Duke, come here!"

Duke whimpered and followed.

Jamie sat down heavily on the porch. Duke sat next to her and put his head in her lap. She might have sort of fainted a bit because she didn't mean to sit, she just did.

Dr. Linn said, "I have to get my phone. Don't move."

Did she think that Jamie had something to do with . . . with that? She couldn't, could she?

Jamie wrapped her arms around Duke. "I'm sorry, Duke. Now I know why you were out. I'm sorry about your owner."

Dr. Linn returned a minute later. She was still talking on the phone.

"Yes, I'm her neighbor, at 1418 48th Street. I have a key to her house, and when she didn't answer I went in. You need to send the police. I think she was killed. . . . Yes, I'll wait right here."

She hung up, typed on her phone, then turned to Jamie. "Are you okay, honey?"

Jamie nodded because she couldn't talk right then.

Dr. Linn held out her hand. "We shouldn't be here right now. This is a crime scene. The police will need to investigate."

Jamie hesitated, then took her hand. Dr. Linn, though petite, was strong and helped her up. "I didn't—I guess—I just wanted to return her dog." Her voice cracked.

"I'm sorry you had to see this."

"You screamed—I didn't know what happened."

She should have run away. Hidden out. No one knew who she was, not really. Jamie was a common name. Why hadn't she lied about her name? Why hadn't she just put Duke in the backyard and walked away?

What were the police going to ask her?

She had a very, very bad feeling that her whole world was going to crumble apart.

Duke pushed his nose against her hand and she scratched him.

III

Detective Gayle Holman interviewed both the neighbor and the teenager who'd found the dead woman's dog. She wasn't buying the kid's story. Something was . . . off.

"What were you doing out after eleven?"

"Walking home."

"You know there's a curfew."

"That's why I was going home."

"Where were you coming from?"

"A friend's house."

"What's your friend's name?"

"Why? I don't know why you're asking me all these questions. I just found the dog last night, took him home because it was late, and brought him back this morning. I was being nice."

"Just answer the question."

"I can't. I don't want to get her in trouble. Her parents weren't home."

"You're going to be in trouble."

"I didn't do anything!"

"Emily Carr was murdered, and you have her dog."

The girl paled. "I didn't hurt anyone. I didn't know her, just saw her when I walked by sometimes."

"Then tell me where you were last night."

"Detective," the deputy coroner said as he approached.

"Stay put," Gayle told the teenager. She moved away so the girl couldn't overhear, and the coroner followed. "What?"

"She's been dead for more than twenty-four hours. I'm guessing closer to forty-eight—the A/C was on, so it's hard to really get a good estimate. We'll know more after the autopsy. Outward appearance of manual strangulation."

"So you're saying what? Thursday afternoon?"

"Morning even. I can't give you an exact time, rigor has come and gone. I would say between early Thursday morning and midafternoon. 6 A.M. to 2 P.M.? That's very rough."

"That girl's lying to me," she mumbled.

"You think she killed the old woman? And returned her dog?"

Gayle had been a cop for twenty-two years, since she was nineteen, and earned her gold shield nearly a decade ago. She'd spent a lot of time with kids in the community—volunteering, coaching a softball team, doing what she could with young teens to keep them out of gangs, off drugs, and in school. With the territory came a lie detector. She knew when the kids were bullshitting her. Most of the time it wasn't serious, and she let it pass. She didn't think the girl was a killer, but she was being unnecessarily evasive.

She left the girl to stew and went to talk to the responding officers.

She'd worked with Officer Riley Knight many times in the past. He was one of the best cops in the field. "What have you learned?"

"A lot. Come out back."

She motioned for Riley's partner to keep his eye on the kid, then walked through the house. Though they'd opened up all the doors and windows to air out the place, it still reeked of the dead.

Emily Carr was a bit of a pack rat, but though cluttered, everything was tidy and clean. Riley said, "Front door was locked—the neighbor confirmed that she unlocked both the dead bolt and main lock when she came in. The back door was unlocked. Half-finished coffee on the table, a plate in the sink with remnants of egg and toast, so I'm guessing she was finished with breakfast."

"I'm with you."

"The dog is a German shepherd mix. Neighbors—not the doctor next door, but the family on the south side—said the dog was barking Thursday morning around ten."

"That's specific."

"The mother—she has two teenage boys who left for school at seven thirty—left the house about ten and heard Duke 'barking his head off.' She was going to talk to Mrs. Carr when she returned, but when she got back at noon, Duke was silent, and she didn't think anything else of it."

"When was the last time anyone saw Mrs. Carr?"

"Dr. Linn called her husband—he's with a patient and can't come right now, but will give a statement at the station later. He's also a doctor. He told his wife he saw Mrs. Carr watering Thursday morning when he left for the hospital. We confirmed with his administrator that he arrived to prep for surgery at seven. But look at this."

Though the kitchen was well-lit, Riley shined his light on the door. There was a faint impression of a partial shoe print, as if someone had kicked the door with the bottom of a sneaker.

"That's good, Knight."

"I aim to please."

"Why haven't you taken the detective exam?"

"I like being a uniformed cop. I leave the detecting to the rest of my family." Riley Knight came from a long line of cops.

"That's not all," he continued. "The door was unlocked. It's been dusted, and CSI has collected evidence from the print, so we're clear."

Still, he didn't remove his gloves and opened the door. "No sign of lockpick or forced entry. But see here?" He gestured to the outside of the door. It had been clawed up—likely by the dog.

"So, the dog is outside, his owner is being attacked, he tries to get in."

"Yes, but something more—the killer didn't exit the way he entered. I sure wouldn't if I'd just killed someone and a dog wanted to bite my head off. There are two other exits—the front door, which was dead-bolted according to Dr. Linn—and a sliding glass door in the den down the hall."

"And that's what he used."

"Yes. It goes to a side patio. On the Linn side of the property, there is clear evidence that he hopped the fence. But there's more."

"You have the killer on video."

He laughed. "No, not yet—but he didn't get into the yard from the side fence. He got in through the *back* fence."

Knight led the way through the deep, narrow backyard that had a small grass area and lots of bushes and trees. The CSI team was collecting evidence at the back fence—a very nice wood-and-brick design. The house behind the Carr home was larger and wider, abutting both Carr's property line and the family to the south.

"Almost done here," the head CSI said. "You were right, Riley— this is how he came in. I can't confirm without testing, but the soil here is similar—and possibly a match to the trace found in the kitchen. And there are recent scuff marks from shoes on both sides of the fence. This brick here? It's loose and recently fell, then was put back. There's a bench on the other side. If the killer used the bench to help leverage himself, he would likely have touched this brick. Maybe it loosened under his weight. He put it back—but I'm going to take it in for trace. Brick is a really shitty surface to get prints from, but we might be able to pull something."

"Would love to get his DNA, too—maybe he cut himself," Gayle said.

The tech laughed. "Only on TV, Detective."

"We need to talk to the owners of that house—they might have surveillance cameras," Gayle said. "Want to join me, Riley?"

"Absolutely. It was bold—jumping over the fence in broad daylight in a neighborhood like this."

"People work. And with all the trees here, he could have been shielded." They walked back toward the house. Gayle saw the hole under the gate. "So the girl wasn't lying. The dog really did dig himself out."

"Lying? The teenager?"

"She was evasive. She pushed my buttons."

"She's fifteen and being questioned by cops. That would make most kids nervous."

"Still—something's up with her. I'm not letting her off the hook yet."

"I have an idea."

"I'm listening."

Gayle listened to Riley's idea, and agreed. "Okay, we'll do it your way." They walked back to where Riley's partner was standing with Dr. Linn and Jamie.

"Jamie," Gayle said, "we can't locate a relative of Mrs. Carr's right now, and Officer Knight is a big animal lover and doesn't want to send Duke to the pound."

His partner snorted. "He can't possibly take another stray in. He has three cats and two dogs as it is."

"It seems that Duke here has bonded with you, Jamie. So we discussed it and agreed that if you want, you can take care of him until relatives have the option of weighing in. If no one wants him, we can help you adopt him."

"Really?" She seemed stunned. "You'd help me?"

"Sure. He likes you, and he just lost his owner. However, he may have seen or smelled whoever killed Mrs. Carr, and there is some precedent for using dogs as witnesses." That was only partly true. Courts were nervous about canine identification.

Gayle squatted in front of Duke. He stared at her. "Duke, I just want to check your paws, okay?" She gently reached down. On the right front paw the claws were worn completely down and two were clearly broken off. "Poor guy."

"What happened?" Jamie asked.

"He was clawing at the back door. When you get home, clean him up, and if they start bleeding take him to the vet."

Jamie's face fell. "Okay."

Riley said, "If you go to the MidTown Vet Clinic on 27th and L, they'll take care of Duke for free." He handed Jamie his card. "Just show them this, I'm friends with the head animal doc there."

"I need your address for the records, and because we'll need to follow up when we find a suspect."

The girl gave her full name—Jamie Blair—and her mother's name, Janice. Her cell number and an address off 65th Street. Definitely a whole world different from the Fabulous Forties.

Gayle wanted to ask her what she was doing on this side of the highway, but didn't. "Okay," she said, "and where do you go to school? Hiram Johnson? St. Francis?"

She snorted. "Johnson."

"Freshman?"

"Sophomore."

"Homeroom teacher?"

"Ms. Fields."

"Okay. We're good here. You want a ride home? It's getting hot, and Duke's paws look sore."

Jamie bit her lip. "I guess."

Gayle sent Riley's partner off to escort the girl, discreetly instructing him to confirm her address; then she and Riley drove around the block to the house in question.

The address was 1407 49th Street. It was a wide, stately home with a large old tree in the front that Gayle would have loved to climb when she was a kid. Knight ran the address. "This is interesting. Officers were called to the house last night for a possible burglary."

"What time?"

"Twelve forty-five. The residents, Cynthia and Brandon Block, returned home shortly after midnight. When Mrs. Block was putting her jewelry away, she noticed that her diamond earrings were missing, along with five hundred dollars she keeps in her jewelry box."

"That's it?"

"When police arrived, Mr. Block said he thought he had an extra credit card in his desk that wasn't there. But all electronics, art, and most jewelry were there. Full inventory pending."

"What kind of thief comes in and just takes a couple things?"

"The earrings were worth twenty thousand dollars."

"You're shitting me. I'll bet she flushed them down the toilet to get the insurance payout," Gayle mumbled.

Murder Thursday morning, then theft Friday night? Could the killer have been staking out the place and thought Mrs. Carr had seen him? If so, why would he kill her for twenty-thousand-dollar earrings? Most thieves would simply avoid the mark, find another. Unless the thief took something that the Blocks didn't report. But then why report the theft at all?

Gayle rang the bell. An attractive, slender woman in her late thirties answered. Even though it was Saturday morning, she was impeccably dressed, with jewelry and makeup. "Mrs. Block?"

"You found my earrings?" she asked hopefully.

"No. We're here about your neighbor, Mrs. Carr."

"Who?"

"She lives in the house behind you. Seventy-nine years old. She was murdered."

Mrs. Block blinked. "Murdered? Oh no. That's awful. Who would do that? I didn't know her well—only talked with her a few times. Emily, I think her name was. She was such a kind older woman."

"Do you have a few minutes?"

"Well, yes, I suppose, though my husband will be home from golf in an hour and we're going out to lunch with friends."

"It won't be long. We believe that the killer may have used your yard to access Mrs. Carr's property."

Mrs. Block shook her head. "Impossible. I was home yesterday morning. I'm sure I would have heard something."

"What about Thursday morning?"

"Thursday? I left at some point for a lunch meeting. I'd have to check my calendar, but I believe I left just before noon."

"So you were home Thursday morning."

"Yes." She frowned. Thinking? Reflecting? Coming up with a lie?

Gayle had been a cop far too long. She was suspicious of everyone. "Do you have security cameras?"

She shook her head. "I couldn't convince my husband that we need them. This can't possibly be a coincidence. The theft. Poor Mrs. Carr."

"We don't know at this point, but may we please inspect your backyard?"

She hesitated. "Okay. Go ahead, but I need to call my husband. He's a lawyer."

Great. A lawyer.

"We already inspected Mrs. Carr's side of the fence and it's clear that someone climbed over from your yard," Riley said.

"This way." Mrs. Block led them down a long hall to a sun room with multiple French doors leading to the backyard. "Please, right through there. I'm just going to call my husband and let him know what's happening."

Gayle and Riley walked outside. The Blocks' backyard wasn't quite as deep as Mrs. Carr's, but it was twice as wide and far more elaborate. A fancy black-bottom swimming pool, covered patio, waterfall, gazebo, long, green grassy area, a stone path that wound around the perimeter. Lots of tasteful decorations, including a stone bench along the back fence where the killer accessed Mrs. Carr's yard. Gayle stopped and inspected the area.

"Bricks. Stone. No footprints," Riley said.

"She was home Thursday morning. She could have seen something, but she didn't say anything."

"An intruder could have gone through the side gate."

"We'll check that next. Did you see what the Blocks have in the house?"

"A lot of stuff."

"Exactly, and that was just what we saw walking out here, yet the thief only took some cash and one pair of earrings? That woman has to have piles of jewelry. Were the diamonds the most expensive? Did the thief know that? Someone she knows? A relative?"

"The property crimes detectives would ask all those questions."

"It feels odd."

"I know the detective who caught the case. I'll call—maybe there's a pattern. Maybe Mrs. Carr's death is related. She might have seen something."

But why was she killed on Thursday if the theft happened the following night? Unless the Blocks didn't notice the missing jewelry until Friday. Maybe they were robbed Thursday morning.

"Thanks, Riley."

Riley stepped to the far side of the yard to make the call, and Gayle inspected the fence and bench. It was marble, with two mates ten feet away on either side. It would be easy enough to jump on the bench and climb over.

She took a couple of pictures, but there was nothing here.

Mrs. Block returned before Riley. "My husband said he wants to help in any way possible. He's heartbroken over Mrs. Carr's death."

"When do your gardeners service the house?"

She seemed surprised at the question. "Tuesdays."

"Any other visitors? Maintenance, pool, guests?"

"Well—I don't think so. My girlfriend stopped by Wednesday to pick up donations for WEAVE, and another friend came by yesterday—we're planning a gala in the spring to benefit pediatric cancer patients. Last night my husband and I were at the theater with friends. That's when we were robbed."

"You're certain the earrings were there Thursday?"

"Yes—I almost wore them Friday night, went back and forth between the diamonds and my emeralds. Picked the emeralds."

"Did you hear Mrs. Carr's dog barking on Thursday?"

"I really couldn't say—there are a lot of dogs in the neighborhood, but our walls are very thick. They rarely bother me."

"No visitors on Thursday?"

"No—my husband came home sometime in the morning because he forgot a file in his office, but I don't remember exactly when."

Riley came over and clearly wanted to talk to Gayle alone. She thanked Mrs. Block and handed the woman her card. "If you think of anything else, please let me know."

"I will. Thank you."

They left, and in Gayle's sedan, Riley burst out, "I talked to the detective in charge. Get this. There's been a string of similar robberies over the last couple of years. All cash, credit cards, and jewels. Nothing over twenty thousand—in fact, the Blocks are the largest score. Most of the thefts were less than five K, but the credit cards have been traced to an ID theft ring the feds are investigating. All the crimes are unsolved. No prints have shown up. There have been sixteen reports over the last three years that match the same MO."

"Which is?"

"Old-fashioned lockpick. Someone who's really good—and has gotten better. In fact, the last few places they didn't connect right away because there was no visible sign of the locks being picked. And the detective thinks sixteen is low—that the thief has probably hit twice that many places, but the victims didn't know they were missing anything. If their ID was stolen, they just dealt with their credit companies."

"No suspects?

"You have one now."

"I do?"

"Jamie Blair."

As soon as Riley said her name, it made sense.

Riley continued, "The target area, according to the lead detective, is 36th to 53rd Streets west to east; J Street to Folsom Boulevard. All walking distance from her house off 65th. She's a nice-looking girl who isn't going to stand out in this neighborhood. The property crimes people have put this on the back burner because the amounts are low. The detective believes that a gang is hitting the houses, young, maybe in their twenties, but they could be off. They also said that because there were no mistakes, they think the places were well staked out, and the thieves know exactly when to go in."

"Who's she working with?"

"No one."

"You just said—"

"That property crimes *thinks* it's a gang. I think it's one smart girl."

Gayle considered. "She found the dog at eleven Friday night. She could have hit the Block house before that, and the barbecue place is definitely between here and her house." She didn't know why she wasn't happy with this news. She didn't want to arrest the girl for burglary. She was fifteen. Send her to juvie? Give her probation? That wasn't really up to Gayle.

"Let's talk to her," Riley said.

"Her life is going to be a mess."

"We don't know that. What we think and what we can prove are two different things. Consider this: She might know what's been going on at the Block house—who's coming and going. I've worked with troubled kids before. That kid is pretty much on her own. I've seen it, you've seen it. Let's see what's what before we make any decisions."

Gayle concurred. "I want to catch Emily Carr's killer, first and foremost. And if Jamie Blair has answers, she'll tell us."

IV

Jamie's mom wasn't home when the officer dropped her off. She was relieved—her mother would have a fit if she was being brought home by a cop.

She made hamburgers for Duke and herself while pondering what she'd overheard at Mrs. Carr's house. The police thought she'd been killed Thursday morning and someone had hopped the back fence that adjoined the house Jamie had robbed. She doubted the owners had realized it yet, but Jamie knew that the wife hadn't been alone Thursday morning. She also knew that there was no way to get into their backyard because the side gate was locked with a combination lock, not a keyed lock. The garage had a side door, and that's the way she went in because it was an easier lock to pick than the front door, not to mention less exposed.

Jamie went to her room and slipped her notebook out from under her mattress. She kept all her notes here when she staked out a place, and then would burn the notebook when she was done. She had to burn this one, too. But first, she wanted to check if her memory was right.

It was. The wife's beefy lover in the black Dodge had been at the house at 9:30 when she'd walked by on Thursday morning. His truck was gone by 11:30. She didn't know when he'd left, but it was between those hours.

She looked back at her notes. He always came on Monday and Thursday mornings during the last two months when she was staking out the street, and the occasional Wednesday. She'd written down his license plate number. He never parked in front of his mistress's house, always three or four houses away, but Jamie knew he went there—she'd watched him several times.

But that didn't mean anything. Did it? Just because the wife was having an affair with the Dodge truck guy didn't mean he killed the old woman. Why would he?

Burn the notebook. Get rid of the earrings.

She bit her lip. "Duke, I'm sorry about your owner, but this is only going to get me in trouble. It's not going to help her."

They didn't have a fireplace, but there was a park a mile away with barbecues and stuff. She'd burned her other notebooks there.

Jamie stuffed everything into her backpack. She'd bury the earrings at the park until the heat died. Her instincts were good, and right now they told her to destroy everything and never talk to the police again. If they wanted the dog, they could have him.

She went outside and opened the garage. As she got her bike out, she saw the police car. It was followed by the detective's car.

Oh shit.

She closed the garage door, locked it, and hopped on her bike as

Officer Knight stepped out of his car. His partner stayed inside. The detective got out of her car.

"Hi," Jamie said, "I need to go do stuff. You're not taking Duke, are you?"

"No, not right now," Officer Knight said, "but we need to talk. Is your mother home?"

"No."

"Do you know when she'll be home?"

Jamie shrugged. "I was just going to the store to get dog food. Can we meet in a couple hours?"

The detective said, "We need to talk now. Let's go inside."

She shook her head. She hated her house. It was a mess, and she was embarrassed. Her neighbors were looking out of their windows. She had always kept a low profile and now? She was the center of attention. Tears burned behind her eyes. For three years no one had suspected she was a thief. Now . . . they knew *something*.

Or was that her guilt? That she was going to burn her notebook that might help them find out who killed Mrs. Carr? She wanted to do the right thing, but she didn't want to get into trouble. She didn't want to be locked up. She just wanted to be left alone.

Detective Holman came up to her. "Jamie, I can help you, if you tell the truth."

She shook her head again.

Duke licked her hand. As if to say everything was going to be all right. But *nothing* was going to be okay.

"Let's go inside," the detective said.

"It's a mess," she whispered.

"Okay."

"The drugs aren't mine. I don't do drugs."

"I believe you."

She took a deep breath, then got off her bike and dropped it to the ground. She unlocked the door and went inside.

Detective Holman and Officer Knight followed her. She'd cleaned the kitchen after lunch, and it was the only place that looked halfway presentable, so she sat at the kitchen table. The cop stood, and the detective sat across from her. She hated the pity in their eyes, because she lived like this.

"I'm going to give you one chance to tell me the truth," the detective said. "If you do, I will do everything in my power to help you. Officer Knight and I have a lot of clout in the department; his brother-in-law is a federal agent and the D.A. is a personal friend of mine. But *you* have to help yourself first."

What did they know? What could she say? How was she going to get out of this?

"I—I don't know what to do."

"The truth. You robbed the Blocks last night. Diamond earrings, some cash, a credit card."

They knew. How had they figured it out so quickly?

"The MO matches sixteen other crimes over three years. But the lead detective thinks there were more that were never reported."

Jamie didn't say anything. She'd robbed forty-five houses over the past three years.

"Based on the evidence, we believe the person who killed Mrs. Carr climbed over the Blocks' fence on Thursday morning at approximately 10 A.M. A neighbor reported that Duke was barking up a storm at about that time, but when she returned a couple hours later, he was silent. We know that the killer came in through the back door—it was unlocked. He left through a sliding glass door on the side of the house, likely because Duke was clawing at the back door. No visible signs of theft. The killer came in, killed her, left. That tells me he knew her."

Officer Knight said, "Her family is out of state. She has no wealth except her home. We don't have a motive. Someone she angered? A thrill killer? If we don't know the motive, it's harder to find him."

"You walk around the neighborhood a lot, don't you?" Detective Holman asked.

She shrugged.

"I don't care about the burglary. I care about finding Emily Carr's killer. And I'll bet if I had a suspect, Duke would know him."

She looked up. "You think so?"

"Based on what we've learned so far? Yes. But I need a direction."

"I'm going to get in big trouble."

"Maybe. But if you help us, I'll help you," the detective said.

Jamie didn't know what to do, but she didn't want a killer to get away.

She reached into her backpack and pulled out her notebook. "I was going to burn it. It's going to put me in jail."

"You're fifteen and have no record—I already ran you." She held out her hand.

Jamie handed her the notebook. The detective and cop read it, both clearly surprised.

"This is very detailed," Officer Knight said.

She shrugged.

"It's confusing," Holman said.

"It's not in chronological order—the number at the top is the address, then days and patterns. I'm good at recognizing patterns. It's just my own shorthand. But I know what you want." She flipped to the page for the Blocks' house. "I'm not good with names, but I know numbers and patterns. A black Dodge truck was at the house every Monday and Thursday morning since I started, um, walking down the street regularly. Sometimes other days, but every Monday and Thursday. Always gone before noon. I figured that the wife was having an affair because he parked down the street. She let him in. That's his license plate number."

"Can you swear that he was there Thursday morning?"

"He was at 9:30 that morning, when I first walked by. When I came back at 11:30 he was gone. That's what that check mark is for, the pattern."

"I'll run him," Knight said and walked out of the duplex.

Jamie looked at her hands. She was done.

"Hey," the detective said.

"I'm not sorry," Jamie said. "I'm sorry I was caught."

"At least you're honest."

"I never took a lot."

"That's why you stayed under the radar for so long."

"Just—just enough to get by. My mom's on disability."

"Your dad?"

"Ditto. But he's not around much. Don't even know where he lives most of the time."

"You don't have to stay here."

"Where would I go?" Now she was angry. "Foster care? Really? I'd never get out of the system. My mom isn't a bad person. She doesn't beat me or anything. She's just lazy and thinks she's a victim of everything. I don't care. I just have three years and I can leave. I took what I absolutely needed to make sure the rent was paid and stuff. I never hurt anyone. And Duke needs me. He doesn't have anyone, either. He's not a young puppy that everyone wants. He's an old mutt." Now the tears were coming, and she couldn't stop them.

"Honey, listen to me. I promised I will help you."

Knight came back in. "Randall Franklin. He owns a gym in midtown—the same gym that Cynthia Block has a membership to."

"Were they in on it together?" Holman asked.

"She had to have let him in the house," Knight said. "She already admitted that she was home that morning."

"Why would she want to kill her neighbor?" Holman thought about it.

"Maybe she didn't know," Knight said.

"Still, why? What's the motive?"

Jamie found the conversation fascinating, and a bit scary. "But you think Duke can identify him."

"Duke—and you. How about a ride along?"

"You're not arresting me?"

"Not now, but you'll have to come clean, then the D.A. will need to make the final decision. But like I said, the D.A. and I go way back. He's tough, but fair—especially with teenagers."

She didn't know what was going to happen, but if she could help put Emily Carr's killer in prison, she would do it.

V

Thanks to Riley Knight, they located Randall Franklin at his gym. He hadn't fled—maybe Block hadn't warned him after all.

Gayle was nervous about bringing a kid into this, but Jamie said she'd recognize him, and they had spotted his car in the lot behind the gym. He was here.

"Officer Knight and his partner are going to stay outside and out of sight." Gayle had already taken off her blazer and pulled her blouse out of her slacks so it wasn't obvious she was a cop. She shifted her holster to the small of her back to better conceal it. "We're going in with Duke. But he has to be leashed. We don't want him to go full-on attack dog, and based on how he destroyed that door, I think that's a possibility."

"He killed Duke's owner." The girl scratched the dog behind the ears as she clipped on a leash Gayle had bought at the CVS down the street. "I'm ready."

Gayle walked into the gym first, the A/C hitting her full force. Jamie followed with Duke. Gayle had only an old DMV photo of Franklin and didn't immediately spot him, but Jamie said, "I see him. He's in the back."

As soon as Jamie spoke, Duke growled and started barking. The teen held the dog back.

Franklin looked over at them, then immediately ran. Gayle said into her radio, "He's heading out back!" She ordered Jamie to stay, then grabbed Duke's leash and ran through the gym. She had one shot.

Franklin was fast. Gayle followed, saw the emergency exit slam shut, and went that way. She burst out in time to see Franklin go around the corner.

She could get into serious trouble for this, but Riley was still down the street. She unclipped the leash. "Get him, Duke!"

She ran after the sprinting dog as he pursued Franklin to his truck. Franklin couldn't even get the door closed before Duke leaped up and sank his teeth into the killer's arm.

"Shit! Oh fuck! Get him off me!" Franklin screamed in pain.

Gayle caught up with Duke. "Randall Franklin," she said, slightly out of breath. "You're under arrest for the murder of Emily Carr."

"Get him off me! Get him off!"

Gayle ordered Duke to let go, but the dog wouldn't. Dammit, this wasn't going as she'd planned.

Jamie did exactly what Gayle told her not to, and came around the corner. "Jamie! Get back!" Gayle pulled her gun. She didn't want to shoot the dog, but if his teeth got into Franklin's neck—she couldn't let the dog kill her suspect.

"Don't shoot him!" Jamie screamed.

Riley and his partner came screeching to a stop behind the idling truck.

"Duke! Come!" Jamie shouted, running toward the truck. Gayle put her hand out to stop her.

The dog let go of Franklin's arm, then the bastard kicked the animal. Duke yelped and fell to the ground. As Franklin was about to kick him again, Gayle said, "Don't you dare! Hands up where I can see them!"

Riley cuffed Franklin and read him his rights. Jamie knelt by Duke. He had blood on his mouth from biting the suspect and was trying to get up, but limped.

"He's hurt," Jamie said. "Please, we have to take him to the vet."

"We do. Because we now have solid evidence tying Randall Franklin to the murder of Emily Carr." Gayle smiled. "And as soon as the DNA comes back from the dog's mouth and victim's neck, I think we can look at murder one." She said to Franklin, "No jury is going to let you off for strangling a seventy-nine-year-old woman."

"I-I-I—" he stammered. "I want a lawyer."

"My pleasure."

VI

Two weeks later, Jamie told the district attorney everything. She didn't want to—she was scared that everything Detective Holman had told her was a lie. That she was going to juvenile detention. That she would be in serious trouble.

But the D.A. told her that if she kept her nose clean and testified against Randall Franklin, plus turned over all the information she knew about the identity theft ring and her jewelry fence, she wouldn't see any jail time. "We'll call it super-secret probation."

"What?"

"If I put probation on your record, then you'll be in the system." He glanced at Detective Holman. "Gayle told me about your home situation. I can get you into a group home."

"No. My mom can't take care of herself."

"But you took care of her by stealing."

She bit her lip. That was true. She didn't know what to do.

"Your mother has to be able to provide for you. You can't steal for her," Holman said.

"I'll get a job. A real job."

"Harder at fifteen, but I like where your head is at. And I think I have something for you." The D.A. handed her a business card. "They're dog groomers and run a dog hotel. They normally don't hire minors, but I know the owner well, and you're old enough for a work permit. It won't be glamorous—a lot of cleaning up after the dogs— but it's a real job, and you're good with animals." He glanced down to where Duke was lying next to her. She had been so worried about him after Franklin kicked him. One of his ribs was broken, but the vet said he was healing fine.

"I just need your word that your thieving days are over. Once a month Gayle or Officer Knight will check in with you, make sure everything is okay."

She turned to the detective. "Why would you do that for me?"

"You did the right thing even though you knew you could get into serious trouble. And you returned the diamonds."

"Why did he do it?" she asked them.

"He's not talking—though I have a plea meeting with his attorney for later today."

Holman said, "We've pieced together some information from what

Mrs. Block said. He used the fence to leave a couple of times when Mr. Block made an unexpected stop home. Mrs. Block said Emily Carr made a comment a few weeks ago about how she needed to put an end to the shenanigans—Emily's word—because Mr. Block was a good man who provided well for her. Mrs. Block dismissed it—but told Randall Franklin. He confessed to her that the woman had seen him a couple of times. That Thursday, he left through the back. Mrs. Block claims she didn't remember when we asked her."

"You don't believe her!"

"No, but I don't think she thought he had killed Mrs. Carr."

"She admitted to the affair, and that she was trying to keep it from her husband," Holman added.

"I think he panicked," the D.A. said. "Brandon Block has a reputation for suing people who make him mad, and Randall doesn't have a lot of money. He didn't want to lose his gym or house, and I suspect Mrs. Carr saw him that morning and gave him a tongue lashing. Dr. Linn confirmed that Mrs. Carr always spoke her mind."

"He snapped," Holman said. "And he will pay for it."

"I really don't like people very much," Jamie said.

"Sometimes, I don't either."

Detective Holman walked her and Duke out of the D.A.'s office. "I asked Officer Knight to take you home. Is everything okay with your mother?"

"She's not happy, but I don't think she's ever been happy."

"Don't let her unhappiness rub off on you. You have a lot of potential, Jamie. You just have to see it."

"Thank you for doing what you said you would."

"Thank you for helping us put a bad guy in prison. You and Duke." Holman bent down and scratched the dog. "You two make a great team."

Songbird Blues

I

It was 1959. Rayne Burns had been gone for three days, and Mister Ridge could still hear her singing in the night, in his sleep. He hoped he hadn't strangled her.

When Rayne Burns sang a song, her voice sounded like brandy pouring from a bottle; a warm, husky flow you'd happily be swept up in. She made you forget. She made you come alive. And Mister Ridge had drowned in her.

We worked at the Rumpus Room—a joint on 57th Street. The doors opened at nine, but nothing really took off until around midnight, once the liquor tide had come in. It was on such a night, two weeks earlier, that Mister Ridge had first heard the voice of the angel.

Two Weeks Earlier . . .

Left. I was vamping, a slow, steady groove down at the bottom end of the piano. Key of A minor.

Right. My brother, up at the other end of the keyboard, was picking out little patterns of melody in the pentatonic, with the occasional blue note. He was good with that, little improvised runs to offset my bass progression.

The piano keyboard was a long, narrow river of variables: eighty-eight keys and almost infinite ways to play them. Get one note wrong and everyone knew it.

My brother and I both worked for Mister Ridge. When he sat at the piano, our job was to play the true notes.

Rayne Burns walked out onto the club's little stage. Red dress and red heels. She walked up to the microphone and into the spotlight, and we went into Gershwin's "Summertime." And it was summertime, and she could sing, and everyone in the room knew it. Only O'Neill, the drummer, had heard her before; he had stood his paycheck on her voice. The band's previous singer had had to be let go (she'd been on the needle one too many times). O'Neill grinned like a cat. He traded a satisfied nod with Hooper on the double bass and with Mister Ridge on the piano. The new girl had the pipes.

"Is there hot water in this building?" Rayne asked the next afternoon, an undercurrent of Irish in her accent. She stood on the staircase of our rooming house, her thin arms wrapped around a bag of groceries, her two hands held flat against it. Her fingers were slender and smooth. Delicate. They had never seen hard work. They didn't need to. Her voice was her work.

"I know this is an old building, but I only get cold water," she said. "And it looks like it flows out of the East River."

The building dated back to 1880; the pipes were all shot to hell. We'd all had problems. She needed to talk to Frobisher, the building's supervisor. He lived down on the ground floor.

She knew him. She had taken the vacant room on the third, the same floor as O'Neill. The drummer had gotten her the gig with the band and had found her a place to stay. He was good with that.

I reached out to carry her bag.

She was fine.

Mister Ridge walked up with her.

"I like the way you play," she said. There was sincerity.

My brother and I were proud.

Mister Ridge paused when we got to her floor. There was no more talking, just that no-words communication that exists between musicians. *The knowing.* We had played together only one night, but we were already in tune, and we were liking it.

She went into her room.

Mister Ridge went up to ours, up on the fourth.

"Who is the girl?" the woodpecker asked. "She's cute." Jack Staines (the "woodpecker") had been creeping down the staircase; he had been watching.

The woodpecker's hands smelt of soap and hung motionless at his sides. His fingers were clean, *always clean,* and red, as though they had been scrubbed under hot water for long periods. The nails were chewed.

I didn't like Staines. Thirty-two, and he'd inherited the building from his grandfather. He lived up on the fifth, above us all, and he knew it.

Mister Ridge left him on the stairs and went into our room.

That night at the Rumpus Room, the band cooked. Rayne held the small crowd in her grip as she tore through the songbook: "Misty," "Funny Valentine," "Stormy Weather," "Fever." She brought the microphone over to the piano and sang "Black Coffee" to us directly. Lady Day in heaven, hear the angel and smile. And when it came around to Mister Ridge's solo, my brother and I took over, and baby, we are a beautiful pair. My brother is indifferent to most things, mostly to me, but when we're together on a keyboard, we go to work. Left hand, right hand. The hot notes.

"I'm a bride of the wind," Rayne said.

She drank some more. We were seated with her in a coffee shop two blocks from our building. I held a cigarette. My brother was a drinker; he held a cup of joe with a jolt of whiskey. We had been there for two hours. Dawn was staggering in with a yawn, rubbing the night-time out of its eyes.

"I had a kid," Rayne said. "Back in Los Angeles." And, after a pause: "I still have her fourth birthday present. It's still wrapped."

She put a hand on the table, facedown.

My brother instinctively reached out and cupped it.

"After she died, I took a Greyhound east, and I haven't been back."

Many times I wished Mister Ridge had been left-handed. I so badly wanted to comfort her, to touch her skin, to feel the heat of her body. I had to make do with nonchalantly nursing our cigarette and feeling the heat of the tobacco.

Rayne kissed Mister Ridge on the staircase at floor three. I got my chance. I reached out and took her right hand. Her fingers were the cherished notes made flesh.

She said good night.

For the next two weeks, Mister Ridge's blood flowed in a major key. He felt good. The band was good, life was good. The whole damned world was good.

And then the angel vanished.

Friday night, and she didn't show up at the club for work. She didn't answer her door when it was knocked, and Frobisher wouldn't open it; she'd paid her rent a month in advance, it was her business what she did.

The night was a wreck.

My brother and I did the thing with the needle: the sweet syrup into the vein and into the soul. Mister Ridge took the hit. He lay back on the bed and thought about the moon and the stars and the end of the universe. And the angel.

There had been no message, no explanation, no reason. She was just gone, plain and simple.

· · ·

Now . . .

Mister Ridge woke up.

Rayne had been singing "Summertime" again, and it sounded like she had been right there in the room. She wasn't. She had been gone for three days, and Mister Ridge hoped he hadn't strangled her.

We helped him sit up.

It was moments before daybreak. A bus passed by down in the street. Mister Ridge climbed off the bed, and my brother and I shut the window. We were lit up in the on/off of the red neon that ran down the edge of the building across the street:

D

R

U

G

S

The last Mister Ridge could remember of Rayne had been a kiss; standing in the hall outside her room three days earlier. It had been the last he had seen of her; the last anyone had seen of her. A wet kiss and tight embrace. In the short space of two weeks, they had become close friends. In that moment, they had become lovers. He knew she soon would have opened her door and let him inside.

Mister Ridge thought again about the photograph of the kid: a postcard-sized photograph, black-and-white, not quite in focus. A kid on a swing in a park.

That wasn't right.

My brother and I helped Mister Ridge put on his clothes. We buttoned up his shirt and tied his shoelaces. We lit a cigarette, and I held it.

Mister Ridge went looking for Frobisher. The building supervisor could damn well unlock Rayne's door and let us look in her room. Maybe she was in there? Maybe she'd been hurt?

I didn't like Frobisher, and neither did my brother. Frobisher had pudgy workman's hands—rough and raw. They were never calm. They fidgeted. The right playing with the left, tugging, forever pulling at loose skin.

Frobisher wasn't in his little office on the ground floor. There was a little, dirty glass window that looked out into the lobby and to the mailboxes. His face wasn't in it. He wasn't in his room, either; it connected to his office by a door. He had a big set of keys, duplicates of every key in the building—we couldn't find it. All we found was an unmade bed, a pinup magazine under it, and a little wooden figurine of a monkey.

Mister Ridge went up to the third floor and to Rayne's door.

I knocked.

There was no answer.

Locked or not, I was going to open it.

I put the cigarette in Mister Ridge's mouth, and I took a slender tuning fork out of his pocket together with a nail file.

My brother was hesitant. He didn't like this kind of work. He didn't like to have to concentrate. He was all about passion and the spur of the moment. He had a streak of violence to him that was like a thunderbolt. He'd rather have simply punched the door open, despite the damage to his manicure.

I forced the nail file into his palm.

I slid the tuning fork into the keyhole and waited. Tricking a lock was like playing ragtime; it only sounded the hell like ragtime if there were two hands on the keyboard.

He joined me. Hesitation be damned, he wanted to get into that room, too.

My brother looked down on everything I did. I was the bottom end of the keyboard; the chord progressions and the bass lines. *The under work.* He was of the noble notes, the melody, the ethereal above. I was just his counterpoint.

We concentrated. Together, with several flicks of his file and the counterpunch of my fork, we unlocked the door and went into the room.

Rayne wasn't there.

The photograph Mister Ridge had remembered was pinned to the wall above the dresser. A single pin. A picture of a little girl in a park on a swing. Rayne's kid.

Rayne's room was the same as our own: single window, bare wood floor, green wallpaper that dated back to the nineteenth century, and a faded picture of a sunflower by that van Gogh fellow hung on the wall. Mister Ridge had the same cheap print on the wall in his room. Every room in the building probably had the sunflower.

Rayne's room didn't make sense. Clothes still hung in the closet. Personals were still spread out across the top of the dresser: lipstick, powder compact, hair brush. If she had gone, she'd taken nothing other than the matching red dress and high-heeled shoes she wore on stage when she sang at the Rumpus Room.

At the bottom of the wastepaper basket next to the dresser lay a little wooden figurine of a bird. I plucked it out. The woodpecker had made it. Everyone in the building had a custom-made, wooden sculpture of an animal. That's how the woodpecker saw us all. Animals.

Where was Rayne's suitcase?

We found it under the bed. I reached under and dragged it out. My brother and I opened it. Inside lay a small parcel wrapped in pale pink paper and bound in a bow. It had the dimensions and weight of maybe a coloring book. The kid's fourth birthday present.

Mister Ridge sat on the end of the bed and took a final inhale on the cigarette. I dropped it to the floor, and he stamped it out with his heel.

As he looked up, he caught sight of a mirror, a little shard of reflection that hung on a nail. Ridge saw himself. Immediately I rose to cover his eyes. My brother did, too. With both of us in the way, he couldn't see himself no more. Mister Ridge didn't like looking in mirrors. He didn't like being reminded he was alone.

We dropped away after a few moments, and he stared instead at the photograph pinned to the wall.

He had a moment of clarity.

The story everyone had been buying had been that Rayne had pulled out and moved on—the bride on the wind. The story was wrong. She wouldn't have walked out without taking the photo.

Mister Ridge had a second moment of clarity. He wondered how he had known about it, how he had known it was pinned to her wall. He hadn't ever been inside her room before.

For a moment, he remembered my brother and me tightening our grip around a neck.

He hoped we hadn't strangled her.

He really did.

II

"She was an overnight girl," O'Neill said. "She's over you in a night and gone the next day. We cats see them come and go all the time."

He gripped his glass of gin with annoyance. He had powerful arms and strong hands with big fingers. And if he had laid any of them on the angel, we'd have broken all of them.

The drummer lost himself in thought. He drummed those big fingers on the table.

I smoked a cigarette.

The late afternoon sun had no chance of entering the Rumpus Room—no windows. The club didn't open until nine, but the bar was open to musicians. Musicians lived outside the clock.

O'Neill's drumming slowed to a faint, unsteady, no-tempo tap of his index finger.

"Our world is changing, my friend," he said. He was almost talking to himself. He took another drink. Tight grip.

Mister Ridge remembered my brother and me taking a tight grip around a neck. He remembered the struggle, and then the relaxation at the slump. As I've said, my brother has a temper. Sometimes, all I could do was to join in and help out. It was better that way for Mister Ridge. It was better for all of us.

"It's this new music," O'Neill said. "It's been bubbling away for a couple of years, and now it's starting to bubble over."

He meant that popular music, that upbeat blend of country and blues the radio stations were all pushing, with those three-minute slices of cheerfulness the kids were all loving.

"You've noticed our crowds are getting smaller, and that they're not getting any younger?"

We had noticed.

"This is the bottom of 1959," he said. "I started playing back in the '20s. I can't play that young music. I only know the old music; the old grooves are the only ones I understand."

He drank another mouthful.

"One day, you and me, we're gonna be gone, man. Just like the girl."

The band played again that night, but it wasn't the same without the girl. Hooper, the bass player, filled in on vocal duties. He was adequate, but it was like comparing lemonade to liquor. The word was put out for a new singer, a new girl, someone as good as Rayne. You may as well go try and catch a falling star.

"Why is Staines called the woodpecker?" asked a man seated on the staircase.

Mister Ridge had just come in the front door of our building. It was after three in the morning.

The man climbed to his feet and held out a badge: DETECTIVE FULTON, 19TH PRECINCT. He was left-handed.

He was called the woodpecker because he was a conceptual artist and his medium was wood. He spent all day up on that top floor of his with few ideas and a lot of lumber. Whittling it, sawing it, nailing it, maybe even eating it, who knew what conceptual artists got up to in the middle of the night?

"You're Ridge, ain't you? The piano player?"

Detective Fulton had two fingers missing from his right hand. He reported that Frobisher had put in a phone call to the police the night Rayne disappeared. Apparently, the building super actually had been concerned about her disappearance.

"You had a thing going on with the songbird, didn't you?" Fulton poked a half-finger. "Frobisher told me. He said he saw you two come in and out together a few times."

Mister Ridge didn't deny it.

The detective wanted to look in our room; apparently, detectives also lived outside the clock. We had nothing to hide that hadn't already been hidden. We took him up to the fourth floor and let him in. He looked under the bed and in the closet. He opened drawers. He picked up some sheet music and remarked that his sister could play. He never said what.

The detective's hands were rough and old, the fingers callused. There was no music in those fingers, no art, no passion, only the cold of winter.

"If you ask me," he said, "I'd say your songbird was murdered."

We damn well did ask.

He showed us, up in Rayne's room.

Across the floor ran a faint, parallel set of scuff marks, about two feet apart. They ran out into the hall, went along to the stairs, and then disappeared.

"Your songbird didn't walk out of this room," the detective said. "She was dragged out."

Mister Ridge heard Rayne in his sleep. She was singing "Summertime" again. He tossed. One note was wrong. It was flat.

He woke up.

There was no singing.

He felt nauseous, and it wasn't from the hit of the sweet syrup we'd given him an hour earlier. It was from the memory of our grip. An intense grip. Around a throat. The struggle, and then the slump.

On the bedside table stood the little wooden figurine of the bird.

It was on/off red in the neon from across the street. Next to it stood a little wooden wolf.

Detective Fulton returned in the morning with two burly uniforms, and the three flatfoots got their hands all over everything: picking up, pulling out, prodding, and poking. They looked in all the rooms and under all the beds. They opened every closet and pulled out every drawer. They made so much commotion that the woodpecker came down out of his lair and sniffed angrily.

And they found nothing.

There were two rooms to every floor. The second on ours was retained by Carnaby, a traveling bible salesman who'd been out of town for a week. His was a room stacked full of the Good Word.

The floor above us, the fifth, the top floor, was the woodpecker's domain. He lived in one room and used the second as his studio. We'd heard he'd knocked a doorway-sized hole through an adjoining wall to link the two.

Rayne's room was on the floor below us, the third. She shared the floor with O'Neill.

One of the rooms on the second floor lay vacant, and the other was the domicile of old man Norwood: an Englishman, a writer, a veteran of the Great War, and a drunk. His hands were covered with cat scratches, and he'd been drunk since 1933. He didn't even know there were other floors above him. His cat was a Persian named Ramses.

There were two rooms on the ground floor: Frobisher had the one with the connecting office, and the second was full of lumber, which belonged to the wunderkind on the top floor, whose only real claim to the arena of the arts was that he had once given Jackson Pollock a cigarette on 42nd Street.

The cops didn't find Rayne. Their dirty fingers found nothing more than eighty odd years of dust, a half-chewed copy of *The Naked and the Dead*, bad plumbing, and Frobisher's photographic studio in the basement. He took pinup pictures down there; we all knew that. And Frobisher was missing. Apparently, there were laws against taking photographs of naked women with their legs spread open. How about that?

We played "Summertime" that night as an instrumental. It gave my brother a chance to show off. He was good with that. Nobody wanted to sing it, anyhow.

Why the wrong note?

It had been eating me. Why would a dream sing one note off-key? What kind of subconscious message was that? What was Mister Ridge's mind trying to tell us?

"Have you seen Frobisher?" the woodpecker asked. Apparently, woodpeckers didn't sleep, either. It was after two in the morning, Mister Ridge had just come into the building, and he was at the foot of the stairs.

We hadn't seen Frobisher. No one had. And the police would have liked to.

My brother and I helped the woodpecker carry some lengths of wood up to his studio; ordinarily, it was one of Frobisher's duties. Mister Ridge offered. We hadn't been up to the top floor, and we wanted to look.

On the way up the stairs, the woodpecker answered the question that everyone who had ever entered the building had wanted to know: *Why wood?*

"I lived in Paris for two years and learned how to paint," he explained. "I came back to New York and rented a studio in Queens. I painted pictures of everything: sunsets, sunrises, naked women reclining, tables laid out with fruit, leather-bound books, and smoldering candles. And every time I finished a picture, do you know what my biggest problem was? How to frame it. Big frame? Small? Plain? Ornate? I undertook a journey of discovery to find the perfect picture frame and, after many months, I discovered what I had been truly looking for: The frame itself. *The wood.* It had been right there all along. Wood is natural, malleable, beautiful, and honest. You see, the frame is the most important part of the picture; it captures whatever you put inside it. It *keeps* it. It has more power and potency to capture and retain perfection than any pretty picture of a canal in Venice, haystack in a field, or bowl of rotting fruit on a table. From that day out, wood became my medium. I had found my artistic truth."

The man was truthfully nuts.

And his studio smelled of soap.

His studio had the same dimensions and layout as our room, only it was stripped of furniture and was a forest of timber, with great abstract chunks of it laid about. And about the only thing these objets d'art looked truly in danger of capturing and retaining was wood rot. And yes, there was a hole in the wall leading into the neighboring room.

We left him.

Mister Ridge went back down to the third and to Rayne's room. Her door was open. He went in and sat on the edge of her bed.

He stared at the photograph of the little girl.

He felt nauseous.

I clawed the edge of the bed. My brother did, too.

Mister Ridge knew he'd seen the photo before; he knew we'd been in Rayne's room *before* he had supposedly gone into her room for the first time.

The sweet syrup don't make the world so clear, or so fluid, or ordered.

He remembered a neck. He remembered my brother and me strangling.

He closed his mind to it.

He remembered Rayne's face; her dark eyes. He wanted to remember that. Nothing else.

What had we done with her body?

He went back up to our room, and my brother and I did the thing with the needle. Mister Ridge took the hit. He lay on the floor and remembered her eyes. Her dark eyes. And her voice. And the taste of her lips. And the next morning she sang "Summertime" again. With a wrong note.

III

"I figure it's either you or the drummer."

Mister Ridge didn't recognize the voice. He rolled onto his back; we were still on the floor of our room. The first stabs of daybreak slid through the window.

A man lit a cigarette—two fingers missing. He was seated on the edge of the bed. He blew out the match and tossed it onto the floor.

It was Detective Fulton.

"Both you and the drummer knew her," he said. "You both worked with her. You were both intimate with her."

How did he figure that?

On the floor next to my brother lay the needle and the other tools of the sweet syrup: the spoon, the cigarette lighter, the bootlace we used for a tie-off, and a little puffy ball of dirty cotton wool. My brother quietly hid the equipment in his pocket.

"You put a woman like that in a building with a bunch of men like you and, sooner or later, you'll kill each other. Or her."

Why?

"Because a woman like that never gives a man what he wants."

I wanted to give the detective a smack in the mouth.

"O'Neill has a rap sheet. He did a nine-month stretch back in the '30s on an assault charge. But my money is on you."

Fulton pointed a half-finger.

"Six years ago, a wife beater was strangled in San Francisco. You were in the picture: a close friend with a passable alibi. The wife still speaks highly of you. The file is still open."

Like I said, my brother had a temper.

"And you're a heroin user. Most of you jazz heads are."

The half-finger was still pointing.

"Why did you kill the girl?"

My brother and I helped Mister Ridge into a sitting position. He wanted another hit of the sweet syrup, but it wasn't a sensible course of action in the present company.

"I also know that Carnaby, that bible peddler across the hall, peddles more than just the word of the Lord to the people. I've had people watching him since April. Did you know he disappeared off the map a week ago? I suspect he knew we were closing in. And Frobisher's reporting the songbird's disappearance gave us the probable cause to walk in and take a look through his sock drawer. Did you know that half of those bibles he's got stacked up in his room are hollowed out?"

We didn't.

"Is that what happened to the girl? Did she get caught up in his narcotics racket?"

She knew nothing about Carnaby.

Fulton shut up. Something had snagged his attention. He put his cigarette into his mouth. He got off the bed and walked over to the closet; the door was wide open, with Mister Ridge's meager assortment of attire on display.

Fulton ran two fingers and a thumb up the spine of the doorway.

The closet was a walk-in kind. You could hang your clothes, throw in your hat and shoes, with room enough for a couple of boxes and odds and ends.

"Would you say that all the rooms in this building are identical in their layout?"

They appeared to be.

"How come the bible peddler's room don't have a closet?"

This thought was significant enough to propel the detective out into the hall and over to Carnaby's door. He unlocked it; he had Frobisher's master set of keys.

He went inside and over to the wall where the sunflower hung. He ran his hands over the wall's surface. He found hinges. It wasn't a wall. The door and frame to the room's closet had been removed and a board had been put in their place to conceal the closet's opening; suitably wallpapered over and with the picture hung. The detective's hands sought a way to open it.

We had followed. We knew what he was looking for: Carnaby's drugs.

"The songbird was just a distraction," he said, intimately running his fingers across the green wallpaper.

We didn't think so.

"A nickel and dime murder to fill up my time sheet. No one really cares what happened to her."

We did.

"Carnaby's narcotics racket is what we're really interested in. The girl was just a pretty little thing that could hold a note."

My brother grabbed the detective and slammed him against the wall and went for his throat. I had no option but to help; within a second, the detective would collect his senses and his hands would start fighting, or going for his gun.

My brother and I did the strangling thing.

Struggle.

Hold.

Hold tight against the struggle.

Hold long.

Slump.

Release.

Mister Ridge didn't like what we had done.

We dragged the detective's corpse away from the foot of the wall and we opened it. We knew how. We knew where the groove lay.

Hidden inside Carnaby's closet lay a cornucopia of pharmaceutical delight: Benzedrine, laudanum, reefer, Turkish opium, the sweet syrup, and who knew what else?

And *Frobisher.*

Mister Ridge had forgotten about that.

He had been of a mind to hide the detective's body inside the closet, but the building's supervisor was already in there, and the air was going off fast.

Mister Ridge remembered: There had been an argument in Rayne's room; we'd made Frobisher unlock it the day after she'd disappeared.

She hadn't been in there.

Frobisher hadn't liked being told what to do. And he'd said some things about Rayne that would have been better off staying inside his head. He'd said he'd have liked to have gotten his hands all over her. He'd said specifically where.

Mister Ridge remembered my brother and me at his neck. We had just about broken it. We had then dragged his body out of Rayne's room and up to our floor; Carnaby's secret closet had been the perfect hiding place for it.

I gathered up some more of the sweet syrup for Mister Ridge and put it into my pocket.

Two bodies inside the closet would smell it up even worse; they'd smell it down in the street. We put the wall panel back into place. There was a furnace down in the basement, which was an even better idea.

It was daybreak; no one was awake in the building. We dragged the detective out of the room (Mister Ridge noticed the faint scuff marks his heels left behind). We dragged the body down the stairs and, on the way down, Mister Ridge began to remember that we had gone this way before.

He thought of Rayne.

It was the most logical thing to do to get rid of a body. Burn it. Why store it in a closet, when you could simply drag it down to the furnace and burn it from existence?

Mister Ridge's head throbbed: *Why had we strangled her?*

We dragged the detective across the concrete of the basement and up to the boiler, and I opened the metal, soot-black furnace door.

There was already a body inside. The smell of it was overpowering.

It wasn't Rayne.

It was *Carnaby*.

He and his nicotine-stained fingers had been in there for more than a week. Unburnt. Mister Ridge remembered that we had needed to buy some accelerant. He remembered there had been an argument with Carnaby about the sweet syrup and its price.

The cops hadn't looked in the furnace. They'd come down to the basement, found Frobisher's photographic equipment and proof sheets of pretty little things and had quit. Anyway, they'd been looking for the man's drugs, not his corpse. Or the corpse of a pretty little thing that could hold a note.

Mister Ridge turned away. He slumped to the floor next to the dead detective and his brain burned.

Why had we strangled her?

What had we done with her body?

Mister Ridge cried.

I didn't know the answers, either. The sweet syrup messes with the clock and the memory of us all.

My brother reached into his pocket and brought out the needle and other tools. I reached into mine.

We did the thing. We all loved the thing.

None of us wanted to think about what might have happened to Rayne, the sweetest girl we had ever known. A girl we'd have given our life for.

Why her?

Mister Ridge took the hit.

He was as far down as he could go.

He lay on the cold concrete floor of the basement and dreamed of our angel.

But he didn't hear her singing. Instead, he heard a typewriter. *Clack, clack, clack.* And then old man Norwood telling his cat to get off the sofa. The sounds were faint, but distinguishable. They were from a room two floors above; traveling down through the plumbing, down through the guts of the building.

The pipes!

Mister Ridge sat up.

Dreams didn't sing *wrong* notes.

We helped him climb to his feet. Raw instinct took him up the stairs, all the way up to the fifth floor, and I knocked on the wood-pecker's studio door.

There was no answer. It was locked. My brother punched it open, and we went inside.

There was no one in the studio.

We went through into the adjoining room. There was no one there either; there wasn't even a bed, just a table and chairs. Where did the woodpecker sleep?

My brother gripped me. He was as desperate as I was. We could feel Mister Ridge's blood pumping.

The daybreak sun struck strong through the windows and cast streaks of yellow through the rooms.

For a moment, all was still.

Silent.

And then the voice of the angel . . . "Summertime."

It wasn't a dream. Rayne was singing, and she was somewhere on that floor. Mister Ridge walked about the two rooms, trying to work out where.

He quickly determined her voice was coming from above. And supposedly only the roof was above floor five, but it didn't sound at all like she was up there, outside. She sounded as though she was inside the building.

The sunflower.

There was no closet in the woodpecker's studio. There was just a wall: green wallpaper and the sunflower. My brother and I found the grooves. It was the same score as down in Carnaby's room: a wallpapered wooden panel on hinges. My brother and I pried it open, and Rayne's voice became louder. Inside the closet lay a narrow staircase that went up to another floor.

Mister Ridge climbed the stairs.

The next floor up was a world of wood; a nonexistent floor between floor five and the roof. The windows were a series of slots of stained glass, architectural flourishes at the top of the building. They let in daylight and, caught in the shafts of the morning yellow, stood the angel. She was dressed in her red dress and red heels. Singing "Summertime." And it was. And she was dirty, and her dress was dirty.

And she was in a cage, a large wooden cage built into the room, floor, attic, or whatever the architect had labeled the place. And the woodpecker lay asleep in his bed in front of it, dreaming a contented sleep as his songbird greeted the new day, caught and kept in his perfect wooden frame.

Rayne saw us. Her dirty hands gripped the wood of the cage's bars. The wrong notes had been on purpose. She'd hoped we'd hear. She'd been waiting.

We woke the woodpecker.

We made him unlock the padlock keeping Rayne captive.

She stepped out.

There were no words; just two musicians and the unspoken knowing of where the song was going.

Rayne's hands tore strips from her dress, and she gagged the woodpecker. My brother and I led him into his cage, and we nailed his hands to the floor. He didn't like that.

We put the padlock back in place.

We put the sunflower back on the wall.

We left the building.

Rayne was free; she was back on the wind. She flew from the city, and we flew with her.

Security

JEFFERY DEAVER

I
March 13

"The meeting's finished?"

"It is," Bil Sheering said into his mobile. He was sitting in his rental car, your basic Ford, though with a variation: He'd fried out the GPS so he couldn't be tracked.

"And you're happy with the pro?"

"I am," Bil said. The man on the other end of the line was Victor Brown, but there was no way in hell either of these two would utter their names aloud, despite the encryption. "We talked for close to a half hour. We're good."

"The payment terms acceptable?"

"Hundred thousand now, one-fifty when it's done. Hold on."

A customer walked out of Earl's and headed to a dinged and dusty pickup, not glancing Bil's way. The Silverado fired up and scattered gravel as it bounded onto the highway.

Another scan of the parking lot, crowded with trucks and cars but empty of people. The club, billed as an "exotic dance emporium," had been a good choice for the meeting. The clientele tended to focus on the stage, not on serious, furtive discussions going on in a booth in the back.

Another customer left, though he, too, turned away from Bil and vanished into the shadows.

Bil, of medium build, was in his forties, with trim brown hair and a tanned complexion from hunting and fishing, mostly in a down-and-dirty part of West Virginia. "Bil" had nothing to do with "William." It was a nickname that originated from where he was stationed in the service, near Biloxi, Mississippi. The moniker was only a problem when he wrote it down, "*B-I-L*," and people wondered where the other *L* went.

"Just checking the lot," Bil said. "Clear now."

Victor: "So, the pro's on board. That was the most important thing. What're the next steps?"

"The occurrence will be on May six. That's two months for training, picking the equipment. A vehicle that'll be helpful. Lotta homework."

They were deep into euphemism. What "equipment" meant was rifle and ammunition. What "vehicle" meant was a car that would be impossible to trace. And "occurrence" was a laughably tame name for what would happen on that date.

There was silence for a moment. Victor broke it by asking, "You are having doubts?" A moment later the man's slick voice continued, "You can back out, you want. But we take it a few steps further, we can't."

But Bil hadn't been hesitating because of concerns; he'd just been scanning the parking lot for prying eyes again. All was good. He said firmly, "No doubts at all."

Victor muttered, "I'm just saying we're looking at a lotta shit and a really big fan."

"This is what I do, my friend. The plan stands. We take this son of a bitch out."

"Good, glad you feel that way. Just exercise extreme caution."

Bil hardly needed the warning; extreme caution was pretty much the order of the day when the son of a bitch you were being paid to take out was a candidate for president of the United States.

II

May 6

The Gun Shack was on Route 57, just outside Haleyville.

The owner of the well-worn establishment was a big man, tall and ruddy, plump with fat rolls, and he wore a .45 Glock 30 on his hip. He'd never been robbed, not in twenty-one years, but he was fully prepared—and half hoping—for the attempt.

Now, at 9:10 A.M., the shop was empty and the owner was having a second breakfast of coffee and a bear claw, enjoying the almond flavor almost as much as he enjoyed the aroma of Hoppe's Gun Cleaner and Pledge polish from the rifle stocks. He grabbed the remote and clicked on ESPN. Later in the day, when customers were present, hunting shows would be on. Which, he believed, goaded them into buying more ammunition than they ordinarily would have.

The door opened, setting off a chime, and the owner looked up to see a man enter. He checked to see if the fellow was armed—no open carry was allowed in the store, and concealed weapons had to stay concealed. But it was clear the guy wasn't carrying.

The man wasn't big, but his shaved head, bushy moustache—in a horseshoe shape, out of the Vietnam War era—and emotionless face made the owner wary. He wore camouflaged hunting gear—green and black—which was odd since no game was in season at the moment.

The man looked around and then walked slowly to the counter behind which the owner stood. Unlike most patrons, he ignored the well-lit display case of dozens of beckoning sinister and shiny hand-guns. There wasn't a man in the world that came in here who didn't glance down with interest and admiration at a collection of firepower like this. Say a few words about the Sig, ask about the Desert Eagle.

Not this guy.

The owner's hand dropped to his side, where his pistol was.

The customer's eyes dropped, too. Fast. He'd noted the gesture and wasn't the least bit intimidated. He looked back at the owner, who looked away, angry with himself for doing so.

"I called yesterday. You have Lapua rounds." An eerie monotone.

The owner hadn't taken the call. Maybe it'd been Stony.

"Yeah, we've got 'em."

"I'll take two boxes of twenty. Three-three-eights."

Hm. Big sale for ammo. They were expensive, top of the line. The owner walked to the far end of the shelves and retrieved the heavy boxes. The .338 Lapua rounds weren't the largest caliber rifle bullets, but they were among the most powerful. The load of powder in the long casing could propel the slug accurately for a mile. People shooting rifles loaded with Lapuas for the first time were often unprepared for the punishing recoil and sometimes ended up with a "scope eye" bruise on their foreheads from the telescopic sight, a rite of passage among young soldiers.

Hunters tended not to shoot Lapuas—because they would blow most game to pieces. The highest-level competitive marksmen might fire them. But the main use was military; Lapua rounds were the bullet of choice for snipers. The owner believed the longest recorded sniper kill in history—more than a mile and a half—had been with a Lapua.

As he rang up the purchase the owner asked, "What's your rifle?" Lapuas are a type of bullet; they can be fired from a number of rifles.

"Couple different," he said.

"You compete?"

The man didn't answer. He looked at the register screen and handed over a prepaid debit card, the kind you buy at Walmart or Target.

The owner rang up the sale and handed the card back. "I never fired one. Hell of a kick, I hear."

Without a word, the sullen man grabbed his purchase and walked out.

Well, good day to you, too, buddy. The owner looked after the customer, who turned to the right outside the store, disappearing into the parking lot.

Funny, the owner thought. Why hadn't he parked in front of the gun shop, where seven empty spaces beckoned? There'd be no reason to park to the right, in front of Ames Drugs, which'd closed two years ago.

Odd duck . . .

But then he forgot about the guy, noting that a rerun of a recent Brewers game was on the dusty TV. He waddled to a stool, sat down, and chewed more of the pastry as he silently cheered a team that he knew was going to lose, five to zip, in an hour and a half.

Secret Service Special Agent Art Tomson eyed the entrance to the Pittstown Convention Center.

He stood, in his typical ramrod posture, beside his black Suburban SUV and scanned the expansive entryway of the massive building, which had been constructed in the 1980s. The trim man, of pale skin, wore a gray suit and white shirt with a dark blue tie (which looked normal, but the portion behind the collar was cut in half and sewn together with a single piece of thread, so that if an attacker grabbed it in a fight, the tie would break away).

Tomson took in the structure once more. It had been swept earlier and only authorized personnel were present, but the place was so huge and featured so many entrances that it would be a security challenge throughout the nine and a half hours Searcher would be at the center for the press conference and rally. You could never scan a National Special Security Event too much.

Adding to the challenge was the matter that Searcher—former governor Paul Ebbett—was a minor candidate at this point, so the personal protection detail guarding him was relatively small. That would change, however, given his increasing groundswell of support. He was pulling ahead of the other three candidates in the primary contest. Tomson believed that the flamboyant, blunt, tell-it-like-it-is politician would, in fact, become the party's nominee. When that happened, a full detail would be assigned to nest around him. But until then, Tomson would make do with his own federal staff of eight, supported by a number of officers from local law enforcement, as well as private security guards at the venues where Ebbett was speaking. In any case, whether there were a handful of men and women under him or scores, Tomson's level of vigilance never flagged. In the eighteen years he'd been with the Secret Service, now part of Homeland Security, not a single person he'd been assigned to protect had been killed or injured.

He tilted his head as he touched his earpiece and listened to a transmission. There was a belief that agents did this, the touching, which happened frequently, to activate the switch. Nope. The damn things—forever uncomfortable—just kept coming loose.

The message was that Searcher and his three SUVs had left the airport and were ten minutes away.

The candidate had just started to receive Secret Service protection, having only recently met the criteria for a security detail established by Homeland, Congress, and other government agencies. Among these standards were competing in primaries in at least ten states, running for a party that has garnered at least 10 percent of the popular vote, raising or committing at least $10 million in campaign funds, and, of course, publicly declaring your candidacy.

Besides the normal standards, one of the more significant factors in assigning Ebbett a detail was the reality that the man's brash statements and if-elected promises had made him extremely unpopular among certain groups. Social media was flooded with vicious verbal attacks and cruel comments, and the Secret Service had already responded to three assassination threats. None had turned out to be more than bluster. One woman had called for Ebbett to be drawn and quartered, apparently thinking that the phrase referred to a voodoo curse in which the governor's likeness would be sketched on a sheet of paper, which was then cut into four pieces—not to an actual form of execution, and a very unpleasant one at that. Still, Tomson and his team had to take these threats, and the ones that he knew would be forthcoming, seriously. Adding to their burden was intel from the CIA that, more than any other primary candidate in history, Ebbett might be a target of foreign operatives, due to his firm stance against military buildups by countries in Europe and Asia.

Another visual sweep of the convention center, outside of which both protesters and supporters were already queuing. Attendance would be huge; Ebbett's campaign committee had booked large venues for his events months ago, optimistically—and correctly—thinking that he would draw increasingly large crowds.

He glanced across the broad street, the lanes closed to handle the foot traffic. He noted his second in command, Don Ivers, close to the rope, surveying those present. Most of the men and women and a few youngsters had posters supporting the candidate, though there were plenty of protesters as well. Ivers and a half dozen local cops, trained in event security, would not be looking the protesters over very closely, though. The true threats came from the quiet ones, without placards or banners or hats decorated with the candidate's name or slogans. These folks would have all passed through metal detectors, but given the long lead time for the event, it would have been possible for some-body to hide a weapon inside the security perimeter—under a planter or even within a wall—and to access it now.

Tomson much preferred rallies to be announced at the last minute but, of course, that meant lower attendance. And for most candidates—and especially fiery Ebbett—that was not an option.

"Agent Tomson."

He turned to see a woman in her thirties wearing the dark-blue uniform of the Pittstown Convention Center security staff. Kim Mor-ton was slim but athletic. Her blond hair was pulled back in a tight bun, like that favored by policewomen and ballet dancers. Her face was pretty but severe. She wore no makeup or jewelry.

Tomson was unique among his fellow Secret Service agents; he believed in "partnering up" with a local officer or security guard at the venue where those under his protection would be appearing. No mat-ter how much research the Secret Service detail did, it was best to have somebody on board who knew the territory personally. When he'd briefed the local team about how the rally would go, he'd asked if there were any issues about the convention center they should know about. Most of the guards and municipal police hemmed and hawed. But Morton had raised her hand and, when he called on her, pointed out there were three doors with locks that might easily be breached— adding that she'd been after management for weeks to fix them.

When he described the emergency escape route they would take in the event of an assassination attempt, she'd said to make sure that there hadn't been a delivery of cleaning supplies because the workers tended to leave the cartons blocking that corridor, rather than put them away immediately.

Then she'd furrowed her brow and said, "Come to think of it, those cartons—they're pretty big. There might be a way somebody, you know, an assassin, could hide in one. Kinda far-fetched, but you asked."

"I did," he'd said. "Anything else?"

"Yes, sir. If you have to get out fast be careful on the curve on the back exit ramp that leads to the highway if it's raining. Was an oil spill two years ago and nobody's been able to clean it up proper."

Tomson had known then that he had his local partner, as curious as the pairing seemed.

Morton now approached and said, "Everything's secure at the west entrance. Your two men in place and three state police."

Tomson had known this, but the key word in personal protection is "redundancy."

He told her that the entourage would soon arrive. Her blue eyes scanned the crowd. Her hand absently dropped to her pepper spray, as if to make sure she knew where it was. That and walkie-talkies were the guards' only equipment. No guns. That was an immutable rule for private security.

Then, flashing lights, blue and red and white, and the black Suburban SUVs sped up to the front entrance.

He and Morton, flanked by two city police officers, walked toward the vehicles, from which six Secret Service agents were disembarking, along with the candidate. Paul Ebbett was six feet tall but seemed larger, thanks to his broad shoulders. (He'd played football at Indiana.) His hair was an impressive mane of salt-and-pepper. His suit was typical of what he invariably wore: dark gray. His shirt was light blue and, in a nod to his individuality, it was open at the neck. He never wore a tie and swore he wouldn't even don one at his inauguration.

Emerging from the last car was a tall, distinguished-looking African American, Tyler Quonn, Ebbett's chief of staff. Tomson knew he'd been the director of a powerful think tank in D.C. and was absolutely brilliant.

The candidate turned to the crowd and waved, as Tomson and the other agents, cops, and security guards scanned the crowd, windows, and rooftops. Tomson would have preferred that he walk directly into the convention hall, but he knew that wasn't the man's way; he was a self-proclaimed "man of the American people" and he plunged into crowds whenever he could, shaking hands, kissing cheeks, and tousling babies' hair.

Tomson was looking east when he felt Morton's firm hand on his elbow. He spun around. She said, "Man in front of the Subway. Tan raincoat. He was patting his pocket and just reached into it. Something about his eyes. He's anticipating."

In an instant he transmitted the description to Don Ivers, who was working that side of the street. The tall, bulky agent, a former Marine and state patrol officer, hurried up to the man and, taking his arms, led him quietly to the back of the crowd.

Tomson and Morton walked up to the candidate and the agent whispered, "May have an incident, sir. Could you go inside now?"

Ebbett hesitated, then he gave a final wave to the crowd and— infuriatingly slowly—headed into the convention center lobby.

A moment later Tomson heard in his headset: "Level four."

A nonlethal threat.

Ivers explained, "Two ripe tomatoes. He claimed he'd been shopping but they were loose in his pocket—no bag. And a couple of people next to him said he'd been ranting against Searcher all morning. He's clean. No record. We're escorting him out of the area."

As they walked toward the elevator that would take them to the suites, Ebbett asked, "What was it?"

Tomson told him what had happened.

"You've got sharp eyes, Ms. Morton," he said, reading her name badge.

"Just thought something seemed funny about him."

He looked her over with a narrowed gaze. "Whatta you think, Artie? Should I appoint her head of the Justice Department after I'm elected?"

Morton blinked and Ebbett held a straight face for a moment, then broke into laughter.

It had taken Tomson a while to get used to the candidate's humor.

"Let's go to the suite," Ebbett said. He glanced at Tomson. "My tea upstairs?"

"It is, sir."

"Good."

The entourage headed for the elevator, Tomson and Morton checking out every shadow, every door, every window.

Ten miles from Pittstown, in a small suburb called Prescott, the skinny boy behind the counter of Anderson's Hardware was lost in a fantasy about Jennie Mathers, a cheerleader for the Daniel Webster High Tigers.

Jennie was thoughtfully wearing her tight-fitting uniform, orange and black, and was—

"PVC. Where is it?" The gruff voice brought the daydream to a halt.

The kid's narrow face, from which some tufts of silky hair grew in curious places, turned to the customer. He hadn't heard the man come in.

He blinked, looking at the shaved head, weird moustache, eyes like black lasers—if lasers could be black, which maybe they couldn't, but that was the thought that jumped into his head and wouldn't leave.

"PVC *pipe?*" the kid asked.

The man just stared.

Of course, he meant PVC pipe. What else would he mean?

"Um, we don't have such a great, you know, selection. Home Depot's up the street." He nodded out the window.

The man continued staring, and the clerk took this to mean: If I'd wanted to go to Home Depot, I would've gone to Home Depot.

The clerk pointed. "Over there."

The man turned and walked away. He strolled through the shelves for a while and then returned to the counter with a half dozen six-foot-long pieces of three-quarter-inch pipe. He laid them on the counter.

The clerk said, "You want fittings, too? And cement?"

He'd need those to join the pipes together or mount them to existing ones.

But the man didn't answer. He squinted behind the clerk. "That, too." Pointing at a toolbox.

The kid handed it to him.

"That's a good one. It's got two little tray thingies you can put screws and bolts in. Washers, too. Look inside."

The man didn't look inside. He dug into his pocket and pulled out a debit card.

Hitting the keys on the register, the boy said, "That'll be thirty-two eighty." He didn't add, as he was supposed to, "Do you want to contribute a dollar to the Have a Heart children's fund?"

He had a feeling that'd be a waste of time.

The hallway of the suite tower's penthouse floor was pretty nice.

During his advance work—to check out the security here—Art Tomson had learned that, in an effort to draw the best entertainers and corporate CEOs for events here, the owners of the convention center had added a tower of upscale suites, where the performers, celebrities, and top corporate players would be treated like royalty. Why go to Madison or Milwaukee and sit in a stodgy greenroom when you could go to Pittstown and kick back in serious luxury?

Paul Ebbett was presently in the best of these, Suite A. ("When I'm back after November," he'd exclaimed with a sparkle in his eyes, "let's make sure they rename it the Presidential Suite.") It was 1,300 square feet, with four bedrooms, three baths, a living room, a dining room, a fair-to-middling kitchen, and a separate room and bathroom actually labeled MAID'S QUARTERS. The view of the city was panoramic, but that was taken on faith; the shutters and curtains were all closed, as they were in the entire row of suites, so snipers couldn't deduce which room Ebbett was in.

In lieu of the view, however, one could indulge in channel surfing on four massive TVs, ultra-high-def. Tomson was especially partial to TVs because when he got home—every two weeks or so—he and the wife and kids would pile onto a sofa and binge on the latest Disney movies and eat popcorn and corndogs until they could eat no more.

Special Agent Art Tomson was a very different man at home.

Only the candidate was inside at the moment. Chief of Staff Quonn was on the convention center floor, testing microphones and sound boards and teleprompters, and Tomson and Morton now sat in the hallway outside the double doors to Suite A. Tomson looked up and down the corridor, whose walls were beige and whose carpet was rich gray. He noted that the agents at each of the stairway doors and the elevator looked attentive. They didn't appear armed, but each had an FN P90 submachine gun under his or her jacket, in addition to a sidearm and plenty of magazines. Although armed assaults were extremely rare, in the personal protection business you always planned for a gunfight at the O.K. Corral.

Kim Morton said, "Wanted to mention: Acoustic tile's hung six inches below the concrete. Nobody can crawl through."

Tomson knew. He'd checked. He thanked her anyway and cocked his head once more as transmissions about security status at various locations came in.

All was clear.

He told this to Morton.

She said, "Guess we can relax for a bit." Eyeing him closely. "Except you don't, do you?"

"No."

"Never."

"No."

Silence eased in like an expected snow.

Morton broke it by asking, "You want some gum?"

Tomson didn't believe he'd chewed gum since he was in college.

She added, "Doublemint."

"No. Thank you."

"I stopped smoking four years and three months ago. I needed a habit. I'm like, 'Gum or meth? Gum or meth?'"

Tomson said nothing.

She opened the gum, unwrapped a piece, and slipped it into her mouth. "You ever wonder what the double mints were? Are there really two? They might use just one and tell us it's two. Who'd know?"

"Hm."

"You don't joke much in your line of work, do you?"

"I suppose we don't."

"Maybe I'll get you to smile."

"I smile. I just don't joke."

Morton said, "Haven't seen you smile yet."

"Haven't seen anything to smile about."

"The two-mint thing? That didn't cut it?"

"It was funny."

"You don't really think so."

Tomson paused. "No. It wasn't that funny."

"Almost got you to smile there."

Morton's phone hummed with a call. She grimaced.

Tomson was immediately attentive. Maybe one of the other security guards had seen something concerning.

She said into the phone, "If Maria tells you to go to bed, you go to bed. She's Mommy when Mommy's not there. She's a substitute Mommy. Like the time Ms. Wilson got arrested for protesting, remember? When they pulled down the Robert E. Lee statue? And you had that substitute teacher? Well, that's Maria. Are we clear on that . . . ? Good, and I do *not* want to find the lizard out when I get home. . . . No, it was not an accident. Lizards do not climb into purses of their own accord. Okay? Love you, Pumpkie. Put Sam on. . . ."

Morton had a brief conversation with another son, presumably younger—her voice grew more sing-songy.

She disconnected and noticed Tomson's eyes on her. "Iguana. Small one. In the babysitter's purse. I stopped them before they uploaded the video to YouTube. Maria's scream was impressive, man, oh, man. The boys would've had ten thousand hits easy. But you've got to draw the line somewhere. You have children, Agent Tomson?"

He hesitated. "Maybe we can go with first names at this point."

"Art. And I'm Kim. By the way, it meant a lot when I met you. You didn't hit the ground running with my first name. Lotta people do."

"The world's changing."

"Like molasses," she said. "So, Art. I'm looking at that ring on your finger. You have children? Unless that is a terrible, terrible question to ask, because they all wasted away with bad diseases."

Finally a smile.

"No diseases. Two. Boy and girl."

"They learned about lizard pranks yet?"

"They're a little young for that. And the only nonhuman in the household is a turtle."

"Don't let your guard down. Turtles can raise hell, too. Just takes 'em a bit longer to do it."

More silence in the hall. But now, the sort of silence that's a comfort.

Inside the suite, he could hear Ebbett had turned on the news—every set, it seemed. The candidate was obsessed with the media and watched everything, right and left and in between. He took voluminous notes, often without looking down from the screen at his pad of paper.

Morton nodded to the door and said, "He's quite a story, isn't he?"

"Story?"

"His road to the White House. Reinventing himself. He went through that bad patch, the drinking and the women. His wife leaving him. But then he turned it around."

Ebbett had indeed. He'd done rehab, gotten back together with his wife. He'd been frank and apologetic about his transgressions and he'd had successful campaigns for state representative and then governor. He'd burst onto the presidential scene last year.

Morton said, "I heard he came up with that campaign slogan himself: 'America. Making a Great Country Greater.' I like that, don't you? I know his positions're a little different and he's got kind of a mouth on him. Blunt, you know what I'm saying? But I'll tell you, I'm voting for him."

Tomson said nothing.

"Hm, did I just cross a line?"

"The thing is, in protection detail we don't express any opinion about the people we look after. Good, bad, politics, personal lives. Democrats or Republicans, it's irrelevant."

She was nodding. "I get it. Keeps you focused. Nothing ex—what's the word? Extraneous?"

"That's right."

"Extraneous . . . I help the boys with their homework some. I'm the go-to girl for math, but for English and vocabulary? Forget it."

He asked, "You always been in security?"

"No," she answered. A smile blossomed, softening her face. She was really quite pretty, high cheekbones, upturned nose, clear complexion. "I always wanted to be a cop. Can't tell you why. Maybe from a TV show I saw when I was a kid. *Walker, Texas Ranger. Law & Order. NYPD Blue.* But that didn't work out. This's the next best thing."

She sounded wistful.

"You could still join up, go to the state police or city academy. You're young."

Her eyes rolled. "And I thought you agents had to be sooooo observant."

Another smile appeared.

"Anyway, can't afford to take the time off. Single-mom thing."

Tomson saw Don Ivers approaching quickly. Tomson and the younger agent had worked together for about five years; he knew instantly there was a problem. Noting the man's expression, Kim Morton tensed, too.

"What?" Tomson asked.

"We've got word from CAD. Possible threat triad."

Tomson explained to Morton, "Our Central Analytics Division. You know, data miners. Supercomputers analyze public and law enforcement information and algorithms to spot potential risks."

She nodded. "Computer game stuff."

"Pretty much, that's right."

Ivers continued, "About an hour ago there was an anonymous call about a white male in a red Toyota sedan. Plate was covered with mud. The driver was standing outside the car and making a cellphone call. The citizen who called 9-1-1 heard this guy mention 'Ebbett' and 'rally.' That's all he could hear. But he saw there was a long gun in the backseat. It was outside a strip mall in Avery."

"About five miles south of here," Morton said.

Ivers continued, "That put all red Toyota sedans on a watch list."

"The caller say anything more about the driver?"

"He was in combat or camo, medium build, bald with an old-timey moustache. Droopy, like gunslingers wore. The computers started to scan every CCTV—public, and the private ones that make their data available to law enforcement. There were two hits on the target vehicles. At nine this morning one was spotted in a parking lot near a gun shop in Haleyville."

Tomson turned to Morton, his eyebrow raised.

She said, "*Twenty* miles south."

"He parked in front of a closed-up drugstore in a strip mall," Ivers said. "The closest active store was the gun shop. We got their security video. The first customer of the day was a bald white male, thirties to forties, with a drooping moustache." Ivers sighed. "He bought forty .338 Lapua rounds. Prepaid debit card he paid cash for. Owner said he was a scary guy."

"Brother," Tomson said, sighing. He added to Morton, "Lapuas are high-powered sniper rounds."

"And he didn't park in front of the shop," she said, "to avoid the camera in the gun shop."

"Probably."

Ivers added, "Then another hit. Two hours ago the Toyota was videoed parked near—but not in front of, again—a hardware store in Prescott, twelve miles away. He bought a toolbox and six three-quarter-inch PVC pipes. No CCTV inside but the clerk's description was the same as the others. Same debit card as before."

"Where'd he buy the card?" Tomson asked.

"A Target in Omaha a month ago."

"Been planning this for a while."

Morton grimaced. "Those towns? That's a straight line to where we are now: Haleyville, Prescott, Avery."

Tomson asked, "Status of vehicle?"

"Nothing since then. He's taking his time, sticking to back roads."

"What would he want the pipes for?" Morton asked. "To make bombs?"

Tomson said, "Probably not. That's pretty thin. You couldn't get much explosive in them."

"A tripod for his gun?" she suggested.

An interesting idea. But when he considered it, that didn't seem likely. "Doubt it. Anybody with a gun that fires Lapua rounds would have professional accessories to go along with it. And in an urban shooting solution like here, he could just use a windowsill or box to support the weapon for a distance shot."

Tomson said, "Put out the info on the wire. Let's advise Searcher."

He knocked on the suite door. "Sir. It's Art."

A voice commanded, "Come on in."

The candidate was jotting notes on a yellow pad. Presumably for his speech that night. He'd do this until the last moment. A transcriptionist was on staff, and she would pound the keys of the computer attached to the teleprompter until just before the candidate took the stage. Open on the table was Barbara Tuchman's brilliant—and disturbing—book about the First World War, *The Guns of August*. One of the first items on Ebbett's agenda as president would be to revitalize the U.S. military—"make a great army even greater!"—and stand up to foreign aggression.

Tomson said, "Sir, we've received some information about a possible threat." He explained what they'd discovered.

The candidate took the details without any show of emotion. "Credible?"

"It's not hunting season, but he could be a competitive marksman, buying those rounds for the range. The camo? A lot of men wear it as everyday clothing. But the license plate was obscured. And he's headed this way. I'm inclined to take it seriously."

The candidate leaned back and sipped his iced tea. After he'd reinvented himself this was the strongest thing he imbibed.

"Well, well, well . . . hm. And what do you say, Ms. Morton?"

"Me? Oh, I'm just a girl who spots tomato-throwers. These men know all the fancy stuff."

"But what's your gut tell you?"

She cocked her head. "My gut tells me that with any other candidate this'd probably be a bunch of coincidences. But you're not any other candidate. You speak your mind and tell the truth and some people don't like that—or what you have planned when you take office. I'd say take it seriously."

"She's good, Artie." A smile crinkled his face. "And I like that she said 'when' I take office. Okay. We'll assume it's a credible threat. What do we do?"

"Move the press conference inside," Tomson said. "The location's been in the news and a shooter would know that's where you'll be."

The conference, planned for a half hour before the candidate's speech at the rally, was to be held in an open-air plaza connected to the convention center. The candidate had wanted to hold it there because clearly visible from the podium was a factory that had gone out of business after losing jobs overseas. Ebbett was going to point to the dilapidated building and talk about his criticism of the present administration's economic policies.

Tomson had never been in favor of the plaza; it was a real security challenge, being so open. The choice had been Tyler Quonn's, but Ebbett had liked it immediately. Now, though, he reluctantly acquiesced to moving the conference inside. "But I'm not changing one thing about the rally tonight."

"No need, sir; the center itself is completely secure."

"The press'll probably like it better anyway," Ebbett conceded. "Not the best weather to be sitting outside, listening to me spout off—as brilliant as my bon mots are."

Tomson noticed that while Kim Morton got the gist of what he was saying, she didn't know the French expression, and this seemed to bother her.

English and vocabulary? Forget it. . . .

He felt bad that his partner was troubled.

Tomson called Tyler Quonn and explained about moving the press conference. The chief of staff apparently wasn't crazy about the idea, but agreed to follow Tomson's direction. Then Ivers opened his tablet and they studied the area, setting the iPad on the coffee table. Tomson explained to Morton and Ebbett, "Assuming he was going to try a shot at the press conference, we'll locate where a good vantage point would be. Get undercover agents and police there to spot him."

Then Ivers added, "I keep coming back to the pipes. The PVC. And the toolbox."

"He could slip into a construction site, fronting as a worker. You know, bundle the gun up with the pipes." Tomson shrugged. "But there's no job site with a view of the plaza."

"There's construction going on there," Morton said, her unpolished nail hovering over the screen. She was indicating a city block about a mile from the convention center.

"What is it?" Ivers asked her.

"A high-rise of some kind, about half completed. All I know is the trucks screw up traffic making deliveries. We avoid that road commuting here."

Tomson picked up the tablet and went to 3-D view. He moved his fingers over the screen, zooming and sweeping from one view to another. He grimaced. "Bingo."

"Whatcha got, Artie?" Ebbett asked.

"You'll be inside the convention center for the rally. But the only way to get into the hall itself is along the corridor behind this wall." He zoomed in on a fifty-foot wall, with small windows at about head height. The windows faced the job site.

Ebbett chuckled. "Artie, come on. It's nearly a mile away. At dusk. Who the hell could make that shot?"

"A pro. And shooting a Lapua round? It's so powerful, what'd just be a wound with another gun would be fatal with a slug like that. Sir, this is a level two threat. I'm going to ask you to cancel."

Ebbett was shaking his head. "Artie, just let me say this: My enemies, and the enemies of this country, want to make us afraid, want to make us run and hide. I can't do that. I won't do that. I know it makes your job tougher. But I'm going to say no. The rally goes on as planned. Move the press conference inside, okay. That's as far as I'll go. Final word."

Without hesitation the agent said, "Yes, sir." Then, given his orders, he turned immediately to the task at hand. "Don, you get a team together. I want eyes on every CCTV from here to that job site, looking for that Toyota. And I want two dozen tactical officers inside and outside the job site. And I need to come up with a different route to get Governor Ebbett into the hall, one that doesn't involve any outside exposure. Not even a square foot."

Ivers said, "I'm on it. I'll call in when I'm in position." He hurried down the corridor.

Tomson said, "I'll find a covered route to get you to the hall, sir."

As he and Morton turned to leave, Tomson glanced down once more at the coffee table, where *The Guns of August* sat. It hadn't occurred to him earlier but now he remembered something; the cause of the First World War, in which nearly twenty million people died, could be traced to one simple act—a political assassination.

In conclusion, my fellow Americans:

This country was founded on the principles of freedom and fairness. And I would add to those another principle: that of fostering. You may remember someone in your youth, who fostered you. Oh, I don't mean officially, like a foster parent. I mean a teacher, a neighbor, a priest or minister, who took you under his wing and saw within you your inner talent, your inner good, your inner spirit.

And nurtured your gifts.

Freedom, fairness, fostering . . .

Together, you and I will invoke those three principles to make our nation shine even brighter.

To make our strong nation stronger.

To make our great nation greater!

God bless you all, God bless our future, and God bless the United States of America.

Governor Paul Ebbett looked over his notes and rose from the couch. He practiced this passage a few more times, then revised other parts of the speech. Little by little, he was closing in on the final version. He still had a couple of hours until showtime.

He smiled to himself.

Little by little.

Which was exactly the way he was creeping up on the presidential nomination. So many people had said he couldn't do it. That he was too brash, too blunt. Too honest—as if there were such a thing.

A knock on the door. "Sir?" It was Artie Tomson.

"Yes?"

"Your dinner's here."

He entered, along with the woman who had saved him from to-mato target practice. He liked her and was sorry she was only a security guard and not on his full-time staff. They were accompanied by a white-jacketed server, a slim Latino, who was wheeling in the dinner cart. Under the silver cover would be his favorite meal: hamburger on brioche bread, lettuce, tomato, and, since the first-lady-to-be was not present, red onion—the sandwich accessorized with Thousand Island dressing and a side of fries.

And his beloved sweet tea.

The man opened the wings of the table and set out the food.

"Enjoy your meal, sir." He turned to leave.

"Wait," the candidate commanded.

The convention center employee turned. "Sir?" His eyes grew wide as Ebbett pulled his wallet from his hip pocket, extracted a twenty, and handed it to him.

"I . . . oh, thank you, sir!"

Ebbett thought about asking, as a joke, if the man was going to vote for him. But he didn't seem the sort who would get humor and he worried the server might actually think it was a bribe.

The slight man scurried off, clutching the money, which, Ebbett bet, he was going to frame rather than spend.

Artie Tomson was giving him an update about the potential assassin, which really was no update at all. They hadn't learned anything from the state police about local threats, or the NRO, NSA, or CIA about foreign operatives. There was a full complement of tactical officers—some undercover in construction worker outfits—in and around the job site. But there was no sign of the bald, moustachioed suspect or the red Toyota.

As they spoke, Ebbett glanced across the living room and noted Kim Morton on her phone, head down, lost in a serious conversation.

Tomson received a call and excused himself to take it.

Ebbett strolled casually to the table and plucked a fry from the basket. Nice and hot. He dunked it in ketchup and, salivating already, lifted the morsel to his lips, as he turned to the TV to check the weather and see if the predicted storm would possibly keep people away. No, it looked like—

Then a crash of china and glass and, with a sharp pain in his back, Ebbett tumbled forward onto the carpet. He realized just before he hit the floor that he'd been facing away from the curtained window and he wondered, with eerie calm, how the assassin, who was apparently across the street nowhere near the job site, had known exactly where he would be standing.

Art Tomson was in the hall, surrounded by a half dozen other Secret Service agents and local police, all facing him as he gave them calm, clear instructions on how to proceed.

One by one, or two by two, the agents and cops turned toward the elevator and headed off for their respective tasks.

Ivers walked up to him and Kim Morton, who stood silently beside the senior agent. Ivers's face was even paler than normal as he displayed his phone. "Here's the answer."

Tomson was staring at the words on the screen. Then he nodded to the door of Suite A. "Let's go."

They walked into the hotel room, Kim Morton behind them.

Searcher, Governor Ebbett, was sitting on the couch, a heating pad on his back.

That was the only medical attention he'd needed after being tackled while about to take a bite of French fry, dipped in what they suspected might be poisoned ketchup.

Tomson said, "Sir, we're awaiting the analysis of the food. But the substance in question is zinc phosphide."

"The hell's that?"

"Highly toxic rodenticide, used to kill rats mostly. Ingest some and it mixes with stomach acid, and a poisonous gas is released."

"What's going on, Artie?"

He nodded to Kim Morton and said, "I'll let my partner here explain. She's the one who thought of it."

With her eyes on Ebbett's she said, "Well, sir. I was thinking that this guy . . . perp, you say perp?"

"We say perp," Tomson said.

"I was thinking if this perp really was some brilliant assassin, well, he didn't seem to be acting so smart. Conspicuous, you know. Parking suspiciously. Talking about the rally in public, while he had a rifle in the back of his car, and he wasn't too concerned if anybody heard him. Wearing camouflage. Buying the PVC pipes and toolbox so we'd think he'd be in a job site. . . . I mean, it just seemed *too* obvious that he was planning to shoot you. And I looked at those windows in the hallway again. I mean, even if he was a pro, that'd be a hell of a shot.

"So what might other possibilities be? I thought I'd call the places we know he'd been: the gun shop and the hardware store. We know what he bought, but what if he'd *shoplifted* something that could be used as a weapon—a tool or a knife or a can of propane to make into a bomb? Nothing was missing at the gun shop, but at the hardware store—where there weren't any video cameras—I asked the clerk if anything was missing. They did an inventory. Two cans of rat poison had been stolen.

"When I saw you go for that fry, sir, I just panicked," Morton said. "I thought whatever I said, you might still take a bite, so I just reacted. I'm sorry."

He chuckled. "No worries. It's not every day a beautiful woman launches herself into me . . . and saves my life at the same time."

Tomson said, "We've closed down the kitchen and concession stands and analyzed the HVAC system. No sign of poison yet. But all of your food and beverages will come in from outside, vetted sources."

"Don't have much of an appetite at this point." He grimaced. "Had to be the fucking Russians. They love their poisons. Look at Litvinenko." The Russian expat murdered in London by Moscow agents, who slipped polonium into his tea. "And the Skripal poisoning in Salisbury—that Novichok toxin . . . Jesus."

"There was no chatter about it in the intel community," Ivers pointed out. "Washington's been monitoring."

"Of course there's no chatter," Ebbett muttered. "They're not talking about it overseas—the communications would be picked up. No, they hired some locals to handle the operation—where the CIA can't legally monitor phones and computers without a FISA warrant. Tell the attorney general I want the bureau and the CIA to check out the known Russian cells and anyone with a connection to them. I want them to use a proctoscope."

"Yes, sir. They've been alerted."

"And the car? That Toyota?"

Ivers said, "Never got close to the job site. Like Officer Morton was saying, it was a diversion, we think. A CCTV in Bronson, about thirty miles east, spotted it, headed out of the state. We're still looking but, after that sighting, it's disappeared. I've got one team going through the hardware store, looking for trace evidence and prints. Other teams are going over the convention center service entrance, kitchen, the suppliers, and onsite staff. We're looking at the tea in particular."

"Bastard messing with my sweet tea?" Ebbett grumbled in mock rage. Then his eyes slid to Kim Morton. "A local security guard took on a pro assassin . . . and kicked his ass."

"I just had some thoughts. It was Agent Tomson and Agent Ivers who did everything."

"Don't play down your role." He looked her over for a moment. "Artie was telling me a few things about you. How you always wanted to be a police officer."

"Oh," she said, looking down. "I guess. That didn't work out. But I'm happy with my life now."

"That's good. Sure . . . But you know my campaign slogan."

She said, "Making a great country greater."

"So what if I could make your happy life *happier*?"

"I'm not sure what you mean, sir."

"What I mean is you did something for me; now I'd like to do something for you. Artie, leave us alone for a few minutes. There's something I'd like to discuss with Ms. . . . I mean, with *Officer* Morton."

"I'll be outside, sir."

At exactly 10:20 that night Governor Paul Ebbett's speech concluded with "And God bless the United States of America." The last word vanished in the tide of screams, whistles, and thunderous applause. Thirty thousand people were on their feet, waving banners and tossing aloft fake straw hats.

Art Tomson, who'd been onstage for the full event, now walked down the steps and joined Kim Morton, who was standing guard at the doorway that led to the underground passage through which Governor Ebbett would exit in a moment.

The evening had gone off without a hitch. In a few minutes Searcher would be in the SUV and speeding to the airport.

"Good speech," she said.

Tomson, who'd heard it or variations of it scores of times, simply nodded noncommittally.

Then she lowered her voice and said, "Thank you."

"For what?"

"Did the governor tell you what he's going to do for me?"

"No."

Morton explained what the candidate had said in their private meeting. "He's going to get me into the state police academy here. He's a friend of our governor, who owes him for something or another." Her face broke into a smile. "And he arranged for a stipend—almost as much as I'm making here. He said one favor deserves another. He did that all because you told him I wanted to be a cop."

"He was asking about you. He thought you were sharper than some of the people working for him." Tomson added with gravity in his voice, "And the fact is, none of us came up with that idea about the poison."

"Just a theory is all."

"Still, in this line of work, better safe than sorry."

Thomson tapped his earpiece and heard: "Searcher's on the move." Into his sleeve mike he said, "Roger. Exit is clear."

Tomson shook Morton's hand. She gave him a fast embrace. Never in his years of being an agent had he hugged a fellow personal protection officer. He was startled. Then he hugged her back and peeled away to join the candidate and his escort hurrying to the waiting SUV.

III

May 24

The main room at Earl's wasn't smoky, hadn't been for years. Even vaping was prohibited.

But the aroma of tobacco persisted, as the owners of the place had made no effort to clean the smell away. Because men, alcohol, and semiclad women somehow demanded the scent of cigarette smoke—if not the fumes themselves.

Bil Sheering was at the bar, nursing a Jack and Coke, looking at the scruffy audience sitting by the low stage and at unsteady round bistro tables. While he knew they all could figure out "Exotic Dance," he was wondering how many had a clue what an "Emporium" was. He wondered, too, why Earl—if there was, or had been, an Earl—had decided to affix the name to his strip joint.

Then his attention turned back to Starlight, the woman on center stage at the moment. Some of the dancers who performed here were bored gyrators. Some offered crude poses and outsized, flirtatious glances. And some were uneasy and modest. But Starlight was into dancing with both elegance and sensuality.

He was enjoying her performance when his attention slipped to the TV, where an announcement was interrupting the game. On the screen was a red graphic: *"Breaking News."*

Somebody beside him chuckled drunkenly. "Don'tcha love it? 'Breaking news' used to be a world war or plane crash. Now it's a thunderstorm, vandals at a 7-Eleven. Media's full of shit."

Bil said nothing but kept his attention on the grimy TV. A blond anchorwoman appeared. She seemed to have been caught unprepared by what was coming next. "We now bring you breaking news from Washington, D.C. We're live at the campaign headquarters of Governor Paul Ebbett for what he has said is an important announcement."

Bil watched the man stride to the front of the room. Cameras fired away, the thirty-shots-per-second mode, sounding like silenced machine guns in a movie.

At Ebbett's side was his wife, a tall, handsome woman on whose severe face was propped a stony smile.

"My fellow Americans, I am here tonight to announce that I am withdrawing from the campaign for president of the United States." Gasps from the crowd. "In my months on the campaign trail, I have come to realize that the most important work in governing this country is on the grassroots level, rather than inside the Beltway. And it's in those local offices that I feel I can be of most benefit to my party and to the American people. Accordingly, I will be ceasing my efforts to run for president and returning to my great home state, where I'll be

running"—he swallowed hard—"for supervisor of Calloway County."
A long pause. "I'm also urging all of my electoral delegates and other
supporters to back a man I feel exhibits the best qualities of leadership
for America, Senator Mark Todd."

Another collective gasp, more buzzing of the cameras.

Ebbett took his wife's hand. Bil noted she didn't squeeze it, but let
him grip the digits the way you might pick up a gutted fish in a tray
of shaved ice to examine it for freshness.

"Senator Todd is just the man to lead our party to victory and"—
Ebbett's voice caught—"make a great nation greater. Thank you, my
fellow citizens. God bless you. And God bless the United States of
America."

No applause. Just a torrent of questions from the floor. Ebbett
ignored them and walked from the room, his wife beside him, their
hands no longer entwined.

The scene switched back to the brightly lit newsroom and the anchorwoman saying, "That was Governor Paul Ebbett, who just yesterday seemed unstoppable on his route to his party's candidacy. But
there you heard it: his shocking news that he is dropping out of the
race. And his equally stunning endorsement of Senator Mark Todd.
Todd, considered a far more moderate and bipartisan politician than
Ebbett, has been the governor's main rival on the primary campaign
trail. Although Todd avoided personal attacks, Ebbett rarely missed
the chance to belittle and mock the senator."

Reading from what had to be hastily scribbled notes on the teleprompter, the blond anchor said, "A lot of people were surprised by
the success Ebbett enjoyed in the primary campaign, which played to
the darker side of American society. His positions were controversial.
Many in both parties thought his nationalist-charged rhetoric was di-
visive. He openly admitted that his campaign phrase, 'Make a Great
Country Greater,' meant greater for people like him, white and Christian. He promised to slash social spending to education and the poor.

"He alarmed those both in this country and abroad by stating that
one of his first acts in office would be to mass American troops along
Russia's borders. Some pundits have said that Ebbett might have tar-

geted Russia not for any political or ideological reason, but because he believed a common enemy would solidify support around him.

"We now have in the studio and via Skype hookup our National Presidential Campaign panel for an analysis of this unexpected announcement—"

"Hey, Bil," came the woman's voice behind him.

Bil turned to see the dancer who'd just been up onstage sidling up to him, pulling a shawl over her ample breasts. Bil wasn't completely happy she'd donned the garment.

He knew she went by Starlight at Earl's but he couldn't help but think of her by her real name: Kim Morton.

She smiled to the bartender, who brought her a scotch on the rocks. The headline dancer began to pull bills out of her G-string. As tawdry as Earl's was, it looked like she had been tipped close to two hundred dollars—for twenty minutes at the pole. She sipped her drink and nodded at the screen. "You did it."

"Me?" Bil asked, smiling. *"We* did it."

She cocked her head. "Guess I can't really argue with that one."

We did it. . . .

They sure as hell had.

Six months ago, the National Party Committee had become alarmed, then panicked, that Paul Ebbett was picking up a significant number of delegates in the primary contests, beating out their preferred candidate, Senator Mark Todd. They were astonished that Governor Ebbett's bigoted and militant rhetoric was stirring up a groundswell of support.

The committee knew Ebbett was lose-lose. If elected, he would destroy not only the party, but probably the economy and perhaps even the nation itself—if he managed to start World War III, which seemed more than a little possible.

Committee Chairman Victor Brown wanted Ebbett out. But backroom attempts to negotiate with him to drop out were futile. In fact, the effort incensed him and fueled his resolve to win . . . and purge the ranks of those who had questioned his ability to lead the country.

So extreme measures were required.

Last March Victor had called in Bil Sheering, who ran a ruthless political consulting company in Washington, D.C. Bil had hurried back from his hunting lodge in West Virginia to his M Street office and got to work.

For the plan Bil came up with, he needed a "pro"—by which he meant a call girl based in the region of the Midwestern state where Governor Ebbett would be holding a big rally in May. After some research, he'd settled on Kim Morton, aka Starlight, a dancer at Earl's with an escort business on the side. He'd found her to be smart, well-spoken, and without a criminal history. She also had a particular contempt for Ebbett since her husband had been killed in Afghanistan, which she considered an unnecessary war, just like the one Ebbett seemed to be planning.

Victor had given Bil a generous budget; he offered Morton a quarter-million dollars to take a hiatus from dancing for two months and get a job as a security guard at the Pittstown Convention Center. She used her charm and intelligence to talk her way onto the security team working with the Secret Service at the rally, earning the trust of the senior agent, Art Tomson.

The day of the rally, Bil, who'd grown an impressive moustache and shaved his head, dressed in combat gear and smeared mud on the license plate of an old hulk of a Toyota he'd bought at a junkyard. He'd made his way toward the convention center from Haleyville to Prescott to Avery, making intentionally suspicious purchases: sniper bullets and PVC pipes and hardware. He'd also made the anonymous call about a man having a phone conversation about Ebbett and the rally with a rifle in the backseat of his car.

Meanwhile, Kim Morton continued to ingratiate herself into the Secret Service operation . . . and get the attention of Ebbett himself. She'd spotted the suspicious man in the crowd, armed with two rotten tomatoes (the kid was an intern from National Party headquarters given a bonus to play the role). Finally she'd offered her insights about the sniper attack being a diversion—poisoning might be the real form of assassination. (There never was any toxin; at the hardware store Bil had not stolen the rodenticide but had merely hidden the cans in another aisle; when they were later discovered the Secret Service would conclude the attack was a product of the security guard's overactive imagination.)

The script called for Morton to tackle Ebbett to "save his life." Following that intimate and ice-breaking moment, Kim Morton had fired enough flirtatious glances his way to ignite latent flames of infidelity. After he'd asked her to stay and Art Tomson had left the suite, Ebbett slipped his arm around her and whispered, "I know you want a slot at the police academy. An hour in bed with me and I'll make it happen."

She'd looked shocked at first, as the role called for, but soon "gave in."

The ensuing liaison was energetic and slightly kinky, as Morton told him she was a bit of a voyeur and wanted the lights on. Ebbett was all for it. This proved helpful, since the tiny high-def video camera, hidden in her uniform jacket hanging strategically on the bedroom doorknob, required good illumination.

She'd delivered the video to Bil, who uploaded the encrypted file to Victor Brown. The head of the national committee had called Ebbett last week and gave him an ultimatum: Withdraw or the tape would go to every media outlet in the world.

After a bit of debate, in which Ebbett had apparently confessed to his wife what had happened (the fish-hand thing suggested this), the man had reluctantly agreed.

Eyes now on the screen, Morton said to Bil, "He's actually running for county supervisor?"

"That's the only bone they'd throw him. He's up against a twenty-two-year-old manager at Farmer's Trust and Savings. The polls aren't in Ebbett's favor." Bill leaned close and whispered, "I have the rest of your fee."

"I've got one more show. I'll get it after."

Bil had an amusing image of himself, sitting in the front row and, as Starlight danced close to him, tucking $150,000 into her G-string.

"This worked out well. You interested in any more work?" he asked. "You've got my number."

Bil nodded. Then he lifted his drink. "Here's to us—unlikely part-ners."

She smiled and tapped her glass to his. Then she shrugged the silky wrap off her shoulders into his lap and walked back to the stage.

CREDITS

ABOUT THE AUTHORS

New York Times bestselling author ACE ATKINS has been nominated for every major award in crime fiction, including the Edgar three times, twice for novels about former U.S. Army Ranger Quinn Colson. He has written eight books in the Colson series and continued Robert B. Parker's iconic Spenser character after Parker's death in 2010, adding seven bestselling novels in that series. A former newspaper reporter and SEC football player, Ace also writes essays and investigative pieces for several national magazines including *Time, Outside,* and *Garden & Gun.* He lives in Oxford, Mississippi, with his family, where he's friend to many dogs and several bartenders.

ALLISON BRENNAN believes that life is too short to be bored, so she writes three books a year and is raising five children. She's the *New York Times* and *USA Today* bestselling author of more than three dozen thrillers and numerous short stories. She currently writes two award-winning series—the Lucy Kincaid thrillers and the Maxine Revere cold case mysteries—and lives in Northern California with her husband, her youngest three kids, and assorted pets.

SHELLEY COSTA's work has been nominated for both the Edgar and Agatha Awards. She is the author of *You Cannoli Die Once, Basil Instinct, Practical Sins for Cold Climates,* and *A Killer's Guide to Good Works.* Her stories have appeared in *Alfred Hitchcock Mystery Magazine, Blood on Their Hands, The World's Finest Mystery and Crime Stories, Crimewave,* and *The Georgia Review.* Shelley holds a Ph.D. in English from Case Western Reserve University, where she wrote her dissertation on suspense, and she teaches fiction writing at the Cleveland Institute of Art. She and her husband live in Chagrin Falls, Ohio.

JEFFERY DEAVER is the *New York Times* bestselling author of numerous suspense novels, including *The Blue Nowhere* and *The Bone Collector,* which was made into a feature film starring Denzel Washington and Angelina Jolie. He has been nominated for five Edgar Awards from the Mystery Writers of America, and is a two-time recipient of the Ellery Queen Readers Award for Best Short Story of the Year. A lawyer who quit practicing to write full-time, he lives in California and Virginia.

ROBERT DUGONI is the critically acclaimed *New York Times, #1 Wall Street Journal,* and #1 Amazon bestselling author of the Tracy Crosswhite series, consisting of *My Sister's*

Grave, *Her Final Breath*, *In the Clearing*, *The Trapped Girl*, *Close to Home*, and *A Steep Price*, as well as the bestselling author of the David Sloane series, and the standalone novels *The 7th Canon*, *The Cyanide Canary*, and *The Extraordinary Life of Sam Hell*, *Suspense* magazine's 2018 Book of the Year, for which Dugoni's narration won an Audiofiles Earphones Award. He is the recipient of the Nancy Pearl Book Award for Fiction and the Friends of Mystery Spotted Owl Award, and is a two-time finalist for the International Thriller Writers and Harper Lee Awards, as well as the Silver Falchion Award and the Edgar Award.

WILLIAM FRANK spent his childhood on naval air stations ranging from French Morocco to Guam. He served as a flight test engineer in the U.S. Air Force and later as a professor of tropical meteorology at the University of Virginia and Penn State. His detective fiction explores the complex world of art theft and its role in international crime and terrorism. A fourth-generation New Mexican, Bill now lives in Santa Fe with his wife, Kathleen Frank, a noted landscape painter.

GEORGIA JEFFRIES is the author of three novels, including *Malinche*, a story of military injustice and border war. Her short story "Little Egypt" appeared in the 2017 noir anthology *Last Resort*, and a family memoir, "The Last Gun of Tiburcio Vásquez," was published in the UC Press quarterly *Boom: A Journal of California*. She is also a contributor to the *Los Angeles Review of Books*, *HuffPost*, and *Written By*. Prior to her work in prose, Jeffries cracked TV's glass ceiling as a writer-producer of multiple Emmy Award–winning series and is the first individual woman to earn a Writers Guild of America Award for Television Episodic Drama. Born in the Illinois heartland, she graduated from UCLA and is a tenured professor at USC's School of Cinematic Arts.

LOU KEMP's short stories have appeared in several anthologies, including *Seattle Noir* and MWA's *Crimes by Moonlight*, where her character Celwyn made his first appearance before *Odd Partners*. She is currently finishing a book of Celwyn's adventures as he becomes a mysterious player in certain historical occurrences. She lives in the Seattle area and believes anything is possible in the land of Oz.

WILLIAM KENT KRUEGER is the author of the *New York Times* bestselling Cork O'Connor mystery series, set in the great Northwoods of Minnesota. He is a five-time winner of the Minnesota Book Award. Among his many other accolades is the Edgar Award for Best Novel for his 2013 release *Ordinary Grace*. He lives in St. Paul, a city he dearly loves, and does all his creative writing in local, author-friendly coffee shops.

JOE R. LANSDALE, Champion Mojo Storyteller, has written novels and stories in many genres, including Western, horror, science fiction, mystery, and suspense. He has written forty-five novels and published thirty short-story collections along with many chapbooks and comic-book adaptations. His stories have won ten Bram Stoker Awards, a British Fantasy Award, an Edgar Award, a World Horror Convention Grand Master Award, a Sugarprize, a Grinzane Cavour Prize for Literature, a Spur Award, and a Raymond Chandler Lifetime Achievement Award. He has been inducted into the Texas Literary Hall of Fame, and several of his novels have been adapted to film. His Hap and Leonard series features two friends, Hap Collins and Leonard Pine, who live in the fictional town of Laborde, in East Texas, and find themselves solving a variety of often unpleasant crimes. These books have been adapted into a TV series for the Sundance TV channel, and a series of graphic novels began publication in 2017.

LISA MORTON is a screenwriter, nonfiction author, award-winning prose writer, and Halloween expert whose work was described by the American Library Association's *Readers' Advisory Guide to Horror* as "consistently dark, unsettling, and frightening." Her most recent releases include *Ghosts: A Haunted History* and the anthology *Haunted Nights* (co-edited with Ellen Datlow).

CLAIRE ORTALDA's short fiction has been published in numerous literary journals, earning her the Georgia State University Fiction Prize and national Hackney Award, among other prizes. She has been an associate editor for *Narrative Magazine*, a founding board member of PEN Oakland, and co-editor of *Fightin' Words*. Her recent segue to mystery writing resulted in her first story in that genre, "Crime on Hold," being published in the anthology *Fish Out of Water*. Her mystery novel, *The Psychopath Companion*, was short-listed for the Del Sol Press First Novel Prize 2017.

ANNE PERRY is the bestselling author of two acclaimed series set in Victorian England: the William Monk novels, including *Dark Tide Rising* and *An Echo of Murder*, and the Charlotte and Thomas Pitt novels, including *Murder on the Serpentine* and *Treachery at Lancaster Gate*. She is also the author of a new series featuring Charlotte and Thomas Pitt's son, Daniel, including *Triple Jeopardy* and *Twenty-one Days*, as well as a series of five World War I novels, sixteen holiday novels (most recently *A Christmas Revelation*), and a historical novel, *The Sheen on the Silk*, set in the Ottoman Empire. Anne Perry lives in Los Angeles.

ADELE POLOMSKI is a graduate of Rutgers University with a master's in creative writing. She has published more than twenty mini-mysteries in *Woman's World*, along with stories in the anthologies *Busted!* and *Noir at the Salad Bar*. "NO 11 SQUATTER" is a tribute to her late mother-in-law, Norma, and to Norma's "assistant," Kareen. The women began their relationship as strangers with different needs, cultural dissimilarities, and communication issues. With seemingly nothing in common, they forged a friendship of mutual respect and devotion. Theirs made for an odd partnership that worked beautifully. Adele is the mother of three children, and resides at the Jersey shore.

STEPHEN ROSS has been nominated for an Edgar Award, a Derringer Award, and an International Thriller Writers Award, and was a 2010 Ellery Queen Readers Award finalist. His short stories and novelettes have appeared in *Ellery Queen Mystery Magazine*, *Alfred Hitchcock Mystery Magazine*, two previous MWA anthologies, and numerous other publications. He has lived in Auckland, London, and Frankfurt; he currently resides on the beautiful Whangaparaoa Peninsula of New Zealand, where his dog Mycroft takes him for afternoon walks.

MARK THIELMAN works as a criminal magistrate in Fort Worth, Texas. Originally from South Dakota, he came south to attend Texas Christian University and the University of Texas School of Law. He and his wife, Betty, are both former prosecutors who live in Fort Worth with their sons and dogs.

CHARLES TODD is the writing team of Caroline and Charles Todd, bestselling authors of the Inspector Ian Rutledge series and the Bess Crawford series, as well as two standalone novels. They also write short stories, including "The Trophy" in *Alfred Hitchcock Mystery Magazine*, "The Pretty Little Box" (Otto Penzler), and "The Piper," a Rutledge mystery published by Harper Witness Impulse. They live on the East Coast, are history buffs, and travel to England as often as they can.

JACQUELINE WINSPEAR's nationally bestselling first novel, *Maisie Dobbs*, garnered an array of accolades, including *New York Times* Notable Book in 2003, a *Publishers Weekly* Top Ten Mystery 2003, and a BookSense Top Ten selection. In addition, the novel was nominated for seven awards, including the Edgar Award for Best Novel. Over the years, her work has won the Agatha, Macavity, Alex, and Sue Feder Awards. Subsequent novels in the series have continued to win awards. Together with *The American Agent* (2019), Jacqueline has now published fifteen nationally bestselling novels in the Maisie Dobbs series, including ten *New York Times* bestsellers. Her standalone novel, *The Care and Management of Lies*, was also a *New York Times* and national bestseller, and a Dayton Literary Peace Prize finalist. In 2019, Jacqueline published *What Would Maisie Do?*, a nonfiction book based upon the Maisie Dobbs series.

AMANDA WITT's fiction has been called "hottest of all" by *Kirkus Reviews* and "arresting" by *Publishers Weekly*. She served as a judge for the 2017 MWA Edgar Awards, holds a Ph.D. in English, has taught writing at various universities across the United States, and is happy to now be settled with her husband back in their home state of Texas. Though mystery is her first love, she also has written four dystopian novels, The Red Series.

ABOUT THE EDITOR

ANNE PERRY is the bestselling author of two acclaimed series set in Victorian England: the William Monk novels, including *Dark Tide Rising* and *An Echo of Murder*, and the Charlotte and Thomas Pitt novels, including *Murder on the Serpentine* and *Treachery at Lancaster Gate*. She is also the author of a new series featuring Charlotte and Thomas Pitt's son, Daniel, including *Triple Jeopardy* and *Twenty-one Days*, as well as a series of five World War I novels, sixteen holiday novels (most recently *A Christmas Revelation*), and a historical novel, *The Sheen on the Silk*, set in the Ottoman Empire. Anne Perry lives in Los Angeles.

anneperry.co.uk

To inquire about booking Anne Perry for a speaking engagement, please contact the Penguin Random House Speakers Bureau at speakers@penguinrandomhouse.com.

ABOUT THE TYPE

This book was set in Centaur, a typeface designed by the American typographer Bruce Rogers in 1929. Rogers adapted Centaur from a fifteenth-century type by Nicholas Jenson (c. 1420–80) and modified it in 1948 for a cutting by the Monotype Corporation.